POWER TO LIGHT THE WAY

THE CHOSEN'S CALLING BOOK 2

GAILA KLINE-HOBSON

Remarks from early readers:

Would you like to be transported to Heaven where you learn to be a warrior for good, fighting evil wherever it exists? Become inspired by the Warrior Team as the members learn skills that will enable good to triumph over evil and for the team to develop such a strong bond that the members work as one. Learn about the Trail of Deliverance, which leads the team members on to their destiny. *Power to Light the Way, The Chosen's Calling Book 2* will enthrall readers.

—**Dorothy Minor**, associate professor of English, retired; blogger as the Book Whisperer, parkdalear.wordpress.com

This story is SO good, I enjoyed it so much. The writing is SUPERB! The story is really really terrific. I am kind of blown away by how good it is, though not surprised given the first book and how much I loved that.

—**Jennifer Rees**, editor of *The Chosen's Calling,* and the *Hunger Games* trilogy, as well as many other books

PREFACE

I am grateful and humbled by the outpouring of support and encouragement I've received from the readers of *The Chosen's Calling*. The messages I received from parents who'd lost a child and found some solace from my words touched my heart and soul.

First, to my family, thank you for your encouragement and patience as I wrote this second novel. Dave, Adam, Jonathon, and Jamie, you have my heart and gratitude for your support throughout the process. I also want to sincerely thank the early readers who devoted their time to read the manuscript and give me valuable feedback to strengthen the story. Laura Vidrine, Dorothy Caldwell Minor, and Jamie Hobson, you have my deep appreciation. I did not take every suggestion, but many of your thoughts strengthened the story and the writing. In addition, I want to thank the incredible artist, Asya Blue, for her amazing work bringing my vision to life for the cover, and for her interior formatting and chapter graphics. Finally, I am deeply thankful the hard work and encouragement of my insightful editor, Jennifer Rees.

Many people requested a sequel so I've written this second installment in the afterlives of Dina, Jo, and Gabe, our beloved warrior angels. I stayed true to the characters and the premise of the story, but some things have changed, as you are about to find out. I think the changes are for the good as the young people evolve and grow into their destinies.

The story is fiction, not theological. The characters, both old and new, are from my imagination. I did a great deal of research, so facts are interspersed throughout the story, but the characters and plot are fictional. I also made up several words that you will not find in a dictionary. I believe the context will help you figure out the meaning of *"lingo-coiner," "crabider,"* and *"cordula."*

I've included quotes from different faiths and spiritual leaders. As in Book One, my intent is to show the commonalities among faiths and focus on how we are more alike than different, even if we come from different backgrounds and faiths.

I brainstormed many possibilities for missions, but none seemed quite right. I researched information for several different scenarios, too. Even with my notes and research, I wasn't enthusiastic about any direction I'd come up with so far. Then, in the midst of research for another plot idea, an article from a news service I never use popped onto my screen. As I read the article, I knew I'd been led to the setting for the mission I was supposed to write. The research and story flowed after that. Some parts were still challenging, but I knew I was writing a message that wasn't fully my own.

May each of us continue to say and do things that give other people hope, especially those who are suffering and grieving. It can be part of all of our missions to be spiritual encouragers. Peace be yours....

CONTENTS

??? WHY?

Jo wiped her mouth and pushed back from the table. "I can't eat another bite, or I'll explode. Can we talk about the mission we just finished?"

Dina studied her friend carefully. "What do you want to talk about? I thought Gavreel, Kirron, and Michael pretty much summed it up before they left."

"I don't know exactly, but I just can't fit it all together in my mind," Jo replied. "I feel so drained, so overcome by the horrors we saw. How are we supposed to get over seeing those things?"

"I don't think we're supposed to get over it or forget it. Kirron told us evil spreads quickly. That's why so many warriors are needed," Gabe reminded her. "I believe we're supposed to focus on the result, not the evil that calls us to fight."

"But, why? If angels fight and fight, why is there never an end? Kirron said he'd faced that demon and slayed him before, eons ago. How's that possible? Do the evil ones have many lives? Is there really any way to defeat those who've fallen to the dark realm?"

"I don't know," Dina whispered as she leaned into her friend. "But I do know we're called to fight them, and we're a good team. We'll work together to fight evil."

"What happens if the dark forces capture us or slay us in battle?" Jo's voice quavered. "That gargoyle wanted to capture Gabe. He wanted to deliver him to the evil one. He thought he'd be rewarded for capturing a warrior in battle. Does that mean we get hauled to the dark side, or does our spirit just extinguish? Or do we return here and refresh to start all over again?"

"I don't know much, but we do have everlasting life, so I don't believe our spirits are extinguished. Remember when we learned to morph into other forms? You asked if we could ever get stuck in another form. Kirron and Gavreel told us we'd return as soon as the creature's lifespan had ended, which is a very short time here. I suppose it's possible an angel could be delivered to the darkness, but we're going to be so well trained and we have one another. We'll have each other's backs."

"That's right," Gabe added. "They keep telling us what a strong team we are and we've only finished one virtue trail and one module of training. We'll learn so much more as we go on. Remember, we have lots more training."

Bruno yipped, turned a circle, and launched into Jo's lap. With his front paws on her shoulders, he pressed his forehead against hers. Sitting quietly for a few seconds, head mashed to hers, the little dog's love and reassurance surged through Jo.

"You're right, boy," Jo cooed. "We'll handle whatever comes our way together. God will give us whatever we need to fulfill the plan. I guess I really need to refresh."

"We all do," Dina told her. "Let's head to our own chambers. We can meet up here when we feel like it. Remember, one knock on each door from the first person here lets the others know someone's in the lounge. See you in a while."

Dina patted Bruno's head and gave quick hugs to Jo and Gabe, then turned and walked to her door. "See you soon."

The others followed her lead. Doors clicked as the teens settled into their private chambers to refresh.

DECISION MAKING

Gavreel, Kirron, and Michael stared at a screen as Uriel approached.

"Is that one of the new teams you wish me to meet?" he asked as he studied the screen.

"Yes, this is Team NMAA. Nathaniel, Micah, Aniela, and Ariel have completed the *Trail of Caring* and their visits successfully. They've mastered the first module of skills adequately and completed a simple mission of leading a mentally disabled child away from danger and reuniting her with her family. They have bonded well. We believe they're ready to traverse *The Trail of Deliverance* with this group, Team DJG+AACB." Gavreel waved her hand over the screen and the image shifted.

Dina, Jo, and Gabe were sprawled on the sofa in their lounge, laughing and playing with a feisty little dog.

"This is the team that's already gone on a level six mission with you and earned the Angelic Medal of Valor, isn't it?" Uriel asked as he watched their interactions.

"Yes, it is. They're really quite remarkable together. We've studied all the squads that are at approximately the same level of training. We're trying to make the best match to navigate *The Trail of Deliverance* together."

"You believe these three are Seraphim, correct?" Uriel inquired. "That they'll progress to the highest ranks of warriors, like us?"

Michael replied, "I have no doubt. Gabe's already discovered fire within his spirit and has used it in battle, coupling his flames with his superior strength and agility. With no battle training yet, he's slain demons and marked the earth with divine symbols."

"Both Dina and Jo have passions and skills well beyond their years, as well as excellent physical abilities," Kirron added. "Their intuition and perceptions are uncanny. They definitely have fire within, but it hasn't been called forth yet."

Gavreel waved her hand across the screen and the image returned to four teens sitting around a table sharing platters of fruit and breads. "These four have performed very well, too. Nathaniel is much like Gabe. There's a spark within him that's undeniable. Micah is much like Jo, musically gifted and very soothing to be around. Aniela has unbelievable ways of making the impossible become possible, like spotting the lost child in dense woods as she followed tricksters leading the child astray. Ariel knew they weren't real bunnies luring the girl far from home. Aniela and Ariel are the glue that bonds this group."

Uriel stared at the screen as the four enjoyed their simple meal. He waved his hand and returned the screen to Team DJG+AACB. After watching their antics with Bruno, he declared, "Very well, I will accept these two teams and assist you with their training. I'll meet all of you at the appropriate spot on *The Trail of Deliverance*."

Uriel turned away. "I have some things to attend to before committing to a training module, but I'll be there shortly."

"I'll bring Team NMAA to the beginning of the trail," Gavreel said. "Michael, will you get Team DJG+AACB? Everyone should be suited up and ready to work."

Michael nodded as the three raised their hands and vanished.

Bruno flipped and ran to the door. He stared silently, clearly waiting for someone or something.

"Bruno says someone's coming," Gabe announced.

"He always seems to know," Dina agreed. "I bet we're going to start training again. Who do you think it will be?"

Before anyone could answer her question, a gentle tapping sounded at the door, and it cracked open. Michael stuck his head in. "It's just me."

He'd barely stepped in when Jo wrapped him in a bear hug. "Daddy! It's so good to see you again. I bet you're going to tell us our time for refreshing is over and we need to go on with training."

"That's right, Pumpkin. All of you need to suit up, including Bruno. You won't be choosing the Virtue Trail this time. We've chosen it for you. I'll escort you there as soon as all of you are ready."

The teens exchanged glances and grins as they headed to their closets to change.

They were ready to face new challenges together. The first trail of virtues had been tough, but it forged them into a strong team who worked well together. They'd earned their gentleness, patience, trust, forgiveness, empathy, and caring amulets on that trail. The introductory training module under Kirron's instruction had been tough, but it was amazing, too, as they mastered the divine gifts of enhanced speed and agility, levitation, invisibility, metamorphosis, and using the space tessellation.

Yes, they were definitely ready to move forward together.

Michael smiled warmly as the team returned. "You look refreshed and ready to commence training. Gabe, pick up Bruno. Join me over here and we'll depart."

The teens moved close to Michael. Jo wrapped one arm around his waist as Dina rested her hand on Jo's shoulder, and Gabe rested his free hand on Dina's shoulder. They knew they were about to use the tessellation to move to the Virtue Trail that had been chosen for them. Michael raised his hand and they were off.

They found themselves next to a beautifully engraved sign. Peacocks and flowers framed the lettering: *The Trail of Deliverance.* Many shades of blue, white, gold, and silver blended to make the sign look like a master work of art.

Dina knelt by the sign, examining the intricate engraving and painting. "This sign is absolutely incredible. The detail makes it so life-like. It looks as if the peacocks could step right off and surround us."

As she stood, still staring at the sign, Gavreel appeared. Four strangers were holding hands, all connected to Gavreel by the girl whose hand Gavreel still held.

Gavreel's radiant smile erupted as she declared, "I want to introduce all of you to one another. You'll be traversing this trail together and our hope is that you all will become masters of the virtues you encounter along the trail."

She dropped the hand of the girl next to her. "I've escorted Team NMAA while Michael escorted Team DJG+AACB. Aniela is standing by me. Next to her is Nathaniel, then Ariel, and Micah. Nathaniel prefers his nickname, Nate."

Gavreel stepped toward the others who waited by the sign. "This is Dina," she said as she patted her arm. "Here's Jophiel, but she goes by Jo," she added as she placed her hand on Jo's shoulder. "Gabriel, Gabe, is holding Bruno, an animal angel who is quite remarkable, as you'll likely see for yourselves."

Gavreel nodded toward Michael. "I'm sure everybody remembers Michael. He's been instrumental in training both teams and accompanying them on missions."

Everyone nodded. "Hey, Michael." Grins crossed each face as they realized they'd said the same thing at the same time as they'd nodded at their trainer.

Michael grinned, too. What a good sign, all seven synching at their first moment together. "I want everyone on Team NMAA to know that Jo is my daughter. I transitioned Home five Earth years before she came, but we've been working together since she transitioned. She receives no more or less attention than any other Chosen One. Gavreel and I work with many teams, preparing warriors to meet whatever comes their way, which is what you're about to face on this Virtue Trail. I hope you're ready to face challenges, problem solve, and become masters of several virtues. Remember all that you've already learned. Remember you're all young warriors training for the same cause. Do your best and don't give up."

Michael raised his hand and disappeared.

Gavreel announced, "I'll be leaving you here as well. Gabe, you can put Bruno down as soon as you step onto the trail beyond this sign. You can introduce him to the members of the new group. Talk amongst yourselves and share your stories as you make your way down the trail. As Michael said, remember the lessons already learned and don't give up. Unity, acceptance, loyalty, integrity, and justice are worthy comrades." With a raised hand, Gavreel vanished.

BEGINNING THE TRAIL

"I guess we better start walking," Nate announced. "We won't get to the end if we don't get going. After you." He made a sweeping bow, indicating they should begin their march. Team NMAA stepped past the trail sign. Dina, Jo, and Gabe stepped on the trail right behind them. When Nate joined the group, the trail began to shimmer.

The path swirled. The brown dirt surface changed to many shades of blue, giving the illusion of water rather than land. The swirling stopped, depositing a rich shade of peacock blue on the trail as far as they could see.

"What a gorgeous color," Jo marveled.

"You say that because blue's your favorite," Gabe and Dina teased.

"Mine, too," Micah offered. "I love every shade of blue, but this one's particularly nice."

Gabe bent over and set Bruno on the trail. After sniffing the now-blue trail, he turned three circles and sat at Gabe's feet.

"This is my dog, Bruno," Gabe told the others. "Actually, he's more like our team's dog now. He loves Dina and Jo about as much as he loves me. He really likes everyone. You should see him with Gavreel. He adores her."

Ariel squatted and whispered, "Bruno."

The little dog glanced her way then looked back up Gabe. "It's all right, boy. That's Ariel. She wants to be your friend. Let's go meet Ariel."

Gabe took a couple of steps and squatted next to Ariel. Bruno sniffed the girl's hand before sitting at her feet and gazing into her eyes. She stroked his head and murmured things the others couldn't hear. Bruno sat there, reveling in the attention from this new girl.

"How come you have a dog on your team?" Nate asked. "I haven't seen any other dogs around here."

"I think he stayed with me because we died together," Gabe said. "We transitioned together so he lives with me here, just like he did before we transitioned. He's acquired enhanced speed and agility so he can keep up with us on missions. He can't levitate, morph, or make himself invisible, though."

Nate squatted next to Ariel, holding his hand close to Bruno's nose. "Well, hello, Bruno."

Bruno sniffed the new hand before rubbing his head against it.

Nate petted Bruno's back while Ariel continued the head massage. "I had a dog before I came here," Nate told the others. "I really love that dog. Her name's Zoe. She's still with my family."

"He likes both of you and that massage you're giving him," Gabe said. "Maybe I should introduce Micah and Aniela to him, too, before we move forward."

"Good boy, Bruno," Ariel and Nate chorused as they stood. Bruno's tail wagged vigorously as he looked from one to the other, clearly expressing his appreciation and requesting more attention.

"Bruno, two more people are waiting to become your friend," Gabe declared as he recaptured the terrier's attention. "This is Micah and that's Aniela. We're going to be spending some time with them, so you need to make their acquaintance."

"You're so cute," Aniela bubbled as she bent to pet the waiting canine. Bruno thanked her with a wet kiss to her cheek.

Micah knelt beside the pair saying, "Pleased to meet you, Bruno. I never had a dog, but I like all animals. I hope you'll like me, too."

Bruno expressed his acceptance with a vigorous tail wag and yip. Micah beamed as he stroked the dog's back as Nate had done.

"My family has three cats," Micah offered. "I miss them a lot."

"I had a cat, too," Jo told them. "Her name's Joy. She's still with my mom and sister. I hope she comes to me when it's her time to transition. I never had any other pet, so I don't know if that'll happen or not."

"So, we're both cat people and have the same favorite color," Micah mused. "I bet we have other things in common, too. I can hardly wait to learn more about you, all of you. I guess we'll find out as we work our way down this trail. We probably should get going." His smile gave Jo butterflies in her stomach.

Dina, who'd been silent during the Bruno Meet-and-Greet, simply said. "Yes, we should. I bet there's something waiting for us just around that bend in the trail."

She walked past them and headed toward the curve a few hundred feet away. The group followed, snickering at Bruno's antics as he leaped and somersaulted his way down the path.

Dina rounded the corner just ahead of the others and found a boulder blocking the trail flanked by huge trees, making it impossible to go any farther. A pole with hooks held two identical cloth bags, a clipboard and pen showing in an outside pocket of each. The top of the pole curved into an ornate curlicue. A shiny gold bell with a blue satin ribbon hung from it. Adjacent to the pole stood a bright blue barrel. An electronic sign flashing neon colors but no words sat on the other side of the can.

"Here we go again," she sighed.

GETTING DIRECTIONS

All seven clustered in front of the strobing sign.

"That sign looks like the one we had to figure out before we earned our Trust charms," Nate announced. "It took us a long time to figure out how to get the directions. Gavreel and Michael told us to remember all we'd already learned. Maybe this is one of those places to apply past learning."

"It took us a while to figure it out, too, but Gabe helped us," Dina said. "Do you suppose this one works the same way?"

"I guess the only way to find out is to try," Gabe replied. "Bruno, come here. Up, boy."

Bruno leapt into his arms, obviously ready for a new adventure. He climbed on Gabe's shoulder, perching like a parrot surveying the area.

Aniela scooted between Nate and Micah, placing her left hand on Nate's shoulder. Micah reached over and gently laid his hand on Aniela's shoulder. Ariel positioned herself between Nate and Gabe, leaving Jo and Dina on his other side. She reached over and laid her hand on the shoulder where Bruno sat, sliding her fingers over one rear foot. Nate placed his hand on Ariel's shoulder while Gabe, Jo, and Dina did the same. They were all now connected by touch.

Seven voices called, "Here we go," as seven hands reached out and touched the top or side of the sign.

The explosions of neon colors erupted into symbols, disappearing as soon as they'd appeared. The kaleidoscope of symbols and colors scrolled faster and faster, but nothing made any sense to the watchers.

"We're not doing something right," Dina declared. "Before, when we touched one another and touched the sign at the same time, the scrolling stopped on a message printed in English. It's not stopping this time. We must need to change something to make it work."

They dropped their hands and looked at one another.

"Maybe we need to rearrange ourselves. Maybe the sign requires a pattern like boy-girl-boy-girl. Since there's one more girl, if Jo came from that end where she's connected to Dina, to this end, where she'd be connected to me, we'd be alternating and it might work."

"It's worth trying," Jo acknowledged as she moved to the other end of the line and placed her left hand on Micah's shoulder. Those butterflies fluttered in her stomach again.

From the new configuration, the seven reached out and connected with the sign. The neon sparks once again shifted into symbols that none of them could read as the frenetic scroll continued.

"Well, that pattern didn't unlock the sign's message. Maybe we need to mix up our teams," Nate offered. "If we alternate members of the two teams so current teammates aren't next to one another, it might work. Let's try that."

"I'll trade places with Aniela," Dina called, "and Ariel can move to the end by Jo. "That way it'll be Ariel, Jo, Micah, me, Nate, Gabe, and Aniela. Our order will go from one team to the other all the way down the line."

The girls moved to their new positions and placed one hand on the shoulder of the person next to them. Again, the group reached out and touched the sign at the same time.

The colorful splashes once more shifted to unrecognizable symbols and scrolled too fast to read.

"What are we doing wrong?" they wondered aloud.

"The idea of a pattern is good," Ariel declared. "We just need to figure out other patterns to try. Any suggestions?"

"How about if we arrange ourselves from tallest to shortest or shortest to tallest?" Micah suggested. "It's just a random thought, but it might work."

"Worth a shot," they all agreed as they shuffled to new positions in the semicircle facing the sign. The new configuration of Gabe, Nate, Dina, Micah, Ariel, Jo, and Aniela reached for the sign.

This time the sign's spinning was markedly slower. Not slow enough to make sense of the symbols that flashed by, but noticeably slower than before.

"Something is better this time, but still not right," Aniela remarked. "We need to change some little thing, but not much."

"Maybe it's not height," Dina proposed. "Maybe it's gender. Look where we are. I am between two guys, but the other three girls are next to one another. Maybe if Micah and I swap places so the three guys are together and the four girls are together, the sign will let us read it."

"Let's give it a go," Micah said as he moved to Dina's other side, so he was next to Nate.

The sign roared to life once more when seven hands connected to it. The explosion of colors faded to silver as navy blue and turquoise symbols whirled around the screen. When the tumbling symbols came to a stop, a message was visible that all onlookers could read.

Your combined auras indicate you are English speakers from Earth. The directions for this task are now being presented in English. Read the message carefully and make sure you discuss and understand what you must do before you begin. Once you begin, you must finish. There is no bypass of this task. You must trust one another and work as teammates to be successful. Listen to one another carefully. Ponder each decision and agree before you place anything in your bag. Once an item is inside, you may not remove it.

Just below that message, they read:

Your first task on this trail,
Which you must finish without fail,
Is to decode this poem and find
Every item you've been assigned.
The hunt you make on this trail
Will be female versus male.
The teams will mix and you must trust
Your teammates' actions are helpful and just.
Canine Bruno is on both sides,
The dog can go where he decides.
New teams will work deciphering the list,
Find each item, making sure none are missed.
Write down the names of things to find,
When found, check each off, noting how they're entwined.
New teams must not part throughout the quest,
And remember: everything might be a test.
Every team member should place items in sacks,
When all are found, make backward tracks.
Return here where the search began.
Place your list in the bag and your bag in the can.
If every item is correct,
The bag will stay and not eject.
If the sack comes back to you,
Check the list to see what to do.
The errors will be marked in pen,
Correct each one and return again.
The first team finished should ring the bell,
Summoning the others to return as well.
The first team wins a special prize,
But helping others would be wise.
No one can advance down the trail
Till two complete bags fill the pail.

"It sounds like we're going on a scavenger hunt," Dina announced.

"That's what it sounds like to me, too," Nate agreed. "Let's read through it a few more times and make sure we all agree about what our task is and how we're supposed to do it."

"Well, it's definitely guys against girls," Jo declared. "Males versus females couldn't be any clearer."

"True, and we can't stop until both teams have finished collecting the stuff," Micah added.

Gabe put in, "And Bruno can go wherever he wants and help both teams. That seems strange since he's male and we have one fewer team member, but whatever."

"It sounds like we have to figure out what to look for before we leave this area, since it says to decipher the list," Aniela commented.

"True. Then we have to write down the name of each thing we think we should find from the hint, or riddle, or whatever they give us to decipher," Jo asserted.

"What do you think it means to notice 'how they're entwined'?" Ariel wondered.

Dina suggested, "I don't think they mean literally laced together, but rather how they're connected, like what's something they all have in common. I think it's another one of those things they want us to think broadly about and figure out as a team. We have to agree before we write it down."

"That makes more sense than finding all the items somehow hooked together. We can't separate to hunt in more places at the same time either since it says new teams can't part during the quest," Nate added.

"If I'm understanding the directions correctly," Jo said, "we have to agree as a team that we've found a correct item before putting it in the sack. Once it's in the sack, we can't remove it. Then we check that item off our list and look for another one."

"It also says every member should place things in the sack, so I think we're supposed to take turns actually placing the items in the bags," Ariel commented.

"When we have everything, we come back here. We put the list in the bag and the bag in the can. If we're right, the sack stays in the can and we ring the bell so the other team comes back. If we're wrong, our bag will come out and we'll have to look at what's marked on our checklist. Right?" Gabe queried.

"That sounds right to me," Micah agreed. "If we have something wrong, we have to figure out what else it could be and go out searching for it. Or, we may have to brainstorm and figure out something else all the things have in common."

"But if we're right and the sack stays in the can, we ring the bell and wait for the others to return. Then we help them find the missing items," Aniela added.

"None of us can proceed until the second bag is in the can and everyone has finished the hunt successfully," Nate acknowledged. "I think we covered the directions pretty well and understand what they want us to do."

As he finished his remark, the sign roared to life again and a new message appeared:

Since you're confident that you understand what to do, each team should take one collection bag from the hook. Teams should separate from one another before turning over the list that's facedown on the clipboard. Read it carefully with your new team. Discuss what you believe you're being sent to seek. When you've written down each item you are to find, go to a tree on either side of the boulder and seek entry to the hunting grounds.

"Let's get started," Micah proclaimed. "I'll grab our bag. Let's move over to that flat boulder over there." He pointed to a mesa-looking rock about a hundred feet left of the sign.

"I'll grab ours," Jo offered. "Where do you want to work on the list?"

"How about that shady spot under those flowering trees?" Ariel suggested.

The girls nodded their agreement before Jo walked over to Micah to fetch their bag. Jo's and Micah's fingers brushed one another as they reached for the two sacks.

Those now-familiar butterflies fluttered in her stomach as he smiled at her and said, "Good luck. I bet you girls do great."

SCAVENGER HUNT DETAILS

The boys sauntered to the flat boulder and clambered on top before Micah turned over the list. Micah held the clipboard in front of him so that Nate and Gabe, who were on each side could see it, too. Bruno nestled next to Gabe, his head resting on Gabe's thigh.

The girls strolled to the grassy patch under the blooming trees, about a hundred feet to the right of the sign. They settled on the ground, sitting in a semicircle so they could see one another. Jo turned the paper over on the clipboard and set it down near the middle of the arc they formed. Everyone could see it in that position.

Both teams read the same message at the same time:

1. This floral display always rings true.
    It lovingly spreads its sapphire hue
    On woodland floors and rolling hillside,
    Attracting hummingbirds far and wide.

    Find: _____

2. King of antioxidant foods,
    Whether eaten raw, baked, or stewed,
    This ball of goodness, though quite small,
    Provides sweet nutrition for all.

    Find:_____

3. With crested head and noisy call,

Whether perched on branch, fence, or wall,
Its plumage stands out from the rest.
Finding one that's molt is your test.

Find:_____

4. Early nesting almost anywhere,
   This red-breasted singer builds with care,
   Protecting each new cyan shell,
   Till a bit you find that fell.

   Find:_____

5. Growing on stalks in tidy rows,
   Always a hit with hungry crows,
   Usually yellow, but not this time,
   Pluck an indigo ear in its prime.

   Find: _____

6. Ornamental minerals with unique hues,
   Favored for centuries as precious jewels,
   Esteemed by many and sacred to some,
   Find a piece of this gem before back here you come.

   Find: _____

7. Growing as bushes or small trees,
   Its flowers and leaves are made into teas,
   Sometimes called the popcorn ball bush,
   One of these balls into your bag you should push.

   Find:_____

8. Spotted on or under rotten wood,
   This small winged creature likes fungi as food.
   In high altitude homes their exoskeletons can be found,
   Scavenge one of these shells you find on the ground.

   Find:_____

You are connected and these things are, too.

You should have deduced they are all _____.

Though noted in common nomenclature,

Each of these items are found in _____.

When every blank is filled, and all eight items are in your bag, return to the starting point and place everything in the can. Happy hunting!

THE GUYS

"Maybe we should do the easy ones first," Micah whispered. "Not that any of them are easy, but I think some are easier than others."

"I know what number two is!" Gabe offered.

"We all know what number two was on Earth," Nate grinned, but I don't think that applies here."

The boys erupted in raucous laughter.

"No, no, I mean the second one on the list," Gabe chortled. "Not the number two you're talking about. Though enough of these could make a very colorful number two."

Uproarious laughter once again rocked the three guys.

"Blueberries," Gabe gasped. "The second one must be blueberries. They're small, sweet, nutritious, and can be eaten raw or cooked. They're one of the superfoods we learned about in health class."

"You're right," Nate and Micah blurted at the same time, grins still plastered on their faces.

"Do we all agree we should write down blueberries for the second one?" Micah asked.

"I agree," Gabe and Nate both responded.

Micah wrote the word in neat block letters on their list.

"Any other suggestions for ones you think are easy that we could jot down before we tackle the rest line by line?" Micah asked.

"I'm pretty sure number three is a bird feather," Nate remarked. "Plumage means feathers and birds perch lots of places, like branches and fences and walls. We have to think of birds that have crests on their heads."

"Cardinals and bluejays have crests," Gabe offered. "There were lots of them where I used to live."

"A titmouse was a crested bird where I used to live," Micah remarked.

Laughter overcame the trio once more.

"Such a weird name, but they do have crests on their heads," he continued.

"Peacocks have crests, too," Nate added to their list. "I bet there are lots of other birds with crests, but they said to use our prior learning. These are the ones we know about, so I bet it's one of these four. What do you think?"

"Maybe we could make a note about those four birds to the side, not on the blank, and see what kind of birds we see when we actually start searching," Micah suggested.

"That works for me," Gabe and Nate replied.

Micah jotted a neat column in the margin by number three: cardinal, blue jay, titmouse, peacock.

"I guess we really are a new team because our words are already synching," Gabe marveled. "It's weird how that happens around here."

"I'm kind of getting used to it now," Nate replied. "It's just the way it is."

Gabe continued, "Number five's an ear of corn. Grows on a stalk in tidy rows and corn is usually yellow. We're supposed to find an ear that is indigo. What's indigo?"

"It's a color word. Indigo is really dark blue that sometimes has a slight purplish cast. It's a very rich color," Nate told him.

"Hmmm. So, we're supposed to find an ear of dark blue corn. I've never seen anything like that, but I guess we'll recognize a corn-field when we see it and hope it's blue corn."

"We're confident about blueberries for two, an ear of blue corn for five, and some kind of crested bird for three. Any others you guys think you know?" Micah asked.

Gabe responded, "Hmmm, number four might be a robin. Red-breasted, nesting, singer all make me think of a robin. Do either of you know what cyan is? That's throwing me off. And a shell would be on a beach or in an ocean, not an area where robins would be."

"Cyan is another color word," Nate offered. "Actually, it's another shade of blue. It's a lighter blue though, kind of turquoise. I think robins lay eggs that color. Maybe we're supposed to find a piece of robin eggshell."

"That makes sense to me," Gabe replied, "because everything else in that riddle made me think of robins. You sure know a lot about colors, Nate. Are you some sort of artist or something?"

"He's a fantastic artist," Micah proclaimed. "I never knew anyone who could draw or paint like he does."

"Dina's like that. She's an amazing artist, too, and she knows lots about art history and artists." Gabe smiled, thinking of the gift she had made for him commemorating his visit.

Micah inquired, "Do we all think a piece of robin eggshell is the answer for number four? Should I write it down?"

"I do," Gabe and Nate responded.

"I do, too," Micah told them with a grin. He printed "robin eggshell" on the line at the end of number four's riddle."

"I have an idea about number one," Micah told them. "Where I used to live there was a flower that spread all over. Sometimes it was purple, but usually it was blue. It blanketed fields and hillsides with this beautiful blue color. The flowers were shaped like little bells so everyone called them bluebells. I don't know if that's their real name or if hummingbirds like them, but the bell shape could go with the 'rings true' part of the riddle. Sapphires are blue so their color goes with that part."

"Sounds good to me," his teammates responded, grins plastered on their faces.

Micah printed "bluebell" on number one's line.

"I wonder how the girls are doing with the riddles," Nate commented, as he glanced in their direction.

"Probably just fine. We already have over half of ours figured out, so they probably do, too. Let's just focus and keep going on the list so we can try to beat them when we actually start the hunt." Micah continued, "I think we're going to have to look at the rest of the riddles line by line and try to figure out the ones we don't have yet."

"The girls are probably doing great," Gabe replied. "Dina and Jo are both good at figuring things out."

At hearing the girls' names Bruno yipped and leapt from the rock. He turned two circles before racing to where they sat under the sweet-smelling trees. He nestled between Dina and Jo, thoroughly enjoying the pats and loving words that greeted him.

THE GIRLS

"So, I've recorded bluebells for number one, blueberries for number two, peacock feather for three, robin eggshell for number four, an ear of blue corn for five, and a piece of turquoise stone for six. We all agree on those, right?" Dina asked as she scanned their list.

Head shakes confirmed their unanimous agreement.

"Time to tackle number seven line by line," Aniela piped. "Unless someone already has an idea."

"I have an idea," Jo offered. "I don't know if it's right, but my grandma and grandpa used to have two big bushes growing on each end of their porch. They got these big flower balls on them. One time they were sort of pink, but usually they were blue flowers. My grandpa said he had to fertilize them when they bloomed that pink color. After that, they always bloomed blue. Grandma said they were called popcorn ball bushes by some people but she liked their real name better, hydra-something."

"Hydrangea," Ariel said. "Of course. That makes perfect sense for that riddle. Some cultures make herbal teas from them. Everything fits with hydrangea. Some of them get big, like a tree, and their flowers are clustered in balls. They can be white, pink, or blue, depending on how acidic the soil is. When your grandpa fertilized his bushes, he changed the acidic level of the soil so the flowers' color changed the next time they bloomed."

"You sure know a lot about plants," Jo marveled.

"Nature's always been my thing," Ariel said. "I love plants and animals. I used to have all kinds of books about them. I didn't know whether I wanted to be a botanist, marine biologist, or zoologist when I grew up, but I knew I wanted to be some kind of scientist who studied plants or animals."

"She remembers everything she ever read about plants and animals, too," Aniela crooned. "She's really, really knowledgeable about things in nature."

"Thanks, Aniela. I guess my brain hung onto facts about things I loved."

"That's how Dina is about art. She knows so much about artists, techniques, art history, and colors. She's an awesome artist herself, too," Jo praised.

"Jo, you're making me blush," Dina blurted. "Should I write 'hydrangea' down for number seven?"

Bobbing heads confirmed their agreement. Dina's ornate cursive recorded hydrangea on number seven's line.

"Number eight seems hardest of all," Aniela observed, "but I bet we can figure it out."

"Well, we know it's small and can fly if it has wings," Jo said.

"And we should look around old logs or other rotten wood since that's where it lives," Dina added.

"But up high, like trees at the top of hills or mountains, since it talks about high altitude homes," Aniela put in.

"Shedding exoskeletons is something some sea creatures do, but also some insects. Since this thing is found at high altitudes near rotten wood and fungi, I am sure its is some kind of bug, probably a beetle or locust. You can see their shells quite often if you observe carefully," Ariel told her team.

"Do you think it's a locust or beetle?" Dina asked.

"I'm not sure. Let's look at the final part of the sheet." She studied the final rhyme at the bottom of the page.

You are connected and these things are, too.

You should have deduced they are all _____.

Though noted in common nomenclature,

Each of these items are found in _____.

"The first blank has to rhyme with 'too' and make sense in the blank, and the second blank has to rhyme with 'nomenclature'." Ariel studied the list their team had mostly completed.

"'Blue' rhymes with 'too,' and everything we have written down can be blue. Since this trail is blue, that makes sense to me," Dina announced.

"That does make sense there," the others agreed.

"Could the second blank's word be 'nature'? Each thing is found in nature. Is there any other word that rhymes with 'nomencla-ture'?" Aniela wondered aloud.

"Brilliant thinking!" Jo crowed. "That makes perfect sense."

"If we have the ending figured out correctly, then number eight has to be some kind of blue beetle's shedded shell. Locust shells are brown, so even though they're found in nature, they wouldn't fit with everything else that's blue." Ariel asserted, "Let's record blue beetle's exoskeleton for number eight."

"Let's do it and get going," three other voices chorused as the girls' team erupted in giggles.

Dina wrote down their ideas for number eight and the final rhyme then stuffed the clipboard and pen back in the outside pocket of their bag.

Aniela grabbed the bag and slung it over her shoulder. "I'll carry it for a while. We can take turns carrying it if that's what everybody wants to do. Okay?"

Bruno raced in circles and did flips as the girls stood and headed to the enormous tree on their side of the boulder. He knew fun was about to begin.

"Do you want to go with us, Bruno?" Dina asked. "If you do, jump up here with me." She held out her arms and caught the terrier as he launched himself. The self-satisfied grin and slurp across her face confirmed his desire. Three other hands stroked his head and back as he perched in Dina's arms. He was starting this new game with the girls.

"We're off, gentlemen! It looks like Bruno has decided to join the winning team," Ariel announced. "Hope you figure out your list soon. Listen for that bell."

"You're so bad," the other girls teased.

"I know, but I couldn't resist since we clearly figured out the riddles first," Ariel murmured. "Guys have no trouble talking smack. I think they know I'm teasing. We'll help them after we beat them."

Gales of laughter and a joyful howl sounded as the girls joined hands and pressed against the tree and boulder, Bruno securely tucked along Dina's side.

THE HUNT BEGINS

The girls stood leaning against the tree and boulder, but nothing happened.

"When we did the trust activity on the first trail, Gabe and I both had to touch the tree and the boulder at the same time to get the tree's vines started," Dina reflected. "Our arms were tied together so we were connected by the black cloth. I'm holding Bruno with one hand, so I don't think we've made a complete circuit of connectedness. Maybe I can get him to stay draped around my neck so I can use my other hand."

She lifted the wiggling dog and draped him around her neck. She slowly removed her hands and he stayed put, his head pressed to the side of hers. "Good boy, Bruno. We're all going to connect to one another and the tree and boulder now. Stay."

A slight rustling and almost imperceptible sway began as the girls connected themselves to one another, the massive boulder, and sentry tree. It wasn't long before the tree's sway was undeniable. Something was happening.

Instead of vines whipping from the tree as they expected, an enormous kite broke from the boughs. The massive thing, shaped like a futuristic jet, hovered over them, four knotted tether lines dangling from the body. Blue swirls pulsed and shifted on the kite's body as it floated above them. It levitated there but did nothing else.

"It's waiting for us! Maybe we're each supposed to grab one of those cords hanging from it," Ariel suggested. "There are four of them and four of us. I'm going for it," she said as she dropped her hands and grabbed the line closest to her.

The strap she now held let out slack and wrapped itself around her torso and flipped her on top of the kite's body. She landed in a seated position, her legs dangling over the edge. The line that had hoisted her aboard now wiggled itself free and attached itself over her lap, anchoring her as a seatbelt.

"Come on, girls, it's great up here! You should see the boys' faces. It's hilarious!" Ariel called.

One by one, Aniela, Jo, and Dina followed Ariel's lead and found themselves seated on their aerial transport device, secured near the edge by the soft lacing that had hoisted them to their perches. Bruno was settled on Dina's lap, her seatbelt wrapped around both of them.

The boys stared, their mouths hanging open as they watched. The girls waved as the kite slowly circled the boulder before whooshing to the far side.

It zipped through an opening in the rock's side. Instead of being in a cavern, as one would expect when entering a rock, the girls found themselves transported to paradise beyond worthy description.

The landscape permeated their eyes and souls as they surveyed the land from above. Uncountable living things wandered among trees as tall as cathedrals and grasses and flowers as dense as the fibers of lush carpet. Woodlands, meadows, and rolling hills stretched as far as they could see. This world was painted every shade of green and splattered with vibrant colors. A clear stream meandered through the land, its gentle murmur humming a welcome. Hums, chirps, songs, and calls of animals came from every direction, not particularly loud, but almost overwhelming in its density. This symphony of nature called them to come explore. Their nostrils flared as the sweet smell of many flowers wafted up and folded around them. The cloying aroma of the air was sweet and fresh. They could actually taste it as well as smell it.

"I feel as if flowers are growing on my tongue," Jo whispered. "My mouth tastes something sweet and satisfying, like the blooms have become a part of me."

"I feel it, too," the others marveled.

The girls studied the topography as their kite slowly circled the area three times. They pointed out things they spotted from the air, like the blueberry patch on one hillside and the spreading bluebells on another. They thought they saw a pile of turquoise stones in a cave opening of another hill. Giant hydrangea bushes seemed to wave as the girls circled near the stream. There were lots of logs and mushrooms among the trees near the hilltop where the bluebells spread.

After the third lap around the hunting grounds, the kite descended near a small sign. It tilted forward slightly, unwound its seatbelt tethers, and gently jiggled the girls to the ground. They stood next to the sign, Bruno at their feet.

They read the sign:

This is the starting point of the hunt. You should return here when you believe you've completed your search. Summon your transporter by connecting to one another and this sign. It will return and take you back to the waiting can.

"Let's get going," Dina blurted. "We should use enhanced speed and agility to go to those hills. We know we can get the blueberries and bluebells, then see if there's really a turquoise pile in that cave and some blue beetle carcasses by those logs where the bluebells are."

"Agreed," the team chorused before a new round of giggles filled the air.

"Bruno loves enhanced running and agility modes. You'll be amazed," Jo told Ariel and Aniela. "He'll go with anyone on our team since we trained him together."

"Let's run to the base of the hill where we saw the blueberries first. When we get there, we can engage enhanced agility to get up where they're growing. Okay?" Dina suggested.

"Sounds fine," the others agreed as they tapped their heels together to engage hyper-speed mode.

Jo and Dina chimed, "Bruno, hyper-speed!"

Their canine companion yipped as he snapped his front paws together and looked up at the girls. His eager expression urged them to get going.

They ran in a pack, equally matched for speed. Their long strides took them to the desired hill very quickly.

They snapped their heels in midair and landed smoothly.

Jo and Dina shouted, "End!" as they snapped to a halt. Bruno followed their command and stopped right behind them, his wagging tail communicating his joy at playing this wonderful game again.

"Three jumps should get us up to the blueberry patch," Aniela declared.

"How about going to that reddish boulder first, then that pine tree that's growing off to the side of the other trees, then land near the blueberry bushes?"

Heads bobbed in agreement.

Aniela said, "I'll start. We're supposed to stay together, so everybody come right away." She stared at her target, tapped her right heel to the ground twice, and made her first leap, landing smoothly on the boulder she'd pointed out.

As soon as Aniela made her second jump to the pine tree, Ariel said, "I'll go now. See you yonder at the blueberry patch!" Her rapid heel tap and leap landed her on the boulder.

"Let's both wait on the boulder and call Bruno, just in case we have to refresh his memory by one of us making the arm circle for him to leap through while the other one catches him as he leaps through the hoop," Dina told Jo.

"Agreed. Who knows how long it's been since we actually used this skill. He might need us to refresh his memory," Jo said. "I'll go up and wait back from the closest edge."

She tapped and leaped, touching down softly and sliding back as far as she could, leaving plenty of room for Dina and Bruno to land.

"We're going to tap and jump up to that big rock where Jo's standing, Bruno. I bet you remember that game, don't you? I'm going to jump now, then you come up to me."

Dina tapped her heel and launched herself at the first target. She landed and shouted, "Tap! Jump!"

Bruno did a flip, landed with tail gyrating, then slammed his front paw on the ground. He reveled in the pats his girls gave him as soon as he landed between them.

"We're going to go again, Bruno. This time I want you to jump in my arms on top of that big pine tree up there." Dina pointed to the tree that was their next springboard.

Jo leaped and landed on a strong branch near the top. Dina landed on one that was slightly below it, but very sturdy, with surrounding limbs she could brace her stance against to catch the catapulting canine.

"Tap! Jump!" she hollered as she held out her arms.

His grin told them he knew his landing was perfect. Jo and Dina beamed at their teammate. He really was an amazing little dog.

"You're going to jump to Jo next time, Bruno. I'm going to come right after you, but she's going to be waiting on the ground right over there where the other girls are watching us. Show them what a good boy and good jumper you are. Go ahead, Jo. I'll set him on the branch right in front of me as soon as you're down there ready to call him."

Jo called, "Bruno! Tap! Jump!"

Immediately, he was at her feet, and Dina was at her side.

"Time to check out these orbs of antioxidant goodness," Dina declared when she landed.

The girls plucked a few from the closest bushes and popped them in their mouths. "Delicious!" they chimed.

Bruno sat on his hind legs and pawed the air with his front paws.

The girls laughed at his cute begging pose before tossing berries one at a time in his direction. He caught every one and begged for more.

The girls stuffed a few more in their own mouths between each toss.

"That's probably enough for Bruno. He'll keep eating as long as we keep tossing them to him, but we need to get some for our bag and move on," Dina declared.

"Last one, Bruno," Jo declared as she tossed a plump one into his open mouth.

"I wish we had something to put the blueberries in, so they don't get smashed in the bag," Aniela mumbled. "Blueberry juice is sticky and can make a mess."

"That's a good idea," Jo agreed. "Let's see if we can find anything that might work as a temporary container for them."

They looked around the ground near the blueberry bushes. Bruno scampered among them, not sure what this new game was, but not too impressed so far.

Several monarch butterflies circled the group. Bruno yipped and chased the orange flashes as they headed toward bushes where other monarchs fluttered.

The girls scrambled after him. Bruno plopped down at the base of a bush and stared at many winged beauties as they clustered on the bush's flowers.

"Milkweed, of course," Ariel announced. "This should work. See this bush? It's done blooming for the season, but that one, where all the monarchs are, is still in bloom. The butterflies are attracted to it because they want to lay their eggs on the plant. The eggs will hatch, and the caterpillars will feed on the milkweed plant. Milkweed's the only food monarch caterpillars eat. We can get two seedpods that have cracked open from this bush that's past blooming."

She plucked two long pods and pulled out some of the seeds and silk that erupted from the pod. "There's room to put a few blueberries in this pod, put the other pod on top of it, and tie them together with some long grass. The blueberries will be protected in the pods."

"You really do know a lot about nature," Jo clucked.

"I told you," Aniela beamed. "Ariel's like a naturalist."

"Thanks," Ariel said with a grin. "I'm glad Bruno led us here."

"Let's go get our blueberries and move on. We're close to the cave where we thought we saw the turquoise piled up. It was on the next hill over from this one." Ariel pointed in the direction of the cave.

"You're right. We need to get a move-on or the guys will pass us!" Ariel smiled. She didn't want that to happen.

Each girl tucked a couple of berries in the milkweed pods before Ariel tied them together with several strands of long grass. Aniela gently placed the pods in the bottom of the bag and checked off number one on their list. "One down, seven to go!" She slung the bag over her shoulder after securing the clipboard and pen in its pocket.

"Let's use enhanced jumps to get to the cave on the next hill. It was about the same elevation as this blueberry patch. That way we won't have to take the time to go down and come back up again," Jo suggested.

"I'll lead our parade this time." Ariel pointed toward the next hill. "We can jump to that bluish-gray boulder from here, then across that valley between the hills to that ledge that's jutting out, then to that wide black spot near the cave opening. We can look around and see if we spot the cave or anything else on our list."

She launched with the other girls and a delighted canine on her heels.

They landed on the huge black spot, which was actually a shadow cast from several trees and bushes packed tightly together just above the cave opening. The canopy's shade camouflaged the opening unless one spotted it from above.

"Well, here we are," Dina cried as she strode into the mouth of the cave. The walls and ceiling of the cave were murals, every shade of turquoise winding into designs and pictures. One image flowed into the next, beckoning one's eyes to travel all around the room. "Wow," she breathed as she took in the spectacular gallery.

The others stood by her side, equally enthralled with the images they found there. They stood gazing around the cavern until Bruno began pawing at the pile of turquoise stones heaped near the center of the room. Musical notes sounded as he flung rocks from the mound.

"Bruno says we need to get back to business," Jo laughed. "Hey! I know that song the turquoise stones are making."

"Me, too," Dina mumbled. "It's one my grandpa used to play in the car sometimes. He told me George Strait recorded it after his thirteen-year-old daughter was killed in a car accident. I never really thought about it meaning so much to him, but now I understand. It could almost be about me. I wonder if Grandpa still listens to that song and if it helps him or if it's too hard to listen to now."

Jo sang a few words, "'And baby blue was the color of her eyes. Baby blue like the Colorado skies....'" The acoustics of the cavern piqued her voice to an unexpected level of perfection.

Aniela and Ariel gasped, "Your voice is amazing. You can really sing."

"Yes, she can. She could be in the Heavenly Choir if she wasn't chosen to be a warrior. Her dad, too. You should hear them sing together," Dina bragged as she hugged her teammate.

"Thank you. Look, Bruno's right. We need to get our turquoise and decide where we're going next."

Jo slid several stones Bruno'd flung back into the pile and picked up one smooth oval of shiny turquoise. "Perfect for our bag!" She held out her hand with the lovely stone.

Aniela held open the bag as Jo nestled the turquoise stone next to the milkweed pods. Jo lifted the clipboard and pen from the bag and checked off number six from their list. "We're a fourth of the way done. On to the next!"

They stepped outside and scanned their surroundings.

"There's the hill with the bluebells spreading up its side," Ariel pointed to the next hill. "That's the stand of trees where lots of logs were on the ground. That's where we were going to search for a blue beetle's exoskeleton. Bluebells first then the beetle carcass?"

Nodding heads affirmed their agreement.

"I'll go first this time," Jo called. "First jump to that oak tree with the wide branches, then to that bell-shaped boulder, then to the near side of the next hill where that grassy patch is."

As soon as Jo launched, Dina called, "Bruno, follow Jo. Tap! Jump!"

Bruno landed at Jo's feet near the top of the oak tree, with Dina right behind him. The other girls landed on branches as Jo, Bruno, and Dina jumped to the bell boulder. Soon, all five were together on a giant patch of emerald grass.

"The bluebells were covering that side of the hill, so we shouldn't have to move far to get to them." Jo headed straight for the patch of brilliant blue flowers.

Bruno raced between his girls, happy to be running again. When they reached the flowers, he somersaulted and landed among the blooms, grinning up at the girls who stood next to the patch of blue. Their laughter assured him they were enjoying his little show.

Dina plucked a stem of bluebells. "Here we go. Number one on our list." Several hummingbirds darted around the bluebells. One hovered near Bruno's face, looking deep in his eyes before zipping away.

"I wouldn't be surprised if that hummingbird was Gavreel checking up on us. She and Bruno are tight," Dina chuckled.

She dropped the bluebell into the bag and checked off number one.

Ariel said, "We're near the stand of trees with lots of fallen logs.

Let's look for the blue beetle carcass and the feather in that area."
She headed there with the others right behind her.

Flapping its wings, a blue jay squawked at the group as they approached the tree where it perched. Observing the girls and dog as they spread out around a rotting log, the jay continued its raucous chant. A feather floated to the ground.

Aniela looked up at the noisy bird. "I know we decided on a peacock feather for number three, but maybe it's supposed to be a blue jay feather. That bird has a crested head, blue feathers, and a raucous call, too. Let's get a blue jay feather and take it with us, not in the bag, but just with us, in case we're wrong about the peacock feather. That way, we'll have one and won't have to search if our bag gets returned with number three marked wrong."

Dina agreed, "That makes sense to me. Maybe we could put a jay feather in the outside pocket with the clipboard till we get back, then we could take it out before we put the sack in the can. You want to look for the feather, Aniela?"

"I know right where to look because that bird lost one while I watched it." She scrambled to the base of the tree and scooped up a blue striped feather from the ground.

Jo and Ariel were bent over, gently sifting bits of bark, pebbles, and other natural debris through their fingers as they searched for signs of beetles. The others spread out and searched the other side of the log.

Bruno ran to the far end of the log and furiously dug at the hollowed opening. He yipped several times as he dug, drawing the girls to him. They saw several beetles scurry further into the log to avoid the dog's pawing.

"Good boy, Bruno! You found beetles in this log, didn't you?" Dina asked as she pulled him back from the log. His paw caught on a rough edge and popped off a piece of the rotting bark. Several dark blue beetle shells lay exposed where the bark had come loose.

"Those are some excellent exoskeleton specimens," Ariel

admired as she gently plucked one from its resting place. "The shells are quite fragile when they're dried out like this one, so we need to protect it before we put it in the bag. I don't see any milkweed pods around here, but we could use some big leaves to make a padded carrier."

"Or feathers," Aniela suggested. "I noticed several feathers under that big tree. "Maybe we could pack some feathers together with long grasses and make a nest or basket for the beetle shell."

"Let's try it. Grab some of those feathers you saw, Aniela. There's some kind of grassy plant near those trees over there"' Ariel said as she pointed to the stand of trees a bit further down the hillside.

Before long, the girls had woven a makeshift basket of grass and lined it with several feathers. Ariel gently laid the beetle carcass on the bed of feathers and tied several more blades of tough grass over the top to keep the exoskeleton from falling out. She gingerly placed the basket in the bag, nestled among bluebell blooms.

"That takes care of number eight. Now what?"

"Let's look around these trees before we go down by the stream. We might find the robin eggshell or peacock feather up here. We know the cornfield was pretty close to the stream where we saw the hydrangea bushes when we were circling."

As Jo gestured toward the trees spreading down the hill, Bruno barked at the sky, his tail whipping the air.

They looked up and spotted the guys circling overhead, waving to them from their kite. They waved back, but whispered, "We'd better get going if our competition has arrived."

Giggles erupted as the girls headed to the grove where many birds trilled and flew from tree to tree.

"Look at all the nests in that huge oak tree," Ariel declared. "I bet there are robin nests somewhere among all those. Let's search the ground first, but we can jump up and check the nests if we don't see anything on the ground."

As the girls fanned out and checked the ground below the

nest-laden oak, Bruno stealthily approached a pair of creatures that strutted below a pair of nearby willow trees. They looked and smelled like birds, but they were huge! As he watched, the biggest one shook its tail and fanned it out erect behind its back, quivering and rustling, the tail feathers sounding like a drumroll. The tail was gigantic and still trembling as the bird screamed like a human baby. The smaller one darted behind a willow. The squawking continued as the big bird sidestepped in slow motion, rattling the elongated tail feathers and shaking its wings. It danced closer to the willow, shimmying its tail and wing feathers as it pranced closer to the other bird.

Dina noticed Bruno frozen in place watching something intently. "Bruno sees something over there. What's that noise?"

"That's a peacock!" Ariel cried. "He's on the ground a few feet from Bruno. Look how beautiful he is! I bet we can find a peacock feather over there."

The peacock sauntered to a rocky wall and fluttered onto it, his tail plumage rattling as he arranged himself on his perch, his eyes still fixed on the other bird that preened herself near the willow tree.

Jo pointed as they walked up slowly. "There's another one by that tree. We may be interrupting something."

"You're right," Ariel agreed. "That male on the rock wall is trying to attract this female's attention. He has romance in mind. Look around quickly for a loose feather so we can get out of here."

Aniela bent and scooped up an iridescent feather, shimmering with an eye marking of blue and gold. "Here!" She held up her find, a perfect tail feather that had been recently molted.

"That's perfect!" the others chimed as they moved toward Aniela.

"Come on, Bruno," Jo called as she headed back to the oak. "You can help us find a blue eggshell. Come on, boy."

"Let's add the peacock feather to our stash and check off number three from our list," Dina said as she admired the feather Aniela still held.

"I'm going to go up into that oak and start looking in the nests on this side of the tree. I won't bother any roosting mamas or babies in the nests, but I'll bet there are some empty nests with eggshells in them," Ariel announced.

"I'll start on the opposite side from you," Dina said as she engaged enhanced agility. "I'm going to start at the top and work down."

"I'll check those nests near the center trunk," Jo declared as she tapped her foot and leaped to the lowest nest in the center of the tree.

Bruno sniffed the ground as he circled the huge trunk.

"There are lots of acorns around here, aren't there?" Aniela asked the little dog. "Scraps of brown everywhere, but we're looking for light blue." She shifted the bag from one shoulder to the other.

"I may have found what we need," Jo called from a branch near the trunk, about halfway up. "This nest looks old, but bits of blue are in the bottom. I'm going to lift the whole nest and take it down to the ground so we can get a better look."

She landed near Aniela and Bruno, the nest in tow. Dina and Ariel joined the group on the ground and peered into the nest Jo held. Just as she had thought, shards of blue were mixed into the nesting material. The eggshell remnants seemed to be those of a robin.

"Bringing down the whole nest was so smart. We can put it in the bag without losing or crushing the fragile eggshells," Dina told her friend.

"So that checks off number four from our list. Now we just need five and six, the blue corn and blue hydrangea flower. We have to head to the lowland for both of those things. The big hydrangea bushes were near the stream, and the cornfield was pretty close to the water, too." Dina checked off number four as Jo slid the nest into the bag that Aniela held open.

Three enhanced leaps later, the girls and Bruno clustered at the base of the hills. "Enhanced speed should get us to the cornfield or hydrangea bushes pretty quickly. Which one do you want to do first?" Ariel asked her companions.

"Let's get the hydrangea first," Jo replied. We know right where they grow, so it will be quick and easy. We won't know if that cornfield has blue corn growing in it or not until we get there and shuck an ear or two. We may have to search longer for the corn."

Heads shook agreement as the girls and dog dragged their feet on the ground to engage enhanced speed. Long strides covered the distance quickly. Before long, the stream lay before them, a sparkling belt of blue and silver stretched as far as they could see.

The guys were headed downstream towards them. Bruno's tail seemed to propel him even faster than enhanced speed when he spied Gabe. The euphoric terrier somersaulted toward the boy he loved and vaulted into his waiting arms.

"I'm glad to see you, too, you little traitor," Gabe murmured as he nuzzled Bruno's ear. "Are you going to go with us for a while or stay with the girls?"

"It looks like he wants to hang with the losing team for a while," Ariel teased as she ruffled the top of Bruno's head. "He's been quite an asset."

"It took us awhile longer to figure out all of the riddles, but we finally got here," Micah declared. "We already found three things, so it's going fast since we finally started searching. That aerial tour of the hunting grounds helped us spy some things before we landed."

"It helped us, too," Jo told them. "Happy hunting, guys! We need to head upstream."

"That's true," Ariel agreed. "We're so curious about what our special reward is going to be that we need to get going. Listen for that bell. Later!" She trotted after Jo, with Dina and Aniela close behind.

"Is she always so full of herself?" Gabe asked.

"She's just teasing. She has a great sense of humor and likes to mess around with people. She's a great teammate. You just have to get to know her," Nate told him.

"Well, at least Bruno's with us now. He seems happy to let them go and stay with us." Gabe set Bruno down.

Bruno yipped, turned a circle at Gabe's feet, pawed his boot a couple of times, and took off toward the hills.

"He wants us to follow him. He probably wants to show us where they found some of the things on the list. Let's go, guys." Gabe activated enhanced speed and zoomed after his dog.

They stopped near the base of a hill. "This is close to where we saw the bluebells and blueberries growing when we were circling," Micah declared. We just have to go higher and pluck some berries and a stalk of those flowers."

"Then we'll search the stand of trees with all the fallen logs for the eggshell and the beetle shell," Nate added. "We should be able to get at least four of the things in this area. That just leaves the turquoise stone for us to locate."

In two leaps, the guys found themselves in the middle of a stand of blueberry bushes. Bruno stood on his hind legs and pawed the air.

"You want some of these, don't you?" Gabe asked as he tossed a plump berry to the waiting dog. He popped a couple in his own mouth before he tossed another to Bruno. "These are delish! Try some."

Nate and Micah popped berries in their own mouths as Gabe and Bruno enjoyed several more.

"We need to break off a little branch that has several berries and get going," Nate told his friends. "It won't take us long to get the bluebells from that next hill, but we have no idea where to find the turquoise. That may take a while. And we may have to search for the beetle shell and robin's eggshell longer than we think."

They stuffed a small branch loaded with ripe berries into their sack as Micah checked number two from their list. "Four down, four to go."

The boys bounded to the next hill and plucked a bluebell stem from the ocean of blue flowers that spread up the hill.

"Number one on our list is now in the bag," Gabe declared as Micah updated their checklist. A hummingbird whizzed around, darting among the boys and hovering near Bruno's face. The little dog sat still and stared at the bird, his countenance captured in his goofy grin.

"That dog seems to know that bird," Nate marveled. "I've never seen a dog stay that calm around a wild bird."

"That may not be just any wild hummingbird," Gabe replied. "Gavreel loves morphing into hummingbird form, and she and Bruno are really tight. That may have been Gavreel, or one of our other trainers. Bruno seems to recognize any of us even when we take different forms."

"Huh. Well, maybe we should ask Bruno where we should go next and just follow him," Micah said as he stuffed the clipboard and pen back into their sack's pocket.

"Where should we go now, Bruno?" Gabe asked.

To his surprise, Bruno raced partway around the hill and stopped in a shady spot, staring intently at the side of the hill.

"Look there. It's the mouth of cave, but you wouldn't even notice it in this shade. Let's look inside," Gabe said. "There's a reason Bruno stopped here."

As soon as the trio stepped inside, the turquoise walls seemed to come to life, pulsating and weaving shades of blue and green all around them. Bruno scratched the pile of turquoise stones in the middle, flinging a stone at their feet.

"Good boy, Bruno! You found our turquoise for us, didn't you? You're such a good dog."

Micah picked up the rock and dropped it in the bag. "Number seven, check. As much as I'd love to explore this turquoise paradise, we need to get going if we're going to find number four and number eight before the girls finish their list."

"You're right. Let's go, Bruno. We're going up to those trees with all the logs lying on the ground."

Bruno raced from the cave, with Gabe, Nate, and Micah close behind. He headed straight for the log where the broken-off end had uncovered several beetle exoskeletons. He sat at the end and stared inside.

"Would you look at that? He knew right where we could find some beetle shells," Nate marveled. "Maybe he went early with the girls so he could spy on their finds for us. Maybe he isn't a traitor. Maybe he's a spy!"

The boys laughed as Gabe ruffled the fur on the little dog's head and announced, "Bond. Bruno Bond."

"So now all we need is the robin eggshell and to get back to the sign before we hear the bell," Micah declared as he gently tucked the beetle skeleton inside a section of pulled-back corn husk and positioned some corn-silks and husks around it. "That should keep it from getting crushed in the bag." He checked off number eight.

"Let's start hunting around some of those big trees," Nate said. "There are probably lots of nests in that grove."

As the guys searched the ground around the base of several trees, Bruno sat quietly staring at the huge oak.

Unlike Bruno, the girls were not sitting quietly. They'd easily located the hydrangea bushes and plucked a blue flower ball for their bag. Dina launched into the biggest nearby tree to survey the land. She pointed, "The cornfields are this way. Not too far. Maybe twenty or twenty-five enhanced strides away."

She joined the other girls on the ground and said, "Let's go get that blue corn and get back to the sign."

They raced after Dina and found themselves at the edge of a huge cornfield.

"Let's pull back some of the husks and look at the ear of corn before we pick it. If it isn't blue, we need to leave it and keep looking for the blue corn."

They spread out to different cornstalks.

Jo called, "This one is just regular yellow corn."

Aniela called, "This one, too."

Dina announced, "This one is sort of reddish-orange. Definitely not blue."

Ariel's first ear was multicolored. "It looks like there are different varieties planted close together. These different colored ears of corn are sometimes called Indian corn because they're the variety natives grew when white settlers arrived from Europe. We just need to keep checking ears till we find the stalk that has blue ears."

They spread out and checked ear after ear. This item was taking longer than they'd expected.

"Look at the ground around that cornstalk in the next row. Those look like footprints around it. Maybe that's the one where the guys found their blue corn," Dina cried as she stepped to the next row and reached for an ear of corn growing just above her head. Sure enough, kernels of dark blue peeked out as she pulled back a section of the husk. "Got it!"

Dina pulled the ear loose and held it out, exposing the sapphire kernels.

"Excellent!" the team chorused.

Dina checked off number five as Jo slid the ear of corn into their pouch. As soon as the clipboard and pen were secured in the outer pocket, the girls bolted toward the sign.

As they connected themselves with hands on each other's shoulders and hands on the sign, their transporter kite reappeared and dropped its tether lines. Without hesitation, they each grabbed a line and were quickly strapped to the kite and on their way back to their starting point.

Bruno yipped as he stood with his front paws on the base of the gigantic oak.

"Hey, Gabe, look, Bruno's summoning us to this particular tree," Micah called. "Look at all the nests up in its boughs. Maybe we need to go up in the tree and look in the nests since we're not finding eggshells on the ground."

Nate and Gabe stood by Micah and looked up, spotting many, many nests in the ancient tree.

"It's worth a shot," Gabe agreed. "Bruno's usually right when he fixates on something. Let's go to different sections of the tree so we can check lots of nests. Try not to touch the nests though, unless you see broken shells and it's empty."

The guys hurtled from branch to branch, peering in nest after nest.

Nate called from near the center of the tree, "Here we go! There are light blue eggshells in this nest. No baby birds, just broken shells. I'm going to get some shells and meet you on the ground." He gently plucked two shells that were roughly half an egg each from the bottom of the nest.

"We did it! That's our last thing to find and we haven't heard a bell yet. Maybe we can beat the girls even though they started sooner than we did," Micah cried as he checked off their last item. "Let's nestle the eggshell pieces near the beetle and pad them with the cornsilk and husk."

As soon as the shells were tucked safely in their sack, the guys charged toward the sign. Hyper-speed and enhanced agility had them there in a matter of Earth seconds, clambering aboard the kite transporter with a grinning Bruno surveying the world below from the safety of Gabe's lap.

THE FINISH

The transporter dropped the girls near the receptacle that still sat by the sign and poles. Aniela pulled the blue jay feather from the outer pocket and stuffed their bag into the can.

The container spun, its sides illuminated with swirls of flashing colors. The hypnotic light show fascinated the girls, until their bag floated from the drum and landed at their feet, squarely in front of Jo.

"Oh, no, we have something wrong," Ariel cried. "Let's see what our checklist says."

She pulled the clipboard from the pocket and saw that item three was circled. The notation by the circle said, "Although a peacock feather is a good choice and much of the male peacock is blue, this feather is multicolored and does not fulfill the requirement for number three. You must think broadly and obtain a feather from a different crested blue bird to finish this task."

Aniela held up the blue jay feather. "Good thing I brought this with us. We can change our answer from peacock feather to blue jay feather and see if it works."

"You're absolutely right," the other girls chimed as they noticed the boys' transporter lowering near them. "Let's hurry and make the change."

Micah, Gabe, Nate, and Bruno approached the blue barrel just as the girls did.

"It looks like we might have a tie," Jo said. "Maybe we should put both bags in at the same time and see what happens. If both teams have every item correct, we definitely have a tie."

"The trainers did say everything was a test. Maybe part of the test is to see how we handle competition among ourselves. Whether teamwork or winning is more important in the end. We were told to help one another finish the task before we could move on together." Nate looked at the others and said, "I'm willing to tie, if everyone else is. It only seems right since we're here at the same time, but it's not just my decision."

"Me, too," Jo agreed. "Girls?"

A chant of, "Together, together!" filled the air.

Micah and Jo stepped up to the canister, holding the two bags above it. They pushed the bulging sacks together as they slowly lowered them to the bottom and released them. They joined the others, watching the light show the can put on for them.

Strobing flashes filled the air with brilliant colors. The container spun faster and faster, bursting into neon ribbons. The streamers swirled above, around, and through the onlookers, connecting them time after time, moving from one to the next. Streaks circled and dipped, eventually uniting above their heads like an enormous umbrella, breaking into sparks and sprinkling down on them. A bright blue flash enveloped the group as the exploding can's light show ended.

No one had any idea what had just happened. They stared at one another, overcome with a euphoric sensation and emotions they couldn't name.

"That was unexpected," a strange voice bellowed.

They spun around to see Gavreel, Michael, and Kirron standing with a man they'd never seen before.

"Team, I'd like to introduce you to Uriel," Gavreel said. "He's going to be in charge of this section of your training."

Speechless and staring at the huge man standing next to Gavreel, the team waited for whatever was coming next.

The trainers glanced from one to the other before Gavreel spoke again. "This is another one of those times when we need to explain things to you sooner than we usually do. Why don't all of you take a seat on the grass while we confer just a moment; then we'll do our best to help you understand what just happened here."

With questioning looks among themselves, the teens sank to the ground without speaking. Bruno nestled between Gabe and Dina, but kept his eyes fixed on Gavreel as she huddled with the Kirron, Michael, and Uriel.

"The Unification is already complete," Uriel marveled. "You saw the unifying streaks surge among all of them and the flash of blue. You know as well as I do, that flash of blue was God's element added to creation. God has chosen this team and endowed these angels with divine power directly. They've been made more powerful before any more training, before becoming fully-trained warriors. Their mobility and actions will be nearly effortless. They'll grasp concepts and understand complex situations by sharing their thoughts and previous experiences. Perhaps, like Gabe, they'll each uncover their seraphim fire. I have a feeling their discoveries will happen long before training and experience usually yield such knowledge."

"There's a great need looming," Kirron added. "We've seen how well both of these groups functioned in early training. Now that they've been united, we must make them understand how crucial it is that they work together to master all virtues and skills."

Michael declared, "They certainly earned their Unity token and reward. I don't remember two teams ever deciding to put their bags in the container together. Usually, the unity happens on the individual teams as they hunt together, and then after one team has won the competition and helps the other team complete the task, they can move on together."

"Let's explain the Unification first, then present the charms and rewards," Gavreel suggested. "They look pretty flabbergasted. That way we can ease some of the unsettledness they're feeling at the moment."

Kirron cleared his throat and announced, "Something quite remarkable just happened and we're going to do our best to explain it to you. Listen carefully as we tell you about the experience you just shared. We'll try to answer all of your questions, but your faith is the real answer to all questions."

"That's right," Michael agreed. "You have been unified into one team by God. You've been fast-tracked, so to speak."

Gavreel smiled at the still-confused faces. "You see, the universe is a life field, filled with life, everything originating from God. Atoms of a spirit coalesce around a field of love to manifest a form. The power to manifest into an entity comes from God's universal force. The life field appears as light and warmth, emanating from a central sun. It seeks a spiritual form around which to congeal and form a living creation. God directed a life force to all of your spiritual forms through the barrel. Its atoms bound you together and transformed you into a higher soul principle than you were individually or as two separate teams-in-training. You were united by the ribbons of light encircling and piercing each of you and connecting you to one another. The blue flash at the end was God's element being added, endowing the creation with its power of life. In this case, your new team was endowed with great power and great responsibility."

"You have been chosen again," Michael added. "You have been chosen to be unified and to serve together. This rarely happens, but when it does, it usually does not happen until much later, when training is complete and missions against evil become the warrior angel's purpose. Unification is often not until the level of Seraph or Archangel that eight or more are united to serve. This is a significant gift. You will now find that movement and action are nearly effortless. You'll understand things easily and reach new levels of comprehension quickly. There are great needs for which you must be ready."

"So, you're telling us we're all staying together as one team from now on because we were united by all of those lights?" Gabe summarized. "Even though we just met the other team and don't really know anything about them, we're now considered a new team? We're supposed to know how to work with one another from one scavenger hunt?"

"You'll learn about one another quickly," the stranger told him.

"You're not just considered a new team. You are a new team. A new weapon for fighting evil. You have been forged into one."

"I don't feel any different. I'm still just me," Gabe announced.

"Unity doesn't dissolve diversity. Diversity strengthens unity. You're each still your diverse selves, but you're more together. You're united, much like spouses become one as they build a life together and share all that comes their way. Their marriage union makes them stronger, and your union has made you stronger. All of you."

"Perhaps if you know more about Uriel, it will help you process all of this," Kirron told them.

Gavreel nodded. "Uriel is an archangel, the angel of wisdom and prophesy. He sparks inspiration and motivation. He visits people to help them gain new insights or make decisions."

"Uriel always directs focus to the one he serves: God," Michael told them.

Kirron continued, "Uriel helps people use their God-given intuition. He helps develop psychic powers and intuitive skills. He provides insights through visions, dreams, and sudden perceptions. He heals the loss of self-respect. He helps people find power in their own value and shine their light in the world."

"Uriel sparks minds with fresh ideas. He urges people to help one another. He motivates people to serve people in need and empowers them to do so. He helps in everyday situations such as problem-solving and finding the right words to say in difficult situations." Michael continued, "He is a very good guy."

"Here's what you need to remember about Uriel in a nutshell," Gavreel told the group. "He lights minds with wise ideas and concepts. He molds negative into positive. He always finds the light in shadows. Most importantly, he knows that all things happen for a reason, and God is the force in all things."

"Is there anything you want to add about yourself?" Michael asked.

Uriel grinned. "Maybe they should know I have an affinity for electricity. I like to spark minds with fresh ideas and sometimes use electrical signs that I'm present. You know, like lights burning out or appliances acting crazy for a bit. Oh, and thunderstorms. I love to arc through lightning. I really like to visit and spark ideas during electrical storms."

The trainers all snickered.

Uriel went on, "Seriously, all of you need to accept that God is unity. The universe is one vast integrated mechanism controlled by the One. Force, energy, and power are all one in origin. God's pure spirit is the director, the controller of the basic energy systems, the I AM, the source, and the center."

He took a breath and surveyed the faces fixed on him. "Divine reality is truth, beauty, and goodness. Love is the sum total of these three qualities. God is love. Love is the desire to do good to and for others. God is the creator and upholder of all reality. Everything. All material creation is perfectly coordinated and connected. God is omniscient, omnipresent, omnipotent, infinite, and eternal."

"So, why is there so much evil in the world that we're being trained to fight?" Aniela wondered. "If God creates everything and God is love, where did all the evil come from, and why does it continue to grow?"

"You're really asking if God created evil," Uriel mused. "Do you think that God would do that?"

"I don't know. I don't understand why there's so much evil and why we're needed to fight it," Aniela stammered. "Where does it come from if God didn't create it? You say everything in the universe originates from God. It just doesn't make sense to me."

"Evil isn't a *thing*. It's an aspect of a relationship. It's part of the miracle of humankind's creation. Humans were created to be creatures of genuine free will. The possibility of love between a person and God springs directly from the person's freedom to choose. The possibility of love entails risk though. It includes pain. Through the exercise of free will, humans have broken their relationship with God. That's what evil is all about."

"I still don't get it," Aniela mumbled.

"Me, either," Jo agreed.

Gavreel stepped forward. "God creates good, but also misfortunes or calamities to help humans grow and learn lessons. Calamity sent from God is always for a good and righteous purpose within the sovereign plan. There are many reasons for weaving trials and troubles into the fabric of human experience. Humans have free will to handle the situations that come their way. Faith should remind us that all things work for good if we believe and trust. God never creates wickedness or moral evil. Humans, however, have exercised free will and chosen to move away from God."

"Perhaps we should tell them a bit about the fallen, too," Michael inserted, "the ones who were expelled from Heaven. They're certainly a big part of the concept of evil."

Kirron continued, "Some sinned and were cast out of Heaven. Their leader is sometimes called Satan. Others use the names Devil, Lucifer, Iblis, Beelzebub, Baal, or the Tempter. Whatever name is used, this being and his rebellious followers are promoters of evil. They've spawned demons who work to capture souls and turn them to evil, as well as tempting humans to sin and turn away from God. Demons' numbers have grown mightily. This is why so many warriors are needed to fight the evil of the universe."

Nate blurted, "Demons are real. Sin is real. Evil is real. Though none of it was directly created by God, God created free will, and the angels' and humans' use of free will led to sin and more and more evil."

"That pretty much sums it up," Kirron replied. "As warrior angels, we lead the fight for God against the evil that just keeps multiplying in the universe. Our missions are always to serve God and save individuals from falling into the dark realm."

"We should get on with it, then, shouldn't we?" Dina asked. "Our training, I mean. We should get going."

"Yes, but before we do, you have earned your Unity charms,"

Gavreel announced. "Each of you, hold out your hand."

Gavreel raised her hand and spun it in the air several times. Each team member held a multicolored charm. It featured the head and arms of eight figures in a circle: one dog and seven humans. Each figure differed in color. The arms of each were wrapped around the figures on each side, connecting all together around the central message. Eight diverse figures connected and encircled the center like intricate lace edging. The center declared: **Unity is an eternal wonder, harmonized strength, and spiritual power.**

"Micah, will you read the inscriptions on the back of the charm, please."

He saw that each figure around the edge was inscribed. His voice resonated as he announced:

> *"Make every effort to keep the unity of the Spirit through the bond of peace."*
>
> The Bible: Ephesians 4:3

> *"So powerful is the light of unity that it can illuminate the whole world."*
>
> Baha`u`lla`h

> *"Unity is strength, division weakness."*
>
> Swahili Proverb

> *"He who experiences the unity of life sees his own self in all beings, and all beings in his own self, and looks on everything with an impartial eye."*
>
> Gautama Buddha

"And hold fast, all of you together, to the Rope of Allah, and be not divided among yourselves, and remember Allah's favor on you... He joined your hearts together, so that by His grace, you became brothers."

Quran 3:103

"Behold, how good and how pleasant it is for brethren to dwell together in unity."

The Bible: Psalms 133

"The wise embrace unity, luminous without ostentation, distinguished without justifying, recognized without boasting, persevering without complaining."

Lao Tzu

"I appeal to you, brothers and sisters, in the name of our Lord Jesus Christ, that all of you agree with one another in what you say and that there be no divisions among you, but you be perfectly united in mind and thought."

The Bible: 1 Corinthians 1:10

As soon as the reading was complete, Gavreel raised her hand, snapping each charm onto each chain. She raised both hands and made eight circles above her head.

Vivid flakes rained down on the newly joined team. Swirls of silver, black, blue, gold, purple, and red melded onto each of their uniforms.

"Your uniforms now bear the favorite colors of all team members," Gavreel told them. "Dina's silver, Gabe's black, Nate's red, Ariel's gold, Aniela's purple, and a double dose of Jo's and Micah's blue. Bruno does not have a color, but now bears the colors of the seven of you. Your team's emblem now reflects all eight of you as well."

They all glanced at the front of their uniforms and noticed the new patch featured there: Team JAMBANGD.

"Uriel, they're all yours. We know the training will progress well under your guidance. We'll present their reward at the end of this module."

UNEXPECTED

Uriel said, "We have much to do, but we'll progress further down the trail before our next challenge. Follow me. Pay attention to everything as we advance to our next stop. I'll be quizzing you."

He strode down the path, one dog and seven youths ambling after him.

Bruno sniffed the ground at the trail's edge and darted to a blue spruce growing off to one side. Something he saw or smelled under the evergreen tree fascinated him.

"Bruno, come. We have to stay with the others," Gabe called. "Come, Bruno."

Bruno sat, staring at something Gabe could not see from the trail.

"Oh, Bruno, we really need to get going. Come on, boy."

Bruno ignored him, entranced by something under the tree.

Gabe strode to the spot where Bruno sat and peered into the shadows. "What is it, boy? What do you see?" He bent over to get a better view under the tree's low-hanging branches.

Near the trunk, a bright blue creature, something like a cross between a spider and a crab, busily wove a web of connected helices. Each helix had a conical surface resembling the shape of a seashell. The spirals interconnected, forming an intricate pattern. One near the edge of the gauzy sculpture clearly flashed a word. Gabe. Gabe. Gabe.

"That's my name," Gabe whispered. "What do you suppose it means, boy?"

One yip and one step forward answered his question.

"I get the feeling I'm supposed to take the piece with my name. I don't know why, but it is summoning me to it."

Gabe dropped to his knees and crawled closer to the blinking section of the network of spirals. The flashing intensified, brighter and faster as he got closer. "I hope I'm right about this."

His fingers met his name. The cerulean spider-crab landed on top of his hand and bound it to the helix he was touching with strong strands of glistening fiber, making it impossible to pull away. It looked into Gabe's eyes as it rubbed its feet on his hand, as if reading or writing some invisible braille message.

"I see why you have been chosen," the little beast said in a surprisingly clear and soothing voice. "You have greatness within you. May you always use that greatness in service to God and others. This gift is one that will strengthen you and your team in every situation. If the others' greatness is anywhere near yours, you are indeed a most powerful team. Take this gift and show it to Uriel. He will know what to do. God be with you."

The creature released his hand as it jumped to a low hanging branch of the spruce. It stared at Gabe before disappearing deep into dense branches.

Gabe pulled the helix with his name. Connected by the web fiber, other helices loosened from the mass, thirteen in all. He stood and tugged the line of spirals connected to his.

They were beautiful. Pearlescent whorls of cascading colors, each one the work of a master artist. One name was embossed larger than the other words and symbols flowing along the spirals. Gabe's name was on the first shell-like piece, followed by Bruno, Dina, and Jo on the next distinct sections. He pulled the strand up further and examined each section. Nate. Micah. Ariel. Aniela. Uriel. Gavreel. Kirron. Michael. The last one did not have a name glistening like the others. It did have other words and marks tracing the curves of the spiral.

Gabe stroked Bruno's head before standing up. "I don't really know what this thing is or what it means, but clearly we are supposed to get it for the team. Good boy for seeing it, Bruno."

"Let's get going now, buddy. The others are probably way ahead of us on the trail by now."

Using enhanced speed, the pair joined the others as they approached two long sofas. The couches faced one another, each one laden with colorful pillows and backed by navy draperies that stretched in an arch and met in the middle of the space between the ends of the divans.

"Oh, gee, this looks a lot like the Board of Insights from our first trail. Not my favorite place to spend time," Gabe muttered. "Maybe this thing, whatever it is, will make it better this time."

"Have a seat anywhere on one of these sofas," Uriel instructed. "I'll explain what we'll be doing when everyone's seated comfortably."

They sat, Micah, Jo, and Aniela on one side, Nate, Dina, and Ariel on the other. Gabe stood near the end of a sofa, Bruno at his feet.

"Um, before we start this part, I have something to show you and tell you about," Gabe announced. "I really don't know what it is, but some creature told me to take it and show it to you, Uriel. The little blue thing said it was a gift and you'd understand and know what to do with it."

Gabe held out his cupped hands, showing the collection of sparkling spiral shells. The one on top of the heap still flashed his name.

Uriel stepped closer and peered into Gabe's outstretched hands.

"You saw a crabider? It—it gave you this?" Uriel stammered.

"I don't really know what the creature was. I'd never seen anything like it before. It was bright blue and looked like a cross between a spider and a crab. It was about the size of my hand. It sounded like a female voice when it spoke to me. It had a nice voice."

"You saw a crabider? It is a very rare and wondrous creation. You're right about it resembling both a spider and a crab. Its silk is very strong. Its gifts are very strong, too. May I see these?" Uriel asked.

Gabe nodded and Uriel gently plucked the still-connected pile of spirals from his hand. As he lifted the stash, all of the names were exposed. There was one with the name of each member of the team and their trainers, and one extra without a name.

Collectively, each team member drew in an audible breath as they saw their names flashing on the sparkling spiral disks. "What is it?" they asked in unison.

"Another unexpected development," Uriel relied. "Just a moment." He raised his hand and made several circular motions above his head.

Gavreel, Kirron, and Michael now stood at his side. "Look what Gabe just brought to the team, including us," Uriel said as he held up the strand of thirteen connected shell-like discs. Their names clearly flashed among the iridescent flood of colors, words, and symbols.

Michael spoke first. "You got this on this trail, Gabe?"

"Yes, sir. Well, it was a little way off the trail. Bruno left the trail and wouldn't come when I called him, so I went to get him. He was staring under a big blue spruce tree and wouldn't budge. I saw something moving in the shadows near the trunk, so I got down on my knees to have a closer look."

"What exactly did you see, Gabe?" Kirron asked.

"The first thing I saw was some sort of blue creature way back, near the tree trunk. Then I saw this beautiful web of spirals all connected. It looked like something from a modern art museum, a sculpture that fused all kinds of seashells together with this gauzy material. It was sparkling, almost hypnotic to look at, even in the shadow of the tree. One section of the web was pulsing with light. Then I saw my name flashing near the edge that was closest to me. Something in my mind told me to reach out and touch my name. When I did, the blue thing jumped and landed on my hand. It instantly wrapped my hand and the disc I was touching in that silk stuff you were talking about."

"You saw a crabider? It touched you and silked your hand to the helix with your name?" Gavreel questioned.

"Yes. Then the crabider, or whatever it's called, pranced on top of my hand. It was like it was reading or writing something with its legs. You know, like blind people do with braille. Then it talked to me before it jumped into the tree and disappeared."

"It spoke to you? What did it say?" Gavreel inquired.

"It's kind of embarrassing to say in front of everyone," Gabe replied.

"You have no need to ever be embarrassed with your team or with us," Michael reassured him. "You need to tell us, all of us, what the crabider said, as exactly as you can remember."

"Well, it had a really nice voice, soothing, almost like waves gently lapping on the shore. It said something like, 'I see why you've been chosen. You have greatness within you. Always use that greatness to serve God and others. This gift is will strengthen you and your team in every situation. If the others' greatness is anywhere near yours, you are a powerful team. Take this gift and show it to Uriel. He'll know what to do. God be with you.' That was all it said. Then I pulled the disk with my name and all thirteen of these came out at the same time, connected with the strong silk."

"Remarkable," the trainers chorused.

"Well, they certainly are fast-tracked," Michael marveled. "So few ever have the experience Gabe just had or receive this gift. Now we all receive the gift together."

"What is this gift?" Gabe finally asked. "I mean, it's beautiful. Does it go on our chains with our other tokens?"

"Have a seat, Gabe," Uriel said as he motioned toward the sofas.

Gabe and Bruno took the end where Nate, Dina, and Ariel already sat.

"This gift from the crabider is very, very rare and very, very valuable. Each helix contains every language from everywhere in the universe. When it's added to each of our uniforms, we'll become fluent in every language. Not just Earth languages used now, but the ancient languages and those from across the universe. That means we'll be sent on missions everywhere in the universe. Novices have never done such a thing. Even seasoned warriors such as we four have mastered only a few languages, limiting where we're sent. Usually studying languages and symbols take eons to master, even with my assistance," Uriel told them.

"How do they work?" Aniela asked.

"They'll become part of the emblem on the front of our uniforms. The helix will connect our essences with every language there's ever been. We'll be able to speak, read, and write fluently in whatever language is used wherever we are sent," Gavreel declared.

"So, why do you think we are getting these things?" Dina asked.

"As the crabider observed, there's greatness in this team," Michael replied.

"And there's significant need to fight evil everywhere in the universe."

"This gift adds to the greatness," Kirron explained, "but you must still be masters of all virtues, well trained, and completely aligned as a team before going on missions. I suggest we get these lingo-coiners on our uniforms and get on with the training."

"Agreed," Uriel, Michael, and Gavreel chimed.

"We need to affix each lingo-coiner individually. As each person holds the disc inscribed with his or her name against the team emblem near the heart, we will lay hands on each of you. Together we will recite this prayer: *Most high God, we thank you for this precious gift of languages. We accept this gift and ask you to guide us in its use so we may serve you.*"

"Obviously, Bruno won't be able to recite the prayer himself, nor will he be able to speak or read the languages, but he'll understand each one when it's spoken. Gabe, we'll have you hold it for him after yours is affixed to your uniform and say the prayer with the four of us as we touch him."

"Does everyone understand?"

Heads nodded affirmation.

"Here we go. Gabe, take the helix with your name flashing and hold it against the edge of your emblem closest to your heart," Gavreel instructed. Michael, Kirron, Uriel, and Gavreel laid both hands on Gabe's head, shoulders, arms and knees.

Five voices joined in declaring, *"Most high God, thank you for this precious gift of languages. We accept this gift and ask you to guide us in its use so we may serve you."*

The shell-like disc pulsed frantically, the silks connecting it to the next disc detached and stitched it to the edge of the team emblem. Gabe's emblem now featured a beautiful iridescent seashell spiraling with embedded words and symbols deep into his essence. He was the first Master of Languages in the group.

The trainers moved to Bruno and each person in the order they were arranged on the strand. They repeated the process time after time until all seven young teammates and one canine were imbued with the gift. They then took turns repeating the acceptance prayer for themselves.

Only one helix remained in Michael's hand, the one with no name.

"Why do you think we have an extra one with no name?" Jo asked.

"Because someone else must be joining this team soon. We don't know who or when, but obviously the plan is for one more to join us on these missions. We'll keep this helix safe until it's needed. Now, get back to work. There's much to do!"

"We'll see you soon, Uriel. Guide this team well."

Kirron, Michael, and Gavreel nodded to Uriel as they placed hands on one another's shoulders. Gavreel raised her hand and they vanished.

FULL ACCEPTANCE

Uriel lowered himself at the end of the couch shared by Micah, Jo, and Aniela. He studied the group that sat on the two sofas before he spoke. "Do you remember Gavreel saying she'd reviewed each of your lives on Earth and knew all about each of you? She did it without being present at the Board of Insights when each of you had to face everything you'd ever said or done. She studied each of your lives very quickly, but she knew absolutely everything about each one of you."

Slight nods told him they all remembered Gavreel's comment. He continued, "Michael, Kirron, and I also studied your lives and know everything about you. Every trainer does this prior to working with novices so that our training is as effective as it can possibly be. You must know everything about one another, too, since your teams have been merged into one. We're going to do some activities to give you insights into one another, then we'll do enhanced-speed life reviews."

"So, we have to go through our whole life on Earth again, like at the Board of Insights?" Gabe asked.

"Yes, but this time you have the insights you learned from doing it before. It won't be as difficult."

"That's hard to believe," Gabe muttered.

Uriel stared at him before he spoke. "Gabe, I know you've learned that every life experience has made each of us who we are now. Trauma and difficulties build resilience and survival instinct. Troubles teach us lessons we can learn no other way. You can't remove the traumas, but you can learn to handle the sharp pieces, learn to use them for good. Every experience is a tool, a tool given by God. Receiving these tools is an extraordinary honor, one that leaves me trembling before God at the astounding grace that's revealed in the lessons we've been given."

"So, you believe the bad stuff that happened to us or that we did are lessons, valuable gifts?" Gabe asked.

"Yes, they are," Uriel told him. "Remember that God is unity. God is love. Everything is connected if it comes from God. It's a great calling to go to others facing life-changing or life-ending transitions. God sends us where we're needed, when we're needed, with the tools that are needed. Many of the strongest tools are forged by adversity and suffering."

"Let's go on with the next step of training now. I want everyone to be silent for an Earth minute and think about something personal and important to you. You're going to tell everyone here about this thing, or person, or activity and why it's so important to you, why it's part of who you are, your essence. We'll go around the group until everyone has shared. I'll start after everyone has had the minute to think about the thing they want to share."

Bruno rested his head on Gabe's lap as the group pondered their words.

Uriel began, "I am who I am today because of my mother. Instilling the love of God in me from the time I was born, insisting I be the best I could be, and help others whenever I could, my mother shared her selfless devotion to God. She was the most intelligent and loving person I ever knew and sensed things about others. I watched her as I grew up, noticing she was always there whenever a need arose in others' lives. My mother encouraged people who felt defeated and planted ideas others could develop. Showing grace through difficult times and kindness to others at all times, my mother was the greatest influence in my life."

He paused, surveying the group. "Who wants to go next?"

No one spoke, so Uriel said, "Fine. We're going to do this. All of us. We'll just go up this sofa and down that one in order of how we're seated. Aniela, it's your turn to share."

She looked stricken at having to speak next. "I'm not really sure what to talk about. I didn't have a person I was close to like Uriel was to his mother. Unlike Micah and his music, or Nate with art, or Ariel with nature, I was never really good at anything. Spending my life in poverty, in a shabby apartment with drug addicts, on the streets, and in a wheelchair, I never had the chance to learn extra things. Being in the hospital so much after my injury, or bouncing from one foster family to another, nothing good ever happened. I liked to dance when I was little, but that all changed. Learning to watch, to look at things carefully, made me very observant. I notice details others don't. I sometimes get feelings about what's going to happen. I guess that's something."

"It's definitely something. The gifts of observation and intuition are valuable," Uriel assured her. The others nodded and smiled at her.

"Jo, you're next."

"I had a really great family on Earth. I loved my grandparents, my mom, and my sister. I had a cat I loved, too. But I guess my dad was really the one who was the greatest influence on who I am. Maybe that's partly because of who he is, but partly because of our shared passion for music. He always encouraged me to sing and helped me learn how to do things with my voice. He and I always loved singing together. Music was a shared heartbeat for us, connecting us by the beat of the song. The vibrations of our voices somehow linked us. We'd exchange glances and smile from within, knowing the music we were sharing was really roots growing and connecting our souls. Dad also taught me right from wrong—well, along with my mom. Dad set a high standard and I tried to live up to his expectations. Everyone who ever knew him loved him and tried to live up to his expectations. He's kind, gentle, and loving, but he can be fierce. That's why he's always been a great warrior. He built those things in me, along with a deep love of music."

"Thank you, Jo. Your brief summation of Michael is quite accurate. Now we all understand how valuable his influence is. You were very blessed to have had him as your father. Your musical gift is undeniably a huge part of your essence. Micah?"

"My family was great, too, but I couldn't pick just one person who's a big part of who I am. Music, though, that goes to the core of my essence. Music has always been my passion. I love to sing and play instruments. My parents always told everyone that I started singing before I started talking. Because I plunked on the piano when I was about three, my mom showed me how to play 'Chopsticks' and 'Twinkle, Twinkle, Little Star.' I played both tunes the first time I tried. She taught me a few other easy songs, and I could play them all. The piano seemed to be a part of me. Before long, I was sitting at the piano creating my own songs. I also learned to play the violin, the clarinet, and the guitar before I transitioned. Although I was pretty good on the other instruments, the piano's my favorite."

"You were a musical prodigy, Micah. You discovered your gift very early and were developing it well. Music truly is part of your essence." Uriel smiled warmly. "Your turn, Nate."

"Um, I guess I'd say art is the most important part of who I am. I started drawing as soon as I could hold a crayon or pencil. Everyone said my drawings were way beyond my years. I loved drawing everything. Like Micah with the piano, paper and pencil just seemed to be part of me. I didn't have to think about drawing or how to capture images on paper, they just flowed from my head through my hand to the paper. I can't really explain it, but creating art was as natural as breathing. I loved drawing, but I loved painting with watercolors and oils, too, controlling the colors as well as the shapes. I was just learning how to sculpt when I transitioned. I loved molding clay into what I envisioned it to be. Stone seemed to tell me what its true form was, what needed to emerge from the stone as I chipped at it. Because I love working in every medium I've tried, I can't say I have a favorite medium for my art."

"You were an artistic prodigy, Nate. You were bestowed a very large gift of artistic ability, and you used it well. Realizing you could and should create art definitely goes to the core of who you are." Uriel's smile encouraged the next speaker. "Dina?"

Dina looked around the group before she spoke. "I feel like I'm copying what others have already said. I had a great family, too, and a dog that I loved. I think all of them are big parts of who I am. I loved to run and play soccer. I was really good at both, so I think they're also big parts of who I am. But, like Nate, art is really the nucleus of my being. My gift might not be as big as his, but I love to draw and paint. I get totally absorbed in my art. I feel that what I draw or paint is born out of my heart, reflecting goodness. I hope that reflection is of goodness within me, and that it brings joy and leads people to love—love the image and the story, and the feelings the image conveys. That's why it flows from me, like a river that has a sense of where it's going before it gets there. Usually the flow is gentle, but not always. At times it rages until it's on the page, saying what it must. It's born rather than created, showing itself for what it truly is, a message that speaks to other souls. I believe that my art connects to my soul, that it's part of me and part divine inspiration. Because my heart has a lot to say, so does my art. Sometimes the message is as free as the wind. Sometimes the message screams to see pain and learn the lessons packed in the painful images. Often the message is beauty, made to enjoy for its own sake. Other times the message is that love is everywhere, look around and see it. My art dances and weaves in and out of my soul before it's finished, capturing its message on the page."

"Wow! You're a whizz of perception and words as well as art, Dina," Uriel marveled. "Maybe you're a writer as well as a visual artist. Painting such fine images with your words may be another gift to be developed."

"Thank you, Uriel. I'm touched by your words," Dina murmured.

"Ariel?"

"God's creations are linked to my soul somehow," Ariel began. "I mean things in nature, animals, birds, insects, plants, even minerals and things that aren't living. I've always loved being outdoors and have been fascinated by every kind of fauna and flora. Perhaps my grandpa, a park ranger, is part of the reason why. He'd show me objects and pictures, and talk to me about things in nature from the time I was a baby. Loving nature is as natural as loving him. We spent so many hours together in the woods during the daytime and poured over his geology, botany, and zoology books in the evenings. I'd memorize the images and names of rocks, flowers, trees, insects, and animals as I studied his books. I remembered a lot of what I learned from his books and could recognize the real things when we were outside. I learned to be quiet and take cues from nature. I know it sounds strange, but most animals weren't afraid of me. If I was still, they'd come very close, sometimes sniffing me. It was thrilling to have wild creatures accept me as part of their world. Grandpa said he'd never seen anything like it, that it was a rare and beautiful gift."

"Your grandfather was a wise man," Uriel told her. "Pure nature connection is a rare and valuable gift, one that you developed well from an early age with the guidance of your grandfather."

"I hope you've had time to gather your thoughts, Gabe. It's your turn."

"Well, this is embarrassing to say, but I was hyperactive and took lots of risks my whole life. I was a tough kid to be around. No one liked me. Until Bruno. Bruno loved me from the beginning. He's all love. His love poured from those alert dark eyes and settled me in a way nothing else ever had. He's a little dog, but has the energy, tenacity, and heart of a giant, coated with pure affection for everyone. He loves moving as much as I do. He could actually keep up with me! Training him gave me the focus I'd never had before. I never thought I really had any talent or gifts until I started skateboarding and doing parkour, with Bruno by my side. I was good at both of those things. I think having Bruno with me gave me confidence. Our hours in the park burned off energy in a positive way so I didn't get in as much trouble at home or in school after I got him. Loving him and being loved by him gave me hope. Bruno is my treasure, my hero, my savior. I don't know if a dog can really be part of a person's essence, but Bruno's been the most important thing in my life. I think our souls are intertwined."

"They may be," Uriel said. "It's a gift to have such a connection to another living being. Your gift of movement has been well developed. You're an impressive athlete, Gabe."

"Thanks."

"Everyone's learned a great deal about their teammates from these moments of sharing. There's still much to learn, however. Next, we're going to go around the group again. This time, each of you will share two things. First, you should share the best moment of your life. Then, you'll tell everyone about thirty seconds of your life you'd relive again if you could and explain why. It might be another wonderful moment you'd relive and savor, but it might be a difficult experience you'd change if you had the chance. Contemplate what you'll say carefully. You must explain why you have chosen both examples from your life. There are no right or wrong answers. We're learning about one another on this path to full acceptance."

The group sat quietly, reflecting on his or her own life, waiting for Uriel to tell them it was time to share.

"Are we ready? Anyone want to volunteer to go first?"

Jo sheepishly raised her hand. "I will, I guess. The best moment of my life was when my sister and I found our cat, Joy, by the dumpster of the apartment building. We'd just moved there from our house on base and we didn't like it or our new school. Then we found that cat. She was so skinny and so hungry, but she purred and rubbed around both of our legs. It was love at first sight with that cat and me. My sis and I brought her inside and fed her a can of tuna and a bowl of milk. We played with her with a piece of yarn after she had a full tummy. She jumped and tried to get the string, sometimes making flips. Watching her made my sister and me laugh. My mom came home from work and she started laughing, too. The three of us laughed together at the antics of that silly cat. It was the first time in over a year, since my dad had died, that we laughed together. It felt so good to laugh again. That's why we named her Joy. She brought joy back to us. That's why it's my best moment. We accepted that we could go on with our lives without being sad all the time, that it was okay to have joy in our lives."

"Thank you for sharing your best moment, Jo. Are you ready to tell us the thirty seconds you'd relive if you could?" Uriel asked.

"I'm having a hard time deciding between two things I'd change if I could," Jo told him. "They're both things I wish I could make different."

"You can share both if you wish, or just tell us one. Your choice," Uriel replied.

"Well, I'd relive the last thirty seconds I had with my dad before he deployed," Jo told them. "I was really a brat, and I made leaving even harder on him. I didn't ever realize it till I saw the scene played on the Board of Insights. I was selfish, only thinking about myself. If I could relive those thirty seconds, I wouldn't say the same things to him. I'd just tell him how much I love him and what a great dad he's always been, how lucky I am because he's my father. I'd relive those thirty seconds because I regret the way I treated him. He didn't deserve my attitude, and I never got to see him again until I transitioned."

"That was insightful and brave of you to share. Do you want to share the second thing you mentioned?" Uriel prodded.

"If I could change another thirty seconds, it would be talking to my mom and sister in the hospital. We all knew what was coming. We all knew I was dying. The leukemia had almost defeated me. My mom and sister never left my side in those final days. It was so hard on them, but their love blanketed me. I wish I'd told them again that I loved them. I wish I'd told them I knew how strong they both were and that I knew they'd be there for one another, pulling each other through the grief. I wish I'd reassured them that I was ready to leave and be with Daddy. I wish I'd told them to find joy sooner this time, that I wanted them to laugh and live. I didn't even try to give any comfort back to them. I was just so mad about the pain and dying that I didn't think about them. I wish I could relive thirty seconds near the end and say the things I should've said."

"That, too, was very brave of you to share," Uriel soothed. "It's hard to face moments we regret, but we learn so much about ourselves and help others learn, too, when we face them head-on. Your visit reassured them and gave great comfort, I can assure you of that. You might not have said the words at the end of your earthly time, but you sent the message when you visited."

"I did feel as if my visit helped them."

"It certainly did. It was a most impressive visit of comfort. So, who wants to follow brave Jo and tell us their best moment?" Uriel coaxed.

"I'll go next," Nate declared. "The best moment of my earthly life was when my big brother came home from deployment. He and I'd always been close, even though he was ten years older than me. He always watched out for me and was almost like a second dad when I was little. He never ever minded having me tag along with him, even though I now realize I must have cramped his style as a teenager. Anyway, I was ten and he was twenty when he left for basic training. I missed him so much when he left. When he finished training, he told us his orders were taking him to a war zone, but he couldn't tell us exactly where. My whole family worried so much about him the whole time he was gone, which was a little over a year. Then one day I was sitting in class trying to figure out a math problem. The room got completely still. You know, weirdly still for a sixth-grade classroom. I looked up and saw him standing in front of my desk, dressed in his camo uniform. He had this great big goofy grin on his face, as if he'd just pulled off the biggest surprise in the world. I guess he had. The look on his face told me he was really proud of himself! My mom and dad were standing in the classroom door, next to my teacher. Their smiles are indescribable. I don't even remember standing up and launching into my brother's arms, but somehow, we were tangled in a bear hug as everyone in the room clapped and cheered. That moment was pure love. It was relief that he was safely home and euphoria because we were together again. That moment couldn't have been any better. It was perfect, even though I cried like a baby in front of my whole class."

Uriel declared, "That's a fine memory and definitely worthy of being your best moment. Thank you for sharing it with all of us. Now for the thirty seconds you'd relive if you could."

Nate hesitated, staring at the ground between his feet. "I'm not sure I should really say what I'd like to relive if I could." He glanced around the group. All faces showed reassuring expressions, though no one said anything. "The thirty seconds I'd relive if I could, would be not getting in the car the night I died. I know I was called here to be a warrior, but if I'm being completely honest, I would change that. I wasn't ready to leave my family or my life on Earth. I was only fifteen and enjoying high school. I was getting better and better at creating art and figuring out who I was as a person. I was blessed with a great family and some really special friends. I never should have gotten in the car with my buddy. He'd just turned sixteen and gotten his license. We thought we were so cool. Joyriding with him was exciting, until it wasn't. When he lost control and went off the road, the excitement turned into a few seconds of terror. We rolled several times before the passenger side of the car slammed against a boulder. I was killed on impact. He survived, but he'll spend the rest of his life in a wheelchair, regretting the joyride we shared. Yes, I'd definitely change the thirty seconds when I climbed in that car."

Dina patted his hand. "I don't think any of us were ready to come here when we were called. We were all so young. But, you have to accept your calling, Nate. You have to accept that your earthly death is part of God's plan and that those years were just a small part of your life. I know it's hard. Sometimes your heart needs more time than your mind to accept things, but think of the good you'll do and the people you'll save. There are better things ahead than any you left behind. It's hard to accept this change, but once you embrace who you are now and what you're meant to do, your regret will be eased. All of us have to keep going forward and accept our destinies."

"She's right," Uriel observed. "You have greatness within, Nate. All of you have greatness within. Rare and true greatness. The combined strength of this group is being melded into a powerful tool for the battle against evil."

"I know I shouldn't regret that I got in that car the night I died. I know I was called here. I've accepted that, but I still regret what I did to my family and friends. My stupid mistake of getting in that car and thinking risky driving was funny and cool put all of them through tremendous pain. I actually encouraged my friend to keep going rather than telling him to slow down. Stupid. Stupid. Stupid."

"I might have been one of the biggest risk takers of all time. I learned at the Board of Insights that I had to accept God's forgiveness. Then I had to forgive myself and others before others could forgive me for things I'd done. We've all done stupid things in the past. We have to forgive ourselves and move on," Gabe remarked.

Uriel agreed. "Dina and Gabe are both honest and true with their words for you, Nate. Your new friends are wise indeed. Who's willing to share next?"

Dina raised her hand in a halfhearted wave. "I'll go next. The greatest moment of my life was with great-grandmother after she moved into our house. She was my mom's grandma. Great Granny, or GG, was getting old and everyone was worried about her living alone. We had an extra bedroom downstairs, so my parents moved her into that room. GG was so smart and so sweet and so funny. She had a hard time walking, but her mind was still sharp as a tack. I loved being with her. I'd brush her hair and smooth lotion on her skin. We did puzzles together, and she taught me how to draw faces and do calligraphy. She was such an amazing artist. I was in awe when she put pencil or pen or brush to paper. Even in her nineties, she could bring beauty to a page. When we were together, she'd tell me all about people in the family and experiences she'd had in her long life."

Dina took a deep breath and continued. "One day, GG said she had a special job for me, if I was willing to do it for her. I'd have done anything for her, so she didn't even need to ask. She wanted me to record a list of who she wanted to get her things when she passed away. She said she'd sign it after I had everything recorded. She said we'd make a beautiful border all around the edges of the words. After her words were recorded in my best calligraphy and we'd created the border together, her last will and testament became a work of art. It was part of her legacy to our family. She said we'd keep it a secret, just between us until the day she died. She trusted me to do this important thing for her and keep it safe until the time was right. I didn't like to think about her dying, but I was so honored. My GG dictated a special message to every member of the family about why she wanted them to have the things she was bestowing upon them. It was just so special, and I got to be a part of the magic she left our family. My mom got her beautiful Tiffany lamp and a ring that had been in the family for generations. GG's message told Mom that the heirloom ring was a reminder of the circle of life that was family, the most precious treasure of all. The lamp, she said, was to light her future with beauty. GG said everyone craves light, that it is light that lets us see beauty and be beautiful. She left me her collection of art books, telling me the masters had nothing on me, but that I should study their lives, techniques, and great works. She also left me a diamond necklace. It was just one beautiful sparkling gem mounted on a chain. She said the diamond was just like me, perfect and needed nothing to enhance its value or beauty. She wanted me to wear the necklace on my wedding day and know she was with me, then and always. She left every child, grandchild, and great-grandchild something special from her life and a personal message. Helping her create her final piece of art was the greatest honor and greatest moment of my life."

"Wow! Your GG sounds like an amazing woman," Nate commented. "As a fellow artist, I understand why that time is your greatest moment. I admire your devotion to one another and to art."

"Thank you, but you might not admire me at all after you hear the thirty seconds I wish I could relive."

Dina took a deep breath, "I wish I could relive the thirty seconds around the time the Tiffany lamp crashed to the floor. I said absolutely horrible things to my little brother that I wish I'd never said. You see, he sneaked up behind me when I was engrossed in drawing and poked me. He wasn't mad or anything, he was just messing around like little boys do. I was so startled, I jumped and screamed, which caused my dog Yodels to bolt and crash into the table with the lamp. Yodels knocked the lamp to the floor and several pieces of glass broke. My pencil made a long streak and ruined my drawing when I jumped. More importantly, Mom's precious lamp from GG was ruined. I was so mad. I shook my brother and screamed at him. I told him I hated him, and that our family was better before he was born, that he was nothing but trouble. He ran to his room crying. I never apologized. I never said or did anything to make him feel better. I just bullied him and left those hateful words hanging over him, poking him again and again when he thought about what had happened. A couple of days later he ran away from home. It wasn't until I faced my life at the Board of Insights that I learned he ran away because of me. He was so upset about the things I'd said. He really believed the family would be better off without him. I hurt him so badly and I never did anything to help him. Instead of being a big sister he could count on, I was the bully who tortured him with my words, which tortured my parents with worry because I was the reason he ran away. My greatest regret is that whole scene with my little brother and the way I mistreated him."

"Lots of siblings say and do awful things to one another from time to time," Ariel said. "It doesn't mean they don't love one another. I can tell how much you love your brother. I'm sure he forgave you, even if you never said anything to him about the scene when the lamp broke. I bet you let him know how happy you were when he came home, didn't you?"

"I did. We were all so happy and relieved when he was found. I hugged him a bunch of times and we played with Yodels together, which he really loved. We laughed so much that afternoon. I think Yodels just knew to entertain us, so we'd laugh and laugh."

"There you go. Your loving attention and shared laughter chased away the harsh words. They weren't poking him anymore."

"It helped both of us feel better when Dad found a stained-glass artist who could repair Mom's lamp. Dad said it was expensive, but worth every cent to see the light in all of our eyes when he brought it home, put it back in its place, and turned it on. Serene light rose with casual elegance from GG's lamp again. Mom said its radiance was a gift to our family, reminding us that we could recover from injuries and should honor one another and our shared lives, which was the best way to honor GG."

Uriel's pure, vibrant smile plunged deep into each young person's soul. "This activity is going very, very well. Jo, Nate, and Dina, you've bared your souls to the group, which is necessary for full acceptance. It's never easy to admit and speak about our regrets, but by facing them and putting them into words that others can understand, you gain greater insight yourself. Who's going to go next?"

Micah stretched. "I'll go next, though what I have to talk about isn't very interesting. I guess the best moment of my life was when I was asked to sing the national anthem before the start of a minor league baseball game. Dad and I were huge fans, so we went to as many games as we could for as long as I can remember. Somehow, our team heard I was a good singer. I still don't know how they knew about me, but maybe my choir teacher contacted them and sent a video of me singing, encouraging them to check out one of their most loyal fans. The team invited me to sing the national anthem at a home game, so of course I accepted. I got to meet the players and coaches. It was exciting to be on the field and look up into the stands. My whole family and a bunch of friends came to hear me. Everyone applauded for a really long time after I finished, but I think my family applauded the loudest. They were so happy and proud. My dad's face radiated such pride. It's hard to describe the joy I felt performing there and seeing my family, especially my dad, so proud of me. I think it's my greatest moment because of how proud they were, but also because my music, which always brings joy to me, encircled everyone with joy that day. It felt so good to make other people so happy."

"You're kidding! That was very interesting," Jo bubbled. "I know exactly what you mean about the feeling you get when you know your voice brought joy or comfort to another person."

"Thanks. That was the easy part to talk about. This next part is going to be harder."

Uriel spoke. "You'll be fine. Remember our goal, full acceptance of one another. We gain great insights of others' essences by what they choose to share. One cannot fully understand or accept another until we know their choices for their best moment and the moment they'd relive if they could."

"If you say so. I just want it to be over."

"Proceed," Uriel encouraged.

"I was kind of a jerk when I was in middle school. I was better by the time I started high school, but I pushed limits when I was twelve and thirteen. I thought I was cool and funny when I said and did offensive things. I guess the time I'd relive if I could, happened in the cafeteria of my middle school. I peeled an orange carefully, so the peel looked like a guy's privates, you know the penis and testicles. All the guys at my table were laughing about it. Actually, we were roaring. We all thought my artistic creation was hilarious. Any way, there was this one boy who was special needs. I think he had Down's Syndrome or something like that. He just wanted to fit in, to be accepted by others, so he was always hanging around. He looked over my shoulder and asked what was so funny. I told him I had made a special sculpture with my orange peel and he could have it if he wanted. He reached for it and held it up. In a loud voice he said, 'I don't get it. What's so funny about a pee pee?' He swung it so the long piece bounced up and down. Everyone saw him and started laughing and pointing. He had no idea what they were laughing about, but he knew it was directed at him. He was so humiliated that he ran from the cafeteria. The orange peel was still in his hand bouncing up and down. I'm sure he could hear the uproarious laughter all the way down the hall. He knew everyone was laughing at him. I was such a jerk. I wouldn't peel my orange like that if I could relive thirty seconds, and I certainly would never humiliate that poor boy. He was so innocent because of his disability, and I preyed on that to get laughs. I regret my stupid, mean behavior. I also regret that I never apologized or did anything to help him."

"You weren't *kind of a jerk* when you did that," Jo growled. "You were a full-fledged jerk. A bully of the worst kind, preying on someone who had no chance against you."

Micah hung his head. "I know. I was a jerk. That's why it's the time I'd relive if I could. But I can't, so I had to forgive myself and ask God and others to forgive me at the Board of Insights. I hope all of you can forgive me, too. I've tried to be better since then, since I realized how awful I was."

Uriel spoke. "Divine forgiveness has come to all of us. We, all of us, must forgive ourselves and one another for our transgressions. Remember, everything we ever said or did, good and bad, has built us into the individuals we are today."

Ariel mused, "We all sinned during our earthly lives and we're all forgiven, or we wouldn't be here. Micah, you aren't that jerk any more. You've moved way beyond that time. You're one of the best souls I've ever met, kind and loving to everyone. Who you are now is way more important than who you were when your hormones were raging out of control."

"Thanks for saying that, Ariel," Micah murmured. "It means a lot."

"Affirmation is important. Three of you still need to share. Who's next?"

"Me, I guess," Ariel replied. "The best moment of my life was outdoors with my family. Surprising, I know."

She grinned as the others all said, "Of course."

"It was winter, very cold and clear. Snow blanketed everything. It made the world bright even at night. My grandparents, parents, and I had gone to town to do some shopping and eat supper at our favorite cafe. When we drove back, the northern lights frolicked in the sky. Ribbons of green, pink, and white swirled overhead and disappeared behind the trees, then rose again in their chase across the sky, with orange and purple shimmers in pursuit. We watched the magical display from the truck's windows the whole way back. When we piled out of the truck, the aurora borealis seemed to have concentrated their chase right over my grandparents' cabin. Streamers of colors poured from the sky and formed what looked like an enormous umbrella over the cabin and all of us standing on the driveway. It was almost as if my family was being cocooned in beautiful neon colors. We stood there looking up, our arms wrapped around one another. We marveled at the miracle we were sharing. Each color seemed to fade into another, swaying and changing, as we watched. The lights glimmered and stretched, grew and shrunk, then grew again. Even though the frosty air nipped at our faces, none of us moved toward the cabin. We didn't go in until the lights marched away, retreated to a part of the sky we couldn't see. My family, all of us, felt God's presence that night. This shared experience strengthened us somehow. I know all about the scientific explanations of the aurora borealis, sunspots and solar storms, but I also know that God gave us this gift, the dazzling natural phenomenon we shared."

"That was quite a moment," Gabe remarked. "Sharing something so special with the people you love must have made it even better."

"Yes, it did. Everything about that time is seared into my memory. The image in my mind is just as clear as the night it happened."

"Are you ready to tell us about the thirty seconds you'd relive if you could?"

"I suppose so. If I could relive thirty seconds of my life, it would be to go back to a huge argument I had with my mom when I was twelve. She told me I couldn't go anywhere until I finished my chores and my book report that was due next week. I wanted to spend the night at my friend's house, but Mom said no. She told me I had to get my bedroom and bathroom cleaned, then tackle that book report. She said there'd be no outings, electronic devices, or TV until all three things were done, even if that meant I was restricted the entire weekend. She even took my phone and hid it! I was so mad! I screamed some horrible things at her. I called her the B-word and said I hated her. She just calmly said that she was sorry to hear that, but she loved me and always would, but she still expected me to get my chores and book report done before anything else. I stomped to my room and slammed the door. I was so mad. I never apologized. It took me quite a while to decide to start cleaning my room, but I finally did it. I really liked the book, too, when I read it. It was Hoot by Carl Hiaasen. I got an A on my book report."

"I was really awful to my mom once, too," Jo admitted. "Probably most kids are when they're growing up. I guess because we know our parents love us, we vent our ugliest emotions on them, knowing in our hearts they'll love us through the meanness and hurt. I wish I hadn't treated my parents badly either, but I know they forgave me. I'm sure your mom did, too, even if you two never talked about it."

Uriel declared, "You're absolutely correct, Jo. Now we're down to two who still need to tackle this task. Gabe? Aniela? Which one of you is going next?"

The last two looked at and pointed at one another. It was clear that neither wanted to jump into the task.

Uriel coaxed, "Both of you have to do it before we can move on to the next activity, so if you don't decide, I will."

The group sat in stone silence. "Fine. Gabe, tell us the best moment of your life."

Groaning, Gabe started. "That's the easy part. The best moment of my life was when I got Bruno. He was the squirmiest, cutest, most playful pup ever! I was eight. Bruno was about four months old. Our neighbors had had him for a couple of months. I'd stop to pet him and play with him every time I saw them out in their yard or out on a walk. He was always so excited to see me. He'd wag his tail so hard it was like he was wagging his whole body. He'd lick my hands and face and crawl up into my lap when I sat on the ground. Anyway, my neighbors were in a bad car crash. Her injuries were minor, but he was hurt really badly and was in the hospital a long time. She talked to my parents and asked them if she could give Bruno to me since she couldn't take care of him with the long hours she was spending at the hospital with her husband. She said it would help them a lot, and they could still see the dog when they were back home. She even said Bruno seemed to love me more than either of them and they felt he was meant to be my dog. She told them how gentle I was when I played with Bruno and that she thought having the dog would help me, too. She was pretty convincing, I guess, because my parents agreed to try it if I'd be responsible for his care and training. The day she gave him to me, I lifted him near my face and told him he was my dog now. We locked eyes and communicated our mutual commitment to one another. This little dog saved me." Gabe stroked the top of Bruno's head. "He's been a love sponge, soaking all that I give him then overflowing back to me. I hadn't had much experience with feeling loved till I got him, but there's no denying he loves me with his whole heart. Just being with him calms me and makes me a better person. He has this power. It's hard to explain, but he's like a divine antidote for everything that's wrong in a person's life. He looks deep within and somehow locks onto an internal spark. He brings peace and comfort just by looking into a person's eyes. I've seen it time and time again. At first it was just with me, but now I see that he communicates deeply with other people too. To me, Bruno has always been a bright star in a profoundly dark world. His brightness reaches everyone. He fills people with love and hope. That voice from my *bright star* calls us to look beyond the darkness to the bright light of love and hope."

Dina said, "Bruno is quite a dog. You're right, Gabe. He brings love and hope to everyone he encounters. I'm so glad he's here with us."

"Yes, from everything I've seen, he's quite a dog. He wouldn't be a member of a warrior team if he wasn't," Uriel stated. "Now for the thirty seconds you'd relive if you could, Gabe."

"Well, Dina and Jo already know this, but I was diagnosed with hyperactivity and attention deficit disorder when I was in kindergarten. I was really wild. I couldn't control my body. I was impulsive and took lots of risks. It seemed like I was always in trouble. My dad wouldn't allow me to take any medicine to help with the ADHD, so I just kept getting into more and more trouble. My dad's solution was his belt. I had so many beatings. My mom took the lashes, too, when she tried to stop him from hitting me. Because every moment in my early life seem pretty horrible to me, I don't know what thirty seconds I'd relive. I can't think of one happy moment in my house with my family until I got Bruno. I guess I'd relive the moment they told me I could have Bruno if I'd take care of him and train him. I was shocked, but so happy. I saw my mom's smile behind my dad when he told me I could keep the dog as long as I'd take complete responsibility for him. I know Mom had convinced my dad to let me try, and that she risked his anger if anything wasn't up to his expectations. She believed in me! I just processed that. My mom believed I could look after the dog and she stood up for me, even though it was risky for her. She was right. I nurtured Bruno and he nurtured me. Bruno never once messed in my parents' house. My mom cared for him when I was at school. I could see she loved him, too. She taught him to sit and stay. He's smart, so he learned those commands quickly. Good thing, too, when my dad was around. No doubt, that's why Mom trained him when everyone else was gone. She wanted him to stay with us, too. I took Bruno to the park whenever I was out of school. Because we played so much, he was worn out when we got home. He loved to run and chase me on my skateboard. I taught him to obey other commands and do tricks. Yes, being told I could have Bruno is the thirty seconds I'd relive if I could. He's the only good thing that ever happened to me, until I met Dina and Jo and we became a team."

"Thanks for sharing that with the newest members of the team, Gabe. I know this activity isn't easy for anyone, but it truly enables us to get to the heart of one another's essences. Aniela, you have to go now. We let you wait till the end, but you have to share so we can all move to the next activity." Uriel smiled warmly at the girl next to him on the couch. "You can do it."

"Yes, you can," Micah reassured her. "We're here for you. Your whole team is here for you."

Aniela whimpered, "I'll t-try. My life on Earth was hard. I always felt as if I were drowning, just trying to get a breath and s-survive. The blackness of most memories clouds my thoughts and takes me back to places I never want to revisit." She paused and took a deep breath. "My parents weren't married and they were both drug addicts. They were dealers, too. I was born in a rundown roach- and rat-infested apartment. I never had proper care. Never. I don't know how I even survived as a baby. My folks were usually high. I was an inconvenience, but a good distraction when they were robbing someone, so they kept me around. There was rarely enough to eat. I didn't know how to do much because no one ever read to me or played games with me or anything. I was tiny for my age. I was certified mentally handicapped not long after I started school. I went to a special ed. classroom. I guess the day I met my teacher is the best moment of my life. Ms. Cross smiled and told me she was so glad I was going to be in her class and that I'd love school. She was right. School became my oasis. Ms. Cross was so kind. I loved her! I really did. I loved her, and I didn't even love my own parents. She showed me how to wash my body and brush my hair. She asked the nurse to get me some donated clothes and a warm coat. Ms. Cross had me go into the nurse's bathroom to clean up before coming into class every day. She made me a basket with washcloths, a fluffy towel, good smelling soap, a toothbrush and toothpaste, and a hairbrush that I kept in the cabinet of the nurse's bathroom. She took home the dirty washcloths and towel every Friday and brought them back clean every Monday. When the soap or toothpaste were about to run out, she got more. I got free breakfast and free lunch at school, so I had more food during the week than I'd ever had before. Ms. Cross gave us snacks in class, too. She read us stories and taught us the letters and numbers and how to write our names and other words. Obviously, she figured out that I didn't have much to eat when I was home, so she got me a back-pack and wrote my name on it in big letters. She put a storybook, a notebook, and some pencils and crayons inside, along with some little boxes of cereal from the cafeteria, a couple of apples, some cheese and cracker packs, and a few other things to eat. She put a purple teddy bear on top of the food. It was the first and only stuffed animal I ever had! I named him Criss Cross after my teacher. I took Criss everywhere! Ms. Cross was the nicest person I ever knew. That's why meeting her is my favorite moment."

"Ms. Cross sounds wonderful," Jo said. "I'm glad she came into your life. She sounds like one of those angels on earth some people talk about."

"I think you're right, Jo. She was such a good person."

Uriel smiled at her. "You're halfway there. Now tell us about the thirty seconds you'd relive if you could. You're a strong girl who's walking into her true destiny. You can do this, Young Warrior."

Aniela stammered, "If I c-could relive thirty seconds of my p-pathetic life, it would be the thirty seconds when my parents were shot and killed, and I was shot in the back as I tried to run away. That bullet in my spine's what put me in a wheelchair. It started the misery of hospitals, pain, one foster home after another, one school after another, and the realization that I didn't belong anywhere. I had no one who loved me or anyone I could love. No one. I was ten, but I looked and acted like I was about five or six. I was mad all the time. No one would keep me because of my violent outbursts. I'd throw things and yell. I could trash a room in a few seconds. I'd try to run over people and animals with my chair. I started setting little fires to get a reaction. They all said I was just too much, a danger to everyone else in the house. I was too damaged. I was in twenty-three placements from the time I was ten, till I died at fourteen. So, the thirty seconds I'd relive, if I could, would be the shooting scene. I don't know if I'd hide instead of running away and being shot, or if I'd charge at the strung-out shooter so he would've ended my life right then like he did my parents."

Stunned silence filled the air as the newest members of Aniela's team tried to process all that she'd just said.

Gabe broke the silence. "I could throw some mighty fine tantrums and trash a room pretty fast, too. I guess we have a skill-set in common that the others don't have."

Aniela stared at his grinning face before bursting into laughter. "Really? You did that too? I guess we're the wrecking balls of this crew!"

"Which leads us to the next step on our journey of full acceptance of one another," Uriel told them. "We're about to view one another's full lives on the screen behind these draperies. Much like the Board of Insights, this showing of each life on Earth will show every moment, good and bad, that formed each of you into who you are today. Unlike the Board of Insights, this is not a reckoning. You do not have to face the negatives of your life, dig through them for deeper meaning, nor ask for forgiveness. Each of you already did that. Our purpose here is to learn all about our teammates so we can understand who they really are and accept one another from that understanding. These will be accelerated, but you will have full understanding. Remember we told you that your gift of early unification meant you'd learn things quickly and easily and movement would be easy? Viewing one another's lives will be your first experience with accelerated knowledge acquisition. You'll fully understand one another's essences from this, just as we trainers did when we viewed them. We'll pause after each person's show for discussion. The board will decide the order of the life summaries."

Uriel raised his left arm and made a sweeping motion. The draperies parted, revealing colors tumbling across the enormous screen. Wisps of brilliant colors scattered and rejoined, merged and parted, filling the screen with God's graffiti. A burst of gold cleared the screen and revealed a striking portrait of Ariel, framed in sparkling gold, studded with golden topaz gems.

She mumbled, "Oh, goodie. I guess we know who's first for this part."

ACCELERATED KNOWLEDGE ACQUISITION

Ariel's portrait faded to black. The colors exploded on the screen as scene after scene from her earthly life rushed before their eyes. Her parents rejoiced after her squalling birth, smothering her and one another with gentle caresses and kisses. The baby grew happy and healthy in a loving home. The toddler soon showed her love of flowers, trees, and anything with feathers or fur. She always wanted to be outside exploring the natural world. As she got older, she hiked and climbed to see the things she wanted to view up-close.

The group watched as she grew and learned how to do many things. They observed her everyday life: school, chores, time with family and friends. They saw her family camping trips and visits to national parks. They watched as she learned to ski and took to the slopes like it was what she was born to do. They followed Ariel's love of photography as she began taking wildlife photos. She started a nature blog where she posted some of her pictures with paragraphs of facts about each one.

She spent as much time as she could with her grandparents at their cabin. Her grandfather, a park ranger, fostered her love of all things wild and natural. They traipsed through the woods together, reveling in all they saw as they wound their way along remote trails and up hills and mountains. He taught her survival skills and how to recognize the plants and animals of the area. Their evenings often centered on beautifully illustrated collections of flora and fauna.

The group smiled at Ariel's Red-Letter Days. They witnessed her enthusiasm for special discoveries in the woods, the magical aurora display she shared with her family, the awards ceremonies at her school when she won top prize at the science fairs three years in a row, and her pride at sharing her photos and knowledge with others on her blog.

The team knew when they saw her Black-Letter Days, too, the days she'd had to face at the Board of Insights as she did her reckoning. They saw the day she wandered off and terrified her parents, then threw a tantrum when she was found, screaming and pummeling her father as he brought her into the house. They witnessed the day she went ballistic at three boys who were throwing rocks at birds, including the aftereffects of a three-against-one fight on her battered face and body. They viewed her confusion and grief when her baby brother was stillborn, and her mother sank into depression. They observed the times she acted out, trying to recapture some of the attention she'd always had as her parents grappled with the loss of their second child.

Images blazed across the screen as her family moved on with life and Ariel grew into a young woman. She went to school, had a busy social life, and loved being outdoors. She spent as much time as possible with her grandparents. The screen faded to black.

"This is hard to see again," Ariel mumbled as the screen roared to life. It showed Ariel intently snapping picture after picture. Birds, berries, flowers, and small woodland creatures all caught her attention. She spotted a deer nibbling leaves just off the trail. She inched closer slowly, moving into a better position for her pictures. She squatted near a bush and focused on the deer. A shot rang out. The startled deer bolted in her direction, closing the gap between them in about two seconds. A second shot rang out. This one met flesh. Ariel's flesh. She collapsed as blood poured from the wound on her neck. She tried to yell for help, but only a gurgling sound came from her mouth. Within seconds she had no strength. The life drained from her body. Her team stared at Ariel the corpse rather than the girl whose life they'd just shared.

The shooter never came to check on her. No one knew if he

realized he'd shot her or not. She laid there alone for hours, her spirit hovering overhead. Shadows deepened as the day grew old. They heard voices calling her name. A search party was nearby, hoping to spot the girl before darkness shrouded the woods and made searching impossible.

A young man spotted her body just off the trail and rushed to her side. He checked her pulse, knowing he wouldn't feel a heartbeat. His whistle blasts summoned others to his location, her grandfather among them.

Ariel stared at the man she dearly loved as he fell to the ground, clasping her hand, moaning her name, and begging for a miracle. His skin was ashen, his face twisted in a grimace she'd never seen before. He screamed then, a primordial scream. It had a raw quality, consumed by pain that had no end. Tears flowed as two of the other men pulled him from his granddaughter's side. His sobs continued as his search party buddies eased him away and made him sit by a tree where he couldn't see what was happening.

A radio call brought others to the scene, with a stokes basket to transport Ariel's body. The investigation lasted many hours after she departed, her grandfather accompanying her away from the death spot. He went as quietly as he could, still whimpering and panting, but temporarily controlling the sobs.

"That was pretty intense," Jo proclaimed. "I feel so sorry for your grandpa."

"He had to break the news to my grandma and then my parents, too," Ariel whispered. "I feel so bad that he had to go through all of that pain because of me."

They watched as Azrael arrived to shepherd Ariel away from the scene of her body's death. They saw her as she transitioned to her new home and began her training as a warrior. They witnessed her bonding with Nate, Micah, and Aniela on the Trail of Caring as the four forged a team. They nodded approvingly as she mastered the use of enhanced speed, agility, levitation, and invisibility.

They smiled as she visited her grandfather as a hummingbird and reassured him that all was fine, that she was fine. They viewed the mission to find and save the missing girl lost in the woods. The screen faded to black and the draperies closed.

"Do you think that hunter knew he shot you?" Gabe asked softly.

"I really don't know. I was squatting down by a bush when I was hit. He might not have seen me. He was looking at the deer running past, not the bush or the girl by it. I wasn't wearing a bright color, so he may not have seen me. When I tried to scream, no words would come out, only a gurgling whimper. It's illegal to hunt in a park, though. He never should have fired that gun at all."

"So, you and Aniela share the experience of being shot, but yours was fatal and hers was paralyzing, but not fatal. You and I both bled out from serious wounds, Ariel," Gabe commented. "I'm seeing some commonalities among members of this team. We shared the experience of bleeding out, though from different injuries. You and Aniela shared the trauma of a gunshot. You and I both visited our family members as hummingbirds and put on a show to convince them that we were really there, Ariel. Maybe we're supposed to figure out the common strands from our previous lives. Maybe full acceptance comes more easily when we focus on things we share rather than what's different."

"Well said." Uriel shifted in his seat. "Everyone should now have a full understanding of Ariel and the life that made her who she is, even though the flash through her life story was accelerated. Are we ready to move on to the next person?"

The draperies parted as every head turned back toward the screen that was again displaying swatches of exploding colors traipsing back and forth. A salvo of blue pops chased the other colors away before revealing a blue frame with inlaid sapphires and turquoise surrounding an incredibly beautiful portrait of Jo.

"I look a little older in this picture than I did when we saw it at the Board of Insights," Jo gasped. "Why do I look different?"

"Because you are different. You see, you transitioned at quite a young age. Having youthful warriors is vital for fighting evil and a tool that we must employ, but no one permanently retains a childhood image here. Can you imagine being forever thirteen? Or forever a baby or toddler? That wouldn't be heavenly in most people's books. Your image will change slowly, really unnoticeably, unless you see the spiritual reflection that's captured in your portrait, like you just did. Your image will modify until you're at the pinnacle of what you would have been if you'd lived to that stage on Earth. For most humans, the pinnacle is in the late twenties or thirties. For a few, it's older, but most peak in image and prowess close to age thirty." Uriel grinned at their flabbergasted expressions. "It's a good thing, another gift. We get to remain forever at our best image when we reach it, or we get to go back to our prime if we lived beyond it."

The portrait disappeared and the black screen split into many small cells showcasing all the moments of Jo's life. The team scanned the ordinary moments and extraordinary moments from the time of her birth. Jo sang time after time. They heard the magic of her voice as she sang solo or with her father. They witnessed five-year-old Jo's temper tantrum and theft of a candy bar from the commissary, and her parents' reactions to the incident. They viewed Michael's deployment and his eight-year-old daughter's behavior at his departure. They watched as a woman and two little girls went on with ordinary life after he left. They stared at the screen as the officers arrived to tell the little family of Michael's death, their grief, and the whirlwind of activities to plan his memorial. They witnessed his funeral and the time after as the three survivors of his family tried to move on without him. They observed the move from base housing when one year had passed and they were forced to go. They saw the new apartment, the new school, and sisters bolstering one another when they had no other friends, the sisters racing one another, and the acquisition of a special calico cat they named Joy. The team smiled when they saw the girls and their mother laughing after so many months of sorrow. Their smiles faded as scenes of Jo's improvement at school, making friends, and racing everywhere with her sister morphed into Jo getting weaker and weaker and having frequent nosebleeds. They sadly regarded the scenes of many medical tests and procedures and the image of Jo withering with each passing day. They heard the declaration of leukemia and saw the effects on her body. The group watched her battle the cancer-enemy that wouldn't relinquish its hold. They gaped at her death scene as her mother, sister, grandparents, and a cat named Joy encircled her with love as she departed.

They viewed her transition, the Trail of Caring passage, and the forging of Team DJG. Her visit to her mother and sister as a blue morpho butterfly brought smiles back to the team's faces. Awe filled the group as they observed Jo training and going on a significant mission with her team and trainers. They witnessed Jo's ability to conquer fear as the team worked to save children from demons. Her serenity in the wrecked school bus was almost magical to watch. They were stunned as she received a Medal of Valor at a council meeting. The draperies slid together.

"We're all speechless," Nate sputtered. "For many reasons."

"You are an impressive individual." Micah smiled as he studied the girl seated next to him. "You had the voice of an angel before you even became one. And that mission! Wow!"

"Um, thanks," Jo mumbled as she tried to quiet the butterflies that had started their flight in her stomach again. "My team did much more on the mission than I did, though."

"You're just being modest," Uriel countered. "You were an integral part of that mission. The Medal of Valor is not given out often, nor lightly. Your performance at every task as a novice was noteworthy and commendable."

"Thank you."

"We've received accelerated knowledge of two of the eight on this newly forged team, one from each of the halves that have been merged. Does anyone have anything to say or ask before we move on to the third showing?"

Silence answered his question, so the draperies opened once more to reveal cascading colors rolling across the screen. Colorful waves peaked and ebbed several times before flashes of red burst on the screen and yielded the space to Nate's portrait, framed in shiny red lacquer trimmed with rubies. The handsome young man smiled warmly, emanating tranquility and confidence.

Cell after cell filled with the moments of Nate's life and rushed before their eyes. They saw his parents' delight at his birth and the loving care he received as a baby and toddler. They watched him grow, developing into the person he'd become when chosen. Scene after scene showed a happy lifetime in a happy family. Nate played happily with his older sister and brother and their beagle, Zoe. The siblings rarely squabbled and truly seemed to love doing things together. Laughter and hugs filled his home. He went to school, did chores, and hung out with friends like everyone they knew. He loved basketball, both as a spectator and player. He rarely got in any kind of trouble. Even as a young child, he was calm and kept himself busy and entertained. Most of all, he loved creating art. Whether sketching, painting, or sculpting, Nate's creations were astounding. Beauty flowed through his hands and transformed a blank page or chunk of clay into a work of art. He beamed with pride as he received multiple awards for outstanding art and when his parents framed and hung some of his pieces in their home. They saw his sadness when his brother left for basic training and again when he was deployed. They shared his joy when Nate's brother returned and surprised him in class. Family times, friend times, or alone times showed the same-yet-evolving Nate: calm, focused, loving, artistic. His body grew tall and strong as his mind and skills sharpened. Then his best friend showed him the driver's license he'd just gotten. They decided to celebrate new freedom together. The screen faded to black.

"Here comes my joyride and death. I was really stupid, as you're about to see."

The screen roared back to life, showing a pair of teenage boys in the front seat of an older SUV. They laughed hysterically as the driver went faster and faster, egged on by Nate from the passenger seat. The car squealed around corners and curves as they headed out of town on a winding highway. Distance and speed were all that mattered. The SUV spun out on a sharp curve and tumbled over and over. Screams replaced manic laughter until it slammed into the boulder that crushed Nate on impact. Nate hovered over the crash, trying to comfort his friend till Azrael arrived to escort him away.

The screen replayed the scenes on the Trail of Caring as he bonded with Micah, Ariel, and Aniela. They witnessed his comfort visit to his parents as a dragonfly, where he created a message with his dragonfly feet in the sand. The infinity sign inside a heart design sent an unmistakable and impressive message. His mother snapped a picture of it and the dragonfly visitor as tears rolled down her face. He rested on her leg a minute before flying to his father's arm. He circled his parents before flying away. They watched the rescue mission he successfully completed. Nate reassured the child and calmed her with his smile and gentle touch as he lifted her and carried her to safety. The grateful expression on the girl's parents' faces filled the group with joy.

The draperies snapped shut once more.

"You were really a good guy, even before coming here, Nate," Dina remarked. "I think your pure spirit was why you were called."

"I don't know about that," Nate replied, "but I led a very blessed life in a very loving family. I know that."

"Let's see who the Board's going to share next," Uriel said as he turned back toward the draperies.

On cue, the draperies parted once more. The board gushed colorful sprays, drenching the surface with puddles of vivid colors until it faded to black and a new portrait came into view.

This frame was light blue with star sapphires and blue diamonds arranged as musical symbols that seemed to chase one another around the frame. Micah's smile and dancing eyes captured everyone's attention.

Scenes of his birth and early childhood raced across the screen. Micah grew in a happy home filled with love and good times. The group smiled as his parents and sister doted on the baby and little boy. Toddler Micah's plunking of real tunes on the piano astounded the group. They were even more awed as his skill grew and he played more complex pieces by the time he was five years old. Micah's singing was magical, as was his easy acquisition of skill with musical instruments. His whole family was musical, but his gifts were obviously the greatest. He sang often with his sister to his mother's accompaniment on the piano or his father's on the guitar. Micah's contentment was obvious when he lovingly cuddled and played with his family's three cats. Attending lots of games with his dad and playing in little league, Micah's love of baseball grew. He developed strong pitching skills and become a fast base runner. He excelled at school through his elementary years and was a favorite with kids and adults alike.

In middle school, Micah pushed boundaries like he'd never done before. He started showing off and talking back to adults. His popularity soared with peers, but dipped with adults as they tried to guide him. The team grimaced as they watched the cafeteria scene when he humiliated the disabled boy with the orange peel. The cavalier attitude of that Micah didn't seem to be the same Micah they'd watched through earlier years. It was shocking to witness the change. Several more scenes centered on a hormonally-driven, unpleasant young man who'd say and do almost anything for attention from his peers.

Micah beamed as he met and shook hands with the baseball players he admired. They heard the coach tell Micah that he'd heard good things about him and that he hoped Micah would work hard to be successful in life, that perhaps one day he'd be able to coach *him* as a professional athlete. Riveted to the screen, the team watched as Micah sang the national anthem at the baseball game, his proud family's joy radiating from the stands.

Micah did an about-face after that baseball game, returning to the focused and pleasant fellow he'd been throughout the first twelve years of his life. When he advanced to high school, a profound change in Micah was apparent to everyone. He was mature, focused, and kind to everyone. His studies, his family, and his musical and athletic passions filled his days. Popular and happy, they watched Micah excel at school, starring in his school's musical and on the baseball team.

A teen party by a river, with music blaring and young people celebrating the end of the school year, rolled across the screen. A bonfire blazed, lighting the area near it. Laughter and music filled the air. The revelers didn't hear the dare or see Micah climb the tree overhanging the river. Most didn't hear the splash either. They heard the distraught call for help as his friend realized Micah hadn't come to the surface after diving into the churning black river below. Frantic 911 calls summoned help. Police, paramedics, and the dive team arrived and sprang into action. In less than an hour, they'd recovered Micah's body from some tangled branches about six feet under the surface. Micah hovered among the boughs he'd climbed just a short time ago, watching them search for and recover his body. He saw the agonized looks on everyone's faces and heard their cries before Azrael arrived and escorted him to Gavreel.

Again, they watched the team's performance on the Trail of Caring, his comfort visit to his friend who'd dared him to jump, and the successful rescue mission. His tender singing to the child as Nate carried her from the woods impressed the group.

The curtains snapped together once more.

"I told you I was a jerk in middle school," Micah offered. "I'm sorry all of you had to see it."

"That was a temporary phase, from which you learned some valuable lessons," Uriel countered. "Remember, everything is connected."

"I guess so, but it's embarrassing to watch," Micah murmured.

"We all made mistakes along the way." Jo's smile was reassuring.

"If there are no further comments or questions, let's see whose life is going to be shown next," Uriel announced.

Fountains of color spurted on the screen as the curtains opened. The colorful gushes splattered and dribbled before fading to sparkling silver drops. An ornate silver frame surrounded a breathtaking portrait of Dina. She, too, looked somewhat different from the image at the Board of Insights.

"I look almost like my mom in this picture."

"You are maturing. Your resemblance to your mother will likely be even stronger as you reach your pinnacle," Uriel told her.

Scene after scene from Dina's earthly life flashed across the screen, extending appreciation for the girl who'd become a young woman of great insights. They saw her grow and develop strong running, soccer, and art skills, as well as perform everyday tasks. They witnessed her successes and challenges. They watched tender scenes of Dina and her great-grandmother, including their completion of The Will art project. They also saw the scenes on the soccer field where she caused a girl's injury, where she cheated on a multiplication test, and where she bullied her little brother when the Tiffany lamp broke. Day after day whirled past, with Dina doing well in school, spending time with her family and dog, running, playing soccer, and creating impressive art. The screen slowed as Dina stood by a lamppost digging in her backpack.

A careening truck headed straight toward Dina as she dug for her phone at the bottom of her bag. It slammed into her, T-boned around her body and the post, taking her life instantly. Her chaotic death scene played. Emergency workers and her brother arrived. Her brother's wails filled the group with agony. The arrival of her parents and the remainder of the death scene added to their shared angst. Seeing her family's and the first responders' pain was difficult.

Everyone relaxed as Dina met Gavreel and went to her new home. They smiled as she talked to her little dog Yodels about her new life. The bonding with Jo and Gabe on the Trail of Caring was undeniable. They marveled at her team's training, their joint training of Bruno, and her impressive visit to her parents as a dragonfly. The paintings she gave Jo and Gabe to commemorate their comfort visits awed the group. They were impressed anew as they watched her participation on her team's mission and the Medal of Valor ceremony. Her knowledge of art, her artistic talent, and her perceptive insights were apparent to everyone.

The draperies closed over the screen, signaling the end of the segment.

"Your poor brother," Ariel remarked. "It was as hard seeing him as it was seeing my grandpa."

"I agree," Dina confided. "I wish he didn't feel guilty and responsible. He was late picking me up and I know that keeps gnawing on him. He doesn't have full understanding yet. He hasn't figured out how to move on with his own life because he doesn't understand the true purpose of my passing. He just blames himself for being late."

"He'll understand when the time is right," Uriel soothed. "We're making fast progress on this task. Your full understanding from the accelerated presentations is impressive. Only three left."

As he turned to face the draperies, they parted, revealing an explosion of red and blue on the screen. Droplets of color melted together and spun around the screen creating a marbled design of all shades of purple, from lightest lavender to deepest eggplant. As the design faded, an amethyst-studded frame sparkled around Aniela's portrait. She radiated warmth, like an extra dose of sunshine had been poured directly into her soul. Her eyes looked as if she'd awakened from an extended sleep, bright and fresh; her gaze seemed to announce, "I see everything."

Aniela's life began in a shabby apartment. A near-skeleton woman screamed a few times, then a scrawny baby's squalls replaced hers. Listless adults lounged on the ratty sofa and on the floor, most oblivious to the birth. Her father was passed out on the floor. One young woman stumbled over. Lifting the baby, she muttered, "It's a girl. You got a girl. I'm gonna clean this mess off her. You got some diapers and stuff?" Aniela's life began with no caresses or kisses. She was swaddled in dirty t-shirt and laid by her mother's side, who'd passed out after injecting. The baby rooted around and finally found a bit of comfort at her mother's chest.

Cell after cell showed a baby and child somehow growing in spite of surviving in a drug abuse display case. Aniela had no toys or books, no adults guiding her, no joy. She was filthy and seldom had enough to eat. No one in her early life loved anything but drugs. Drugs decomposed her mother's body to the point she was little more than a walking corpse. The listless or violent adults who cycled in and out of her life were all about the same. Aniela was trapped in a web of pain. As acts of depravity happened all around her, she became a little girl who tried to fade into her surroundings.

Scenes from her elementary school days flashed across the screen. They saw the amazing Ms. Cross and the tenderness she ladled over Aniela. The group smiled as they saw Aniela's first smile, wrapped in a Ms. Cross hug. The scenes at school were happy. Aniela learned how to care for herself, finally had enough to eat, and experienced the joys of stories, games, and learning. They saw the special backpack stuffed with supplies and food that Aniela toted to and from school each day. The purple bear, Criss Cross, was welcome in class and had a special small chair all his own. Aniela smiled more and more often, and her petite body filled out a bit. She stayed with Ms. Cross for two years before moving to the next teacher, who also showered her with the extra attention she so desperately needed. She learned to read and write in spite of the lack of early exposure to words and became a puzzle whiz. She could assemble a puzzle faster than anyone had ever seen. Her visual perception was remarkable. She learned to dance in P.E. A passion for movement that she'd never experienced before flooded over her. She moved gracefully to the beats she heard in her head.

She attended the same school four years, just a couple of blocks from the rundown apartment building where she lived. She thrived in the sheltered environment of school. Then she had to go home, back where there was no food or nurturing, but plenty of escalating violence. Back to the place where actions had to be severed from thoughts. Back to where mere survival was an accomplishment. Back to her cage of fear. Until the cage burned down and threw them into life on the street. Aniela no longer went to school. She became a lost kid who fell between the cracks in a large city. No home. No school. No love.

Aniela grew a little as the years rolled by, but she remained tiny. Her small size aided her parents as she performed on the street. People stopped and watched a child they thought was about five do complex street dancing—popping, rooting, and liquid dancing. Many would drop coins or dollar bills into the can she set on the curb. Her parents took her tips, after they'd pickpocketed onlookers who were mesmerized by the tiny child. Sometimes they'd give her a dollar or two to get something to eat, but the cash mostly went to their addiction and buying more product to sell to others. Everyone and everything became a way to facilitate the next fix.

Once a day they'd visit a soup kitchen nearby, if her parents weren't too high. Aniela could eat as much as any adult there and would stuff bread in her pockets for later. Life on the streets became her world. She watched her mom deal and get high. Her dad only came around looking for money or a fix. He was gone more than he was around. Aniela spent much of her time in the shadows, trying not to be seen but always seeing.

The screen faded to black, and a full screen image of a frenzied man waving a gun came into view. They knew what was coming next from Aniela's earlier sharing, but it was hard to see the scene play out before their eyes. The demented man screamed for drugs and wouldn't accept that they had none at the moment. He needed them now. Aniela's father walked toward him with his hands up. "We ain't got none, man. Can't give you what we don't have. Put that piece away." The shot reverberated under the overpass as Aniela's father crumpled to the ground. His life fluid drained from him in a puddle of garish scarlet. Her mother screamed and rushed at the shooter. The second shot dropped Aniela's mother near her father's body, crimson spewing from her before she landed. Life ebbed from both of their bodies as they lay in a puddle of their mingled blood. Aniela gasped as she bolted away. The third and fourth shots dropped her in a fountain of red. Sirens roared nearby as the shooter ran away.

The screen fragmented into many cells again, racing through four years of images. There were scenes of hospital stays, surgeries to remove the bullets and repair the damage, and Aniela's recovery from the bullets to her spine. They saw her get her wheelchair and learn how to use it. She was in and out of so many foster homes and different schools. No one kept the girl who acted out for very long. Her physical and emotional pain worked in tandem and took over her brain. Aniela was overcome by the hopeless life she'd led, the constant betrayals, the abandonment by death, and grief. She was engulfed in despair, drowning in a private ocean with a deadly undertow. The team watched as she sank deeper and deeper into depression that no one could help.

The screen shifted to full-screen view once more. Death came to Aniela with slow rattling gasps. It was neither kind nor quick. The virus put her in the hospital, all alone except for the frazzled nurses who tried to make her comfortable. She struggled for each breath on the ventilator. She sucked in her final breath and broke the earthly tether. Azrael wrapped his arms around her before they departed from that lonely hospital room, something they hadn't seen in any other transitions.

The curtains closed slowly, quietly, as if they, too, were over-whelmed by the scenes that had just played.

Aniela hung her head, as if still ashamed of the life she'd led and the person she was. Her sorrow permeated the air, seeming to marinate everyone and everything within range of the screen.

Uriel spoke softly as he lifted Aniela's chin to look into her eyes. "You led an earthly life dominated by evil, yet you never succumbed to the evil all around you. You suffered far more in your short life than most do in many decades of life. The greatness within you is evident from your mere survival. You survived so much and you learned so much, things that most never have to learn. I don't mean academic learning or how to develop gifts that were bestowed in your essence. I mean that you created your own tools of survival through dire circumstances, tapping into some inherent intuition. You became a keen observer as you survived, which led to your insightful ability. You were given the life you were given because you were strong enough to live it. Never hang your head in shame about yourself, Aniela. You have as much greatness within as any other individual chosen to be on this remarkable team."

Aniela nodded, but was unable to speak. She hadn't yet recovered from watching her life on Earth played for the second time.

"I know that was an intense presentation, even in accelerated format," Uriel admitted, "but everyone has to know everything about each team member, whether their life plays as a Disney show or a horror movie. We'll move on now."

The curtains parted, revealing a kaleidoscope of colorful shards shifting around the screen, the patterns and movement seeming to sync in a soothing beat. Bright colors gave way to black as a black lacquered frame with golden and silver flecks emerged around the divine portrait of Gabe.

The multifaceted screen flashed images of Gabe's life, starting with his C-section birth. They watched scene after scene of his dangerous, risky behaviors and frazzled parents trying to keep up.

Frustration burgeoned and the patience waned with each passing day. Repeated spectacles of parental fights, yelling, and beatings filled the screen. His father was home less and less but was always angry and violent when he appeared. Gabe's kindergarten temper tantrum and many other episodes of trouble at school played. They watched as Gabe began bullying his younger brother. Everyone smiled when they saw him hold a squirming puppy in his neighbor's front yard and laugh as puppy kisses wet his face. Every time he saw the pup in his neighbor's yard, Gabe romped and played with it, giving and receiving love.

The group nodded as they viewed the scene where Gabe was told he could have Bruno if he took total responsibility. They enjoyed watching the years between eight and thirteen when Gabe trained Bruno, hung out with him, and developed incredible skateboarding and parkour skills. Life seemed somewhat better after the dog joined Gabe's family. Gabe and Bruno were at the park several hours a day, running and playing, expending energy. Gabe grew into a tall strong young man as Bruno grew into a bright athletic dog in his prime.

A full screen image displayed Gabe and Bruno playing frisbee in the dog park, their delight evident as Bruno fetched toss after toss of the plastic disk. Then Bruno landed on a huge dog that launched into attack mode, killing Bruno with vicious bites to his neck. Bruno's death and the man's comments that he should control his animal propelled Gabe's swift kick to the man's head. The onlookers were horrified as the melee of the big dog's attack on Gabe filled the screen. Pandemonium reigned as others in the park tried to help and first responders arrived. Police officers and paramedics tried to stanch the blood flow from Gabe's body while the big dog was hauled away by animal control. An attempt to revive Gabe in the ambulance as the life drained from his body failed. Bruno landed on Gabe as he hovered over his body in the trauma center; there was no doubt the pair would transition together. Azrael escorted Gabe to Gavreel, Bruno cradled lovingly in his arms.

The screen shifted to the Trail of Caring, showing Gabe's first journey with a group of four boys. They heard Gavreel's instructions to join a new team and try again as she moved Gabe back near the beginning and the others off the trail. They let out a collective sigh of relief as he successfully completed the trail with Dina and Jo. Team DJG's training was impressive. All were astounded as they viewed Gabe's athletic prowess. Gasps filled the air when Gabe's feet erupted in flames as he flipped while doing enhanced jumps. Everyone was moved as they watched Gabe's comfort visit to his family and his performance on the mission. Witnessing Gabe's ability to fight demons and kill them with flaming kicks awed everyone, even the two who'd been with him on the mission. The symbols Gabe burned on the ground, and the Medal of Valor ceremony added to the mystique of the young angel warrior who'd brought all of them the gift of languages.

The draperies snapped shut as baffled stares centered on Gabe.

"Dude, that was seriously amazing," Micah squeaked. "How do you make your feet flame like that?"

"I don't make it happen. It just happens when I flip while I'm in enhanced mode. The Council said I discovered a divine weapon within myself and knew how to use it instinctively. I don't understand it myself," Gabe replied, "but I'm glad I could kill those gargoyles and Pukwudgies before they captured those kids."

"What's that extra initial token you got after you burned the crystals on that ledge?" Ariel asked.

Team DJG members shot looks among themselves, but no one spoke.

Uriel declared, "These three were instructed not to discuss this particular amulet with anyone. But, you're now a team and must have full acceptance, so I'll explain. It is a Soul on Fire charm. It's rare and powerful, much like the Gift of Languages helix Gabe brought us. This charm is created when a warrior angel discovers a power within for fighting evil. Gabe's discovery of his fire within unveiled his true identity as a seraph. When he charred that crystal with his feet, and changed its physical form, his essence as a seraph became undeniable. Gabe is young and untrained, but he will quickly rise to the rank of his calling. It's almost certain that Dina and Jo are also seraphim because they, too, received the Soul on Fire charm. All of you are likely seraphim since you've been aligned as a new team and fast-tracked with Unity on just the second virtues trail."

"What does that mean?" Aniela asked softly. "I mean about being seraphim?"

"It means that you'll become very powerful warriors. You were chosen to be warriors and then chosen again to be unified as this new team. Your training will be accelerated and intense. At level five, you'll be trained to fight with flaming swords, imbued with power from God to destroy evil."

The seven stared at Uriel but said nothing. The draperies parted once more as Uriel declared, "We're to our final viewing."

"But, we've seen all of our lives already," the group chorused. Their chuckles almost drowned out Uriel's response.

"Almost all of your lives," Uriel told them. "Watch and learn."

A young terrier licked pup after pup as she whelped four in all. They grew into feisty puppies under the watchful eye of their mother. Mama had lots of milk and caressed them gently with her tongue. Their first home was a sturdy wooden box tucked next to a wood burning stove, lined with a fluffy towel. It was delightfully cozy. As they grew, the pups learned how to climb out of the crate and toddled around the kitchen. A loving woman cooed to them, cuddled and petted them, and cleaned their box every day. She wore long skirts that were so much fun to pounce upon! She laughed at their playful antics and often stopped to stroke their heads. After a few weeks, she gave the pups plates of finely chopped meat and mashed vegetables. She'd hurry them out the door as soon as they finished eating and set them in some springy stuff she called grass. She kept saying, "Do your business. Do your business." When one of the pups piddled in the grass, Long Skirt Lady gave it a bit of meat, a pat on the head, and said, "Good dog!" Before long, all four pups were eager to piddle in the grass and get a piece of meat. Long Skirt Lady got really excited when a pup made its poop outside in the grass instead of the kitchen. She praised, petted, and gave meat for that, too. In just a couple of weeks, the litter had learned that the grass was for piddles and poops, not the kitchen floor. The grass was fun for frolicking. The pups chased one another and wrestled as they grew bigger, stronger, and ready to leave their mama. Strangers came by to look at and play with the puppies. One by one, the strangers took the pups away. Bruno was carried away by a man and boy.

Bruno's new home was lonely. He whimpered a lot. At first, the boy petted him and played tug of war with a knotted rope. That only last a couple of weeks. The man and boy were not gentle like Long Skirt Lady. They yelled a lot, at each other and at him. These people threw things and made loud noises by slamming things down. When he got scared and piddled on the floor, they screamed and threw him outside. They often yelled, "Bad dog!" They were mad at him all the time. He tried to lick their fingers to say he was sorry, but they just shoved him away. Bruno chewed on a chair leg when his teeth hurt. The man threw him against the wall as he roared, "That's it! No more. You are a huge mistake! We're not putting up with any more from you!" Bruno slinked around the edge of the room, trying to escape the man's rage. The man snatched him by the scruff of the neck and said, "No more. You aren't going to be here any more!" He roughly carried Bruno up onto a wagon seat. He drove the wagon a long way, then flung the pup to the ground and drove away.

Gabe stared at the screen, his hands clenched into fists. His eyes declared his rage, though his mouth stayed still.

Bruno laid on the ground, oblivious to the dirt and commotion all around him. Wagons clopped down the street and people walked past, no one concerned about the pup that laid at the edge of the road, immobilized by pain and sorrow. Bruno finally roused and dragged himself up. He limped a few steps and collapsed behind a barrel setting at the end of the building. He drifted in and out of fitful sleep, lonely and scared, but unable to move. Hunger and thirst plagued him. He whimpered from time to time, but had strength for no more than that. Days passed but he could not move.

Then he heard the rustling of a skirt. Maybe Long Skirt Lady had found him! He whimpered softly and tried to yip, but no bark would come, only the faintest whine. The lady crouched near him and offered her hand. Instead of sniffing it, he tilted his head and closed his sunken eyes. He tried to roll over to show his belly, the most submissive gesture he knew, but he didn't have the strength. He opened his eyes and licked her outstretched hand. She gently ran her hand down his head and back. He was so thin it was like dragging her hand over a rough rock wall, with ridge after ridge and hollow after hollow meeting her fingertips. This baby was starving to death! She eased her hands underneath the pup and lifted him with absurd ease; he weighed less than a bag of flour. He whimpered as she lifted him. Now that he was closer, she nearly gagged at the noxious ammonia stench. He'd been too weak to move when he could hold his urine no longer. In spite of the smell, she cuddled the tiny pooch to her chest. He snuggled his head against her throat, his gratitude undeniable. As she turned, clutching the emaciated puppy, her face came into view for the first time.

The group gasped as they recognized Gavreel. It was a different place and time, and the face was bruised, but that woman was definitely Gavreel! They all saw the scabbed-over gash around her neck where the pup's head rested.

She hurried home with the near-dead pup. After filling a basin with warm water and gently easing the tiny boy into it, Gavreel lovingly caressed his body with sudsy hands until the filth and odor were washed away. Fresh warm water soothed his pain as she rinsed the foam. With the pup wrapped in a towel and set by the fireplace, she mashed some meat, bread, and milk together. Dozing in the towel, Bruno looked so innocent and weak. She tenderly lifted the puppy-towel bundle to her lap. Gavreel dipped her fingers in the gruel and held them to his mouth, letting him lick them clean. He slurped the delicious fingers over and over before drifting into the deepest sleep he'd had in the weeks since leaving Mama and Long Skirt Lady. He awoke when sunlight streamed in the only window. He was wrapped in the fluffy towel and in the arms of the woman who'd saved him. He watched her a few minutes as she dozed peacefully before he stretched and licked her chin. Her laughter, soft voice, and gentle strokes reassured him that he was home.

The screen fragmented into many cells, showing Gavreel's loving care as Bruno recovered and grew into a vibrant and happy dog. The pair spent almost every minute together, even when she went to cook at a nearby inn and tavern. He curled up by the stove and rarely took his eyes off her as she worked. He followed her everywhere. She patiently trained him to follow commands and do tricks. Before long, her little dog won the hearts of the inn's owners and patrons.

Years passed as woman and dog lived meagerly, yet comfortably together. Life was better for both of them together than it had ever been apart. Their mutual adoration was indisputable.

The screen shifted to full view mode again. Flames and black smoke billowed from the building where Gavreel rented a ground floor room. A yellow glow illuminated the night sky as the fire quickly spread. Acrid smoke filled the air. Heat radiated from the building, so strong it could be felt across the street. Somewhere close by, a bell clanged. Crackling sounds and shouting voices broke the quietness of the night.

The scene shifted to Gavreel and Bruno, cuddled together in her small bed. Bruno roused as the bell clanged and voices shouted. Sensing danger, the little dog pawed frantically to wake Gavreel. She sprang up, clutched Bruno, and bolted toward the door. The ceiling collapsed as they got about halfway across the room. They were buried in burning debris, pinned down by a gigantic support beam. The window blew out, sending sizzling shards of glass raining into the now busy street, along with the haunting sound of Gavreel's death scream.

Still clinging to her beloved dog, Gavreel hovered over the frantic scene as the orange flames consumed the entire building. Nothing and no one escaped. Azrael transitioned several souls from that location, starting with a special woman and her dog.

The screen shifted to its multifaceted view and showcased Gavreel's and Bruno's everlasting life together. They were happy in their service as she became a powerful warrior and transition counselor for new recruits. Bruno gave comfort to many young ones as they faced their new lives in their new home and on many missions.

The screen went full view, showing Gavreel studying her DMD screen, Bruno at her side. A slideshow of beatings and abuse whizzed by, finally stopping on a view of eight-year-old Gabe, sobbing and cowering in his closet, clutching a stuffed dog. Bruno cocked his head and pawed at the DMD. "You're right, boy. As much as I love you, we have to do something to save this boy. Clearly the time is right for you to go on a solo mission. I will take you there and set up the scene. The rest will be up to you. I know you'll know what to do to save him."

Gavreel made gestures none of them understood, but Bruno morphed into a puppy. She held him close and kissed the top of his head. They gazed into one another's eyes for the longest time. They vanished together and reappeared in a maze, where Gavreel wandered, Puppy Bruno still clutched to her. The pair came to an opening and stepped into a yard. It was the house next to Gabe's parents' home! Gavreel approached the couple raking the lawn, thatching it to remove the dead grass. She smiled warmly and showed them the pup she held. She spoke softly, but with an unmistakable urgency and commanding tone. She told them that this puppy, named Bruno, would be coming to them, that they were to take care of him and love him for a short time, but that his true home would be with the boy next door, and they'd know when the time was right to pass him to Gabe. She directed them to encourage the boy and dog to spend time together, that they'd see clearly that they were meant to be together, but only when his father would accept the dog into their home. She assured them that they'd both survive a difficult time ahead, to have faith in one another and the end result of the challenge they'd face. She turned and walked back into the maze.

The woman sat bolt upright in bed. Her startled husband turned toward her mumbling, "Are you all right?"

"Yes, I guess so. I just had the strangest dream. Some woman carrying a puppy said the pup was going to be coming to us for a short time and that we're supposed to take care of it, but that it's really supposed to be with Gabe next door. She said we'd know when to give the dog to Gabe, at a time when his dad would let him keep it. The dream woman told us—you and I were together in the yard in the dream— that we'd face a difficult time, but we'd both survive. It was so strange."

"It sounds like it, but dreams are like that sometimes. I wouldn't mind getting a dog, but I don't think I could keep it for awhile, then give it away." Her husband smiled. "I guess we should get up. That yard isn't going to thatch itself. It will take us several hours to get the yard cleaned and fertilized."

The screen honeycombed again, with scene after scene showing Bruno's arrival and life with the couple next door. They saw days whiz by as the pup grew. He loved both of them and the boy who often came to play. They witnessed the couple's car accident and Bruno alone in the kitchen day after day, as the woman came home late each night and left early each morning. Scenes flashed, including one where the neighbor begged Gabe's mother to let her give the dog to Gabe. Gabe's mom assured her that she'd to talk to his father and try to convince him, but that the request might be more effective if it came directly from her. They knew what would happen next. Gabe and Bruno would be united.

Bruno's life with Gabe rushed by, including their joint transition as Azrael escorted them to Gavreel. His training with Team DJG and quick bonding with Dina and Jo ended the Bruno segment.

The drapes eased together once more.

Gabe scooped Bruno up and held him close to his face. Their eyes locked on one another. There was no judgment in their shared gaze, only love. Bruno sent a mental message they all could hear and understand: "Your eyes have been opened. You let my light in and the demons that haunted you were chased away. I've been your spark in the darkness, as Gavreel was mine, and I was hers. The darkness holds no power over us because we know pure love. We have the power to light the way."

"That, young warriors, is the epitome of full acceptance," Uriel declared. "Together, you have the power to light the way for countess others."

All eyes were still fixed on Gabe and Bruno.

Uriel continued, "The board has presented each of your lives with radical honesty. Each one of you has had to own and accept the outcomes of his or her individual life. You now know all there is to know about one another. Are you willing to do the same for every other teammate? To fully accept another soul is to love entirely, to give part of your essence that you will never reclaim. Do each of you fully accept one another as Gabe and Bruno have done?"

Bruno settled on Gabe's lap and stared at Uriel. One yip declared his acceptance of everyone on Team JAMBANGD.

"Bruno has led the way. Each of you must declare your answer to my question. Do each of you fully accept one another?"

"I do," resounded around the group, the declaration clear from everyone.

"These Acceptance tokens are now yours. They should remind you that the true power of acceptance is love."

They looked at the gold charm that looked like conjoined heart outlines surrounding a circle. Each of their names was intricately engraved on one of the hearts. The center simply said, "**WITH ONE VOICE...**"

The flip side of the charm revealed tiny buttons on each heart. When pushed, a golden heart popped out with words inscribed.

"Dina, will you read the words you find on each embedded heart, please?"

"When you accept yourself, the whole world accepts you."

Lao Tzu

"It is your duty to be exceedingly kind to every human being, and to wish him well; to work for the upliftment of society...until we change the world of man into the world of God."

Baha'i: `Abduu'l-Baha, Page 90

"Accept one another, then, just as Christ accepted you in order to bring praise to God."

The Bible, Romans 15:7

"Do not hate anybody, because that hatred which comes from you must, in the long run, come back to you; if you love, that love will come back to you, completing the circle."

Swami Vivekananda

"Do nothing from selfish ambition or conceit, but in humility count others more significant than yourselves. Let each of you look not only to his own interests, but also to the interests of others."

The Bible: Philippians 2: 3-4

"The Devil flatters us that we are very righteous while we are feeding on the faults of others...If you would have God's mercy on you, have mercy on one another."

John Smith, LDS Guide

"There is no 'way' to be. You are. It is enough."

Lao Tzu

"Your duty is to treat everybody with love as a manifestation of the Lord."

Swami Sivananda

"Finally, all of you, be like-minded, be sympathetic, love one another, be compassionate, and humble."

The Bible: 1Peter 3:8

Dina pushed the button to close the final pop-out message of acceptance and looked at Uriel.

Uriel gestured, adding the newest tokens to their chains. "Tolerance and acceptance make fertile soil for seeds of change. Let's get moving down this trail. There's still quite a bit to do before we are dispatched on our mission."

ESCAPE, PART I

Ambling down the blue path, the team marveled at the wonders all around them. A breeze rustled the leaves and grasses and caressed their skin with its gentle touch. Birds trilled joyously, their songs as soothing as loving lullabies. Clouds scuttled overhead, creating one fluffy masterpiece after another. Sweet scents wafted over them, ever-changing as they walked along the path. Everything seemed to work together to meld their spiritual wholeness and connectedness.

"Here we are," Uriel announced as he pointed to an enormous boulder blocking their passage.

"Here we go again," seven voices whined before erupting into laughter.

"I'll be leaving you shortly. You must tackle the next part of the trail's challenges together, with no one but your team. Please, connect with one another for tessellation transport to the exact location. You have many strengths as a team. Utilize everyone's gifts. Gabe, make sure you have a good hold on Bruno for transport. Remember integrity and tenacity are important virtues. Don't give up. You'll need this."

Uriel pushed a scroll into Nate's hands before he raised his own hands and the team vanished.

"I'm leaving now." Uriel raised his hand again and was gone before anyone could say anything.

"This reminds me of the cave room during the trust challenge on the first trail," Jo told the others. "I know most of you were blindfolded, but I could see it from the top of the boulder. This place is beautiful like that cave was, but there's a lot of things that are different, too."

Aniela scanned the massive room. "It's quite similar, Jo, with the pulsing lights, glimmering gems, and whatever all those sculpture things are; but look at the maps and pictures scattered on the walls. This flat stone in the middle of the room wasn't in the first cave, either."

"That flat stone looks like a table, a perfect place to look at this scroll Uriel gave us," Nate declared as he sauntered to the table stone and unfurled the scroll so everyone could read what it said. A bright light settled on the flattened scroll. In fancy script and framed by ornate vines and symbols, they read this message:

Somewhere inside this stony lair,
A creature dwells that's now quite rare.
An ancient brute with rooster's head,
And taloned feet known to shred,
Winged beast with body of a serpent,
This deadly fiend's no longer sent
To the worlds of man and beast
To punish sinners or to feast.
With one breath, or look, or touch
It's victim's life it will clutch.
Avoid contact if you can,
But for its attack you must plan.
Only a weasel is immune
To a cockatrice's glance of doom.
Death's summoned by a rooster's crow
Or glimpsing itself in a mirror's glow,
These alone are the only ways
If the cockatrice you must slay.
With ruthless power it will prove
Why this warning you should behoove.

As they finished reading the ominous poem, the scroll lengthened and more writing appeared:

Your mission: find your way out of the cockatrice's den. There are three areas from which you must escape. You've been transported to the first section. As you see, there is no obvious way out. You must find the hidden door and figure out how to open it. Clues for solving this puzzle are everywhere. Rest assured, the creature is not in this first chamber, but it may be in either of the next two. The beast may lurk anywhere after you leave this room. Be wary! You must find your way out before the cockatrice finds you.

In order to escape, you must work together to collect and solve the clues. Each room has different clues and methods of escape. The way is not easy. Listen to and honor one another. Keen observation, logic, your gifts, and teamwork will see you through.

In the second chamber, you must solve each riddle and use those answers to get the ultimate answer: the way to the next chamber.

Your third and final chamber requires you to navigate through a maze and find the hidden tunnel. Twists and turns are not always what they seem. Stay together. Remember, the key to Heaven's gate is love. Carry it with you always. It will be the power that keeps you safe and well.

"So, we have to have to figure out how to get out of this place by collecting clues and avoiding something called a cockatrice," Micah summarized.

"I've never heard of a cockatrice," Dina offered, "but it sounds pretty awful. Head of a rooster, legs with talons, on the body of a serpent, with wings. Sounds like some kind of mutant dragon."

"And it can kill you by just looking at you, breathing on you, or touching you," Jo murmured. "It sounds very dangerous."

"But we have some hints about what to do if it finds us," Gabe reassured her. The poem said weasels are immune to the cockatrice's deadly stares. The sound of roosters crowing and seeing its own reflection in a mirror can kill it, so we just need to plan our defense using that information before we move to the next part."

"If we have three rooms to get through, I guess we'd better start searching for the clues in this one." Ariel walked toward one of the maps on the wall and studied it intently. "I don't see anything here that looks like a clue. It just looks like a map of some old kingdom."

Aniela scanned the room before walking to a detailed painting of children playing with kittens. She studied it before declaring, "I think I've found something." The others crowded around. "See this part right here, where the yarn is tangled on the floor next to the basket? It looks like a piece to a jigsaw puzzle, doesn't it? I wonder what will happen if I trace over it with my finger." She reached out and ran her finger over the image of tangled yarn. The section she touched clattered to the floor, a perfect jigsaw puzzle piece.

"I thought so!" she beamed. "We have to find pieces and assemble a puzzle to solve the way out of this place."

"You're brilliant!" her teammates crowed.

"Let's spread out and see how many pieces we can find," Nate suggested. "We have no idea how many pieces there are or what the picture will be when we put them together, so it may take a while."

"Maybe there is something on that old map, now that I know what I'm looking for," Ariel announced. "Worth another look." She walked back where she'd started looking. "Well, I'll be! I think the corners of this map might be the corners of our puzzle. This fancy design in each corner looks like it may be more than a design." She traced over the two straight edges and around the twists and turns of the decorative line. The piece fell to the floor. She traced the other three corners, and all fell from the map. "I have the puzzle's corners!" she announced. "I'm going to put them on the table by the scroll."

The team found piece after piece hidden in paintings, maps,

sculptures, and lights. A few minutes passed, but no one found any new pieces.

"Maybe we have them all," Ariel suggested. "Let's start assembling the puzzle and see if we can figure out our exit."

"It looks like we have thirty-six pieces here on the table," Micah called. "There are the four corner pieces from the old map and sixteen with one straight edge, so that means the outside edge has twenty pieces in all. If we get that part together, the middle should be easier."

"Group them by color," Aniela said. "It's easy to see where they go if they're sorted by their main color."

"The corners are mostly blue, like the map's water, and so are the straight edge pieces. The others are mostly speckled like this granite, with bits of blue," Ariel observed. "You don't suppose this puzzle is a picture of this table rock, do you?"

By the time Ariel had finished her remark, Aniela had the outside edge hooked together. "More than half way done." She smiled at her teammate's astonished faces.

"You really are a puzzle whiz!" Gabe declared.

They watched with wonder as Aniela snapped one piece after another into its correct place. When she finished, the image of the table rock was unmistakable. The puzzle was complete, but there was one piece left over. "I wonder why there's one extra. It doesn't make sense since the whole puzzle is done."

"Maybe that leftover piece is the key to unlocking the door from this room. The picture is of this flat rock, so maybe the door is somewhere on it or near it," Dina suggested. "I think we need to search the entire surface and the floor around it."

Seven pairs of hands searched the top and sides of the table rock, but no one found anything unusual, just the smooth surface of granite. Then they crawled around the floor around the rock searching the nearby floor for anything that looked or felt unusual. No one noticed Bruno sitting on his hind legs staring at the end of the table.

"Hey, Gabe, look at Bruno. What's he doing?" Nate asked.

"He's trying to show us something," Gabe said as he stroked Bruno's head. "What is it, boy?"

Bruno didn't flinch or take his eyes off the slight overhang on one end of the table rock.

"He's looking on the underside of this edge," Gabe declared as he felt along it. His fingers crossed an indenture. "I feel something," he announced as he laid on his back and looked up at the spot that felt different. "Hand me that leftover piece, would you?"

Ariel handed him the piece.

Gabe lined up and pressed the puzzle piece into the indenture he'd felt. It was a perfect fit!

The light over the table strobed as the table rock slid over, revealing a metal trap door with a golden ring handle. The door looked ancient and heavy.

"We did it!" the team cheered as they clustered around the portal to the next part of their challenge.

"Now we need a plan," Jo reminded them. "Before we go where the cockatrice might find us."

ESCAPE, PART 2

"**S**he's right," Micah said. "We need to know what we'll do if we see the beast."

"I think we should take the scroll with us, for one thing," Nate declared. "We might want to reread it, or maybe a new message will appear as we get further along."

Heads shook in agreement.

"Let's take this and keep it with us, too," Aniela said as she held up an ornately framed but lightweight mirror. "I took it off the wall right over there. The poem said seeing itself in a mirror would kill the cockatrice. Seems like this is a weapon they put here for us."

"Good thinking. We might be able to morph into weasels if we need to, but we can't really read and try to solve riddles if we take that form," Ariel declared. "I guess we can morph into weasels if we hear something strange or see the cockatrice before it sees us."

"Anybody good at animal sounds?" Dina asked. "Remember, the sound of roosters crowing can kill it."

"One of us could morph into a rooster and crow if comes near," Jo suggested. "The first one who spots it could morph and crow. That sound would be a pretty clear signal to the others that the cockatrice is near."

"What are we going to do with Bruno, Gabe? He might growl or something if he sees the creature first and alert it to where we are." Micah looked at Bruno tenderly, but with concerned eyes.

"Well, I suggest one of us hold him while we search for the riddles and try to figure them out. He seems to understand being held quietly when we levitate, so maybe whoever's holding him should levitate if he seems tense. That would give a different view of the room, too, and might help find the riddles."

"It probably goes without saying, but we need to stay as quiet as we can," Micah added. "We don't want to disturb the creature if it's sleeping or distracted by something other than us."

"So, we have our plan. Are we ready?" Jo asked.

Nate and Dina reached for the golden handle and pulled. The heavy door lifted slowly as they pulled back. They eased it down so that it settled next to the opening with only the slightest rattle.

The temperature dropped and a new smell hung suspended in the air as they stared into the opening. It was not stairs as they'd expected, but a winding slide that grew darker the farther from the opening it wound, seeming to lead to infinite darkness as it snaked away.

"Well, isn't this special? We get to slide into The Cockatrice's Den of Horrors," Nate observed. "I'll go first, if nobody objects. Maybe the next person should wait about ten seconds and then slide down. If Gabe's holding Bruno, we'll all be together at the bottom in a little over a minute."

"If you're leading, you should hold this in front of you, like a shield." Aniela held the mirror toward him. "That thing might know the bottom of the slide is a good hunting ground. It might be waiting."

"Thank you, Aniela. What a great idea! I'll take the mirror, and you bring the scroll." He sat on the edge of the slide and settled the mirror in front of his torso and head, holding it by the strong wire on the back. Count to ten and follow me, one at a time." He pushed off with one hand and disappeared as he rounded the first curve.

"I'll go next," Dina muttered as she plopped on the edge of the slide. "See you at the bottom." Her push sent her speeding down and out of sight.

One by one, the others followed. They all landed safely and quietly on a thick mat at the bottom.

The room was a fortress of stone, a mosaic of humble rocks come together to hold something ancient and strong. The stones stood mute, yet the visitors sensed the whispers of the ages, the souls of those who'd come before them to this place.

"This is hallowed ground," Dina whispered. "Do you feel the power here?"

"I do," Jo replied. "I feel vibrations, like something is reaching out to us."

"Maybe those vibrations can lead you to one of the riddles we have to find and solve," Micah suggested. "Can you hum or sing what you're feeling?"

"I don't know, but I'll try." Jo sang softly:

"What should we know?
Where should we go?
What should we do?
We're listening to you."

As she sang, vapor flowed from her mouth and floated in a winding ribbon to a painting of a rainbow over trees. The vapor swirled around the painting before dissipating.

"Jo's song is leading us to that rainbow picture," Gabe declared. "Maybe our first riddle's there."

The group huddled around the picture, examining it closely, but saw nothing that looked like writing or a riddle.

"Could we be wrong about this picture?" Jo mused. "I don't see anything."

"Let's look on the back," Aniela theorized. "Maybe the riddle's hidden." She lifted the picture and turned it over. As soon as she did, a beautifully printed card floated into Jo's hand.

"What does it say?" the group chorused.

Jo read aloud, ***"What's at the end of a rainbow?"***

"It is one of the riddles!" Aniela exclaimed. "A pot of gold? That's what they say."

"Too obvious!" Ariel exclaimed. "It's a riddle, so we're supposed to think of the less obvious."

"In that picture, it was trees," Jo offered. "Maybe a certain kind of tree with a name that could be a play on words?"

Ariel studied the painting. "I don't think so. Those trees look like three ordinary blue spruces."

"Well, this trail we're on is blue. Ariel said they're blue spruce trees, so those trees might be the answer," Nate suggested.

"It doesn't make sense," Dina said. "What's at the end of the rainbow? Blue spruces. Three blue spruces. It doesn't make sense."

"Yes, it does," Micah hypothesized, "if the trees are just what forms the answer. Look at this." He traced the line between the three trees in the painting. "Downward slant, upward slant, downward slant, upward slant. That makes the letter W! What's at the end of the rainbow? The letter W!"

"I think he's right!" Jo asserted. "That makes sense, and it's a pretty good riddle."

"Do we all agree? Is our first answer W?" Dina asked.

Bobbing heads affirmed the team's agreement.

"Let's write down our answers as we solve the riddles. Maybe that quill pen over there works. We don't have any paper except the scroll, but we could record on it, don't you agree?" Dina strode to an old-fashioned desk with a beautiful quill resting next to a candelabra. As she approached, she could feel increasing vibrations. She spread the scroll open on the desk.

"There are more vibrations over here," she told the others. "Another riddle might be close by. I'm going to see if I can use this quill to write down our first answer, but we should look around this old desk."

The group clumped around her as she recorded "W" in striking calligraphy just below the writing on the scroll. "This quill pen is cool. It makes lines that are so sharp and clear. Look at the beautiful stand where the pen rests. Isn't it magnificent?"

She lifted the quill base, exposing a card that was tucked underneath. This one floated into her hand.

"Look, we have our second riddle. *'We're tall when we're young, but short when we're old. What are we?'* Definitely a riddle," Dina declared. "Any ideas?"

"Maybe a pencil? It's long when it's new, but it gets shorter every time you sharpen it as it gets older," Gabe suggested.

"That makes sense, but maybe we should see if we can come up with any more ideas before we write it down," Ariel replied.

"Lots of people my parents knew smoked cigarettes," Aniela offered. "They're bigger when they're new and burn down to small butts."

"That makes sense, too," Ariel agreed. "That would apply to cigars and pieces of wood. They all get smaller as they burn."

"So, three of our possible answers involve things that burn. That seems like it's important," Micah added.

Bruno leapt on the desk and stared at his people. He sat at attention in the space between the scroll, quill base, and candelabra.

"Of course! Good dog, Bruno!" Dina patted his head. "He's telling us to look right here on the desk, where the riddle came from when I lifted the base. I think the answer is 'candles'! There are candles in this candelabra and they get shorter when they're old."

"Wow! You and Bruno are right," Nate agreed. "Does everyone think candles is the right answer to this riddle?"

Yeses all around confirmed their answer before he added the word candles next to the W.

"There's so much to look at in this room. It's so cluttered, not at all what I'd think you'd find in a cave." Gabe looked all around. "Where should we search next?"

"Jo and I both felt vibrations as hints about the first two riddles," Dina reminded them. "Did any of you feel vibrations or something like static electricity? That feeling may be part of the search."

"Maybe if Jo and Micah sing softly, we'll get some of that vapor to lead us to another riddle," Gabe suggested.

Micah warbled softly, *"Where's the next riddle? Where can it be?*

We need to find number three."

He smiled at Jo, and she joined him as he repeated the ditty. As soon as Jo started the song, vapor spouted from both their mouths, swirled together, and meandered across the room. It spun into intricate curlicues and surrounded a leather-bound book in a cluttered bookcase.

"This book seems to be calling us," Micah declared as he lifted it from the shelf. "Riddle three, where are you hiding?" He examined the front and back covers, but no card or writing was on either side. He opened the book, but found nothing inside the cover. It must be here, maybe in the middle of the book somewhere? He quickly thumbed through the pages and gently shook the book to see if anything would fall out. Nothing.

"Sing again, while you're holding that volume," Dina said.

As soon as the song began again, a card floated from the back of the space where the book had sat and landed on top of the book in Micah's hands.

"Here we go! Third riddle: *I am an odd number. Take away a letter and I become even. What number am I?'"*

"That one's easy," Nate asserted. "I've heard it before. My big brother used to do riddles with me all the time. The answer is seven. Seven's an odd number and if you take off the letter S, you have the word even."

"He's right," Aniela said. "Look at the spot where the card was hidden. It's the seventh spot from the left and the seventh spot down from the top of the bookcase. That seems like proof that 'seven' is the right answer."

"You really are amazingly observant," Gabe marveled. "Between you and Bruno, we won't miss anything."

Dina said, "I'll record 'seven' if everyone agrees."

"I wonder how many riddles we have to find and solve," Ariel murmured. "W, candles, and seven doesn't sound like a full answer, so I know we need more. Any ideas where we should look next?"

Gabe called, "I wonder if there's something near this grandfather clock. I feel like static electricity is pricking my skin." Bruno nuzzled his neck. "Bruno feels it, too."

"The pendulum doesn't seem to be moving," Nate observed. "Do you think it's working?"

"Maybe not as a clock, but something's happening here," Gabe said. "Do you feel that static?"

"I do, so I guess we should search around the clock and see if we find another riddle. Maybe I can open the case and look inside. The door won't budge. If the riddle's inside, I don't know how to get it. It's too heavy to move, so the riddle wouldn't be on the back or underneath it."

"I'll levitate and look on top of the clock," Gabe offered. "I see something up here," he called. "Hooray! It's our next riddle." He plucked a card from the top of the long case clock and returned to the ground, with Bruno happily draped around his neck.

"Read it, Gabe," his teammates chimed.

"What occurs once in every minute, twice in every moment, yet never in a thousand years?"

"We blink?" Jo suggested.

"We blink way more often than once a minute. Not in a thousand years? That means it's not something we actually do." Dina looked at her teammate fondly. "But you got us started trying to come up with an answer that makes sense."

"The clue was on top of an old-fashioned clock, so it might have to do with time, or it might have to do with being raised up, or on top of something," Ariel suggested.

"Is this one your brother told you before, Nate?"

"No, I don't remember it, but it's a play on words."

"Minute, moment, and thousand years are all amounts of times, but I agree with Nate. This is something to do with the words, not time," Dina whispered. "Read it again, Gabe."

"What occurs once in every minute, twice in every moment, yet never in a thousand years?"

"Perhaps the word **'in'** makes a difference. What happens once 'in' a minute, twice **'in'** a moment, but not at all **in** a thousand years?" Dina asked again, stressing the word **'in'**.

No one responded to her question so she continued. "What if it's the letter M? The word minute has one M, the word moment has two M's, and a thousand years doesn't contain an M at all."

"That's true! You just figured out our fourth riddle," Nate beamed. "It makes sense to me. Everyone agree?"

Their agreement encouraged Dina to record M on the scroll next to W, seven, and candles. "That's four answers, but they don't make sense together yet. We must have more to find if we have to put the answers together to find the escape hatch from this room." "We should stroll around the room and see if any of us feel the vibrations or static anywhere else," Micah suggested.

"Riddle, oh riddle, where can you be? We need to find you to be free!" Jo crooned, just above the volume of a whisper. She wandered around the perimeter repeating her ditty when an ornate sculpture of an elephant caught her eye. She examined it carefully, fascinated by the lifelike image. For some reason she couldn't explain, she felt compelled to stroke the elephant. She ran her hand over the wide back then along its belly. To her delight, she felt another card fastened to the underside of the pachyderm. "Here's another one," she announced when she pulled the card free.

The others joined her by the sculpture and asked her to read riddle 5.

"*Forward I am heavy, but backward I am not. What am I?*"

"Yikes, what could be heavy one way, but backwards it's not heavy?" Ariel asked.

"Maybe a load of something? The truck or trailer is heavy when the load leaves, but when it returns, it's not because it was unloaded and the truck or trailer is empty," Micah suggested.

"Possibly, but it may be another play on words, not an actual thing," Aniela told him. "I don't really think the answer is load."

"Yes!" Nate exclaimed. "It is another word play."

The team looked at him, waiting for more.

"The riddle was on this elephant. Elephants weigh about a ton when they're adults."

"So?" chimed his teammates.

"So forwards, the word is **ton**, but when you look at the letters backward you have **n-o-t, not.**" He grinned. "A ton is heavy and when the letters are reversed you have the word not. *'Forward I am heavy, but backward I am not.'*"

"You really are good at riddles," Dina commented. "You just figured out our fifth one. Should I write ton with our other answers?"

Aniela, with the mirror's wire looped over her arm, studied a huge poster of circus acts from some bygone day. The poster featured a ringmaster in the center with a megaphone. Acrobats filled one ring, lions and tigers another, clowns cavorted in the third, and an elephant wearing a funny hat balanced on two stands in the last ring. "I never saw a circus, or any other show," she murmured. "They must be fascinating to watch."

Her teammates glanced at the poster and returned their attention to the scroll where Dina had recorded the answers to the riddles. "Our answers are W, M, seven, candles, and ton. What can all of that mean?"

"I bet they're hints to something we have to spot, like the puzzle pieces in the first room. Let's look for candles or seven of something and see if the rest of the answers are around one of those words or pictures," Jo suggested.

"Like this candelabra on the desk," Dina reminded them. "It has seven arms and holds candles. Seven and candles are two of our answers. Could we be looking for something on the desk near the candelabra?"

"Or maybe, it's right here on this poster," Aniela announced softly. "This section with the elephant might be what we need."

Her team crowded around, eager to hear what their observant friend had discovered this time.

"An elephant represented the word ton when Jo found the riddle, right? Look at the hat on this elephant. It has flaming candles on top. Seven of them. Now look at the stands where the elephant's balancing. Look at the design on each one." She traced over the gold lines on the red stands. The seven zigzagging diagonal lines clearly made W and M by sharing the fourth line, the one that connected the letters.

"She's right!" Gabe concluded. "I can see it clearly now that she's pointed it out to us."

"I wonder what we have to do to find the way out, though," she wondered. "Tracing around the edges of the picture didn't make anything happen like it did when we were gathering puzzle pieces."

"Possibly, each of us has to trace it," Micah suggested as he dragged his finger around the image.

Each team member followed his lead and traced the elephant, balancing stands, and funny candle hat. Nothing happened.

"They told us to use prior learning," Jo reminded the group. "Remember both signs only worked when we were connected and when we all touched them at the same time. Maybe it's the same thing here."

"You're probably right," Ariel acknowledged. "Let's try that."

The team formed a semicircle around the poster, with one hand resting on the shoulder of the person next to them and one hand stretched out to touch the elephant section of the poster. Bruno still hung around Gabe's neck.

The poster now felt warm, noticeably warmer than the air temperature of this craggy chamber. The elephant's two balancing stands spun faster and faster, cascading red and golden embers clustered and congealed on the floor near the team.

"Look, those stands are opening our exit," Dina observed. "Aniela has the mirror. I'm going to grab the scroll from the desk."

The pool of embers swirled and spread a molten-looking path across the room.

"I guess we're supposed to step onto this trail," Gabe whispered. "Bruno and I'll go first this time."

As soon as his foot met the scarlet trail, he was sucked into the meld, like he'd stepped into quicksand. In just a second, he was gone from view.

ESCAPE, PART 3

"**A**niela, you should go next or give one of us the mirror," Nate said. "Gabe and Bruno shouldn't be alone, wherever they went, without the mirror. That cockatrice must be in the last section since it wasn't in this chamber."

"I—I guess I'll go," Aniela stammered as she held the mirror in front of her head and upper body and stepped onto the rippled crimson stream. She, too, was sucked into the liquified stream of red and gold.

"I bet more than one of us at a time could step on this molten flow and go wherever it wants us to go. Want to try it with me, Jo?" Micah reached for her hand.

Euphoric butterflies flapped in her stomach as Jo stepped on the portal pathway, her hand comfortably cupped in Micah's, her eyes locked on his smiling face. The pair plummeted out of sight.

"Interesting," Nate mumbled. "Should we try it together, too, girls?" He linked arms with Dina and Ariel. Together, they marched forward and were swept from the room of riddles.

Reunited under an enormous maple tree, the group stood in awe as ruby and gilded leaves swayed on the branches, rained down, and swirled around the group. There seemed to be a message in the leaves' motion, but no one was sure what it was.

"We're at the start of some kind of maze," Gabe told the others. "We're still inside the cave, but these moss-covered walls stretch as far as I could see when I scanned the area from high in the tree." He pointed to the thick wall of green with just one opening, about the width of a door. "This tree blocks you from going anywhere but that opening. The paths through this thing shimmered and kept changing. I don't know how we're supposed to find our way through it."

"Well, we all know we have to do it, so we may as well get going," Ariel declared. "Everybody, stay close together and alert."

"Do you want one of us to carry Bruno for a while?" Dina asked. "Your arms and neck must be getting tired."

"That would be great for a little while," Gabe admitted. "I'm sure he'd like to cuddle with you, too."

Bruno kissed Dina's cheek as she nestled him in her arms. Their mutual joy was apparent to all.

As soon as the final member stepped through the opening, it clanked closed, barring anyone from exiting the way they'd entered the labyrinth.

"That's not good," Aniela whispered as she scooted closer to Gabe.

They soon discovered that the puzzle of paths split and turned in many directions. The walls were frigid, the moss stiff and prickly to the touch, like it was forever frozen. The chilled air had a dark and threatening feel. It seemed to want to suck the breath from them, slow them, make them lose their focus, goading them somehow.

They wandered through the narrow passages clumped closely together. It seemed to get dimmer the farther they went. Taunting voices whispered from the walls, encouraging them to split apart and search for the exit to save themselves from the cockatrice. The best and smartest would find the way out. The others deserved their fate. They weren't worthy of being warriors.

"Don't listen to those voices," Dina blurted. "They want us to betray one another. If we betray one another, we're betraying God. We have hundreds of ways to fail this test, but I know separating the group is an instant fail. We have to stay together. We have to walk through our fears. Together."

An unknown voice hissed, "You think you're so smart, Dina! We know about you. We know what you did in your earthly life. You're nothing but a cheater and a bully, a phony. You're trying to bully the others into doing what you want, cheating them of free choice."

Dina stood frozen, Bruno clutched to her chest. She shifted him to her shoulder. He draped over her shoulder comfortably and nuzzled her face.

Jo and Micah linked arms with Dina. "Follow your own good advice, Dina. Don't listen to that voice. It's taunting you with your personal fears about mistakes you made in the past. It's trying to distract you and keep you from moving forward with resolve," Jo told her friend.

Dina clenched her jaws and stepped forward, her teammates' arms still looped through hers. Her wide-open eyes focused straight ahead. She had no map, but she knew her faith and intuition would help her through this trial.

Jo sang softly, "Life's a dance, you learn as you go..." Her breath swirled ahead, beckoning the group to follow.

Micah repeated, "Life's a dance, you learn as you go..." His breath, too, puffed forward.

Together, Jo and Micah repeated the song line over and over as they marched forward. To their amazement, a section of the maze wall shimmered and parted, opening a new path.

"It appears we're supposed to go this way." Micah gestured toward the opening.

"You and Jo singing that song line over and over created this opening," Nate marveled. "Maybe music, or certain words, something like that, voiced repeatedly causes the walls to shift and show us the way out."

"You silly, silly boy!" the hissing voice jeered. "Silly, silly boy is going to make this team crash! You're good at helping things crash, aren't you, Nate? You're all going to crash on this task if the silly, silly boy has his way."

"Don't listen to that, Nate. It's scoffing at you because you're on to something," Gabe reassured his teammate. "Part of this maze's purpose is to torment us about things from our pasts. I bet it's training for dealing with demons who try to take over our minds. If we listen and let that voice get to us, we won't get out of here."

"So, the weird wild one thinks he's so smart now!" the voice taunted. "You're so weird even your own father didn't love you. No one is going to listen to you, Gabe! You're wrong, as usual!"

"Let's get going," Ariel prodded. "Maybe if we move away from this opening the voice will stop."

The troupe proceeded forward as Aniela muttered, "We can do this. We CAN do this." One by one, her teammates joined her. "We can do this!" rang softly from each mouth, Jo's and Micah's voices turned it into a chant that they all repeated over and over.

A section of the wall glinted in the dim light. The glimmer grew into a flash and another opening in the wall appeared before them.

"All of us repeating the same thing created another opening!" Ariel declared. "The first opening came after the line of the song was sung over and over, now this one is after all of us chanted the same thing. I'm sure Nate was right. Repeated sounds or melodies are the key to getting out."

"Well, let's get going," Aniela pleaded. "I really, really don't like it in here."

"None of us do," Ariel soothed. "We'll keep moving to find the path out."

Jo smiled. "That's right. Do you have a favorite song, Aniela? Maybe we can sing it together as we walk."

"I like 'Somewhere Over the Rainbow.' Ms. Cross liked it, too. We used to listen to it in class if someone needed to calm down."

"I love that song! Did you ever see the movie *The Wizard of Oz*? The main character, Dorothy, sang it so beautifully."

"No, I never saw that movie, but I know the song."

"We learned about that song in my freshman choral music class," Micah offered.

"It was written in 1939 by two Jewish men in America. They

won an Oscar for it in 1940 because of the movie, but it was really written about Jewish people and what they faced from the start of World War II. It takes on a whole new meaning if you think about it being about Jewish people and what they endured through the Holocaust."

"Let's sing the first line of it over and over and see if we find which way to go next," Jo suggested.

"Somewhere over the rainbow, way up high..." Jo and Micah smiled at one another, clearly enjoying their duet.

"Sing it with us this time, Aniela," Micah coaxed. "Everybody should sing it. Maybe the wall will open sooner if more voices are lifted."

"Or maybe that cockatrice will find us," Gabe countered.

"Good point," Micah acknowledged. "Let's sing softly, but you sing, too, Aniela."

Aniela's voice blended well with Jo's and Micah's. She clearly relaxed a bit as she repeated the line over and over as they walked. White vapor puffed from Jo and Micah as they sang and walked on each side of Aniela. The vapor seemed to rush ahead, as if it had some important place to be.

Once again, they noticed that a section of the wall shimmered and dissolved. A new opening loomed before them.

"Here we go again," Nate announced. "I hope we don't have too many portals left to find. It seems like we've been in here a long time."

The group had moved about ten paces from the latest opening when Aniela squeaked, "What's that?" She pointed to a pile of something against one wall of the maze, about a hundred feet ahead of them. It was silent and unmoving. The cold stones around them closed in as they stared where she pointed.

"Everyone should stay calm," Jo whispered. "We can't let fear control us. We can't let the unknown throw us into panic. We have each other, and we know we have to get through this maze together.

You have the mirror, Aniela. If that's the cockatrice curled up by that wall, you can hold the mirror up to fight it. Or give it to one of us, and we'll do it."

"I've carried it all this way," Aniela declared, "I'll keep going with it."

"What if the rest of us should morph into weasel form until we get past it?" Ariel suggested. "Just in case."

"I'm going to stay as I am and stay with Aniela," Gabe said, "but I think the rest of you should morph or go invisible. Dina, give me Bruno back so you can morph."

The voice hissed, "Leaving the mirror in the hands of the slow one. She won't know how to use it! You don't know how to do much, do you, Aniela? Dumb, dumb Aniela. Dumb, dumb team for trusting her with your only weapon!"

"Don't pay any attention to that voice," Gabe told her. "It's part of the test. We all know you aren't dumb. You'll do fine."

A weak smile crossed her lips. "I wish I was as brave as the rest of you. I'm really scared."

"That's completely understandable, but being scared is what lets the bravery come out. You can do this."

Bruno stretched over and pawed her shoulder.

"See, even Bruno knows you've got this."

A young woman brandishing a mirror like a shield, a young man with a terrier draped around his neck, and a pack of five weasels stealthily approached the heap next to the wall.

The top of the heap lifted, showing that it was not the cockatrice, but a young man dressed in dark green and brown. His dark clothing and skin nearly camouflaged him against the mossy wall in the dim light. With his head down and knees pulled up tightly to his chest, the heap hadn't looked human, but now they could clearly see that it was.

"Bax!" he cried. *"Fadlan. Bax!"*

"He spoke Somalian," Gabe marveled, "and I understood it. He said go away, please, go away."

"I understood it, too," Aniela murmured. "This language thing is pretty cool."

"Salaam alaykum," they said together. Hello.

"Idaa!" Leave me alone!

"Maxaa khaldan?" What's wrong? Gabe smiled at the young man.

"Eeyaha! Eeyaha duudrjoogta ah!" Dogs! Wild dogs!

"These are not wild dogs. None of us will hurt you." Gabe told him in perfect Somali.

"Morph back to yourselves," Gabe said to the five weasels near his feet. "He'll see that you're not dogs at all."

Dina, Jo, Ariel, Nate, and Micah now stood next to Gabe and Aniela. "Hello," they said together in his language.

A shocked young man gaped at the group of people who now stood where he knew he just saw five wild dogs. Everyone understood his comment in his native tongue. "I don't understand. I am scared."

Together they told him, "Stand up. You can go with us."

"No! That wild dog will try to eat me!" the stranger shouted.

Laughing, Gabe replied, "This is Bruno. He is a tame gentle dog. He likes everyone."

"Leave me alone!"

"No! We will not leave you. You can stay with us."

Gabe handed Buno to Jo, then reached down to help the young Somali to his feet.

The young man scrambled out of his reach. "Leave me alone. Please."

"We can't do that. It isn't safe for you to be alone."

"Who are you?"

"My name is Gabe."

"My name is Jo."

One by one, each member of the team introduced themselves

to the disbelieving young man. Nate, the final member to tell his name, added, "What's your name?"

"My name is Guleed."

Nate knelt next to the young man they'd just met. "Pleased to meet you, Guleed. We need to go. It is dangerous to stay here. We need to get out of this place."

"I saw a strange beast. I am scared.

Team JAMBANGD exchanged worried looks. The cockatrice was nearby and now they had a stranger among them, one who didn't seem able to protect himself or help them.

"Maybe we could explain about the cockatrice and let Guleed carry the mirror since it doesn't appear that he can morph into a weasel or go invisible. We have to get him to go with us. We can't just leave him here and go on without him." Gabe looked at each of his teammates with sorrowful eyes. "We can't leave him here as prey for the cockatrice. I don't understand why he's in this maze. He doesn't seem to be doing the same challenge we are, and he doesn't seem to have any divine powers, but I know we can't go on without him. At least I can't. I remember what it was like to be afraid and feel all alone. I won't leave him."

"We won't leave him, or you, either," Jo asserted. "We just have to get him up and moving with us. I have this strange feeling. Something's about to happen."

"I feel it, too," Dina and Ariel replied.

Nate and Gabe knelt on each side of Guleed and spoke softly and quickly in Somali. Guleed pointed down the passage. They nodded and pulled the newcomer to his feet. Aniela demonstrated how to hold the mirror up like a shield using the wire on the backside, then handed it to him.

"Thank you."

"Seriously, let's get going," Jo prodded. "This static electricity feeling is getting stronger and stronger. Some force is close."

"Someone needs to stay behind Guleed," Micah suggested. "If

he's holding the mirror in front like a shield, he won't have any protection if the cockatrice attacks from behind."

"I'll stay right behind him," Gabe announced. "I can walk backwards and watch behind."

"I'll stay next to you," Nate told him. "We'll be the rear guard."

"Jo and Micah, why don't you sing something and see if that frosty breath opens the way out," Ariel suggested. "Music might soothe everyone as we walk."

Jo grinned and sang, "Heigh, ho, heigh, ho, it's out of the maze we go!"

First Micah, then the others joined in whisper-singing her song parody. Even Guleed managed, "Heigh, ho, heigh, ho!" and a small smile. He drummed on the mirror's frame with his open hand.

After only a few dozen steps, the wall began to shimmer, revealing a new passageway.

"Here we go! Here's our next turn," Micah announced.

The wall closed quietly as the group entered the new passage. Stunned, they stopped in their tracks. At both ends of the passageway stood pairs of cockatrices! They saw not one beast, but four! Busily grooming one another, the creatures didn't notice the newcomers in the middle of the dim hallway.

The voice hissed, "You really did it now! Look where you are. The actual nesting area of two pairs of ancient cockatrice. I bet they're hungry. Too bad there's no place to run or hide!"

Fear clutched the group. Guleed pressed himself against the mossy wall, as if commanding his body to be part of the surface.

"That's right, Guleed. Stay tight against the wall," Gabe whispered. "Sit like you were when we found you. Tuck yourself up as compactly as you can and hold the mirror over you like a shielding umbrella. Hold that wire tightly with both hands and don't look at the creatures. They can kill by looking at you. Keep your face hidden under the mirror!"

"We need to go invisible and be ready to fight if the cockatrice attack Guleed," Gabe continued. "Jo, can you cloak Bruno with your invisibility?"

She clutched the terrier close to her as she nodded her affirmation.

"We don't want to kill these creatures if we don't have to; we are invading their nesting area, after all. But, we can't let them get Guleed. Watch carefully. Go invisible!" Gabe's raspy whisper punctuated the seriousness of the situation.

The hall now looked empty, except for a trembling heap of brown and green tucked under a mirror. The heap waited for whatever was coming. He knew that sooner or later, his involuntary noises or his smell would draw the creatures to him. That was the way with every predator in his homeland. Sharp senses and remorseless kills helped the fittest survive. Still, he stood no chance against four of these rooster-dragons. He had no weapon and no choice but to depend on this turtle-style defense and these strangers who walked with a wild dog and made strange things happen.

From one end of the labyrinth, a keening sound erupted. It was a crow of sorts, but short and wrapped in a hiss. Not your usual crow. Not the kind that was supposed to be deadly to the cockatrice. This sound was met by another from the opposite end of the mossy hall, a warning. Whether the warning was to or for one another was unclear.

The two smaller cockatrice flapped leathery wings and landed atop the mossy walls, surveying the scene below. A vibrating mirror leaned near one wall, and their mates stood staring at the peculiar heap.

In that frozen second between stand-off and fighting, the cockatrice's eyes flicked from one another to the mirror. Their eyes showed no fear. They weren't sure what they were seeing, but it didn't belong in their nesting area. They'd been invaded in their home.

Sauntering from each end, the cockatrice approached the

middle where the strange pile chattered and shook. Their talons scraped the stones and echoed through the narrow passageway, but there were no other sounds. They smelled the fear. Whatever had invaded would be easy prey.

Two pairs of angry eyes declared a primal rage entwined with an indomitable will to survive. Vicious jaws snapped hooked beaks as they drew nearer. Guleed could hear the power in those snaps. He knew they could shred him easily. With nowhere to hide and nothing to do, Guleed could only wait and feel. Feel the hard cold wall pressed against his back. Feel the wire cutting into his hands as he clutched the mirror over himself. Feel his bones rattling and his heart pounding as fear surged. Feel the tears trickling down his cheeks as his fear overtook him and turned into terror.

Quick thrusts of talons scraped the frame of the mirrored shield as shrieking crows and cackles resounded next to Guleed. The pair of males were intent on their mission to oust this invader in their den.

The attack was interrupted by unseen forces. Somehow, something unseen was on each of their backs yanking at their wings and distracting them from their prey. Whatever gripped their wings was strong and intent on pulling them away from the quivering mass behind the shield. Both cockatrice gyrated in circles trying to buck off whatever had this hold on them. The beasts' shrieks of pain and anguish echoed through the hall. These invisible enemies riding their spines could not be reached by beak or claws.

The tumult of snapping, scraping, and frenzied whirling moved the males away from their intended victim. The females swooped from the top of the walls towards their mates. Their cries were defensive and clear: We, too, will fight. We will defend our mates and our nests. They lurched repeatedly, trying to catch whatever had this power over their mates. Then they found themselves, too, overpowered by something on their backs clutching their wings and making it impossible to defend. The four roared and shook, clamored and spun, bellowed and bucked, but they made no headway in dislodging whatever had hold of them.

Jo's angelic voice rang through the cavern, singing a very old song:

"God is our refuge and our strength,
our ever-present aid,
and, therefore, though the earth gives way,
we will not be afraid..."

A second voice joined the song as the lines were repeated over and over. Streamers of white smoke puffed near the heap on the floor. The cockatrice twirled and twisted in frazzled attempts to free themselves. Ribbons of white encircled and bound each pair of cockatrice, the gauzy web too strong to break. The creatures were muzzled and blindfolded by the streamers that just kept coming. The strands spun around the mirror, too, shrouding the reflective side.

The song echoed through the chamber as more and more white vapor changed into the strong fibers that bound the beasts and mirror.

Aniela shouted, "We can return to visibility now. The cockatrice are harmless now that they're like mummies. She made herself visible first, perched on the back of one of the females, her hands still clinging to the tops of the now useless wings.

One by one, the group made themselves seen. Dina reappeared on the back of the other female, Gabe and Nate on the backs of the males. Jo and Micah were squatting on each side of Guleed, blocking an attack from either side where the mirror didn't cover Guleed's body. Ariel stood protectively near the front of the mirror-shield.

Jo stood, Bruno tucked close to her side. "You can stand up now, Guleed. The danger has passed. It's okay. Put down the mirror and look at what's happened to the beasts."

Hesitantly, Guleed lowered the mirror. His unblinking stare and statue-like pose declared that his brain was trying to make sense of all he was seeing. His eyes and mouth were frozen wide open in stunned surprise. He was temporarily incapacitated, paralyzed as he tried to process the scene before him.

The four cockatrice wranglers leaped to the floor near the others. Micah murmured, "Give me your hand. I'll help you up."

Guleed stared at him but did not reach out. He was trying to remember how to speak, trying to remember at least one word. None came to him.

Gabe went to his other side. "It's okay, Guleed. Micah and I will help you up, then we'll try to find the way out of here. You'll see. Everything's all right now."

They pulled bewildered Guleed to his feet.

"You did great, Guleed," Jo soothed. "You stayed silent and tucked under the mirror just like we told you to do. You were so brave to stay so quiet with the cockatrice so close and not being able to see what was happening. We're going to move away from this area now. Come on, walk with Bruno and me."

Guleed stared at Jo, gently holding and stroking the little wild dog. He nodded slightly and sidestepped away from the bound pairs of cockatrice who were still flailing and screeching.

Jo raised her voice in song, *"Then sings my soul, my savior God to thee…"* Micah's voice joined hers as they rejoiced surviving the cockatrice den.

Clouds of white vapor rushed from their mouths as they sang. It spun into a whirlwind, stretching to the top of the wall before spinning into it, ricocheting off, growing exponentially, and spinning around the group who gaped at the spectacle. Glittering blue strands mingled with the white, creating a striped funnel cloud. Their clothes and hair flapped like flags as the wind pushed them together, back to back and side to side. It was exciting, feeling the pure power of this wind as it rushed at them, swirling and sculpting. Whatever was happening now would leave them different. They all knew that.

The wind was not a passive backdrop in their battle to be freed from the maze. It had become one of them, roaring as it slammed into the wall. The mossy barrier crumbled and the wind blew the team like confetti outside the confines of the cockatrice den.

They found themselves standing under the biggest and most colorful tree any of them had ever seen. Its gigantic heart-shaped leaves, in every color that could tumble from a giant crayon box, waved at them. The wind died down, so it was just a gentle kiss on each of their cheeks, enough to spin a few of the heart leaves around their feet.

"We did it! We made it out of the maze, and we're all fine!" Ariel beamed.

"You are more than fine," Uriel declared as he stepped from behind the trunk. "You are utterly amazing."

CHOICES WE MAKE

U riel stared at the group that stood before him, speechless and motionless as he surveyed the team. "Please, have a seat or stretch out under this magnificent cordula tree. You'll find the grass as soft and comfortable as any bed you've ever stretched out upon. We can refresh a bit and enjoy the view of the vibrant leaves as they rustle above." Uriel slid down and rested his back against the smooth trunk. He scooped up a handful of white and blue crystals that lay on the ground near him, staring at the bits in his cupped hands. The others surrounded him on the ground, gazing up at the harlequin canopy of leaves. Gabe and Nate whispered to Guleed and motioned for him to sit between them.

Guleed stared at Uriel as if he'd just pulled a hippopotamus from his pocket. The sparks in his brain were desperately trying to connect the dots and make some sort of sense out of all that was happening. Instead, he felt like his brain was short circuited. Nothing made sense.

"I've never heard of a cordula tree," Ariel said. "I'd remember seeing a picture of one. It's spectacular."

"No, you've never seen one of this species before. They haven't existed on Earth for eons. Cordula is actually the old Latin word for heart. It is a fitting name."

"Well, it appears you have been fast-tracked again. This is not the usual exit point from the cockatrice chambers. Most warrior trainees have several more tasks on the *Trail of Deliverance* to complete before reaching the end." Uriel smiled at the group.

"First, I'm going to ask the others to join us here." Uriel raised his arm and made several circular motions in the air.

Gavreel, Michael, and Kirron appeared next to him.

Guleed, wide-eyed and terrified, tried to leap up and escape. Gabe and Nate held him, murmuring softly and reassuringly in Somali. As soon as Guleed calmed, Gabe sprang to his feet and wrapped Gavreel in a bear hug.

"Thank you, Gavreel. You're just the most amazing individual I've ever met! You saved Bruno the pup, and you loved him for so long. I can't believe you gave him up for me. You told me once that I'd understand some day when I asked why no one ever came to help me. You came and you brought Bruno. You two saved me. I can't even imagine how hard it was to let Bruno go."

Guleed watched Gabe's embrace of this woman who'd just appeared and listened intently to the words Gabe showered on her. He didn't understand what Gabe said, but he could understand the sincerity of the moment.

"Bruno saved me, too, as you saw. He's a remarkable creature and has been a hardworking and devoted angel since our transition. I still love him, as I love all of you." She smiled at every person gathered under the giant tree. "We both knew it was the right time, and you were the right person for him to devote his life to next. You needed him far more by that time than I did. He's become an integral part of this team, and we still get to see and love one another. He understands an angel's calling, as you're beginning to understand yourself." She pecked Gabe's cheek. "Have a seat by your newest teammate, Gabe."

"It seems we now know for whom this is intended." Gavreel pulled the helix from her pocket, Guleed's name sparkled where no name had been before. She spoke in Somali to the trembling young man.

"I am Gavreel. This is Michael and Kirron. The man who met you by the cordula tree is Uriel. We are all angels. Everyone here will help you feel at ease and understand what is going on as you transition to Heaven. You have been chosen, Guleed."

"Ch—chosen for what?"

"Chosen to serve God in fighting evil, like what is happening in your homeland on Earth. You've been chosen to join this team of young warriors who protected you and freed you from your state of torment, your personal anguish. You were in limbo, and now you are not." Gavreel smiled warmly.

"What? I don't understand anything you're talking about."

Gavreel continued, "You have transitioned from your Earth life to your everlasting life. Because of the life you led on Earth, your transition required a different entry, one of introspection and inner spiritual cleansing. Few who enter from this route become warriors, but you have been chosen. Your soul has been purified."

"Let me add something," Michael said. "Guleed, you were a warrior of survival your entire life in Somalia. You did many things during that lifetime that you had to face during your time alone in the cockatrice den. You had to feel the terror you inflicted on others. You suffered greatly yourself, but you imposed great suffering on many people. You had to see and reflect on all the things you did. That's why your life flashed through your mind over and over while you were confined, why you couldn't stop thinking about some things. Facing that pain and terror is what allowed you to be released from the maze with this remarkable team. The whirlwind that freed you also connected your essence to theirs. There is greatness within each of them, so there must be greatness within you, too. As Gavreel said, you have been chosen."

Gavreel spoke again. "First, let's get you in the team's uniform, Guleed. Just stay right where you are." She raised her arms and gestured.

Guleed stared at the form-fitting jumpsuit that now clothed him and felt the chain around his neck.

Gavreel blew a handful of blue glitter she pulled from her pocket toward the group of young people. The sparkly bits swirled around all nine before merging into their uniforms' fabric. Their team emblem now featured another G. They were Team JAMBANGGD.

"What's happening? How is this possible?"

"You have been officially connected to this team. We added more blue because it's your favorite color, and the letter G to the emblem to represent your name. You are a warrior angel in training, Guleed."

"I need to explain this and add it to your uniform." She held up the helix with his name gently glowing. She explained the gift of languages he was about to receive. Now it made sense why these people could speak perfect Somali and understand everything he said! The elders among the group practiced the acceptance prayer in Somali with Guleed and told him to hold the lingo-coiner over his heart at the edge of the team emblem. He recited the prayer as they rested their hands on his head, shoulders, and arms.

Incredulous that he understood everything when they switched to English, Guleed stared down at the gently pulsing symbols on the lingo-coiner. "I don't know how this is possible, but I really like this thing."

"It is a divine gift. Very rare and very precious. It will serve all of us well. It already has, as you were discovered and delivered."

"I believe you'll like the other divine gifts you're about to receive, too, Guleed," Kirron told him. "It may seem a bit overwhelming right now because so much is happening at once, but your help on the mission we have been assigned is vital. That's why you were placed with this fast-tracked team and why you, especially, are fast-tracked."

"I don't know what you mean," Guleed told them as he fingered the bracelets on his left wrist. "What does fast-tracked mean? What are divine gifts?"

"Fast-tracked means you were chosen by God to become a powerful warrior much faster than most. You'll learn quickly and acquire needed skills easily. We'll work with you to gain the skills that these warriors already have. Divine gifts are gifts from God.

They'll help make you a mighty warrior." Gavreel smiled at him again, that smile that oozed comfort and reassurance.

"How do you know I am fast-tracked?"

Uriel replied, "The power of the blue strands that merged with the whirlwind. Those blue stripes are God's direct intervention. God added strength to the funnel to break through the wall and swirl all of your essences together to form this team."

"You have not had the time to learn with and bond with your teammates yet, but God chose this team to protect you and free you. God chose you to be a warrior, on this team," Michael added. "You'll soon discover how fortunate you are to have been joined with these warriors."

"Let's do the accelerated life showings. He'll understand more after seeing each of their histories. Then we'll show his life to the others. His life will take some discussion. We must ascertain full acceptance before moving forward." Kirron strode to the maze wall. With a leaf from the cordula tree, he tapped the wall nine times, one tap for each warrior whose life stories he called forth. "You're about to see every event in each person's life up to this point, Guleed. You'll understand each person fully after these viewings. Then your life will be shown, and we'll discuss the events that shaped you and why your entry was different from the other members of your team. Get comfortable and make sure you can see this section clearly."

Warrior after warrior's life stories zipped across the wall, showing every moment of each life on Earth, the training, and missions to this point, including the time spent on the *Trail of Deliverance* and in the cockatrice den. A flurry of vibrant cordula leaves swirled against the wall, clearing it so only the bare wall showed once more.

"Amazing. I don't know what else to say. All of you are amazing. The things you can do are amazing. I don't really understand any of this, but I know you saved me from the maze and those creatures. This little beast isn't a wild dog. I never saw one that wasn't wild, but this one isn't. I see that now."

Uriel spoke softly. "This group fully accepted one another ear-lier on this trail. They fully accepted you by their actions to protect you and free you from your confinement. Full acceptance of each team member is vital. So, I must ask and you must answer this question: Do you fully accept each member of this team?"

"I do!" erupted from every mouth, the two words loud and clear from Guleed.

"Then this is yours." Gavreel handed him the Acceptance charm, nine conjoined hearts with each of their names edged the center sec-tion where **With One Voice** was engraved. "Look at it. Read the front and back then it will become the first token on your chain."

As soon as he looked up, Gavreel gestured. The charm locked onto his chain and an extra heart was added to the charms of the eight others. They were now a confirmed team of nine.

"This part will be difficult for all of us," Michael announced. "Guleed's life on Earth was very different from any of ours. Many things happened to him, and he did many things to others for which he had to atone. His life will not be easy to watch, but we must watch it together and remember that he was chosen in spite of the years he spent on Earth. There is a reason for everything."

Two brown and white cleric butterflies flapped from the lowest limb of the tree and landed on Guleed's knees. They perched there until cordula leaves spun once more, filling the blank wall with their colorful gyrations. When Guleed's portrait appeared, the butterfly pair winged to the frame. His face shone with an intense expression, his eyes declaring his watchfulness. The leaves swirled across the portrait, replacing it with his birth scene. His mother looked very young and scared. She screamed on the dirt floor of a tiny crude tent, with only a ragged piece of cloth under her. Two other women were with her, one about her age and one a little older. They were gentle and encouraged her to push with each contraction. The younger one wiped her forehead with a damp cloth and held her hand. The older woman was positioned to catch the baby when he emerged from his

mother. After several screams, the lusty cry of a newborn replaced the agonized screams of his mother. "You have a son," was all she said. The younger woman worked rapidly to clean him and lay him next to his mother as the other woman attended her.

The birth scene ended, and the view fragmented into many cells showing Guleed's early years. He lived in a makeshift domed tent of plastic sheeting and blankets patched together with ropes and sticks. He was the first born to his fourteen-year-old mother. She'd delivered five siblings by the time she was twenty. Two of her babies died in childbirth or shortly after. Everyone was malnourished; there was never enough food nor clean water. Many people were ill and died from infectious diseases. He attended a small school for only two years and was sent to herd the goats and sheep when he was eight years old.

Lions, leopards, cheetahs, hyenas and jackals were constant threats. They preyed on livestock and people as they tried to survive the harsh conditions of Somalia. Regular fighting between al-Shabab jihadists and Somali government forces created chaos in their lives. Frequent mortar rounds, improvised explosive devices, arson, and arbitrary executions were commonplace. Al-Shabab recruited boys as young as nine to join them with the promise of one meal a day and a few coins. It was not a request, but an expectation. Boys were taken to training camps to become soldiers for the jihadists. Girls and women faced brutality on a daily basis. Clan militias were as violent as animal predators.

Guleed's village resisted the aggressive child recruitment campaign by sending young ones into the countryside. Many children, most of them unaccompanied, fled their homes to escape involuntary servitude. Mortar rounds and fires destroyed the patchwork village of flimsy shelters and slaughtered the livestock nearby. Guleed plastered himself to the ground, shrouded by savannah grasses when the first rocket struck the herd. His father was killed when a mortar destroyed their dwelling. His mother, brother, and two sisters, were filling water jugs when the attack occurred. They weren't killed that day, but their lives would never be the same. His mother was widowed with four children under eight. No home. Nothing but the clothes they wore and the jugs they'd taken with them for water. Men who weren't killed in the attack were taken into custody. Everyone in the village bore the same burden. Families were fragmented and every shelter shattered or burned.

A band of women and children walked for days on a dusty road toward Mogadishu. They'd heard that there were camps for displaced people where humanitarian aid was available. It seemed their only chance for survival. Water, food, and shelter were their focus, staying alive their goal.

Guleed's mother with four young children became part of the 2.6 million Somalis living in internal displacement camps. These refugee camps burgeoned with victims of the ongoing civil war that ravaged their country.

His mother made a hut of sticks and plastic sheeting on the allocated space in the informal settlement. She was allotted a speck of land and the plastic sheeting on the condition that she register with the UN's World Food Program and pay a percentage of the ration she received to the "gatekeeper." Jumbled plastic shelters crowded tightly against one another. The tarp and fabric metropolis stretched for miles in every direction. Poor sanitation, no access to clean water, and thousands of people heaped together became their reality. Illness, violence, and theft were constant.Guleed became adept at stealing food. He'd raid unattended huts and knock people over, snatching whatever they carried. He was fast and learned the layout of the camp quickly. He could tuck himself away until no one looked for him, just another thieving boy. It was the only way his family ate the first few weeks in the camp.

Guleed's family's first food aid was delivered by WFP workers. A month's supply of rice, beans, flour, and cooking oil were stacked inside their shelter. They felt rich! Their stomachs would not ache and grumble this day. This day, they'd feast on rice and beans!

The landowner and the gatekeeper arrived as soon as the aid workers left. They claimed half of the rations to cover the building materials Guleed's family had received; it would be 30% every month after that. Refusal to give half meant eviction from the camp. There was no choice. They had nowhere to go. Danger was everywhere. At least here, they had their little dwelling and some food. It wouldn't be a feast after all, just another meager meal to help their supplies last.

Day after day, week after week, Guleed wandered the camp searching for food to snatch. It never occurred to him that stealing other people's food resulted in their suffering, and sometimes their deaths. He just knew he was always hungry, and his little sisters cried for food. His little brother and mother didn't cry, but they gobbled up everything he brought home. As an eight-, then barely nine-year-old boy, who'd become the man of the house, Guleed thought only about himself and his family. His world wasn't any more than that.

One day, after they'd lived in the camp a little over a year, a group of about fifty men carrying guns rampaged up and down the streets. They hunted for girls and young women, grabbing the ones they wanted. Anyone who resisted was shot on the spot. Men's laughter followed the gunfire as they celebrated their kills. Death or torture and sexual servitude were the only choices of the chosen females.

Guleed's eight-year-old sister was among the militia's chosen. Her mother clutched her daughter's arm and tried to pull the girl away, a vain attempt at protection. The bullet took the woman's life instantly. Guleed's mother was dead at twenty-three. The girl's shrieks drowned out the men's laughter as the shooter hoisted her over his shoulder. Thrashing and kicking earned her a sharp crack over the head. Unconscious, her limp body was hauled elsewhere.

Guleed heard the shrieks from several streets away. He raced home and burst through their hut's opening. His six-year-old brother and two-year-old sister sobbed, huddled together next to their mother. The woman lying in the dirt was lifeless. Her dark eyes were open, shouting the terror she had felt as she died. The pool of crimson grew as more blood drained through the bullet hole. Her face, so beautiful in life, was frozen in grotesque terror.

Aside from the pounding of his heart, none of Guleed's muscles would move. He was frozen in place, staring in the half light of their shelter at a scene he couldn't explain and would never forget. His mother was dead.

They were orphans. He was only nine, but he understood life that had suddenly gotten much worse than it had ever been. How was that even possible?

Guleed, finally able to shake himself from his shocked stupor, shook his brother's shoulders. "What happened? Where is Bilan? Where is our sister?"

His brother's sobs allowed no words. His tears had already wet the front of his shirt. When he tried to speak, he choked on the first syllable he tried to utter. He struggled to breathe against the crying. He sank to his knees, no longer able to stand and face the enormity of his grief and terror. He sobbed into his hands, his tears dripping between his fingers and splattering his mother's shoulder.

His baby sister thrust herself against Guleed's legs. Her desolate wails were more than crying. Her breathing was ragged as she collapsed at his feet. Her gasping sobs echoed from the walls of their hut, announcing that she was drained of all hope. The pain that flowed through her and from her was palpable. At the age of two, her childhood had ended.

"Come, come out here with me," Guleed commanded as he herded his young siblings through the tent's doorway. "Sit here against the hut in this patch of shade."

His young siblings did as he ordered. They sat, deflated, against the wall of their plastic home. They made no attempt to conceal or even wipe away the tears that continued to flow. Pain poured from every pore of their small bodies. In a matter of minutes, they'd gone from gregarious children to people whose brains had been shredded from the inside. They were hanging on by a thread.

People from the neighboring shelters emerged, what was left of their empathy triggered by the ferocious cries of agonized children. The woman who lived next door, his mother's friend, scooped up his little sister, stroking her back and talking softly in an attempt to calm her. "It's all right, little one. I have you. It's all right." Still cradling his sister, the woman eased down next to his brother. She wrapped one arm around him and pulled him next to her. He buried his face against her side.

"Do you know what happened here? Do you know where my sister Bilan is?" Guleed pleaded.

Many voices answered at once. The women and children who were left knew exactly what had happened. A clan militia came again. They wanted girls and young women this time. They took what they wanted and killed all resisters. There had been a lot of gunfire.

"Where is Bilan?" he asked again.

"A man in the militia carried her away. She wasn't moving, but I don't think she was dead," another woman told him. "The men were laughing as they carried or dragged the girls away. There were many men and they all had guns."

"These men took my sister and murdered my mother?" His voice dripped sorrow, but was peppered with fury.

Sad nods finally answered his questions.

Guleed's chin trembled as he tried to hold back his grief and rage. Everything became a blur. He breathed heavier than he'd ever breathed before as he tried to cling to reality. He felt his world unraveling, the tapestry of his early life becoming a disarray of strings scattered at his feet. He opened his mouth again, but the keening that erupted was a frequency that shattered his own heart.

He fell to the ground, his throbbing pain replaced by an emptiness that was even more painful. He'd never felt grief this bad before. Despair gripped him. He lost himself when reality slammed into him. He'd moved beyond reason, beyond calming, beyond life in this camp. The raw pain inside him was too much to contain. His spirit raged, ready to erupt.

Guleed still sat between Gabe and Nate. He stared at the wall that had just played the first nine years of his life, his fists clenched and tears streaming.

"I became a different person the day my mother was murdered and my sister was abducted," Guleed managed to say. "I did many, many bad things."

Uriel spoke softly. "You did change that day, Guleed, and you did many things that most people will never understand because they didn't live the life you did. But all of us, you included, were made to be who we are, with our flaws and gifts. All things are connected. Your earthly life, like everyone else's, melded you to be the person you are. Your experiences will be assets in the missions ahead."

Gabe added, "As you saw, I was good at getting into trouble. I had a knack for making people mad and no one but Bruno liked me until Dina and Jo." He smiled at his "sister-friends". "I know I was forgiven for the things I did, so I had to forgive myself. You're going to have to forgive yourself, too."

"You do not know the things I did yet, except stealing food for my family," Guleed replied. "I think some things are unforgivable."

"Only pure evil is unforgivable," Michael told him. "You did not function to spread evil. You functioned to survive as long as you could in an environment that most cannot even fathom, let alone survive."

"We must show the last part of your earthly life, Guleed." Uriel tapped the cleared area where two butterflies still perched. The cordula leaves wove a kaleidoscopic pattern that cleared to a scene of Guleed's mother's body being lowered in a rectangular hole by several people. The neighbor woman stood there, still holding the baby girl. Guleed and his brother scooped dirt over their mother with their hands, working as a team until the hole was filled. They piled rocks over her grave to keep the predators from digging up her body. It was done. Their mother was gone from them, just like their father. Maybe their parents were reunited in whatever came next.

The viewing space fragmented into many cells showing Guleed's life after he buried his mother.

The UN workers came to take them away from their neighbor's shelter the next day. They had a special place for orphans. A two-year-old, six-year-old, and nine-year-old would not be allowed to live alone in the camp. As they walked down the littered street, Guleed bolted from his siblings and the aid workers. He was fast and disappeared around a corner before either adult could reach the corner. He was nowhere in sight. He heard them call his name and grimaced as he saw his brother's and sister's tears start again. He had to go. He knew a boy his age would stand a better chance alone than trying to take care of younger ones. The two of them would be more likely to stay together if it was just the two of them and not three.

Guleed tucked into his hiding hole until they left. He eased out and headed the opposite direction. He was scared and utterly alone, but it'd been his decision, so he had to try to handle it.

He managed to survive the first few months by stealing food as he had so often done and sleeping in one of the many crevices or cavities he'd discovered and used as hiding holes. He was lonely, filthy, and increasingly brutal as he robbed people of food and money. Theft, seasoned with a bit of pain for the victims, became Guleed's release valve for the pain he felt every minute of every day. Others should suffer, too. That was just the way it was.

The monsoon season demanded that Guleed's world change. He could no longer sleep in trenches or craters with rain pelting him and the ground turning into a muddy basin that threatened to drown him. He decided he'd curl up by the door of one of the buildings nearby after everyone had left the area. The overhang would be more protection than the open holes he'd been using to sleep. He could curl up so small, he'd be almost invisible in the corner of the doorway. He was ten now but could still tuck himself so tightly he almost disappeared. He had the bag he'd snatched from an old woman. It was handy for carrying his meager possessions, all of which he'd stolen. It held an extra shirt, the length of colorful fabric he could cover himself with when the wind was strong, and the last third of the loaf of bread he'd snagged earlier in the day; the bag would be soft enough to curl around on the stone stoop.

Sleep came like a sledge hammer falling. Guleed hated to give in to the defenseless hours when he'd be oblivious to his surroundings and vulnerable. But he could fight the need no longer. Though unwelcome, sleep came instantaneously as he assumed a contortionist's position around his bag. His body twitched with fiery sparks, his fight or flight mode still engaged as he drifted to that place where his thoughts intertwined with memories and longing. He dreamt of things past, things that would never be again. He saw the countryside and his mother and father. For a moment, he felt whole again, almost happy, as he smiled at them. Then the monster pounced. It snatched his sister Bilan, roaring and snarling at everyone nearby. He saw his brother and sister sobbing next to his dead mother; he saw his remaining siblings wailing and unable to speak as they buried their mother and again when he left them for the last time. His sleep became a violent whirl of colors and scenes, replaying things he'd seen and things he'd done. Solitude and slumber summoned his tribe of hideous phantoms.

Guleed startled awake when he felt the jab of metal on his back. Men surrounded him, all of them carrying rifles like the one that had jabbed him. His heart thudded in his head. He couldn't breathe. He pulled his protesting muscles up, trying to force his always-obedient legs to run. But they twitched and refused to run.

He heard footsteps, even louder than his pounding heartbeats, and knew there were even more men than the ones he could see. There was no escape, and there'd be no mercy—he knew that.

Two men jerked him to his feet. They bound his hands behind his back and looped a rope around his neck. He'd been captured by a patrol, probably Al-Shabab. He'd heard the talk of what happened to those they "recruited." He thought he understood what would come next. He'd be taken to a training camp. He'd be trained to do their bidding, to kill or be killed.

The air was heavy as the humidity pressed down. The scent of rain mingled with the squalor of the street and the stench of these men. A jagged streak of hot silver severed the sky. A boom crashed a split second later, drowning out the voices. The first drops of rain, like bullets on their skin, pelted all of them, captors and captives alike. After the first drops, the clouds unleashed a torrent of water, driven by a wind so fierce it threatened to flatten them with every step. This storm was as violent as the men who surrounded him. Guleed felt his feet slipping on the mud as he fought the howling wind and lashing rain. As he stumbled, the noose around his neck pulled him up and forward. He commanded his lungs take in air, to help him survive.

The troop of men and boys muddled along several rain-slick streets until they reached a truck parked behind an abandoned building. The boys were tossed into the back of the truck and told to sit against the far wall. Nine of them did as they were ordered, their spirits too deflated and their fear too massive to resist. Several young men piled in the back with them, cursing the storm that had soaked them and cut short their hunt. The truck roared to life, jostling them away from the known. Ahead stretched the unknown, an emotional no-man's land where survival would be the only important thing.

The truck lurched, rocking side to side on the ragged pavement. The men's chatter subsided after a while. Some may have dozed, but it was impossible to tell in the darkness. Finally, the brakes squealed, and everyone lunged forward as the truck stopped. Earnest voices barked commands as they were herded from the truck's trailer to their new world.

Guleed blinked his stinging eyes, trying to see clearly all that was around him now. He saw huge tent walls rise out of the darkness. Only a few minutes ago, the blackness was absolute. Now the black sky of night was fading to the silent charcoal of dawn. Soon, dove gray would give way to the actual colors of the world, the colors that were hidden under the night sky.

The sun peeked above the vista of massive tents. Armed men stood near some tent doors and others were scattered around the encampment. Silence greeted them as they were herded to a tent down a central row. Captives and captors entered a tent where the mingling scents made their mouths water. Bananas, mangos, and guava were piled on the tables. Steaming cups of tea waited at two tables. The boys were told where to sit, with their captors interspersed among them. As soon as everyone was seated, girls and young women brought in plates, heaping platters of canjeero and steaming pots of chopped meat. They were served as many of the canjeero as they wanted and a huge ladle of meat. They could have as much fruit as they desired, too.

Guleed had never seen so much food! Maybe this place wouldn't be so bad if food like this was part of it. Timidly at first, but then with fervor, Guleed gulped down his plate of meat and four canjeero. A banana and a mango rounded out the biggest meal he'd ever had. His protruding hard stomach declared he couldn't eat another bite. This sensation of fullness was foreign and almost uncomfortable now that he'd stopped gobbling the food before him.

With breakfast stuffing their bellies, the boys shuffled to another tent. This one had woven mats and cloths scattered on the floor. Told where to lie down, each boy was ordered to sleep, to prepare their bodies for training. Guleed had no idea what that meant, but his full belly and nearly sleepless night beckoned his departure from wakefulness. Within seconds, sleep pooled on his eyelids and buried him in slumber. He slept the sleep of the exhausted, deep and void of anything he could remember when he woke. It had been a long time since he'd slept without the monsters tormenting him.

The scene on the wall faded and swirled into many cells. Days of training in the camp and tasks he was forced to do filled each cell. The message of jihad was drilled into him. Guleed's speed and ability to hide were assets as he planted explosive devices. He could fade into the background to listen, gathering information and relaying it to the officers in camp. Many people died as a result of the information he relayed and the explosions he set. So far, he was too valuable to be used as a suicide bomber.

Three years passed. Guleed's body grew somewhat bigger, but he was still small for his age. His skills grew deadlier. He was obedient and devoted to the cause that had rewarded him with food, a bit of money, and the comradeship of the men with whom he served. At thirteen, he was an accurate marksman and adept at handling crude explosives.

Scenes played showing armed entry by Kenya into Somalia. Soldiers attacked Al-Shabab strongholds. As the armed groups ashore diminished, maritime pirates seized the opportunity to recruit and use the same children who'd been disarmed and demobilized. Guleed was one of them.

Guleed quickly learned how to drive a fishing boat. This, along with his small size, agility, and superb marksmanship made him an excellent pirate. He became the moral dilemma of the sailors he approached. Shock hit the men as they realized this "soldier" was not a man or a professional. This "soldier" was a child, not their equal in age, strength, training or understanding. Men on ship after ship were hesitant to shoot a boy, with dozens of other children behind him, even if he was holding a gun. The sailors had to choose between defending their own lives, their ships, and their shipments or taking the lives of children. Most would not consider shooting down a ship filled with children. As a result, Guleed seized ships and amassed cargo and humans to be ransomed. He liked life on the sea and the power he felt. He was at the forefront of Somali piracy as it metastasized into Somali's only booming industry.

At sixteen, Guleed had grown taller and stronger. He was no longer the boy who used his child image as a weapon against those he approached at sea. He was a testosterone-filled young man, more brazen, more violent, more filled with bitterness about the tragic life in which he was trapped. As Somalia smoldered and descended deeper into poverty and became the world's leader of atrocities against humankind, Guleed's spirit festered as he fell deeper into his own abyss of self-awareness. His future was nothing more than a sea of rough waves and certain death. He was utterly devoid of hope. His gloom and despair became intoxicating blackness, evil darkness overtaking his thoughts. His moves were all variations of the same theme: survive. He would do what he had to do until the end finally came.

Guleed's crew was directed to dock in a village in Puntland where they were due to receive a shipment of AK-47's, RPG-7's, and F-1 hand grenades. The hawala dealer had made a 50% deposit in Mogadishu, but Guleed would pay the rest when he took delivery of the weapons. He'd done this several times before. Carrying a large sum of money to pay the balance was risky, but easier here than in Mogadishu. He was glad the dealer had agreed to drive the shipment out of the city.

Guleed and five crew mates hung out near some ramshackle buildings, at the entrance to the alley that ran between the sagging structures. This location had a clear view up the only road coming into the village from the south. Early and fully armed, the pirates kept their backs to the wall as they watched and waited for the delivery. Villagers avoided the area where they stood, knowing these young men were as dangerous as they were young, flaunting their power over their shoulders. These men wouldn't hesitate to shoot anyone who interfered in whatever business they had here.

Guleed knew the arms smugglers often traveled with women and young children, pretending to be a family headed home. If they were stopped, the young ones made excellent human shields. If all went without interference, the woman might have a few coins tossed her way. If not, women and children were expendable.

An old car bumped along the dusty road, approaching slowly. Two men filled the front seat. A young woman and two very young children filled the back seat. They were clearly looking for something.

The car eased up near the cluster of armed men, pulled hard to the left and reversed several car lengths down the alley. The driver ordered the woman to get out and open the trunk with a key he tossed at her. Her trembling hand dropped the key as she tried to wiggle free from her son's clutching hands. Tears filled his eyes as she shouted, "Guleed, stop! You have to let go of me. I have to open the trunk of the car before he gets mad."

Helpless to do anything but obey, she cowered as he leaned over the seat. His fist punched her face as she reached for the fallen key. "Get that trunk open now, Bilan, or there will be a lot worse coming your way!"

She tumbled out of the car, trying to hold back tears and get a breath. She felt like someone was choking her, though no one was near. Whimpering, both children watched their mother stumble to the back of the car. She tried to send them mental messages, "Hush, babies, hush. If you make him madder, it will be worse for all of us." She fumbled with the key and popped open the trunk. She inched along the back fender, trying to get back to her babies before they erupted in wails she wouldn't be able to stop, causing blows she wouldn't be able to stop.

The front-seat occupants threw open their doors and emerged, both armed with enough fire power to kill everyone in this village. Both held a young child as a shield.

They backed toward the open trunk, never taking their eyes off the six young men who laughed with one another as they approached.

"No need for all of that," Guleed soothed as he approached. "We have something you want, and you have something we want. Just a friendly business deal. If we wanted to shoot you, it would have happened already."

"G-Guleed?" a soft voice murmured. "Guleed, is it really you?"

He stared at the young woman who stood near the rear fender of the car. He blinked several times, but there was no denying the resemblance. "Bilan?"

"Yes, Guleed, it's me!" Her voice trembled as tears flowed in earnest.

"You two obviously know one another, but we need to finish this deal and be on our way. There is no time for idle talk. Where's the money? You still owe half."

"First, we see the goods," Guleed snarled. "If the goods are what we're expecting, you will get your money."

"Open the suitcases. You'll find everything you ordered in these five cases. The 100 F-1s are in the smaller bag. The four largest cases hold the AK-47s and RPG-7s."

A quick look inside each case confirmed that the contents were as promised. Guleed handed over an envelope of cash as each of his companions backed away carrying a suitcase in one hand and a gun ready to use in the other.

"I will take this woman and her children, too," Guleed told the men.

"No, you will not. They are mine," the driver barked. "I chose her as a girl and made her a woman. She bears children well, better than my other wife. She has not quite reached fifteen years and has already born me two sons. She obeys now, and I seldom have to beat her. All I have to do is move toward one of those boys and she is obedient."

"You will never beat my sister or one of her children again,"

Guleed hissed. "No man uses his own son as a shield. They are coming with me whether you like it or not."

Bilan whimpered, "Please, Afweyne. This is my brother Guleed. I have not seen him for more than six years, since the day you made me yours. He just wants to see me and meet his nephews. You know I named our firstborn son after my brother Guleed. This is him. Please, let me talk with him a little while, then we will head back to Mogadishu. Please."

"No! We are leaving now. My business with this pirate is finished. You have no business with him. Get in the car! I'll finish my business with you later."

Afweyne pushed her toward the open door. She stumbled headlong into the edge of the door, cracking open her forehead. Blood gushed from the gash and ran down her face. She lay in a stunned heap, unable to speak or get in the car.

Guleed rushed toward her. "Bilan! Bilan, are you all right?"

The bullets tore through Guleed's shoulder just before he reached his sister. He fell inches from her, his weapon useless at his side.

The men saw the bullet holes oozing crimson down his sleeve and shirt front. Bilan saw the person, her Guleed. She saw the pain on his face and knew he still lived. She raised her arm, reaching for him.

Afweyne grabbed her wrist, yanked her up, and slammed her into the backseat. He threw the two terrified boys on top of her and slammed the door. He piled into the driver's seat and gunned the engine as Guleed tried to get to his feet. Rather than driving away, Afweyne threw his car in reverse and accelerated hard.

Bilan did not see what happened because she was bent over, gathering her sobbing sons from the floorboard. She heard the crack of bones and the agonized scream though. She felt a hard bump as they moved backwards and another bump as the car sped away. She thought she heard, "Forgive me." as the car sped away.

Guleed's vibrant eyes that once watched everything now stared vacantly. His lips were agape in a stiff, stifled scream position. His legs were twisted unnaturally. The dark red pool spread down his arm, chest, and on the ground where his crumpled body rested.

His spirit surveyed the scene. He watched the old car race away. He saw two of his crew race back to where he lay. He heard them shouting and saw the villagers scramble into their homes and shops. No one was going to help a fallen pirate. No one was going to get involved in whatever had just happened here.

Guleed floated, watching the chaos his crew mates created, when Azrael appeared. "I will take you where you need to go, Guleed. You must spend time alone and face what must be faced before your transition is complete."

He remembered nothing after Azrael touched his shoulder until he found himself trapped in the labyrinth, unable to escape the place or his thoughts. He wandered a very long time, hiding from the beast that lurked there. Finally, the others found him.

Cordula leaves swirled as the display ended. The pair of butterflies that had been affixed to the wall flew back to Guleed and fluttered near his face. Together, they ordered, "Stand up, Guleed. Our time here is short, and you must know we are still with you." The pair transformed into a young couple who pulled a disbelieving Guleed to his feet.

"Mother? Father? You are here?"

The couple wrapped their firstborn son in a tight embrace. His mother declared, "Son, you have faced and survived so much. You must now devote yourself to your destiny. You have much to do. You will be a warrior and make us proud. Your father and I are serving together as guardians, but you will be a warrior! We cannot stay with you, but know that we love you and believe in you. Your brother is on his own path, but your sisters need you."

Guleed clutched his parents until his father intoned, "We must go, and you must do what you must do to become a warrior. Be not afraid, for we are with you. You carry us in your heart, as we carry you." The pair vanished as soon as his father finished his statement.

Guleed sank to the ground, bewildered and speechless, but grateful to have seen his parents. Brilliant blue leaves spun away from the other colorful leaves and danced around the brethren below the ancient tree. These leaves, like sails without boats, were untethered messages, ones they did not yet understand.

Uriel stood and walked once around the tree, studying the blue leaves that arranged and rearranged themselves around the group. He rested his hand on the trunk as a royal blue leaf landed on his shoulder. He addressed the group. "God is love. To God, we are all beloved. God brought us forgiveness and grace. God has never encouraged or condoned war, but does let people exercise their free will. People have often chosen to fight one another, and evil gains strength in such times. God chose Guleed and sent him to this team. Together, we will teach him what you have already learned, young warriors. You will be trained in some new skills together then we will depart to handle a mission in Somalia. We will prepare."

Uriel took a step forward. "You will receive your Justice charms for the last section of the cockatrice den challenge. Your unselfish and accepting care of Guleed, before you knew anything about him, proved that you instinctively leave judging to God. You did not have to know who he was or what he'd done in his life to accept him. You accepted him without judgment because God put him on your path. He did the same with all of you because he did not run and hide, two things he's adept at doing. Your intrinsic sense of justice was also apparent in your treatment of the cockatrice. You chose not to slay the beasts even though you had a mirror with you. You understood that you had invaded their nesting area and that they were only behaving instinctively to protect their home and one another. By defending Guleed without killing the cockatrice, you showed honor, respect, and justice for God's creations."

Gavreel spoke softly. "We have several things to discuss before training resumes. First, let me present these cordula leaf charms. These Justice charms recognize your acceptance of one another, your fair treatment and forgiveness of choices each person made in the circumstances they lived through, and your justice mindset in handling all that comes your way." Gavreel raised her hand and sent a blue heart-shaped leaf charm into the hands of each young warrior. Each was engraved with the words: *JUSTICE: A JUDGEMENT THAT IS FAIR AND FORGIVING.*

"Press the small leaves on the back of your charms," Gavreel instructed. "Ariel, will you read each message aloud as it emerges from the leaf?"

Ariel pressed each leaf and read the enclosed messages.

"Those who judge will never understand, and those that understand will never judge."

Buddha

"See that you are merciful unto your brethren, deal justly, judge righteously, and do good continually."

Book of Mormon: Alma 41:14

"Verily! Allah loves those who are just."

Quran: Surah al-Hujurat 49:09

"Judge not, and you will not be judged; condemn not, and you will not be condemned; forgive and you will be forgiven."

The Bible: Luke 6:37

"You therefore have no excuse, you who pass judgment on someone else, for at whatever point you judge another, you are condemning yourself, because you who pass judgment do the same things."

The Bible: Romans 2:1

"For behold, my brethren, it is given unto you to judge, that you may know good from evil; and the way to judge is as plain, that ye may know with a perfect knowledge, as the daylight is from the dark night."

The Book of Mormon: Moroni 7:15

"Never judge another man until you have walked a mile in his moccasins."

Native American Proverb

"Don't take revenge. Let Karma do all the work."

Buddha

Ariel pressed the final button and looked up at Gavreel. The Justice charms snapped onto each of their chains.

FINISHING UP

Michael and Kirron stood on each side of Uriel. "We also need to address your performance in the first two sections of the cockatrice den," Kirron announced. "You demonstrated great perseverance and tenacity as a team in searching for the puzzle pieces, assembling the puzzle, finding the hidden door, seeking and solving all the riddles, and making your way out of the labyrinth. Every step of this challenge strengthened you as a team. You honored one another's strengths along the way and never gave up, even though the tasks were demanding. Guleed did not do the first two rooms with you, but he was in the maze far longer than you were in the den. He had to face himself and the things he'd done over and over. He never quit, just as none of you ever quit at the tasks you faced. You proved time and time again that you are stronger together than any one of you is on your own."

Michael added, "I hope all of you realize that tenacity is more than endurance. It's a combination of endurance, stubbornness, and faith. It's the absolute certainty that what you're doing or looking for is going to happen. It's more than hanging on. It's a mindset. Tenacity serves warriors well. Without doubt, you're the most tenacious group of young warriors I've ever met."

"I'm pleased to present these Perseverance and Tenacity charms to each of you." Kirron gestured, and a new amulet landed in each of their hands. This one was an open heart with an infinity symbol overlapping the heart. Gold and silver sparkled around the words that were engraved along the heart outline: **Success lies with perseverance and tenacity.** "Gabe, why don't you read the messages embedded along the back of the infinity symbol. Just press each bump and the wisdom will emerge."

Gabe pressed the first bump and read aloud:

"And let us not grow weary of doing good, for in due season, we will reap, if we do not give up."

The Bible: Galatians 6:9

"When a person is devoted to something with complete faith, I unify his faith in that. Then when his faith is completely unified, he gains the object of his devotion."

The Bhagavad Gita

"It does not matter how slowly you go as long as you do not stop."

Confucius

"Persevere! You will not win immediately, but definitely."
"Never give up. Great things take time."
"In the confrontation between the stream and the rock, the stream always wins- not by strength, but through perseverance."

Buddha (3 quotes)

"Strength does not come from physical capacity. It comes from an indomitable will."

Mahatma Gandhi

"Allah is with those who patiently persevere."

Al-Quaran: 2.153

As soon as Gabe read the final message, the Perseverance and Tenacity tokens snapped into place.

"We commend you on another virtue, which you confirmed your mastery of while in the cockatrice den," Michael told the youths. "We watched and saw your support and loyalty for one another throughout each chamber, but your performance in the maze section was exemplary. You did not succumb to the taunting voice that mocked you and tried to humiliate you. Instead, you supported one another, time and time again. You demonstrated your understanding that honor lies in loyalty." He pulled a handful of charms from his pocket. "Bruno gets one of these to hang with his initial and acceptance charm. That dog exemplifies loyalty, so it's fitting that he displays that he's a master of the virtue."

The Loyalty amulet was a wolf's head resting on a ribbon banner. **Loyalty is honor** was engraved on the ribbon. Michael passed out a silver charm to each trainee. "Aniela, will you please read the messages that pop out when you slide your finger around each ear and each pointed end of the ribbon." Michael encouraged her with a smile.

She traced around the parts as she was told and read each message that emerged.

"Loyalty is hard to find. Trust is easy to lose. Actions speak louder than words."

Buddha

"Loyalty is the first job of God."

Yogi Paramahana Yoganada

"Never let loyalty and kindness leave you! Tie them around your neck as a reminder. Write them deep in your heart."

The Bible: Proverbs 3:3

"Friends love through all kinds of weather and families stick together through all kinds of trouble."

The Bible: Proverbs 17:17

As soon as Aniela had read the last verse, the Loyalty token snapped on each of their chains and on Bruno's collar.

The young warriors looked expectantly at their elders. They sensed more was coming but thought it best if they waited for one of the trainers to speak. This waiting was gentle, like the caress of a beach breeze, natural and subtle.

Uriel didn't make them wait long. "None of us have ever had this experience with our trainees before," he told the group, "and we've had too many trainees to count. I know that we've told you repeatedly that you're a strong team and that there is greatness within you. Two of this team proved the strength once again as they discovered an embedded weapon within. Just as Gabe called forth flames from his feet by doing flips in enhanced mode, Jo and Micah discovered their own secret weapons."

"What? We didn't have any weapons," Jo protested. She glanced at Micah. He shrugged his shoulders, his confusion as apparent as hers.

"Oh, but you did," Gavreel replied. "You may not realize it, but you discovered and used a very powerful weapon."

"I don't understand," Jo murmured.

"Your gentle spirit, your concern for others, your faith, and the gift of your magnificent voice combined with the same qualities from Micah. When you sing together in faith, you call forth your weapon." Gavreel smiled at the baffled pair.

"I've sung with lots of people, including you, Dad," Jo protested, "and there's never been a weapon erupt from my singing before."

Michael's eyes fixated on his daughter. He blinked before he spoke. "Yes, we've sung together many, many times. We make beautiful music as a duet and as soloists. We've always shared a passion for music. We can soothe those who are distressed and make people happy. Our combined voices are nothing like yours and Micah's though. That's why your weapon never emerged when you sang with anyone but him."

"I still don't understand, Dad. What are you talking about? What's this weapon you seem to know about, but I don't?"

"Your passionate and faithful singing voice called forth steam from within your soul. It started in the first chamber of the cockatrice den. Remember the swirling puffs that led you to some of the puzzle pieces and riddles? The steam wasn't a weapon yet, but it was a sign of the power within you, Jo. It helped you find things you needed to find. It was a sign that your power could be called forth when it's needed to help others."

Gavreel took over the conversation. "When you got to the maze, you discovered that your singing combined with Micah's could literally find the way."

"This doesn't make sense to me. We all figured out that repeatedly saying or singing the same thing over and over opened the portals to new sections of the maze," Micah countered. "Aniela started saying, 'We can do this!' over and over, and we joined her. All of us saying that with her made the wall shimmer and open. It wasn't just Jo and me singing that opened the walls."

Michael looked lovingly at the young man who just spoke. "But you and Jo singing together in faith has great power. I don't know how to explain this except to say it straight out. You, Micah, are my daughter's soulmate. Your souls together exude divine power from within. Think about what you've learned since meeting Jo. You have many things in common. Both of you love cats, the color blue, and music. You're both gentle, humble, and kind. You both think of others before yourselves. If you'd lived to adulthood, you would have found one another and married. I can tell you've felt something special for her since you met. You sensed your connection even if you didn't understand it."

"Dad, you're embarrassing me," Jo stammered. "You're talking crazy."

"No, I'm not. You've felt funny near Micah since you met him. You sensed something different, too, but you didn't understand it. Those butterflies in your stomach aren't just because you have an ordinary crush. That's your divine fire igniting because your soulmate's near."

"We've told you before and we'll say it again, there are many things you know nothing about," Kirron added. "Soulmates and divine power from their pairing is another one of those things. All of us recognized it as soon as the first puff of vapor appeared in the first chamber, Jo."

Gavreel beamed. "This is a wonderful thing. Everyone has a soulmate. It's part of the magnificent plan and epitomizes connectedness. You two are just more fortunate than most because you found one another at such young ages. Most have to wait much longer to find their true soulmate, if they ever do. You discovered your combined power and used it so well, which is astounding. None of us have ever discovered soulmates during training."

Uriel nodded heartily as Gavreel finished her comments. "We're amazed that we have these Souls on Fire tokens to present to this team. They're different than the ones Gabe brought to the team when he discovered his fire within and his internal weapon, but they represent the same accomplishment. They will go right next to your black initial Souls on Fire charm, if you have one. If not, they'll be centered on your chain. Look at them carefully. They're very special. They were formed from the white and blue funnel that spun you into a team and broke through the wall to free you. Uriel collected the bits near the tree and they transformed in his hands."

Uriel pressed an initial charm into each of their hands. Like the black ones that Gabe, Jo, and Dina wore, these initials were fancy script letters. Each bore the words, "The human soul on fire is the most powerful weapon." The engraved words wound around each letter's shape. These charms were made of sparkling white marble with striking blue veins. They represented strength and power. At each endpoint of each letter's shape there was a gleaming sapphire. The message was clear: God was the alpha and the omega, the beginning and the end. God's direct power would always be with them. The charms snapped on their chains as soon as Uriel waved his hand. The Loyalty charm nestled between the black and white initials dangling on Bruno's collar.

Uriel's, Gavreel's, Michael's, and Kirron's amulets were tornado funnels, not letters, but made of the same white and blue marble. The blue veins twisted around the white like a spring. The funnel shape was clear. Small sapphires ringed the large oval opening at the top of the funnel cloud and a large sapphire sat at the bottom like a period at the end of a sentence. The 'human soul of fire' inscription wound around the blue spiral. When Uriel waved his hands again, the trainers' newest charms joined the crowd that already hung there. Just like the black star, the funnel token stood out from the rest. It was slightly larger and hung centered by the star. One could see the power pulsing from the pair hanging side by side.

"The next section should be a fun reminder for everyone as we help Guleed gain the skills you already possess. After our time on the training course, we'll give you time to reflect and refresh before we do new skill training. Is everyone ready to tesselate to the course?" Uriel asked.

The group stood and smiled at Guleed. "You won't believe what's going to happen now!" they chorused. Laughter erupted as the youth and elders placed hands on one another's shoulders to connect for transport.

Before Guleed could respond, they disappeared. Cordula leaves swirled into a smiling face on the ground where the group had just rested.

TRAINING MANEUVERS

Guleed gawked at the flat expanse ringed by some kind of pavement. "Where are we? How did we get here? Why does this road have so many narrow lanes?" he asked.

Uriel laughed as he replied, "We are in another section of Heaven. This part is used for physical training, especially running. We came here using the space tessellation. We'll teach you about that in a little while. This isn't a road, Guleed, it's a running track. The lanes are for people who are running. The surface gives good traction. If everyone stays in their own lane, no one crashes into another person."

"Why would anyone run on such a road? Where does this road go that the running people need lanes?"

"The track is mainly for training, for practice. Sometimes tracks are used for competition to see who's the fastest. It doesn't go anywhere, it comes back right where we start," Uriel told him.

"This seems like a stupid thing to do," Guleed remarked, "to run on a road that doesn't go anywhere but comes back to where you started running. Why run if you don't go anywhere and just wind up back where you began? I don't get it."

The others tried to contain their laughter as Uriel attempted to explain the concept and use of a running track to someone who'd never seen one or heard of such a thing.

"Maybe we should just teach him about enhanced speed and let him run with the others. He might understand the track's usefulness after he's run on it for a while," Kirron offered.

"You'll love running here," Gabe piped up. "Just give it a try after one of these guys explains what to do."

"Kirron, will you do the honors since you introduced enhanced speed to all of the other trainees?" Uriel asked as he backed up so he was next to Gavreel and Michael. "I'd like to watch your technique."

Kirron shot him a look that almost shouted, "This is a set-up for your entertainment."

Kirron stood in front of Guleed. "Humor us and run with Dina and Nate to that fence way across the clearing and back, going as fast as you can. I want to see which of you three is the fastest runner. I'll shout the word, 'Go!' I want the three of you to run to the fence and back. Do you understand?"

Guleed looked at him. "What do you mean when you say, 'Humor us'? Are we supposed to do something funny when we run? I can make good animal sounds. Should I do that when I run?"

"No, no, just run as fast as you can when I give the signal. 'Humor us' is just an expression meaning to just do what I am saying to do even if you don't want to do it." Kirron tried to keep the hint of amusement out of his voice.

"There is nothing funny about following orders," Guleed grumbled. "I do not understand this expression. If I didn't do what I was told, I would have been beaten or killed. What's funny about either of those things?"

"Nothing, Guleed. It was a bad choice of words. I want you to run to the fence and back as fast as you can with Dina and Nate when I shout the word go." Kirron smiled at him. "Okay?"

"I guess so. At least you're not having me run on the road to nowhere," Guleed said. "I will run to the fence and back."

Nate and Dina flanked Guleed and waited for Kirron's signal.

The moment Kirron started the race, the spectators burst into laughter. "I think you and Guleed are both humoring us," Uriel told his friend.

Kirron grinned, "Happy to oblige. I'll have to remember to be very literal in how I say things to Guleed. All of us will. He's never seen or learned things that we take for granted. He understands the language we are using, but it will take time until he processes the things that he's never seen or experienced. Idioms and slang terms are hard for many native speakers to understand, so having them translated and trying to make sense of their meaning will take a bit of practice. If you recall, we practiced all the other divine gifts until they were mastered."

Michael remarked, "Guleed's as fast as Dina and Nate."

Kirron replied, "I'm not surprised. His survival often depended on his speed and stealth."

As Kirron finished his statement, the teens reached the fence and began their return trip. They were so close together that it was impossible to declare who was in the lead.

The three stayed neck-and-neck the entire race, blowing past Kirron in a tie. They were met by applause as they returned to the group.

"Wow! You three are good runners!" Uriel exclaimed. "Even before engaging enhanced speed, your performance is impressive."

Guleed grinned at the praise. "I never knew a girl could run like that, Dina. You are as fast as Nate and me."

"I always loved to run. I ran with my big brother all the time. I pushed myself to keep up with him, so I'm used to running with guys," Dina told him. "You'll be amazed when you experience really fast running, though."

"Which is what all of you are going to show him right now," Kirron said. "All of you line up on the track. Bruno, too, right behind you, Gabe. Guleed, stand here by me where you can see everyone."

The teens lined up, side by side, with Bruno standing right behind Gabe, waiting for Kirron's signal.

"Watch carefully, Guleed, and be ready to tell us what you observed when they finish this race. Runners, engage enhanced speed and go!"

They snapped their heels together and took off. Guleed's mouth hung open as he observed the length of their strides and how fast they rounded the curve at the end of the track. When he couldn't see them anymore, he turned to Kirron. "How can they go that fast?"

Before Kirron could answer, they heard laughter and saw the group returning from the opposite direction. They seemed to be flying they were running so fast. Guleed watched as they all snapped their heels together and landed on the spot where they'd begun. Even the dog did this.

"That, Guleed, was a demonstration of enhanced speed running," Kirron told him. "Your uniform, including your boots, will help you do many things extraordinarily well, like running faster than you ever dreamed possible. What did you observe, other than their speed, when you watched this race?"

"All of them, even the dog, snapped their heels together when they started and stopped running," Guleed told him.

"That's correct," Kirron praised. "The heel snap on the ground engages enhanced speed. To stop running at hyper-speed, you have to snap your heels together in midair, before you land. It takes some practice, but that's what we're here to do. You're going to run with the others next time. You'll snap your heels together right before you start running and then run as fast as you can. This track is 25 miles. You'll circle it with your team and return right here. You must snap your heels together in midair to have a smooth landing. Otherwise, you'll stumble and tumble on the ground. Are you ready to try it?"

Guleed's smile answered the question as he joined the others at the starting line.

He heard Gabe say, "Hyper-speed!" as they tapped and bolted away.

Very soon, youthful laughter filled the air. The runners were almost back. All but one landed smoothly. Guleed rolled on the ground but kept laughing. He lay like a turtle on its back and tapped his feet together. "I don't think I landed right, but that was fun!"

"Learning when to snap your heels together takes some practice," Gabe told him as he pulled him to his feet. "You'll get it before you know it, though. It took us a while to teach it to Bruno, but even he has it perfected."

"Let's do the start and stop drill. You won't run all the way around the track this time, Guleed, but stop when I tell you to stop. I'll be on the inside of the track watching and telling you when to stop and go. You might have to practice the stops a while, until you feel confident with them."

They group ran together until Guleed mastered stopping enhanced speed. It only took a few more attempts until he was stopping with them.

"You have enhanced running now, Guleed. We're going to run to another part of the training grounds to work on the next skill. Follow me. I'll stop and start a few times so be ready for that. Uriel, Michael, and Gavreel will meet us there."

Kirron dashed away with eight teens and a dog in hot pursuit. When he stopped, everyone but Guleed knew exactly where they were.

"Here we are, Guleed. This is where you'll learn about and practice the next power your boots enable you to do."

He pointed to the flat boulder staircase. "We'll start here. One at a time, each of you jump to the highest step you can without any enhancement. Watch what they do, Guleed."

Each teammate bounded to the highest point they could with one jump. All landed on the third or fourth steps. Each jumper returned to the ground as soon as they made their landing. Finally, Gabe was the only one who hadn't demonstrated his leaping skills. Instead of running straight at the boulders like the others had, he ran toward the nearby tree, slammed into it and catapulted himself to the seventh level.

Applause echoed as trainers and trainees alike commended his impressive parkour skills and high leap.

"Your turn, Guleed," Kirron announced. "You're going to do one step at a time to see how high you can leap. Jump on the first level, then step back down."

Guleed easily jumped onto the lowest level.

"Now, go to the second one and come back down."

It was still easy. Without being told, he immediately sprung to the third level as soon as he'd returned from the second. He made the fourth level, too, but slammed into the edge of the fifth and toppled down.

"I guess I can jump to the fourth one, like the other guys, except Gabe." Guleed looked at the trainers. "Now what?"

"Now I am going to measure how far you jump with this device." Kirron took the coiled wire from his pocket that he'd used to measure the other trainee's jumps. He flipped it out on the ground. "This wire is the starting line, Guleed. You can get a running start if you wish, but you must start your jump behind this line. This device will accurately measure each jump, no matter how many times you go and then give us an average length. Are you ready?"

Guleed backed up a few steps and ran toward the wire. He launched himself into the air just before the wire. It was an impressively long leap. He returned to the others, smiling broadly at his successful jump.

"Do it again, Guleed. We'll have you jump several times and my device will average all of them."

Guleed did as he was told, jumping and landing ten times before Kirron told him that was enough. Kirron lifted the wire and snapped it in the air. Bright red lights flashed and then "Guleed: average jump 3.6 meters / 11 feet 9.732 inches" flashed before them.

"Hey, that's exactly what my average was," Gabe remarked. "Guleed, our jumps averaged just the same."

"That's because you're both so athletic," Kirron responded. "They're very good averages." He snapped the wire again. This time the red display of Guleed's average disappeared, and the wire wound itself into the tiny tight coil Kirron had taken from his pocket. He slipped it back into the same pocket and looked directly at Guleed.

"Your boots are designed to protect your feet and lower legs. They also give you extra power when running and jumping. You already learned about the running enhancement. I'll show you how to improve your jumping now. Watch my feet as I explain this to you and demonstrate."

Kirron backed a couple of steps away from Guleed and the others who whispered among themselves.

"This is so cool, Guleed. You'll love it," Aniela said softly.

Kirron continued, "You know you snap your heels together one time to start the hyper-speed running mode and that you stop and land safely by snapping your heels in midair. If you want to jump higher than you can on your own, you need to tap the heel of your right boot on the ground. One tap helps you make one high jump. If you tap your heel twice quickly, your boots will help you make multiple high leaps. You always have to look at your landing destination so your brain and the boots can sync the assistance you need. Let me demonstrate."

Kirron tapped his right boot and bounded to the top of the boulder staircase. "Guleed, you and a couple of the others join me up here."

"I'll go up with you, Guleed," Aniela offered. "It's easy. Just like Kirron said, tap your right boot on the ground, look where you want to land, and jump. Watch me, then come on up." Aniela landed smoothly and waved down at the others.

"That doesn't seem possible," Guleed whispered.

"It's possible. Just try it," the other encouraged. Laughter broke out as they realized they'd uttered the same comment at the same time. The blended team was already synchronized.

"I can go, too, if you want," Micah offered. "It's amazing. Follow me up."

Before Guleed could reply, Micah was waving at him from the top of the boulders.

His teammates and the other trainers started chanting, "Guleed! Guleed! Guleed!"

He gathered his courage and sprang. He found himself next to Kirron at the top of the rocky formation. Aneila and Micah patted him on the back. "Look at the view, Guleed. It's awesome up here."

The group sailed down the boulder stairs and joined the others on the ground.

"Let's practice single jumps a few times until Guleed's comfortable with them, then we'll show him multiple leaps."

The teens happily obliged, cavorting from one high spot to another. Guleed no longer needed encouragement to try this new skill. He chortled along with the others as they chased one another from one lofty point to another.

"That's enough!" Kirron called. "Come back down."

Eight laughing teens and a grinning canine surrounded him.

"This is a great thing, to jump like this!" Guleed exclaimed.

"We're going to practice the two-tap mode now," Kirron told them. "Guleed, you must understand that there's a lot of momentum force when the multiple jump feature is activated. You have to pay close attention. Plan your jumps before you start and look at each landing point. Only you can activate the power and show it where to go by visualizing your landing spots. You drag your right foot backwards like this to end the multiple leap mode." Kirron demonstrated.

"Watch me as I demonstrate the multiple jump. I'm going to jump to the top of the boulder staircase, then to the top of that tree, and finally to the top of that hill. I'll be back in a minute."

Kirron tapped his right foot twice and bolted to each place he'd declared before he left. He swiped his foot back as soon as he landed.

"You can use the multiple jump mode to come down as well as to go up, as you saw as I returned. Everyone is different, but most trainees find they can comfortably spring ten to twenty times higher or longer than they could with their own power. Don't try to do leaps that are too high or too long before you figure out what

POWER TO LIGHT THE WAY

you're capable of using the boost. Everybody ready? Leave one at a time so you don't crash into one another."

The team leapt from one location to another, chasing and laughing. They enjoyed frolicking with one another. Observing the skills of each member of the blended team, including Guleed, the trainers delighted in the lively chase.

"Time to return!" Kirron called as he waved his arms.

As soon as all had gathered, Kirron told them to have a seat on the ground. "Guleed, you've clearly mastered two divine powers, enhanced speed and agility. You're now as proficient in these skills as your teammates. Your boots are great assets, but now we'll focus on some other important features of your uniform and the powers they bring."

Guleed grinned. "I do like these boots and what they help me do!"

"You'll like the other stuff you're about to learn, too." His teammates barely got the synchronized comment out before laughter overtook them again.

"Moving on," Kirron announced. The group stifled their laughter and focused on him. "If you need a new perspective from above, you can levitate."

The others watched Guleed's face as Kirron backed up a few steps and started his demonstration of levitation. "To activate levitation mode, you run the index finger of your left hand around the first bracelet on your right wrist. You then raise your right index finger in the air, making clockwise circles. The more circles you make, the higher you'll go. To come back down, you make counterclockwise circles with your index finger. To deactivate levitation, you tap the bracelet five times quickly. Watch me now."

Kirron circled his bracelet, raised his index finger, and made four circles in the air. He rose about twenty feet. "Every circle is about five feet or one-and-a-half meters, so four circles raised me about twenty feet, or about six meters." He made four counterclockwise circles and floated back to them. He tapped his bracelet five times.

Guleed was speechless. He stared at Kirron, looked up, then back at Kirron.

"It's quite easy. You'll like levitating," Gavreel inserted. "It's not magic, but it is a useful divine power."

"You won't have any trouble with this," Dina told him. "We can go up with you if you want."

"I will try," Guleed finally said.

Everyone stood. Gabe commanded, "Sit, Bruno!" The terrier immediately sat at Gavreel's feet.

"Bruno can't levitate so he has to obey a sit-stay command if one of us isn't holding him," Gabe explained. "That's a good boy, Bruno. Sit by Gavreel."

The group rose about ten feet in the first levitation. The grin on Guleed's face told them he was ready to go higher. They went up and up, waving at the four elders and dog on the ground. They came back down as soon as they heard Kirron call.

"That was really something!" Guleed cried. "I can't decide which one of these new powers I like best!"

Michael spoke up, "They are all very useful and exciting. I think you should take turns holding Bruno when you levitate. Remember, he has to be calm and quiet with any team member if he's on a mission where levitation is required. He's used to rising with Gabe, Jo, and Dina, but one of you might have to take him. He should be used to everyone."

"Excellent suggestion, Michael," Kirron said. "Gabe, why don't you take him up the first time, come down and hand him over to Dina or Jo. The others can observe how you hold him while he levitates."

Gabe scooped up his dog and rose about twenty feet, Bruno tucked like a football at his side. Bruno happily thumped his tail but did not squirm or make any sound. Gabe returned and handed him to Dina. She rose about twenty-five feet, with Bruno securely tucked at her side. She handed him off to Jo, who handed him off to Micah. The terrier was passed from teammate to teammate until only Guleed had not levitated with him.

"Your turn, Guleed," Gabe announced. "You hold him like this against your side, with your hand on his chest between his front legs and your elbow near his tail."

"I do not know if I can do this. I have never ever touched a dog. They were all wild in my country. They are dangerous creatures. The packs would attack and kill animals and people. I know everyone says that this Bruno creature is not a wild dog, and he has seemed calm around everyone else, but I do not trust him."

"Bruno is part of our team, Guleed. He won't hurt anyone, including you. You can trust him, and I want him to know he can trust you. Try petting the top of his head." Gabe smiled at the newest team member.

Guleed reluctantly touched the top of Bruno's head and pulled his hand back.

"That was a good start, Guleed," Jo encouraged. "Do it again."

Guleed reached out again and stroked Bruno's head a couple of times. Bruno didn't move or make a sound.

"Try running your hand down his back now," Nate suggested. "Dogs like to be petted. You can make friends with them by letting them sniff you and then petting them gently."

With lots of encouragement, Guleed got braver about petting the little dog.

"Why don't you sit down and hold him on your lap for a bit," Gavreel suggested. "You'll quickly discover that Bruno likes to be held and that he won't hurt you. Just keep petting him and talk softly to him. He's a very loving little dog."

Guleed plopped on the ground, his legs stretched out in front of him and a worried look on his face. Gabe set Bruno down and said, "Sit with Guleed, Bruno."

Bruno looked from Gabe to Gavreel to Guleed. He walked to

Guleed and gingerly stepped on his thighs. He sat facing the trembling boy, staring into his eyes. They gazed at one another without moving.

Gabe suggested, "Pet him, Guleed. He's trying to be your friend. He isn't going to hurt you. He's never hurt anyone."

Guleed softly stroked the little dog who pressed his head against his hand.

"See! He likes you petting him. He's asking for more!" Gabe told him.

Guleed smiled. "He isn't trying to bite me, even though my hand is close to his mouth."

"He doesn't bite anything but food," Gabe told him. "He likes food!"

"I like food, too, Bruno," Guleed snickered. "Maybe we can like food together."

Bruno licked Guleed's hand, as if answering with a kiss. Guleed jerked his hand away. "He's tasting me! This dog just tasted me!"

"He isn't tasting you," Gabe reassured him. "When dogs lick a person or another animal, they're giving kisses. Bruno just kissed your hand."

"Oh, you're making that up," Guleed replied.

"No, it's true," chimed from everyone who was watching. They smiled at one another as they acknowledged another synchronized response.

"It's true, Guleed," Gavreel blurted. "Now you've seen how calm this little dog is. He won't hurt you. You have to master levitating holding him before we can move on. You'll absolutely love the next divine skill we're going to introduce you to, after you finish this one. But if you don't want to learn how to become invisible, let's stop for today and give you time to get to know Bruno better."

"Invisible?" Guleed squeaked. "We're going to learn how to become invisible?"

"You are going to learn how to become invisible, Guleed. All of the rest of us already know how," Uriel told him. "But Gavreel's right. If you aren't brave enough to levitate with a little dog, you aren't ready for invisibility." The others saw the wink Uriel made to Gavreel before he started talking.

"I want to learn how to be invisible," Guleed declared. "So, if I must hold this creature that licks but does not bite, I will try."

"I'll levitate up and down with you a couple of times, just to make sure you're okay," Gabe told him. "Then you can prove to the elders that you're plenty brave enough to do it alone."

Gabe pulled Guleed to his feet and lifted Bruno. "Hold him just like this." Gabe tucked Bruno at his side once more. He handed him to Guleed and adjusted Guleed's hand, so it had a secure grip on his beloved dog.

"Let's just go up two circles' height and come back down the first time," Gabe suggested.

Guleed nodded. They rose about ten feet. Bruno stayed as calm and quiet with Guleed as he did with everyone else.

"Go back down and we'll go higher next time," Gabe murmured. "You're both doing great."

After landing smoothly, Gabe suggested, "Let's go up five circles' height this time. Are you ready?"

"I'm ready," Guleed declared as he raised his index finger and began making circles. Together, he, Bruno, and Gabe rose high above the others.

"It's time for you to go up alone holding Bruno. Let's go back down then you can levitate again and prove you're ready to move on to invisibility."

They landed smoothly. Guleed announced, "Now this little beast and I will rise with no one else with us. We will prove we are brave and ready to learn more."

He immediately made circles with his raised index finger. Guleed and Bruno rose and rose, until they were out of sight.

"Why would he go that high?" Gabe cried. "What if he drops

Bruno from way up there?"

"I'm sure they'll be fine and be right back," Jo said. "He wants to learn how to become invisible. He probably thinks he has to prove his bravery to all of us."

Gavreel offered, "I'll go up and talk to him if they're not back shortly, Gabe. I think Jo's right. He's trying to prove his bravery and manhood to us."

She'd no sooner finished her comment when they could see something descending.

"Here they come!" Uriel announced.

Guleed landed and set Bruno on the ground. "We were brave and went higher than anyone else, the little beast and me. That cloud up there tickled us when we went through it."

"It looks like you're ready to learn invisibility now that you've clearly mastered levitation," Uriel declared. "Kirron, your techniques are clearly working well, would you like to continue with invisibility, or should one of us take over?"

"I'll continue," Kirron replied. "I'm sure fast-tracked Guleed will master invisibility quickly."

Kirron turned to Guleed once more. "What we're about to share with you is a tool we use frequently on missions. It's a tool and should never be viewed as a game. You must always use it seriously and only to do good. Invisibility is never used to frighten people or pull pranks. Do you understand?"

"Yes, sir."

"Good. We become invisible only when absolutely necessary. If anyone misuses the power, it's stripped from that warrior *forever*. There are no exceptions, no extra chances. If you misuse invisibility, it will be taken away, and it will never be returned to you. This divine gift should be cherished and respected. Do you completely understand what I've just told you, Guleed?"

"Yes, sir."

"Let's go on, then. To engage and disengage invisibility mode, the action is exactly the same. If you're visible and do what I'm about to show you, you'll become invisible. If you're invisible and do it, you'll return to visibility. It's another power you access through the bracelets. You cross the underside of your wrists forming a T-shape, making sure the three bracelets on your right arm touch all three bracelets on your left arm. When they're aligned so they're all touching, they form a complete circuit of power. You rub the bracelets together three times like this." Kirron moved his right arm upward, downward, and upward again as everyone watched.

Kirron disappeared, but could still be heard as he said, "To return to visibility, cross your bracelets again and rub them together three times." He was standing before them once more.

Guleed's face froze in confusion. His brain neurons couldn't process the information from his wide eyes fast enough. Then, a grin crept across his face, quickly stretching from one side to the other, showing every one of his bright white teeth.

"My bracelets have this same power?" he asked. "I can do what you just did?"

"Yes, but you must remember that it's a tool for good in serving God. It must be taken very, very seriously."

"Oh, I'll take it seriously. I promise. Can I try it now?"

"Go ahead. Show us how you do it."

"I put my right arm bracelets on top of my left arm bracelets and make sure they all touch like this. Then I go up, down, up with my right arm and I disappear."

"You did it, Guleed! You're invisible!" rang from his teammates' lips.

"Come back to visibility now," Kirron called.

Guleed stood next to the group, the wide grin still plastered across his face. "This is a dream come true."

"It's a divine power, given by God to aid on missions. Always remember how valuable it is," Kirron stressed.

"Let's show him about moving when we're invisible," Dina suggested. "He should know about that, too."

"Guleed, all of you are going to become invisible now. I want everyone to take a few steps. Guleed, notice how you feel when you move when you're invisible. Everybody, go invisible."

The group vanished. When Kirron called, "Become visible!" they reappeared, scattered in all directions, many steps from where they'd started. They quickly walked back to Kirron.

"What did you notice about moving when you're invisible, Guleed?"

"Walking was like enhanced running. I went very far, but I only took five steps. I had to take many more steps to get back here when I was visible. Why?"

"Do one of you want to explain it to Guleed?" Kirron asked the trainees. "I would like to hear your version of the information I explained to you when each of you learned about this skill."

Dina offered, "I think I remember everything you told us. I'll try to explain it to him."

"Proceed," Kirron told her.

"Kirron told us that we're weightless when we're invisible so we can move farther easily. Our bodies here aren't the same as our flesh-and-blood bodies on Earth, but there's more to them than when we're invisible. When we're visible, we're in our soul mode. Our souls can be seen by everybody here and by some people on Earth. When we become invisible, we're operating as just our spirit. Our soul and spirit are connected, but they're separable. Your soul is your essence as a human, but your spirit is that immaterial part of you that connects you to God."

"Very good, Dina," Kirron praised.

"I think I understand this," Guleed stated. "When we become invisible, there is no body at all, just our spirits moving so we move farther faster."

"That's true," Dina reassured him, "and that's why we have to take the gift of invisibility seriously because we're able to maneuver through our souls and spirits. It isn't a game. It's very serious."

"Dina's correct. You must always revere your total being as you were created. God bestows this gift for good, but it can be stripped away if it isn't honored and used correctly." Kirron smiled. "You've learned many new things, Guleed."

Gabe added, "Everyone should know that Bruno can't become invisible on his own, but he can become invisible with one of us if we snuggle him against us. Just like with levitating, he can go with any of us, but we have to hold him tightly and cover him with our invisibility."

"That's a good reminder, Gabe," Gavreel observed. "Guleed, are you ready for more, or have you had enough for one training session?"

"I like these things you are teaching me," Guleed replied. "I like that I can run fast and jump far. I like that I can rise high in the sky and that I can become invisible. I even like that I can hold that dog-that-licks-but-does-not-bite. I am ready for more of these special things you are giving me."

"Very well, we'll continue," Gavreel said. "Everybody, take a seat while we explain this to Guleed."

"This will be fun!" Guleed's teammates elbowed one another and giggled.

Gavreel continued, "One of us will be with you the whole time for this section, Guleed. It's vital that you listen carefully and do exactly what we tell you. Don't leave anything out and don't add anything. Like invisibility, metamorphosis must be taken very seriously."

"I do not know this word, metamor-something. What are we going to be doing?"

"Metamorphosis, or morphing for short, means changing body forms. Going from the shape you're in as a human to the body or shape of another living thing."

"What? I will become something else? I have never heard of

such a thing. No one in Somalia ever spoke of such a thing. I do not think this is possible, even here."

"It's possible. It's another divine gift your teammates are all skilled at already."

Everyone shook their heads. "You'll be amazed how fun it is to be something else for a while." Raucous laughter shook the group.

"I do not know what is so funny, but I am ready to try this new thing. What do I have to do?"

Michael declared, "The first creature we learn to morph into is a butterfly. Butterflies are nonthreatening creatures found almost everywhere. They symbolize rebirth and hope, among other things, in many cultures. Butterflies have simple body structures so they're easy to shift into.I have never had a trainee yet who didn't thrill at the first experience of flying as a butterfly. They're a popular form for comfort visits and dream visits to those who are grieving."

"I'm going to become a butterfly? I'm going to fly?"

"Yes, for a little while, then you'll come back to yourself." Michael smiled. "I think you'll like it."

"We never, ever morph into another human's form," Kirron told him. "You were created exactly as you're supposed to be in your human form, to be who you are with your unique gifts. There are evil demons who morph into another's human form and wreak havoc in that person's life. Other demons enter the bodies of living people and overtake their lives. Helping someone who is possessed by an evil spirit or spirits is one of the hardest battles we ever fight. This gift of transformation is from God and we must only use it for good. I feel I need to say it again: we never shift into the form of another person."

"Okay, we never become another person, but we can become a butterfly and other things," Guleed said. "What do we do to make a change like that?"

"Let's see if the young ones can teach him what he needs to do," Gavreel suggested. "It will be a good way for us to assess if they still have the invocations perfectly memorized."

"We can teach him," Aniela assured her. "I'll start. The first thing you do is cross your wrists tightly against your chest, like this." She demonstrated the action. "Then you have to recite a prayer. We have to teach it to you, and and you will need to practice saying it till you have it memorized."

"So, the bracelets touch each other again and are held tightly over my heart?" Guleed asked.

"Yes, and then you say the prayer while you visualize the thing you want to change into." Aniela beamed, savoring her ability to teach something that she already knew to someone. It was a new experience for her and she liked how it felt.

"Let's take turns practicing the prayer with him line by line, then putting all the lines together," Nate suggested. "I'll do the first sentence."

"I'll help him with the second sentence," Aniela said. "It's a short one."

"I'll do the third one," Jo said.

"I'll do four," Gabe offered.

"I'll take the last one, then," Dina said. "Let's all practice the whole prayer with him when he's learned each line."

"I'll teach him the return-to-self invocation," Micah offered, "after he has the longer one memorized."

"You have a great plan," Gavreel encouraged. "Ariel, why don't you recite the whole prayer first so Guleed can hear it and understand the meaning before Nate starts practicing the first line separately?"

"This prayer is partly from Proverbs in the Bible, Guleed. We have to do things we don't understand and trust God to help. This is the invocation you have to memorize:

Great creator of all creatures, from mini beasts to massive, you who created me and sustain me, hear my prayer today. I beseech your help to take another form. I know you see the image in my mind and know what's in my heart. I trust you, God, with all my heart, and do not lean on my own understanding. Help me take this form so I can serve you well."

"That was perfect, Ariel," Gavreel praised. "Nate, you're up."

One by one, Guleed's teammates drilled the lines of the invocation with him, linking each new line to the ones before it, until he had the entire prayer perfectly memorized.

"That sounds perfect, Guleed, but now you must learn how to return to your true form. You cannot cross your arms or speak when morphed in other forms, so the prayer that Micah's going to practice with you must be said over and over in your mind as you visualize yourself in your human form. Micah, your turn." Gavreel watched as Micah positioned himself in front of Guleed.

"This part is from Proverbs, too," Micah told him, "but it's only one sentence and a lot easier to learn. This is what you repeat in your thoughts until you morph back to your true self:

Those who trust in themselves are fools, but those who walk in wisdom are kept safe."

After just a few repetitions, Guleed had the line memorized. The trainers had him say the morphing invocation once more to make sure he hadn't forgotten any of it, then declared that he was ready to morph. Kirron agreed he would stay right with him and send the telepathic messages when it was time to return to human form. The others would all morph, too, but were free to flutter and play as they wanted.

Gabe knelt before Bruno. "We're going to morph into butterflies, Bruno. You can watch us, but you need to stay right here. Sit! Stay!" Bruno thumped his tail and sat obediently staring at Gabe.

"Morph!" Kirron commanded.

Bruno listened carefully as each warrior recited the invocation and whisked away on fluttering wings. A dozen winged beauties flapped around him, then fluttered in different directions. One pair stayed close together, but the others scattered then floated back together.

Bruno gawked at orange and black monarchs flitting across the sky with yellow swallowtails, black swallowtails, a painted lady, and a pair of blue morphos. One butterfly was much larger than the others, but it, too, fluttered smoothly across the sky. The giant butterfly was orangish-brown with black markings and had long narrow wings. A yellow swallowtail stayed right next to it no matter where it went. It landed gracefully on flowers and trees before it chased some of the other flyers.

Bruno yipped happily when he saw and heard his team returning in human form.

Guleed chattered delightedly with the others. "I was flying! I was really flying! I really like this new power. It lets me fly!"

"Told you you'd like it," his team chorused.

"What kind of butterfly did you morph into, Guleed? Jo asked. "It was the same kind your parents were at the cordula tree. I never saw butterflies like those before."

"I don't know its name," Guleed replied, "but it's very common in Somalia. We see them in the countryside and the city."

"You became a papilio antimachus," Ariel told him. "They're the biggest butterflies in Africa, and some of the biggest in the world. They can have wing spans of eighteen to twenty-three centimeters."

"You really know so much about things in nature," Gabe remarked. "I don't know how you remember it all. Your brain capacity must be at least double mine."

Ariel blushed. "Um, thanks. I just loved looking at pictures and reading about anything in nature."

Kirron smiled. "You did well morphing into a butterfly, Guleed. We're going to change into dragonflies next. Dragonflies can fly very fast. They're agile and can change directions quickly. Their four wings can move independently of one another. Try testing all of those things when you soar as a dragonfly, Guleed. Also, practice landing and taking off several times. Are you reading to recite the transformation invocation?"

Bruno cocked his head as he listened to the people surrounding him recite the prayer again. A dozen pairs of iridescent wings whisked around him, then scattered in all directions. He watched the aerial acrobats as they raced across the sky, dipping and diving, rolling, making figure eights and full circle turns, and doing loop-the-loop maneuvers. Every dragonfly daredevil darted crazily in this aerobatic competition.

Bruno's tail thumped as Gabe asked, "Did you watch us doing stunt flying, boy?"

Guleed marveled, "This morphing thing just gets better and better. I could fly upside down and make all kinds of turns."

"How are you feeling?" Gavreel asked.

"Me? I feel wonderful. I feel better than I ever have," Guleed bubbled.

"He doesn't have any effects from shifting either. He fits right in with this team."

"Just like we did with the others, we should practice shifting between butterfly and dragonfly forms without returning to human form," Michael suggested.

"Yes, that's important," Uriel agreed. "If you have morphed into one form and need to change to a different form besides your human form, you must mentally recite the invocation prayer while picturing the new form you wish to take. It can feel funny, especially if you're flying when you do the change. You might feel like you're falling, but it won't last. We'll start as butterflies and transform to dragonflies when Kirron sends us the telepathic command to do so. Are you ready to try, Guleed?"

"I'm ready to become anything that lets me fly," he assured them.

"Remember to say the five sentences in your mind when you hear my message to shift to dragonfly form," Kirron reminded him. "Go butterfly!"

A dozen voices repeated the prayer. Bruno watched his teammates disappear once more and studied the colorful wings that propelled the beauties away from him. He watched as each one swam across the sky, constantly rotating and tipping their body angle so their flight looked erratic. A few circled back toward him, but most flew out of sight.

Bruno witnessed several sets of colorful wings change to iridescent shimmers. They chased one another, maneuvering to avoid being tagged by the perceived "It." Joy filled the air as they zipped after one another, enjoying the chase. Not prey and predator, but creatures that enjoyed the chase immensely.

The sound of laughter came from every direction as Bruno watched the people return. His joyous tail thumps welcomed them back.

"The last form we will take during this training session is a hummingbird," Gavreel told them with a wink. "Remember, hummingbirds fly every direction. Make sure you try going backwards, sideways, and hovering, as well as zipping around frontwards. It's absolutely delightful to take hummingbird form for a while."

"I do not know what this thing is you are talking about," Guleed announced. "How can I picture it in my head if I do not know what it is?"

"I'm sorry, Guleed. I should have thought about where hummingbirds live and realized you wouldn't have seen them in Africa," Gavreel said. "They're amazing little birds. There are over three hundred varieties, but they're only found on the islands of the Caribbean Sea, and in North America, South America, and Central America. They have iridescent feathers and long beaks for sucking nectar from flowers. They're incredible flyers. They're the only birds that can fly backwards, sideways, upside down, and hover. Their wings flap in the shape of the number eight and make a humming sound because they flutter so fast. I'll transform and hover near you so you can study the shape of a hummingbird before you visualize it."

"You might feel a bit strange when you take hummingbird form," Kirron added, "because birds have more complex bodies than insects, with bones and organs that insects do not have. The strange sensation shouldn't last long once the shift is made."

Gavreel nodded, crossed her arms, and recited the now-familiar invocation. A brilliant hummingbird hovered near Guleed's head. He extended his arm. Gavreel the hummer landed on his outstretched hand and gazed into his eyes.

"This bird is so tiny, but so magnificent to look at," Guleed marveled. "Are they all green and red like this one?"

"No, there are other colors. Remember, Gavreel told you there are over three hundred species of hummingbirds," Michael told him. "They're all astounding flyers."

"Are you ready to shift into hummingbird form?" Kirron asked.

"Yes. I think I will like being a beautiful little bird."

"Let's go, then."

"Oh, I almost forgot to tell you something important," Michael announced with a wink. "You expend a lot of energy flying as a hummingbird so feel free to suck nectar from any of the flowers around here or munch on mosquitos, flies, or spiders that might be near."

"I have never heard of anyone eating those kinds of bugs. In my country, people do eat locust when they swarm so maybe it is not so different. I will try it if you say I should."

Laughter erupted among the others and the hummingbird on his hand hopped from foot to foot. Guleed shot them a puzzled look. He didn't understand what made these people laugh so much.

Gabe chuckled, "Michael's joking with you, Guleed. He did the same thing with me the first time I transformed into a hummingbird. No one expects you to actually eat bugs. He was just trying to get a reaction from you. The flower nectar is very sweet and good. I do recommend that."

"So, I do not have to eat bugs?"

Laughter broke out once more, but Michael managed to say, "No, Guleed, you don't have to eat bugs."

"I do not understand what is so funny, but I am glad I do not have to eat the bugs. I did not like locust, so I do not think I would like them either."

"No one's laughing at you, Guleed. I hope you understand that," Uriel declared. "Laughter is one of those things that helps relationships grow strong. Laughing and crying together strengthens bonds like very little else. Affectionate laughter isn't meant to hurt anyone. It's playful teasing, showing affection among people who care about one another."

Stifled chuckles peppered the transformation invocation as everyone took hummingbird form. Just as before, Bruno maintained his sit-stay and stared at the iridescent darts that surrounded him. Two tiny birds hovered near his face and dipped their beaks lovingly on his nose before zipping away. They chased one another to a clump of bright pink flowers. Both hovered a long time, sucking the sweet nectar. Bruno studied them as they drank and zoomed away.

Flashes of color flowed in graceful arcs back and forth around the meadow, a sky dance filled with spins and dips. The tiny birds painted a picture of beauty, grace, and pure love of motion. Their aerial dance was poetry, celebrating the purity of life and movement.

Bruno's fascination lasted through the entire hummingbird dance. He jerked his head from side to side when one flew near him. He wanted to keep it in sight as long as possible. His tail thumped delightedly when certain birds came near, but he never stood or attempted to chase after them.

Laughter and chatter surrounded Bruno once more, met with voracious tail thumps from an excited terrier.

Guleed was ready to explode. "That was fantastic. I might not have known what a hummingbird was before we flew like one, but I will never forget it. I could do anything in that body! Up and down, fast or hovering, forwards, backwards, sideways! It was all so exciting."

"Gavreel and Gabe especially like hummingbird form, too," Michael declared with a grin.

"What's not to like?" Gabe asked. "Flying in every direction is pretty hard to beat. You can get up now, Bruno. You were such a good boy."

Bruno ran to Gavreel and put his front feet on her knee. She bent over to pet him, and he poked his nose against hers. He then ran to Gabe and did the same thing. As soon as he'd exchanged nose pecks with them, he raced to the flower clump, stood on his hind legs sniffing the blooms, somersaulted, and raced back to the group. Exuberant laughter filled the air.

"That dog-that-licks-but-does-not-bite is a funny animal," Guleed announced. "I did not know animals would smell flowers."

He was imitating Gavreel and me after we morphed," Gabe explained. "We both pecked his nose before flying to those flowers and drinking nectar. We did spins and flew away. He was showing us he knew it was us, even as hummingbirds."

"Everyone, sit down. We need to make sure Guleed really understands what this gift of metamorphosis is all about before we move on," Uriel declared.

"Guleed, why do you think you're able to take different forms?"

"You told me that it is a gift from God, a divine gift. God can do anything, even something as unbelievable as changing from one thing to another."

"That's true, but why is it possible? How is it possible?" Gavreel prodded. "There's more to this gift than acknowledging that God can do anything and that God gave the gift."

"I must admit that I do not know. I have seen and done so many things that I never would have dreamed were possible. I can't even begin to explain why we can do this marvelous thing."

"Our profound Dina explained it well to her early teammates. Perhaps she'll share her thoughts again, with her new teammates," Gavreel declared. She smiled encouragement.

Dina smiled back, but hesitated before speaking. "I'm not sure about this, but it makes sense to me. I think we experience our true selves when we change forms. I think everyone's true form is life energy. That energy is the pure life. I know it sounds weird since we all died on Earth, but I think it's what's meant by everlasting life. It's why we could transition here when our earthly bodies died and why we can change to different forms now. Because we are human, our very being, our life force, can pass through a body, our human body or ones we visualize. Our life energy can pass through a mind or a soul. I could feel my life force when I was a hummingbird. I was still me, but I had the instincts and capabilities of a different body. My life force is what makes me, me. I'm the force whether I'm a butterfly, dragonfly, hummingbird, or any other living thing. It doesn't matter what the body is; the force that moves it is life. As a result, we can transform, because we're part of everything God created in the universe. We are all life."

"So, who we are is energy, not really a body," Guleed said.

"That's what I think," Dina told him. "Humans received this gift, this power, from God. This gift was not bestowed on other creatures. That's why Bruno, even though he's very smart and intuitive, can't morph. He was formed as a dog, so the gift is not inside him."

"You must be the smartest person if you figured this out," Guleed said. "It makes sense when you say it, but I could not have thought of it myself."

"Guleed, you must also know that morphing makes some feel shaky or unsettled. You do not seem to have had any feelings like that. You must understand that it is possible to be stuck in a body if you have transformed and something traumatic happens that causes you to forget the return-to-self invocation. It's very, very rare, but it has happened. If you're stuck in a different form, it is until that physical body dies and the life force transitions. Time is very different here than on Earth, so it is quite a short time. That's why butterflies, dragonflies, and some birds are popular forms. Their life spans are very short so being stuck is very short. Do you understand the risks of metamorphosis, Guleed?" Kirron asked.

"I do," Guleed said. "I accept being stuck if I get to fly. It is worth the risk."

"We have covered so much on *The Trail of Deliverance* and this first training module to teach Guleed the powers he needed to be on par with his team. He still has a few more things to learn, but we made excellent progress. I think you need to rest, reflect, and refresh before we tackle more." Uriel spoke softly but sincerely. "You all have demonstrated once more the greatness that has been assembled in this team. I believe Gavreel is planning to escort you home and explain the care of his uniform to Guleed. Gavreel, they're all yours."

"Connect with one another to go home," Gavreel told the group. "I'll escort you to the home of Team JAMBANGGD. There are a few changes."

Gabe scooped Bruno up as his teammates laid their hands on one another's shoulders. The group vanished as soon as Gavreel raised her arm.

HOME

Gavreel landed with the team at their home. The front resembled each of the former teams' previous homes, but it was noticeably wider. A splendid veranda fronted the entire house. Swings still hung on each end. Groups of tables, comfortably cushioned chairs, and sofas welcomed everyone to the porch. Hanging along the roofline above the railing, brilliant flowers spilled over the edges of hanging pots. Glazed pots, all of them works of art, glistened in red, purple, black, silver, gold, and many shades of blue. Dazzling blooms made eye-catching displays as they nestled among the seating and tables. Huge pots speckled with the team's colors flanked the double front doors, their exquisite blossoms stretching upward and outward.

"Here we are, team. You'll find most of it very similar to how it was it was when you left, but there are some changes since your teams are now consolidated. Your personal spaces are exactly the same, but the porch and lounge have undergone some minor changes to reflect the union of your teams." Gavreel pointed up the three steps. "Let's sit on the porch a bit and talk before we go inside."

They climbed the stairs and chose seats where they could all see one another, everyone but Guleed. Frozen in place and speechless, he gawked at the porch and all it held.

"Come, check out this swing with Bruno and me, Guleed," Gabe called. "It's really comfortable and fun to swing back and forth."

Guleed didn't move. He gazed both directions over and over. "I have never been anywhere so grand," he murmured. "I saw some grand houses in Mogadishu, but they were guarded, and no one could get close. This is even grander."

"It is a beautiful home. Your beautiful home," Gavreel told him.

"I—I have never lived in anything but a shelter with a dirt floor," he sputtered. "I do not know how to belong in a place like this."

"You'll get used to it very quickly," his teammates chorused.

"Please, choose a seat so I can explain a few things before we go inside," Gavreel urged. "Check out the swing with Gabe or sit in one of these empty chairs."

"I will sit with Gabe," Guleed said as he strolled to the end of the porch and eased down on the opposite end of the swing. He mimicked Gabe's position by putting one arm on the armrest and the other along the back of the swing.

"We can swing back and forth by slightly pumping our bodies forward and back like this," Gabe said as he made the motion. The swing slowly rocked. "The more you rock your body, the faster the swing will rock with you. Bruno and I like to rock."

Guleed flashed a smile of pleasure. "This is like being anchored on the boat, with the waves gently rocking you. I like this swing."

"Good," Gavreel said. "When we go in the lounge, you'll see some changes from the lounges your two teams had before. There's nothing too drastic, but all of your team colors have been blended into the decor. There are now eight doors leading to your private chambers rather than the three or four that you previously had. Two chamber entrances are now on each of the side walls, and the other four are still along the back wall. Your doors are still your favorite color with your initial on each door. Since there are two A's and G's, you'll know which one is your entrance by the color. The line art connecting your doors now contains all of your team colors, too."

"We each have our own room?" Guleed asked incredulously.

"You actually have more than one room that is all your own, Guleed. Everyone can explore the lounge changes together, then do whatever you want as I show Guleed his private chamber and how to take care of his uniform. Are you ready to go in now?"

"I know I am!" Gabe blurted. "I don't care too much about the colors in the lounge, but I sure am ready for food!"

The others laughed. "We're all ready for food," Nate replied. "We had quite a workout since we left, with doing the trail, the cockatrice den, time at the cordula tree, then training. I'm starving, too."

"We get to eat now?" Guleed asked. "It has been a very long time since I put food in my belly. It has been making some loud noises since I did all that running and jumping."

"Remember that prize you could earn for winning the scavenger hunt? You've earned a banquet. We can have it now if everyone's ready to eat."

"YES!" chimed from the team.

"Since all of you want to eat first, we'll have your banquet before we do anything else. Allow me." She raised her arms before turning the doorknob to enter the lounge. Wonderful aromas made them sniff deeply.

"I hope the ice cream dream machine is part of this banquet," Aniela whispered. "I love ice cream."

Gavreel winked at her as she raised her arms again.

The group rushed through the open door and headed to the table. It was ready for them with nine places set and frosty glasses of fruit punch already poured. The center of the table and kitchen island were laden with food.

"Help yourselves, young warriors. I'm sure you'll find some sustenance that will please your palates." Gavreel smiled at the group as she made a sweeping gesture toward the steaming platters, bowls, and trays.

Guleed froze in his tracks as he scanned the lounge and the feast that was set for the group. The others grabbed plates and piled on their favorites, but Guleed just stood and stared at everything that surrounded him.

"Guleed, come get some food and slay that growling beast you said was in your belly," Nate urged.

Guleed looked down at his abdomen. "I did not say I had a beast in my belly. Do you think I do?"

His teammates' laughter exploded. No one could say a word as they settled on chairs around the table. Finally, Gavreel managed, "There's no real beast inside you, Guleed. It's just another one of those expressions. Nate meant that you should eat so that your hunger pangs will go away and your stomach will stop making noises. Some people call stomach sounds growling because they sound like an animal growling. That's called figurative speech. It doesn't mean exactly what it says."

"I do not understand why people say things that they do not really mean, but I am glad that I do not have to kill some beast in my belly."

His teammates' laughter rocked the room as he approached the table where everyone but Gavreel was already seated.

"Get one of those plates from the table and fill it with whatever you'd like to eat," Gavreel directed. "There's plenty of food so get as much as you want, but save some room for dessert. We have a special treat for the end of the meal."

"I do not know what many of these foods are," Guleed marveled, "but they look and smell good enough to eat."

"They're all good!" the group chimed with full mouths.

Guleed picked up a plate and tried to spoon some food onto it. The food slipped off the spoon and splattered back on the platter. "This food that looks like red worms with brown chunks does not want me to eat it. It is not worms, is it?"

Chortles sounded around the table once more. Gavreel fought to keep a straight face and explained, "That's spaghetti and ground meat. It is quite delicious. Most people eat it by twirling the noodles around their fork before trying to lift it to their mouths. It's similar to baasto, but is covered in a tomato sauce with ground meat rather than chopped onions, carrots, and potatoes mixed with the meat.

Let me help you get some on your plate." She ladled a couple of large spoonfuls onto his plate. "What else looks good to you? How about some of these sambusa?"

"Yes, please. I love sambusa. The spicy meat and vegetables inside the pastry are delicious."

"Have you ever eaten pizza, Guleed?" Micah asked.

"I do not know this word pizza, so I do not think I have ever eaten it."

"Gavreel, we should introduce him to pizza at his first heavenly feast," Micah declared. "I don't know any teenager who'd turn down a slice."

"Very well. How about you try pizza with ground meat on it, Guleed?"

"And lots of onions," Gabe suggested. "That's my favorite, ground meat, onions, and lots of cheese."

Gavreel flicked her hand and a large flat pan with a steaming cheeseburger pizza appeared on the island next to the platter of spaghetti.

"I'm grabbing a slice of that, too," Gabe announced as he approached from the table. "Grab your slice, Guleed, then I'll get mine."

"Me, too," Nate and Micah blurted as they sidled up next to Gabe. "Nothing beats pizza!"

"Ice cream beats pizza," Aniela called, "but pizza's really good."

"Sit down where you took the plate, Guleed, and start eating. You can get as much as you like, so feel free to get more if you want it, but save some room for Aniela's favorite food."

After Guleed was seated with his teammates, Gavreel filled her own plate and joined them. She enjoyed their banter and laughter. She couldn't remember ever training a finer group of young warriors.

"I like the red noodles. What did you call it?"

"Spaghetti!" sounded around the table.

"Tell us what you think of the pizza," Micah prompted.

Guleed examined the triangle on his plate. It is big."

Gabe told him, "Some people cut it up and eat it with a fork, but most people lift it like this and just bite off the slice, starting at the pointed end." He took his first bite, savoring the flavor that filled his mouth.

Guleed mimicked Gabe's method. Delight crossed his face as he chewed. "This is so good! I've never tasted something so wonderful. I like pizza!"

His teammates laughed again, Guleed joining them this time.

Gavreel smiled, enjoying the sight of Guleed being carefree, enjoying a simple pleasure. He'd had so little time to be a child and so few pleasures.

The group emptied several platters and bowls before Aniela announced, "I am going to have my sundae now. Anybody else?"

She walked to the machine setting on the end of the kitchen island and lifted one of the bowls next to it.

"Guleed, what's your favorite kind of ice cream?"

"I have never had anything called ice cream before."

"You've never had ice cream?" Aniela was incredulous.

Gavreel interrupted their conversation. "Why don't you get him a small bowl of your favorite, Aniela. He can try small samples of everyone's favorites and see what kind he likes best. Make it with a fourth of a cup of ice cream and the toppings you like, then give it to him and get your own."

"That's a great idea, Gavreel." Aniela placed a bowl on the machine's flat palatte and said, "Please, give me a fourth of a cup of chocolate ice cream with chocolate syrup and peanut butter chips on top."

The machine sprang to life, with lights flashing and a whirling sound from deep inside. Aniela's order filled the bottom of the bowl. She carried it to Guleed. "This is my favorite. I hope you like it."

Everyone watched Guleed as he dipped the spoon into the concoction and raised the bite to his mouth. Utter bliss crossed his face he swirled the ice cream around his mouth. "This is the best thing my tongue has ever tasted!" he cried. "It's as good as pizza, but it's so cold. I have never had anything so cold." He scooped up another bite and plunged it into his open mouth. "Mmmm!"

"I'm glad you like it, Guleed. I'm going to get mine now."

He nodded as he scraped the remainder in his bowl into the spoon.

"I'll let you taste my favorite next," Ariel told him as she moved behind Aniela who was lifting her bowl from the dispenser tray. She set a bowl on the palate and ordered. "Please, give me a fourth of a cup of mint chocolate chip ice cream with chocolate syrup drizzled over it and bits of crushed mints on top."

She delivered her favorite concoction to Guleed. "Here you go. Here's a different kind of ice cream. This one's my favorite kind of sundae."

"Mmmm, this one is good, too. I like this stuff you call ice cream. I do not know why you call it Sunday, though. Is today Sunday? Is it the only day you can eat ice cream?"

His teammates burst out laughing once more, leaving Guleed perplexed. "I, again, do not see what's funny. I have no idea how long I was in that maze. I do not know what day it is. If you call the food Sunday, I am thinking that is because it the only day you eat it."

Gavreel told him, "You're not really wrong, Guleed. The food and the day of the week are spelled differently, but the concoction is thought to have been created on Sunday. There's lots of disagreement about where it was created, but local governments in many places forbade selling sodas on Sunday because some churches objected to it. It's been said that one soda fountain owner decided to serve a soda-less ice cream treat only on Sundays to obey the law. Instead of pouring soda over ice cream like usual, he poured just the syrup over the ice cream and put a cherry on top. One story maintains that the creator's last name was Sonntag, which means

Sunday in both the Swedish and German languages. Some say he named his creation after himself, but nobody knows for sure. Any way, the concoction became very popular, so he sold it on other days, too. Before long, other places began serving ice cream topped with syrups. People were afraid that churches would be offended by putting Sunday on the menus, so they changed it to sundae."

"You know so much," Aniela told Gavreel. "I'm glad you tell us things like that."

Gavreel smiled. "I'm glad you enjoy listening and learning new things."

One by one, each teammate shared their favorite combinations with Guleed until he declared. "I am so happy to have eaten this excellent food, but I do not think I can eat another bite. My belly is hard with so much inside it."

"We've all eaten enough," Jo put in. "I'm really full, too."

"Speak for yourself," Gabe mumbled as he stuffed another cookie in his mouth. "I still have a bit of room in my food containment chamber."

"Do you ever get full?" Jo teased.

"Occasionally, but we only eat every so often around here so I have to take advantage of it when I can. It's not gluttony if I only eat every two or three months," he theorized.

Gavreel spoke up, "I need to show Guleed his chamber now and explain some things to him that all of you already know. We'll leave you for a while. Feel free to hang out together in the lounge or head off to your own chambers for some alone time. As you've probably already noticed by the door colors, Jo's and Aniela's blue and purple doors are on each side of the fireplace on this side wall. Micah's blue, Ariel's gold, Nate's red, and Gabe's black doors are along the back wall. Guleed's blue and Dina's silver doors are opposite Jo's and Aniela's on the other side wall. Guleed, please, come with me." She stood and motioned for him to follow.

GULEED'S CHAMBER

Guleed chattered as he followed Gavreel across the lounge. She turned the knob and told him, "This is your space, Guleed. The others may come into it if you say they may, but if you want to be alone, this is your area, and they will leave you alone. You may also go into each of their chambers, but only when you are given permission. Sometimes, we go into one another's spaces to observe, but you must always ask and be granted permission to enter another angel's private chamber. Do you understand?"

"Yes, behind this door is mine. Others can come in, but I must say it is okay. I can go in their rooms, too, but only if they say it is all right."

"Correct." They stepped through the doorway and the door clicked shut behind them.

"This is your private kitchen and living room. Your refrigerator and pantry are filled with things you like to eat. You may take as much or as little as you like. Your food will always be restocked when you take some. If the food needs to be heated, set it on the stove and it will instantly warm to the perfect temperature and texture. You may eat here or in the lounge with the others. It's your choice when and where you eat if you choose to eat when you are not on training maneuvers or on a mission. You do not have to eat here, and you never have to void waste, but you may eat for pleasurable feelings and companionship. The longer you're here, the less often you'll feel compelled to eat."

"This is like a palace!" Guleed exclaimed. "This is just for me?"

"Yes, this is *your* heavenly home," Gavreel confirmed. "This thing on the wall is a TV. It will show images similar to what we watched on the maze wall when the cordula leaves swirled and made pictures. Just say what you want to watch, and it will appear on this black screen. It's for entertainment. You can say, 'Show me something funny,' and a funny program will come on. Gabe likes to watch skateboarding competitions on his, and Micah likes baseball games and symphonies. The others don't watch their TVs much. It's up to you whether you watch or not. Some people find watching shows relaxing, and others prefer doing other things. If you want music just say, 'Play,' then name the music you want to hear. The music will play until you say to stop the music."

"This room is beautiful. I have never seen such fancy furniture. The colorful blankets thrown over the ends of the long chair remind me of my homeland. The pictures on the walls do, too."

"The furniture where the fabric throws are arranged on each end is called a sofa or a couch. Three or four people can sit on it at a time, or you can lie down on it and rest. The fabric throws and artwork were selected to make you feel at home in your new home; everything is Somalian."

"I like it very much. I like the little statues of the giraffe and elephant on that table, too."

"Follow me to your bedroom and closet now, Guleed. You have to know how to change clothes and care for your uniform when you're not wearing it."

The pair strolled down a short hall, past an open door to Guleed's bathroom and through a doorway at the end. "This is your bedroom, Guleed. This is your bed. You do not need to sleep any more, but many still find pleasure in sleeping so you may sleep if you choose to do so. Like eating, sleeping is for pleasure and the desire for it will lessen the longer you are here. Many teenagers sleep a lot and find they still want and need to sleep, especially near their transition times. It's an excellent way to refresh if you choose to sleep."

Guleed stared at the huge four-poster bed made of hand carved wood and the colorful bedspread that stretched across it. "I do not sleep on a mat on the floor here? I have never slept in a bed."

"You may sleep anywhere you choose, but I think you'll find your bed very comfortable. At least try it," Gavreel suggested. "You just pull the fabric covers back, climb in, rest your head on the pillow, and pull the covers back over you. I'll show you." Gavreel pulled back the bedding, stretched out, rested her head on the pillow where she slid in, and adjusted the covers over herself. "This is a wonderful place to refresh."

She stood, flicked both hands twice, and headed across the room. They bed was perfectly made again. "This door opens to your closet, Guleed. This is where I'll show you how to take care of your uniform."

"What is a closet?" Guleed asked. "This is another word I have never heard."

Gavreel smiled. "A closet is a space for storing things like extra clothes and shoes. Most bedrooms have closets as part of the room. Let's go inside your closet and I will tell you what you need to do to change clothes and store your uniform when you're home."

Guleed followed her and gawked at the shelves lined with folded shirts, shorts, and shoes. More shirts and long pants hung from a bar. "Is this a store?"

"No, Guleed, these are your clothes and shoes for when you're home and not wearing your uniform."

"I never had more than two shirts and two pairs of pants. I cannot believe this is all for me."

"It is. See that round platform at the end of the closet?" She pointed.

"That's where your uniform is stored when you're not in it."

"So, I always put the uniform on that round thing when I take it off," Guleed said. "Well, yes and no," Gavreel replied. "You don't put it on the platform after you take it off. You can only take it off if you are standing on the platform. Step up on it and I'll explain what you must do."

Guleed did as she asked, and shimmers surrounded him. "What's happening?"

"Everything's fine. Your essence activated the force field. This platform is programmed with your essence. Only you can activate it by stepping on it. It recognized your essence when you climbed on top of it. It's the only place you can remove or put on your uniform. Don't do anything yet, just listen. You take your uniform off by running your hands down your thighs like this, from the top of your legs to your knees. If you just swipe down, your uniform will come off and you'll be naked. You'd do that if you wanted to take a shower or bath. If you want to change to some comfortable clothes rather than stay naked, you swipe your hands down and back up quickly while you visualize what you want to wear. If you want that pair of black shorts and that gray t-shirt, you look at them and think of them. They'll automatically clad your body when the uniform's removed. Try it. Not naked mode, but other clothes mode. Look at what you want to wear and swipe your hands down and back up quickly."

Guleed went through the motions and marveled when he saw the bright blue shirt and black pants on his body. "Where is the uniform?"

"Step down here and look at the platform," Gavreel told him.

Guleed's mouth gaped as he stared at the uniform hovering right behind where he'd been standing. The boots were at the side of each uniform leg, the chain of charms and bracelets on the platform between the boots. Shimmers surrounded the ensemble.

"The platform is protecting and refreshing your uniform," Gavreel explained. "You change clothes on the platform every time. It's the only place where the uniform can come off or go on. Only your essence can activate your platform. Each angel has their own platform for uniform security."

"This is another amazing thing," Guleed remarked. "I have seen and done so many amazing things since coming here. Nothing here is like what I knew in Somalia for the sixteen years I lived."

"You are right about that. Somalia, with all its problems in recent decades, is very far from being like Heaven. Your everlasting life is a great improvement over your earthly life. You will have to work hard and learn much, but you are more prepared for the role of warrior angel than many when they begin."

"Why do you say that I am more prepared? I know less than my teammates."

"Yes, you know less about skills and powers you gain here, but you faced evil your entire life and survived untold violence, starvation, squalor, diseases, and deep grief. You've seen far more than most. You won't be shocked by evil that is rampant in the universe. Most new warrior trainees are shocked by the things they see and must face on missions. Many must adjust to and accept their calling after experiencing things far less than you survived."

Guleed hung his head. "Yes, I experienced much in my life, but I was part of the violence. I hurt and killed others. I was evil on Earth. I have much shame."

Gavreel raised his chin and stared in his eyes. "You were not evil, Guleed. Many of the *things* you did were evil, but they were not your choice. You were just a boy trying to survive. You were forced into service of evil ones, first the clan militia then the pirates. Except for stealing food when you and your family were starving, you never once chose to go out on your own and harm others. You managed to survive in that violent environment without adult supervision and training in the way you should go, but never intentionally chose to be evil or enjoyed it. You just followed your instincts to survive. I think that may be why God chose you to be a warrior, in spite of the life you led. God knows your heart. God forgave you as you faced your actions in purgatory, chose you to join the most powerful team I've ever seen, and fast-tracked your training. God purged your spirit and made it clean. You must accept these gifts from God just as you accepted the divine powers you perfected today. You're vitally needed on the looming mission."

"I wish to help fight evil. I wish to stay here in this wonderful place. I do not know what I can do on this mission, but I will try to help."

Gavreel smiled. "Good. One more thing you should know about your closet. Any time you change clothes, just leave them on the platform. It will refresh the clothes and put them away for you. You'll always have clean things to wear."

"I have never seen so many clothes in one place. I cannot believe they're just for me."

"They are. You can wear any of them when you're not in uniform."

"I like these clothes I'm wearing. They're very soft and smell nice."

"I'm glad. Let me show you your bathroom now, Guleed. I know you've never used indoor facilities, so I'll show you how things work. Follow me through this door."

Guleed followed Gavreel, his bare feet padding over the cool tiles. "My feet have never touched anything so cool as this floor. It is a wonderful feeling."

"I like to feel cool tile, too," Gavreel told him. "There's something soothing about walking on a cool surface. This thing is your sink. This handle turns on hot water and the other one cold water. If you turn them both on part way you can get warm water. This is soap for washing your hands or face. You push the handle down and liquid soap squirts out. Try it."

Guleed turned on both faucets and pumped soap on his hands. He rubbed them together, fascinated by the foam and scent the rubbing created. He ran them under the running water and watched the foam slip down the drain.

"This is a toothbrush and this is toothpaste," Gavreel explained. "You squeeze a little toothpaste on the bristles of the toothbrush like this, then rub it all over your teeth to clean them. The toothpaste leaves your mouth feeling clean and cool. Take your toothbrush now and scrub your teeth with it."

Guleed cautiously rubbed the toothbrush over his front teeth and smiled. "This tastes almost like Ariel's favorite ice cream!"

"It is minty, but you don't eat it. You spit it out in the sink and rinse your mouth with water when you have brushed all your teeth. It makes your mouth feel good and takes away bad tastes that might be left from some foods."

Guleed glanced up in the mirror. Foam dribbled from the corners of his mouth. "Oh, no! I have the rabies disease! I am foaming at the mouth. This is very bad! It must have come from the dog-that-licks-but-does-not-bite. I have been around no other animals."

Gavreel chuckled, "Oh, Guleed, you don't have rabies. There are no diseases in Heaven. That's just foam from the toothpaste. Just like the soap on your hands made foam when you rubbed it with water, the toothpaste makes foam when you rub it over your teeth. It's fine. Bruno has no diseases."

"Are you certain?"

"Completely certain. As soon as you've brushed all of your teeth with the foam, spit out what's in your mouth into the sink, get a mouthful of water and swish it around, then spit it out in the sink, too. As soon as you've rinsed your mouth with water, hold your toothbrush under the running water and rinse it off, too, then put it right here."

"Step over here now. This is a bathtub. If you want to sit in water and wash yourself, you turn on the water faucets here and adjust the temperature to how cool or warm you want the water to be. When the water fills the tub about halfway, you take off all your clothes and climb into the water. Some people like to sit in a tub and some like to lie back and lean on the tub to relax in the water. You can put body wash from that bottle on the cloth and wash all parts of your body. It gets foamy just like the hand soap, so you have to splash water on yourself to rinse it off. Some people like bubble baths, so you can pour some of the liquid under running water and it will make lots of bubbles in the tub. When you're finished bathing, push this button and the water will drain. When you step out, grab one of these towels and dry yourself. Wear or carry your towel to your closet platform and pick the clothes you want to wear. The towel will be refreshed by the platform and put back in your bathroom."

"I have never sat in water before. In Somalia, there is little water, except ocean water and during the monsoon floods. We wash with a wet cloth, but no one I ever knew sat in water."

"It's a pleasant experience. You may want to take a bath and try it. Or you can take a shower. This is your shower stall. See that nozzle? Water comes out of it when you pull out and turn this knob. If you leave it to the right, the water will be cool. As you turn the knob to the left, the water gets warmer and warmer. Right in the middle is half cold water and half hot water, so it feels warm. If you go all the way to the right, the water will be very hot, so be careful. Most people find the temperature they like best and leave the knob positioned there. Then when you pull it out the next time, the water is your perfect temperature. Just like with a bath, you put the body wash on the cloth and rub the foam all over. The water spraying from the nozzle will rinse off the soap. When you're done, push the knob in and the water will turn off. You have towels here, too."

Gavreel looked tenderly at her latest charge. "Guleed, there's something else you need to know about your chambers. Since you didn't have a home with your family when you transitioned, I'm not sure what you'll see when you look, but we'll look together this time."

"What will we look at together?"

"Come with me again, and I'll show you."

They walked back to Guleed's bedroom. Gavreel knelt near his bed. "Come down here with me, Guleed."

Guleed knelt by Gavreel. "Is it time to pray?"

"It's always time to pray, but that's not what we're doing at the moment. I want you to lean over and put your face near the floor. Tiny cracks will open, and you'll be able to observe areas and people from your earthly life. Most angels see the rooms of their prior homes and the places where they spent the most time, like school or sports fields. I'm not sure what you'll see, but we'll face it together. It may be hard for you to see some of the things you will see, but it's important that you look."

When Guleed leaned down, a fissure opened. His view was of a Somali refugee camp orphanage. Three large tents stretched before him. Each tent had woven pallets on the floor, with a piece of cloth on top of each pallet. Each tent had ten rows with ten pallets in each row. Flies swarmed everywhere. Hundreds of children milled around inside the tents or in the empty space between the tents. Most were very young. Many were crying. All looked very sad. Guleed stared at a little girl who looked like his sister Bilan when she was taken. She appeared to be eight or nine. She tried to soothe a pair of toddlers who leaned against her sobbing. "It will be all right. You can stay here by me," she murmured.

"I think that's my baby sister Fatima," Guleed cried. "She was only two the last time I saw her, but she looks my sister Bilan. Bilan was eight when she was taken. Fatima would be eight or nine now, too."

"I'm sure it is your youngest sister," Gavreel mused. "She looks like a person with a kind heart. It seems she's doing as well as one can do in a refugee camp. She is still alive and trying to help others."

"I wonder where my brother is now. He would be twelve or thirteen. I hope he did not run away and leave Fatima alone. I hope he is not part of a militia and doing things like I did."

"If we move to a different part of your chambers, we'll have a different view," Gavreel told him. "Let's move in by your sofa and see what appears when we look through the crevasse that will open there."

The pair walked to the living room and knelt together in front of Guleed's sofa. A new crack appeared as soon as Guleed's face was near. The new scene showed Bilan in a bedroom with the two boys Guleed had seen briefly in the car that brought the weapons. His sister and his nephews, the oldest one his namesake. Bilan's face was bruised and swollen. She limped as she tended the baby.

"He beat her! Look at my sister's face! He beat her." Guleed's hands were balled in fists as he watched his sister lovingly change the baby boy then cuddle him to her. He saw the tear trickle down her cheek as she held her son. "She is barely fifteen, and already she has a four-year-old son and another baby. He must have made her a mother as soon as she became a woman!"

"Her life has been hard, too," Gavreel responded. "Very few people in Somalia live lives that are not tremendously hard. Her struggles and her pain have been different from yours and Fatima's, but her journey is just as difficult. I believe that's why we're being sent on the mission to Somalia. The time is right to conquer evil in at least a small part of your homeland. You were chosen to help this team do that. So even though these things are hard for you to see, they should strengthen your resolve to help fight the evil that's rampant. You may make things better for some of the people who struggle to survive there."

"I want to help make things better for my sisters and others. I want to make things worse for that man who hurt Bilan." Guleed stared at his sister as she rocked the baby and watched her older son roll a small truck around the floor.

"Let's see what your kitchen floor will show you when you activate the portal there," Gavreel suggested. "Both of your sisters are busy soothing little ones."

Guleed watched sadly as the group with which he'd sailed held a transport ship at gunpoint. The crew became captives as the young men from the pirate ship took control of the vessel. "They'll try to get ransom money for the sailors and the return of the ship after they steal the cargo," Guleed declared. "These men are in great danger if they try to fight, now that their ship has been boarded. I never noticed how scared the men looked when we captured them and their ships. They knew they might be killed."

They watched the pirate occupation of the cargo ship a few minutes before Gavreel spoke. "Do you want to see if the others are still in the lounge or would you prefer to stay in your own chambers by yourself?"

"I wish to see what my team is doing. If they are all gone, I will try a bath and resting on that giant bed you say is all mine."

"I'll follow you back," Gavreel told him as she patted him on the shoulder.

TEAM TIME

Guleed found the rest of the team sprawled on the huge sectional sofa, all wearing casual clothes rather than uniforms.

"Hey! Welcome back!" chimed the seven on the sofa. Laughter punctuated their remark.

"You obviously learned about your closet platform," Ariel observed.

"Yes, Gavreel showed me that and other things in my beautiful home. All of you went to your closets, too, I see."

"We did. We all took showers to refresh and put on comfortable clothes before coming back here to hang out for a while," Jo told him.

"I did not take a shower, but I brushed my teeth and watched below. I did not like anything I saw in my homeland."

The group shot concerned looks at one another and then at Guleed.

"Looking at your old life is really hard," Aniela murmured. "I don't like looking at anything except Ms. Cross's classroom. Sometimes I like to watch her and remember, but I don't like to see anything else from my earthly life."

"I saw my sisters and my pirate crew. I didn't like seeing how hard their lives still are when I have so many wonderful things here."

"Come, sit on the sofa with us," Gabe urged. "Bruno wants to kiss your hands again."

"I will sit, but I do not really want the dog-that-licks-but-does-not-bite to taste my fingers again. I know you say it is kissing from a dog, but I do not like the way it feels."

His team chuckled as Guleed eased onto the cushion farthest from Gabe and Bruno.

Jo called, "Gavreel, will you come and sit with us a while? I'd like to talk about some stufff."

Gavreel eased down next to Gabe. Bruno snuggled on her lap, but stretched out a front leg so it rested on Gabe's arm. He kissed Gavreel's hand as she stroked his outstretched leg. "Thank you for the kisses, sweet boy. Yes, I missed you, too."

"What do you want to talk about?"

"Well, for one thing, can you explain how Guleed got in the cockatrice's den and why he didn't come to Heaven like the rest of us? I know Uriel talked about it some, but I don't understand."

"As you saw from the accelerated telling of his life story, Guleed chose to survive in a very harsh world. He did many things that hurt others. He accumulated a hefty account of negative acts in his lifetime, yet he never hurt others for pleasure or just because he could. After he was captured by the militia, he followed orders so that he might survive. He was a child with a child's perspective. His acts were evil, but his heart was not. He never asked for forgiveness nor faced the evil acts he'd committed while he lived, though. That's why Azrael escorted him to one of the purgatory stations. There are several different varieties, but Guleed was placed in the den of a predator because he'd lived in fear of predators his whole life. All alone, he had to face fear as great as what he'd created in others' lives. He had to suffer through watching the things he'd done to others loop through his mind. If he admitted to himself the evil he'd committed and asked for forgiveness, God would save him and he'd have a role in everlasting life. Most who've been redeemed, go to the lowest rank of angels, that of messenger. It's extremely rare for a warrior angel to come from a purgatory station. Guleed was chosen by God and chosen by your team. His spirit was purified as his essence mixed with your team. God and your team rescued him from the cockatrice den to fulfill his true destiny."

"Okay, I understand that better now," Jo conceded. "My dad really embarrassed me when he said Micah and I are soulmates.

Why would he say that, Gavreel?"

Gavreel gazed at the gentle young warrior before answering. "He told you that because it's true," she said softly. "His intention wasn't to embarrass you."

"Still, it's crazy. I know our teams are unified, and we've all accepted one another, but I haven't spent much time with Micah. I don't know how anyone could declare we're soulmates."

"Jo, finding your soulmate is a rare and wonderful gift. You were very young when you transitioned and had no experience with personal connections except with your immediate family. Finding the personal connection that's the other half of your essence is a beautiful thing. Can you be honest with yourself and your team and admit that being around Micah felt different than being around anyone else?"

Jo stared at Gavreel. "I don't know what you mean."

"I mean those excited, fluttery, tingly feelings you both got every time you were together, especially when you touched. Everyone could see it. There's a particular joy that's radiated when soulmates are near one another."

Her teammates nodded slightly, acknowledging Gavreel's words.

"We trainers recognized the fires in both your souls being stoked when you two were in the first room of the cockatrice den. As you hunted for clues to escape, your mouths discharged just a bit of the steam. That was from each of your fires within. The intensity built the longer you two were together and the more you sang together. When the vapor from both your mouths blended and made things happen, it was obvious you'd found and called forth your internal weapon. It's strong when you and Micah speak together, but especially strong when you sing together. You saw the power of your combined voices when you opened portals in the maze. That whirlwind that freed everyone is an undeniable weapon."

"So, you're sure he and I both have fires within our souls, and they're strongest when we sing together?"

"Absolutely certain. There's nothing wrong with those butter-flies-in-the-stomach feelings you get when you're together, either. They're signals that your essence is in a heightened state. Holding hands, gentle touches, and having arms around one another are all ways the feeling builds and your internal fires are strengthened."

Micah smiled at Jo. "Well, soulmate, I guess Gavreel just encouraged us to enjoy the feelings we've been having, to embrace the feelings and one another."

"On that note, I am going to leave you to rest and refresh. When one of us comes again, it will be to finish training. Guleed will learn about the DMD and tessellation and be caught up with all of you. Then we'll begin battle training. Level two is very early for that, but you are fast-tracked and need is escalating rapidly. Be ready for an intense session when I see you again."

She lifted a snoozing Bruno and set him on Gabe's lap before vanishing.

"Well, paint me mortified!" Jo declared the minute Gavreel left.

Dina studied her sister-friend. "Jo, are you embarrassed because everything's happening so fast? Since our team has to know everything about one another to be successful on missions, we're all aware of things we might have kept private on Earth. You two are lucky. Think about it. We all died before any of us had any romance on Earth. You and I were fortunate because both of us grew up with loving parents. I saw loving touches between my parents when I was growing up, and I bet you saw them between yours, too. They loved us so well because they loved one another first. I'm pretty sure my parents are soulmates. They completed one another and made one another better. Your parents may be soulmates, too. Remember what your dad said when you two returned from your comfort visit? He said how wonderful it was to touch your mom again, that resting on her arm was as much for him as it was for her."

Jo murmured, "I'm sure you're right about our parents, Dina. You always know what to say."

"Just don't get carried away with a bunch of kissing in front of all of us," Gabe quipped. "In my opinion, Bruno is the only teammate that should be allowed excessive public displays of affection!"

Laughter sounded once more when Bruno sprang up and licked Gabe across the face. Bruno escalated the laughter as he made his way around the sectional, kissing each team member's cheek. When he made it to the last team member, he did not kiss the closest cheek as he had done to every other person. Instead, he jumped on the back of the sofa and draped himself around Guleed's neck. He rubbed his head against Guleed's cheek.

"Do not do it, dog-that-licks-but-does-not-bite! I do not wish to have your slobber on my face. I do not wish to have your slobber anywhere."

Bruno was encouraged by the laughter he'd evoked so kept rubbing his head on Guleed's cheek.

"Look, he listened to me. I am glad he has not laid one of those slobbery kisses on my cheek."

A grinning Bruno then kissed Guleed on the lips. Bruno leapt off and ran to his and Gabe's door as Guleed sputtered and the team roared.

Gasping for air, Gabe sputtered, "Well, Bruno kissed everyone goodnight and headed to our door. I guess we'll go refresh on our bed. See you in a while." He followed his still grinning dog to his chamber door.

"We should probably all get some rest before they come for us," Ariel announced. "See you soon."

The team stretched and everyone headed to their chamber doors. The lounge emptied quickly, except for Jo and Micah.

"I'm sorry you're embarrassed they said we're soulmates," he whispered. "I, personally, am delighted. You're the most amazing individual I've ever been around. I feel better around you than I've ever felt."

"I feel things, too, but my dad embarrassed me when he said that in front of everyone."

230

Micah lifted her chin, gazed in her eyes before closing his, and leaned closer. His kiss was slow and soft. Everything fell away except the two of them as their breath mingled and their essences ignited. Warmth spread through their bodies as they leaned against one another, spreading new and indescribable sensations. This kiss was comforting in a way that words could never be.

When he pulled away, he whispered, "Thank you."

"For what?"

"For being you." His voice wavered from the tension between them. His breath was shallow and shaky. "For being you, the most amazing individual I've ever encountered."

They stared deeply into one another's eyes as if searching for definitive proof that they were what the others claimed they were: soulmates. Curiosity, wonder, and love flooded between them.

"Thank you, too," Jo squeaked. "You made me feel a lot better. Your touch is very comforting."

"Let's head to our chambers now," Micah blurted, "or I'm going to keep kissing you. I believe I could become addicted to kissing you. You'll fill my dreams as I refresh."

Jo traced his cheek with her finger before heading to her chamber door. "See you soon, sweet Micah. I'll dream of you, too."

TIME TO TALK

Jo bounced into the lounge, popping sweet juicy grapes into her mouth. She crossed the lounge and pounded once on Dina's door, their signal that someone was in the lounge and to join them if desired. She didn't knock on the others' doors, though. She was hoping for some time with just Dina.

"Hi!" Dina called. "Guess you're here first again. You really look refreshed! You look positively radiant today." Dina settled on the sofa by Jo.

"Want some grapes? They're really sweet." Jo held the bunch out for Dina to pull some from the cluster.

"Thank you for saying what you did last night, I mean about soulmates," Jo told her. "I needed to hear that from someone my own age."

"No problem. I do think our parents are probably soulmates. I don't know about anyone else's, but I know my parents had a loving marriage and made a loving home for our family. They seemed to complete one another and just know what the other needed. It was so natural."

"I want to tell you something, but I want it to stay just between us. Okay? Micah kissed me before we went to our chambers last night!" Jo blurted.

"Really? Tell me more," Dina urged, studying her teammate's face.

"It was unbelievable. He told me how glad he was that they said we were soulmates and how he felt wonderful when he was around me. Then he lifted my chin and kissed me tenderly on the lips. It's hard to describe, but it was like our essences ignited when we kissed. I felt as if I were on fire but not burning. It was the best feeling I've ever had."

"So, do you accept that you two are soulmates now?"

"I guess so, but it still seems strange to me. My dad really embarrassed me when he talked about it in front of everybody. He didn't give me a chance to think about it, to process the idea. Telling everyone that we'd have married on Earth if we had lived longer and found one another there was pretty embarrassing."

"I get that, but I don't think he meant to embarrass you. He was just trying to explain. If he knows you found your soulmate, he's probably happy for you, but also maybe a little sad."

"Why would that make him sad, if it's supposed to be so great?"

"Think about it, Jo, from a different perspective, as Gavreel's always telling us to do. Michael's been the most important male in your life, both on Earth and here. You've shared how important he is to you and how he had the biggest influence on you. Your dad knows that if your soulmate is with you, he's no longer number one in your eyes. You aren't Daddy's little girl anymore; you are your own young woman with a new exciting male in her life. He might feel a bit displaced and have to process that himself."

"You're so smart, Dina. I never even considered that."

"He knows you're both young but not too young to feel what you feel. Seeing the steam that came from both of you and blended to make a weapon was impossible for him to deny, but it's still something he has to have time to adjust to and process."

"How old do you think we are by Earth-years now? Time's so different here. I have no idea how long it's been since we transitioned."

"I was thinking about that since I saw my portrait and I looked so much like my mom," Dina told her. "Maybe we could see if the calendar is still hanging in my parents' kitchen. It might give us some idea. Want to look with me?"

"Of course. Let's go," Jo said as she jumped to her feet.

The girls giggled as they flounced to Dina's door and into her bedroom. As they knelt together and Dina's face got close to the floor, the expected fissure opened and allowed them to look into

Dina's former home. The month of August showed on the kitchen's calendar. Her mom was busy frosting a cake, while her dad sat at the table watching her.

"I can scarcely believe our baby boy is a teenager today!" she announced. "It doesn't seem possible that he's already thirteen and that his brother will be heading back to college next week. The house will be so quiet again with just one kid and one dog here with us."

"Time's a funny thing," her dad said. "Sometimes it seems so fast and other times so slow. It's hard to believe that he's a teenager, though."

Yodels danced on his hind legs, trying to get a better look at the cake. His white muzzle announced his advancement in years.

"If this is August second and my brother's turning thirteen, it's been nearly three years by Earth time since we transitioned! That means we're sixteen, Jo. Sixteen!"

"No wonder our portraits looked so different," Jo mused.

"No wonder the guys were so hungry when we got back here!" Dina chortled. The girls shared a good laugh as they stood to head back to the lounge.

"Let's see if the others are up and want to join us," Jo announced as they walked back. "I wanted some time with just you before everyone came. Thanks for talking with me. I feel like I can tell you anything, like I did with my sister before I transitioned."

"I feel the same way, though I never had a sister. I'm glad you've become my sister here," Dina replied as she wrapped Jo in a hug. "I'll go this way and pound once on each door and you start on the other side. We'll see who joins us if they hear the signal."

Before long, the sectional rocked with laughter as Team JAMBANGGD exchanged stories and teased one another. Bruno entertained the group by zooming around the room every time the laughter reached a certain level. On his return trip, he stopped by the front door and sat down staring at it.

"What is the dog-that-licks-but-does-not-bite doing?" Guleed asked as he finished his second banana.

"He's telling us someone is coming," Gabe, Dina, and Jo declared together.

A tap on the door verified their response.

"It's us," Gavreel called as she poked her head in. "Are all of you refreshed and ready to start work again?"

Gavreel, Kirron, Michael, and Uriel joined the young team on the sectional.

"Everyone will need to change into their uniforms, but first we want to talk to you about Guleed's comfort visit. He'll be doing that before we resume training, but his will be different from all of yours. We've decided that Guleed must make a dream visit because of the circumstances of his life and the pending mission." Gavreel smiled, but concern showed on her face. "Everyone, go change and come right back. We'll explain more as soon as everyone's suited up."

Uriel added, "Dream visits are more difficult for a beginner, but they offer the opportunity to speak to the one being visited. You saw that when Gavreel visited Gabe's neighbor to explain about Bruno. This will be similar. Guleed has no home to visit, but he has two living sisters he's observed from his chambers. Although it's unusual, we've decided he'll visit his sister Bilan. He'll deliver a message from us, as well as bring comfort to her. Because dream visits are difficult, and the place he's visiting is so dangerous, two of us and one of you will accompany him on this visit. Jo, please, prepare yourself to make your first dream transport. Someone young with your natural gentleness and instinctive communication skills may be needed."

Jo shot a look at her father, then Micah. Both looked concerned as they studied her reaction but said nothing.

"Go! Everyone suit-up and get right back here," Kirron barked. "We have much to do this session and must get started."

PREPARING FOR GULEED'S VISIT

Kirron spoke as soon as the group reassembled on the sectional. Jo sat between Michael and Micah, both of whom held one of her hands in theirs. Jo kept her eyes fixed on Kirron. "Thank you for returning so quickly. Uriel is going to explain what's going to happen as soon as we finish this discussion."

"Everyone's going to Guleed's chamber momentarily. Kirron and I will hold open the tessellation so we can all watch the dream visit. Gavreel and Michael will accompany Guleed, Jo, and Bruno through Bilan's brain. As you might recall, Gavreel wandered through a maze before visiting Gabe's neighbor in a dream. Those twists and turns were actually her brain. The entire brain is active during dreams, from the brain stem to the cortex. We'll watch Bilan sleep in order to determine when she's reached the rapid-eye movement phase, because most dreams happen during REM sleep. The mid-section of the organ deals with emotions when one is awake and asleep. The amygdala, which is associated with fear, is very active during dreams. Dream visitors from here try to skirt around this section, but sometimes that's impossible. Visitors with evil intent head straight for the amygdala." He took a deep breath before continuing. "Everyone's brain is somewhat different, but the cortex is responsible for the content of dreams for everyone. That means the cortex is their destination. As they slip into this part of Bilan's brain, Michael and Gavreel will trigger a pleasant memory from your shared youth, Guleed. We reviewed your life again and decided on the day your father came home with new lengths of fabric for each of you. Before the fabric was changed into new garments, you and your sister chased one another around, letting your cloth billow behind you like parachutes. You laughed, enjoying the impromptu toy the fabric had become. Do you remember what you said to Bilan right before your mother made you give her the cloth?"

Guleed cleared his throat. "I told my sister that she would look beautiful in the new pink and orange baati that our mother would make, but she couldn't look more beautiful than she did right then with the fabric around her head framing her happy smile."

"That's right. You were both happy at that moment," Gavreel told him. "Nothing scary was happening around you, and your love for one another was strong. We'll enter her dream as you're playing. Michael and I will stay in the background and will not speak or do anything unless something happens that calls for our intervention. Jo will remain silent, too, unless you need help to convince Bilan of our message."

"I am not sure what I am supposed to do in this dream visit," Guleed told them.

"Me, either," Jo fretted.

"Or why you're taking Bruno," Gabe added.

Kirron declared, "First and foremost, your job is to bring comfort to your sister. She's been in deep grief since your transition. She had just found you again, and you were ripped from her once more. Her husband's not happy with her or the emotional state she's been in since that day. Her sons are irritable much of the time because they sense their mother's mood. Afweyne's violence with her and the boys is escalating because she can't stop her tears when he orders her to do so. To save her from further harm, you need to convince her that you're all right and watching over her and her sons."

"Which leads us to the next reason we're having you make a dream visit rather than a comfort visit in morphed form," Michael told him. "You must convince your sister that you'll be coming again, next time with your team of angel warriors and four seasoned warriors. If you or Jo are holding Bruno, she'll be amazed, since she also believes all dogs are wild and dangerous. Seeing gentle Bruno will help convince her that there's something very special about this dream. She'll recognize you, Jo, and Bruno, so she'll know the mission is underway, but she must give no warning to anyone in the compound. She must keep her sons close so they're not harmed. You must convince Bilan that she'll soon be freed from the clutches of the man who's abused her since she was snatched nearly seven years ago."

"I hope Bilan is not frightened by seeing me with a wild dog and a stranger in her dream," Guleed declared. "I am glad that we can talk, but I do not know if I can convince her that we will be coming again to help her."

Michael continued, "She must know and understand that she has inheritance rights, that the compound where she's being held will become her property when her husband is dead. The money he has accumulated will become her money. Although the money was gained by deplorable methods, it will be used to help others when she has control. She'll no longer be destitute nor dependent on a vicious man. People will try to convince her that she must leave, but she must stand firm, knowing that it's her property and will remain the home of her sons. His other wife bore him no children, so she won't have the same inheritance rights. She will be allowed to stay in the quarters she's always had and be provided for, but she will not have control of the assets. Bilan has been chosen for this responsibility."

"I am not sure Bilan will believe anything I say," Guleed said. "I have not been with her for years, not since we were children. Our lives were very different, but I know we both did what we had to do to survive."

"Bilan's suffering has been great, but the time is almost here for her to fulfill an important part of her journey," Gavreel announced. "You must convince her that the compound must become an orphanage and school for some of the children who've lost both parents and are all alone in the world. She must understand that she should contact SOS Children's Villages. Fatima has been cared for by this organization since you left. The people who run this organization will help Bilan secure her property and educate her in what needs to be done to house and care for some of the children in their charge. Bilan will reunite with Fatima and bring her home, as well as others who need her. She'll become an SOS mother to orphaned children, keeping them safe and nourishing their bodies and souls. Afweyne's other wife will also become an SOS mother to those who need her. She's also vital in saving many children."

Kirron studied Guleed's face before adding, "This is something else that's very important for you to understand. We know that the man who kidnapped Bilan and has inflicted suffering on her since she was eight years old, is under the control of powerful demon named Aka Manah. Aka Manah literally means 'mind made evil.' He's the demon of evil intention and evil thinking. He controls many, including Afweyne. The longer a person is under Aka Manah's control, the eviler they become. Afweyne has succumbed to evil. His heart and mind are black. We'll try to free him from the evil, but it's not very likely that we'll be able to do that. There can be no redemption for him if he refuses to admit his evil ways and ask for forgiveness. That's why our mission will likely be to slay him along with the demons surrounding him. There are many demons in human form in his weapon-running organization, just as there were in the clan militia that ravished many innocent Somali lives. He's not a demon himself so your nephews are not halflings, Guleed, but Afweyne is as evil as any demon. He has absolutely no conscience."

"We will be going to Somalia to slay Afweyne and demons?" Guleed gasped.

"Yes, and hopefully, Aka Manah will be among them," Kirron affirmed. "I toppled him once, centuries ago. But he has resurfaced with the intention of destroying another civilization. Your homeland's society, Guleed."

"Our mission will not happen until after your visit and after further training," Michael told him. "The situation's worsening so we must act soon. Which means we need to get your visit finished and your training started again. Are you ready to speak with your sister in her dream?"

"Like most things here, I do not understand how this is possible, but I will try," Guleed told them.

"It's crucial that each of you remain connected to one of us until we reach Bilan's cortex," Gavreel instructed. "Jo, you should carry Bruno and hold Michael's hand. Guleed, I'll hold your hand as we wander through the folds and crevasses of your sister's brain. We'll remain silent until we reach the cortex. You'll know we're there because we'll see her dream. I'll let go of your hand when we've reached our destination. You can step away from me and speak to your sister. She'll see you change from the boy in her dream to the young man she saw in Puntland. She will hear you and be able to speak with you. Remember, you must first bring her comfort, then relay the message about our impending mission and her mission after we leave."

Guleed's nod signaled his readiness to begin.

"Let's follow Guleed to his chamber," Kirron declared. "We'll watch Bilan and see if she is ready for the visit."

The group paraded after Guleed as he made his way to his door.

GULEED'S VISIT

Guleed knelt by his bed and lowered his face to the floor. The crack that opened showed Bilan standing next to a large bed. Afweyne was there, too. As they watched, he punched Bilan's face, shook her violently, and threw her on the bed. They heard him yell that she was quickly becoming worthless. He vowed she'd be back on the streets if she didn't stop crying all the time and meet his needs. He ranted that he would give his sons to his other wife when he threw her out, that his sons were still young enough that they'd accept their new mother quickly.

"I will go to my sons' new mother now!" he screamed. "She's always ready to take care of me. Even though she's not borne my children, her ways are desirable. I will make her very happy when I give my sons to her." He slammed the door as Bilan sobbed on the bed. Guleed's hands became white-knuckled weapons as he watched the scene.

The team witnessed Bilan's tears soak the pillow and heard her gasping wails. Everyone knew this was more than crying. Bilan's desolate sobbing declared she was drained of all hope, and her heart was broken. She cried until there were no more tears, just emptiness and sorrow. She drifted into a fitful sleep, her breath ragged with intermittent gulping breaths. Her eyelids began to flutter.

Gavreel proclaimed, "It's time, Guleed. Stand up. Kirron and Uriel will open the view into Bilan's psyche, so the others can watch your visit. Jo, drape Bruno around your neck and take Michael's hand. Guleed take my hand. We'll go now. Remember to stay connected until I release your hand. You can speak to her when I let go of you." Guleed felt something against his palm but said nothing and did not release his hold on Gavreel's hand.

Kirron and Uriel made gestures none of them recognized and held their fingers together forming a roof over the crack. The bedroom scene shifted to a dark maze with many twists and turns.

Bruno nuzzled Jo's cheek as she settled him around her neck and took her father's hand. He smiled at her as he intertwined his fingers through hers. They moved next to Gavreel and Guleed.

Michael and Gavreel took one another's free hands. They raised their joined hands above their heads, made a circular motion, then punched upward several times. They vanished from Guleed's chamber and reappeared in the maze.

Gavreel and Michael dropped hands, but clutched Jo's and Guleed's hands as they walked. The gloom of the labyrinth made their images barely perceptible, but they could see Gavreel and Michael tugging the others along the dim passageway. No one spoke as they moved quickly around several bends.

After several more steps, they reached a brighter part of the maze. Still holding Jo's and Guleed's hands, the trainers stood side by side and raised their free hands. They traced their hands along the wall, as if writing a message with their bare hands on Bilan's brain.

The scene shifted from an empty blank space to a village of fabric and plastic tent-houses. A boy and girl chased one another around, shrieking and laughing as colorful cloth ballooned behind them. They heard a woman call, "That's enough. You'll get your new garments dirty before they're even made. Bring me your cloth now."

Young Guleed spoke, "My sister, you will look beautiful in the pink and orange baati that Mother will make for you from this cloth, but you could not look any more beautiful wearing it than you do right now with the bright colors framing your smile."

As those words were spoken in the dream, Gavreel released Guleed's hand and prodded him forward, into the bright scene.

Young Guleed now became the Guleed they all knew. He smiled at his young sister, who let the cloth drop over her shoulders as she stared at her transformed brother.

"Do not be afraid, Bilan. I will never hurt you." Guleed took a step toward his little sister. "You must listen to me and remember everything I tell you. I know my words will sound strange, but everything I tell you is true."

"How, how are you now grown up?" Bilan stuttered as she backed away. "I am still a small girl and you are big. I do not understand."

"I will try to explain. After Afweyne killed me with his car, I spent a long time facing the life I had led and the things I had done. I am now an angel because a team of warrior angels freed me from the beast's den. I am training to be an angel warrior with them. I am visiting you in a dream because there are several things you must understand."

"I do n—not understand. I...I do not believe you."

"You may not understand, but you must believe. We just watched you before you cried yourself to sleep. We saw Afweyne hit you, shake you, and throw you on the bed. We heard him tell you that you are worthless and that he is going to throw you out and give your sons to his other wife, the one who cannot have children. He is a very bad man. I do not want him to hurt you anymore."

"How, how could you know this? He and I were alone in my bedroom." Little girl Bilan was now young woman Bilan.

"I told you, we watched you. We were waiting for the right time to visit in your dream. I have come to bring you comfort and important information. I want you to know that I am watching over you, and I am always with you in your heart."

"Guleed, if that is really who you are, why do you keep saying 'we'?"

"Because I am now a part of a team of angels. I have been chosen to fight evil with them. My team is watching. Some of them are here with me."

"You are lying. You are standing here before me all alone, telling me things that are impossible. Go away! Do not haunt my dreams!"

"He's not lying," Jo said as she stepped next to Guleed. "My name is Jo, and this little dog is Bruno. We are on Guleed's team."

Bilan backed further away. "Do not let that wild dog near me! My sons need me."

Guleed stepped toward her. "I know it seems impossible, but Bruno is not a wild dog. He licks a lot, but he does not bite. They have told me that he is kissing when he licks. I do not know if I believe that or not, but he seems to be a gentle creature."

Jo moved next to Guleed again. "Watch Guleed pet Bruno's head. You can touch him, too, if you want."

Guleed gingerly patted Bruno's head. Bruno looked tenderly at him and wagged his tail, but never moved from his perch around Jo's neck. "See? He let Guleed pat him. Do you want to touch him?"

Bilan shook her head no.

"You don't have to, of course, but I thought you might want the experience of touching a dog. He's a very good little boy. He has a gift for comforting people."

Bilan stammered, "Why, why are you here?"

"I'm Guleed's friend and teammate. So is Bruno. We're both angels, too. We're here to support Guleed as he delivers a very important message to you. He didn't have confidence that you'd believe him, but I want to assure you that everything he's about to tell you is true and will be happening. You must believe him." Jo smiled at Bilan as she finished speaking.

"Please, listen, Bilan," Guleed began again. "I hope you know I love you and want you to go on with your life. You cannot keep crying over me. My nephews and other children need you. You must be strong for the little ones. I want you to know that I am happy now, and I am going to be doing important missions to fight evil. You also have a mission to fulfill."

"I have no mission. I have only survival," Bilan murmured.

"You have survival and a mission," Guleed told her. "My team and I will return after a bit of time has passed. You will know our mission is at hand because you will recognize Jo, Bruno, and me. You must take your sons some place safe when you see us arrive. Bring them to your bed chamber or some other safe spot in the house, far away from where we are."

"Why? The compound is guarded and safe. Afweyne pays many men to keep his home safe from intrusion. Little Guleed likes to play on the grass between the wall and the house, so we are outside often."

"It will not be safe for you to be there when we arrive next time. If you see us, you must take the boys away, get them to safety. You may be shocked to learn why we are coming. This man, Afweyne, is an evil man. He has done so many bad things and gets pleasure from hurting others. He no longer knows right from wrong. His mind is filled only with what he wants and how he can inflict suffering. He is surrounded by demons masquerading as humans who encourage his thoughts and actions. Angels are coming."

"Afweyne is a bad man," Bilan whispered. "He likes to hurt people."

Guleed continued, "I know. I have seen it. The angels who are coming will likely slay this evil man and his entourage of demons. You will be freed from the torture and bondage you have lived through since he stole you from our family and murdered our mother. You will inherit his property, this compound, his money, and other assets. Many will try to convince you this is not true, but it is true. Stand firm against their claims and refuse to leave the compound until the matter is settled. There is a metal box in his dressing room that contains all you need to know about his holdings. Get it immediately after you see us. Take it to your room and hide it. Call the SOS Children's Villages right after Afweyne is gone. Our sister Fatima is there. You should ask for her to be brought to you here and ask for someone to come and help you arrange to become an SOS mother for other orphans. The people at this place are good people who've been working hard to care for many children. Fatima has been with them since we buried our mother."

"You are going to kill Afweyne?" Bilan blurted. "I can't say this saddens me because I have wished for his death many times. He has hurt me over and over; I have lived in terror nearly seven years. I never recovered from seeing our mother shot and knowing it was because she tried to save me from him. Then he killed you as you tried to help me. I do not see how slaying him here is possible, though. He is well guarded and has many powerful weapons."

"We are angel warriors," Jo told her. "We're sent on missions to fight evil in the world. Our next mission is here, to fight the evil that surrounds you and free you to be a ray of goodness in this land where there is much suffering. We'll try to free Afweyne from the evil, but if it's not possible, he will be slain."

"Guleed, how do you know that Fatima is at this SOS Children's Village? Is our brother there, too?"

Guleed smiled at his sister. "I only saw Fatima. She looks so much like you did at that age. Fatima will be delighted to be back with you, though she won't remember anything. You can ask about our brother."

"I'll rescue Fatima as soon as I can," Bilan promised.

"You are a loving sister and mother, Bilan. Fatima was so young when she became an orphan. She doesn't know what it's like to be loved by a mother or a sister. You'll become the most important person in Fatima's life and a surrogate mama to many more. You are needed to nurture more than just the two children you brought into the world. You're going to turn this compound into an orphanage for SOS Children's Villages. You'll bring joy to Afweyne's other wife as she joins you in this mission and becomes another SOS mother. Together, you two will save countless children. Your mission will soften the suffering of many Somali children."

"We must go now," Jo said. "We have preparations to make before we come again. Remember everything that Guleed has told you, Bilan. Do not be afraid any more. You'll soon be free."

"I love you, Bilan. I will free you. I promise you that." He pressed something in her hand as he spoke.

Guleed and Jo backed away, toward the dark wall. They joined hands with two others that Bilan had not noticed. Guleed waved before they stepped out of view. As they departed, Bilan sat upright in bed. She held a scrap of pink and orange fabric in her hand.

NECESSARY PREPARATIONS

Silently, the warriors and an obedient terrier wound through dark twists and turns before transporting back to Guleed's chamber.

"That was fine dream visit," Uriel declared. "You delivered comfort and information just as you were instructed."

"It was well done," Kirron agreed.

"Both of you were outstanding," Gavreel praised. "Guleed, you remembered everything we told you to convey. I'm confident you convinced Bilan of the truth of your words. And, Jo, your support was perfect, gentle and reassuring. Having Guleed pat Bruno was brilliant."

"You both moved like seasoned dream visitors," Michael remarked. "You handled yourselves admirably. Gavreel and I just had to escort you to the proper location, and you handled the rest."

"Thank you for taking me to visit my sister. Thank you for helping me accept what I was saying was truth, Jo."

"The others already have this, but you definitely earned yours, too, considering the fine visit you just made." Gavreel pressed a gold charm in Guleed's hand.

He studied the amulet he held. The center section was circular and bore the words: **"Never let *your* fear or *your* needs stop you from giving comfort to others."** Surrounding the center were seven triangular pieces with golden filigreed edges that reflected light in every direction.

"This charm is like the sun. I can almost feel the warmth from it," Guleed marveled.

"After you read the inscriptions on the backside of each ray, it will be added to your chain," Gavreel explained.

Guleed savored the words he read, valuing each quote from the Bible, Quran, Book of Mormon, Buddha, Hippocrates, and the Youruba Proverb. "These are all very wise," he declared just before the golden sun charm clamped into place.

"We're now moving to the training center. Guleed will be caught up to the rest of you after we show him the center, teach him about the DMD and tessellations, then let him transport the group a couple of times. We'll begin a new phase of training for all of you after that. Please, stand, and connect to one another for transport," Kirron told the group.

The group quickly assembled. Micah's arm wrapped around Jo's shoulder as he whispered in her ear, "You were magnificent on that dream visit, Jo."

She smiled, trying not to let anyone else see her trembling, as pleasant tingling from his touch surged through her body.

The group stood in front of the enormous glass doors of the training center. As they stepped toward the building, the doors opened, welcoming them to the center's lounge. Everyone but Guleed had seen the area before. Guleed surveyed his new surroundings. He noticed the pleasant smell of healthy growing things as he studied the countless plants filling the room. Crystal statues sat on the floor and tables, and crystal baubles hung from many branches. Dancing prism specks darted around the room. A lovely, serene sound was barely audible, yet soothed all who entered. He noticed many seating areas, most of them filled with uniformed teams studying strange devices they held.

"What are those things?" Guleed asked.

"Those are Dynamic Milestoning Devices," Kirron replied. "We call them DMDs for short. They're one of the things you'll learn about in this training session."

"We'll get to the DMD training shortly," Gavreel added, "after you've seen the rest of the training center. Notice that there's at least one trainer with each group of trainees seated around the lounge. You can tell there are many different teams by the variety of colors on the uniforms. Follow me, please." She led the group to the back wall of the gigantic lounge.

"Notice all of the doors along this wall. These doors lead to the control centers for each level of operations. This one on the far left is for level-one missions. Your teammates now have access privileges to this level-one door, since they've successfully completed a level-one mission and moved to level-two training, Guleed. You do not yet have direct access on your own, but you can accompany any of us through this door. When you finish the mission for which we're preparing, you'll have access on your own. To enter the restricted area, you must press your hand against the door. If your essence has been programmed into the door, it will open for you. If not, it will remain closed. Michael, why don't you go in and wait for each trainee to join you in the entryway? We'll let them all test their individual access to level one."

Michael pressed his hand against the door and stepped inside.

"One at a time, each of you press your hand on the door and join Michael," Gavreel urged. Before long, only Gavreel and Guleed stood outside the level-one door.

"It's our turn, now, Guleed, step through the door with me this time."

Uriel spoke as soon as the final two joined the group. "Guleed, when we go around this corner, you'll see why so many young people are needed to become warriors. This level shows only level-one missions. These are considered the easiest missions, but they require high levels of gentleness and caring. Most teams stay at this level for several missions and then move up to the next level where more skills are needed. There's a huge backlog of needs at every level. Teams who demonstrate extremely strong gentleness and caring qualities might stay at this level longer or even permanently, but most teams advance after a few successful level-one missions. Only the strongest trainees with the widest array of skills advance to the highest ranks of warrior angels, Archangel or Seraph."

"The team you've joined will not repeat level-one missions, Guleed. All of you have been chosen to advance quickly, so we're just showing you this area so you gain understanding of the need. Let's step around the corner so Guleed can see the level-one area for himself," Gavreel instructed.

Guleed's mouth gaped as he stepped into the immense room. It stretched farther than he could see. The ceiling and walls pulsed with countless hexagonal cells, each showcasing scenes of need. Encasing each compartment was a lighted strand of green, yellow, red or black. Some had a solid outline, but many were flashing.

"What are all those things on the walls and ceiling?" Guleed asked. "And who are all of these people in here?"

Kirron answered, "These cells show the locations where level-one missions are required. The colored edge prioritizes the missions. Even though a need is real and growing, the green light around the edge means there's still time before sending a team. Yellow means the danger has grown and requires attention as soon as possible. Red indicates imminent danger. Flashing red is crisis. If the evil is not conquered, the segment goes black. When darkness has overcome someone, the need moves to a higher level. It may move to level two, or it may jump all the way to the highest level. Every mission is different, which is why we train warriors to think critically so they can figure out things regardless of the situation. The people you see here are all angels. Most are level-one teams learning about the need or about their assigned mission. Some are trainers, and some work in this section all the time."

"Why are there so many more red outlines than green?" Guleed wondered.

"Because evil spread quickly," Michael told him. "Evil is powerful. Many people succumb to the temptations that are placed before them."

"Let's take them to the level-two control center now," Gavreel suggested. "They are technically level-two trainees, even though we know they're being prepared for a higher-level mission. They all need to see the needs at level two before we move on to tessellating and DMD usage. Follow me, please."

The troupe paraded after Gavreel as she exited the way they'd entered. As the level-one door closed behind them, they gathered next to the second door. "Stay together, please. It's usually very crowded in this section."

Gavreel's hand opened the door, just as Michael's and the others' had at level one. They scooted through the opening, with Uriel and Kirron bringing up the rear. Just like level one, there was a small foyer leading to the main room.

This room also stretched farther than they could see, but the ceiling was much higher than level one. It was so high they couldn't make out what was happening in the cells that covered it. They could see that most were outlined in red.

"There must be twice as many mission needs shown here as level one. The ceiling is so much higher, and every wall displays so many more scenes. There's almost no green or yellow here," Dina remarked.

"That's because many level-one missions escalated and moved here. They need immediate attention, or they'll flash, or go black, causing them to move up to an even higher level."

"What are all those big things in the middle of the room that have so many people looking at them?" Guleed asked.

"That's the control center for this level," Kirron explained. "Those silver uniformed individuals are Principalities. You saw some in level one and will see them in each level's command center. They program DMDs and closet platforms, among many other things. This rank of angels is permanently assigned to data tracking and organizational duty. While they're not warriors, they are crucial in making missions successful. Principalities get data from the Council, organize the data, monitor needs, and track missions. They have command over lower angels and direct the fulfillment of divine orders, meaning they can make changes to original orders if the mission requires a change. Watching over large groups and communicating in ways that other ranks of angels cannot, set the Principalities apart. They're superior communicators. Dina, Jo, and Gabe saw even more Principalities at the Council Edifice, working outside of the actual council chamber."

"So, if we see solid silver uniforms, we know those angels are Principalities and they're like the managers of things that happen everywhere?" Gabe asked.

"Basically, yes. They're in direct communication with the Council at all times and have the latest information about all decisions made by the Council. They keep track of and dispense information to everyone else in every capacity."

"We need to move along," Gavreel announced. "Let's find a seating area big enough for all twelve of us and train Guleed in the tessellation."

The group shuffled over to two smaller seating areas that were side by side. A quick move of a few chairs created an oval of chairs beckoning them to sit.

Uriel spoke again. "Guleed, you've moved with the group quickly from one place to another several times. This is done using the space tessellation. Your teammates have already learned how to use it and assumed the responsibilities that come with this great gift. What we are about to share with you is one of the greatest secrets of the universe, if you're willing to assume the gift and the responsibilities that go with it. Are you willing to do so?"

"Yes, I am," Guleed replied.

Uriel held out his hand and showed Guleed the golden grain he held. "This grain holds all the tessellations of the universe. It holds every location in the heavens. It's the map of the universe that will allow you to use space travel to move anywhere instantly.

This grain updates automatically when new places are built, or old places are destroyed. You don't have to do anything. The Principalities take care of the constant updates once you have accepted the gift. You must understand, Guleed, that this wonderful gift is a great responsibility and is only used in service for God."

Guleed stared at Uriel, not sure what to say.

Gavreel broke the silence. "Guleed, you must willingly make the Oath of Acceptance and abide by it throughout your eternal life. If you break the oath at any time, the grain will be stripped from you. If that happens, you'll be moved to the lowest rank of angels in the lowest level of Heaven. You'll be starting over as a novice and will never again have the opportunity to become a warrior. You've been chosen and fast-tracked to become a warrior, so that would mean you'd forsake the gifts you've received and not fulfill your destiny. Do you fully understand the seriousness and value of this gift of space travel?"

"Yes, I do," Guleed responded.

Uriel asked him, "Are you willing to accept the Grain of Space Tessellations?"

"I am," Guleed announced.

"Very well. Please, stand, Guleed, and put your hands in praying position in front of your chest. You'll hold your hands in that position until I tell you to put them down," Uriel instructed.

Guleed stood with his hands steepled by his chest.

"The four of us will administer the Oath of Acceptance, one line at a time. You must repeat it clearly and exactly as we say it to you. Do you understand?"

"I understand."

Uriel spoke first. "I do solemnly swear, as one of God's chosen angels, that I willingly accept this gift of Space Tessellations."

Guleed repeated the first line. Michael faced the newest trainee and recited the second line. "I solemnly affirm, upon my honor as a warrior angel, that I will use this gift only in service of the greater good for God."

As soon as Guleed finished the second line, Gavreel intoned the third line. "I further swear that I will safeguard the knowledge of tessellations with vigilance, never revealing any information about this gift to anyone, anywhere, ever."

Guleed's perfect recitation of the third line cued Kirron to administer the fourth and final line. "I promise to uphold the traditions, integrity, and high standards set by the angels that came before me whenever using the Space Tessellations, so help me, God."

As soon as Guleed completed his proclamation, Uriel pressed the golden grain between his eyebrows. The four trainers chorused, "In so much as you have spoken the Oath of Acceptance in this company, we now bestow upon you this great gift. Use it wisely and well, remembering always that it is a powerful tool for doing good works and serving God."

His team beamed and applauded as the trainers backed away, placing their own hands in praying position and saying, "You must now touch the spot between your eyebrows where the grain entered your soul with the tips of your fingers, then lower your hands to chest level again. You will tilt your steepled hands down and back up three times to activate the tessellations grain. When you've done this motion, say 'I thank you, God, for this gift and your trust in me as your servant.'"

"Congratulations, Space Traveler Guleed. You may put your hands down now," Uriel told him. "Have a seat with your team."

Gavreel told the group, "The identification code for your home has changed since your team has changed. Your home's identification is WHL6JAMBANGGD."

Everyone but Guleed exclaimed, "Warrior Heaven Level 6 Team JAMBANGGD!"

Gavreel smiled at Guleed's confused expression. "You see, Guleed, you must always know where your home is, so you can return to it when you've space traveled anywhere. You've been in Sector WHL6 since you transitioned, except for the dream visit. It's a vast area, though. You've only seen part of it, so you need to memorize your home's location, so you can always return to a familiar place. The acronyms used to identify locations are all logical. WHL6 stands for Warrior Heaven Level 6 and the rest of the letters in your home's identification is your team's name, the one on your uniform's emblem."

"Right now we're in the training center. The identification for this location is WHL6TCB1."

His teammates chimed, "Warrior Heaven Level 6 Training Center Building 1!"

"We're going to let Guleed check out his space traveling ability now."

Michael stood and pulled Guleed to his feet. "Visualize your home, brush your hand over the spot where the grain was inserted, and raise that arm above your head. That will take us there. If you're traveling with someone else, you must be touching or looking directly at them. Tell me the code for your home."

"WHL6JAMBANGGD."

"Perfect. He put his hand on Guleed's shoulder. Take me there."

As soon as Michael finished his directions, the pair vanished.

"He did it!" his team cheered.

Almost immediately, the pair returned. Guleed's smile announced his opinion of this new ability.

"Excellent!" Michael praised. "How do you feel?"

"Excellent!" Guleed bubbled.

"Let's try one more transfer with just one other person," Kirron suggested, "then we'll have him try to move the group."

"I want you to take me to Warrior Heaven Level 6 Enhanced Agility Training Area 1," Kirron told him. "That's where you learned about enhanced jumps. What do you think the identification code is for Warrior Heaven Level 6 Enhanced Agility Training Area 1?"

"Um, would that be WHL6EATA1?" Guleed offered.

"That's exactly right. You seem to fully understand the acronym system. Let's go." Kirron put his hand on Guleed's shoulder just before they disappeared.

As soon as they reappeared, Kirron declared. "Smooth. Time to try a group transport."

"How about returning to the cordula tree?" Uriel suggested.

"Always a nice place to visit," Gavreel agreed. "Everybody, stand up and make a complete circuit of connectedness. Guleed, visualize the beautiful cordula tree and the code WHL6CTAE."

"What's the AE stand for?" the group asked, snickering that they all asked the same question.

"Alternate Exit. Warrior Heaven Level 6 Cordula Tree Alternate Exit. We told you it wasn't the usual exit from the cockatrice den."

Gigantic blue leaves swirled around their feet as they stood under the magnificent cordula tree. Vibrant leaves waved at them as they stared up.

"How do you feel after moving twelve souls with you?" Gavreel asked him.

"I feel fine. I do not notice anything except excitement when I move on the tessellation. It is exciting."

"Yes, it is exciting," she agreed. "Let's go back to the training center now."

Seated once more, the team waited for the next direction.

"Gabe, I see you still have your team's DMD attached to your bracelet, and Aniela, you have the other one. Please, remove them and bring them to full size so we can explain this device to Guleed."

As soon as the DMDs were enlarged, Gavreel continued. "These are Dynamic Milestoning Devices. You saw some when you arrived at the training center. They hold all records of the space tessellation, travel using the tessellation, and your team's missions. It's the ultimate data storage instrument. It will record everything and give you as much information as possible about your missions. This is the full size. You saw the shrunken size when Gabe and Aniela removed them from their bracelets."

Michael picked up the instruction. "It's easy to use. Any of your hands will open the case because it's programmed with your essences and with ours. The only others who can access your DMD are the programmers, the Principalities we told you about earlier. You must keep the device with you at all times, but it doesn't matter which team member has it."

"Notice that the cases now feature the letters JAMBANGGD rather than the previous DJG or NAMA." Uriel smiled. "Those Principalities are organizational geniuses. They're on top of everything that happens."

The group admired the fancy script letters engraved among the swirls of silver, gold, rose, bronze, black, and copper.

"Aniela, please, show Guleed how to close and shrink the device when it's open," Uriel prompted.

"It's easy. You run your hand over the flat bottom of the device from one side to the other and then back again." As soon as she did that, the domed half snapped closed and concealed the screen. "To shrink it, you tap it three times on the domed side like this." It shrank to the size of a dime. "You put it on your bracelet like this to transport it. It will be so stuck that you won't be able to remove it unless you know the trick."

"What is the trick?" Guleed asked.

"First, try to pull it off my bracelet," she said grinning.

Guleed tried several times. "I am not strong enough. I definitely need to know the trick."

Everyone laughed.

"It won't come off unless one of us does this," Aniela said as she ran her index finger around the edge three times then tapped the top three times. It came off in her hand.

"The device is held in place by a very powerful energy," Gavreel explained. "Hand the device to Micah and let him show Guleed how to bring it up to full size."

Micah tapped the DMD three times. The tiny disc returned to

the size they'd seen earlier. "To open it, you roll your hand over the domed side one way and then back the other way." The domed top rolled away and tucked into the flat bottom side. The black screen was now visible.

"Your turn, Guleed. Take the DMD from Micah. Close it, shrink it, and attach it to your bracelets."

Guleed successfully secured the miniature disc and declared, "I did it."

"Yes, you did. Now remove it, bring it back to full size, and open the dome so you can see the screen."

Guleed beamed as he held up the device for everyone to see.

"Ask the device where your next tessellation destination is, Guleed. The screen will show you a picture of the location and the code. This time you'll be moving the group to a location outside of your home sector, so the code will not begin with WHL6."

Guleed leaned close to the DMD and bellowed, "Show me our next tessellation destination, please."

"You don't have to be that close or speak that loudly," Gavreel told him. "Just stand or sit comfortably and speak normally."

Bursts of bright colors exploded on the screen, their chaos and predictability like massive fireworks overtaking the night sky. Each flash drew a pattern on the screen, unique and breathtaking as they merged their brilliant light and vivacious colors. The fiery sparks swallowed up the black screen, burning with impatience as they rushed to transmit a new message to the team. The blazing splotches, trails, and arcs joined to form a picture of a strange structure. Many interconnected spheres formed a giant steel structure sculpture similar to an atom. One sphere was the center of the structure with massive rods joining other spheres to the central one. Supporting pillars hoisted the spheres in their raised position and held them there. All were made of polished metal, so shiny that they reflected the surrounding sky and landscape. The ground was perfect circles of every imaginable color, overlapping one another like scales. New colors emerged where two or more circles converged. The shimmering reflections on the lower surfaces of the spheres, the connective rods, and pillars were a random patchwork, whimsical and festive. This showcase of colors with no pattern summoned them. The code "HCA" flashed at the top of the screen.

"Oh, the Principalities are treating this team!" Uriel exclaimed. "I haven't been to Heaven's Creativity Atom for a long time."

"I don't think any warriors have," Michael acknowledged. "We've been too busy to linger there."

"We won't be able to linger there during this visit, either," Kirron proclaimed, "but it will be a memorable experience for the group."

"Are you ready to take the group to HCA, Guleed? It's on level one so all angels regardless of rank can go there. That means you'll be taking us out of this sector. It may feel different from earlier travel using the tessellations." Gavreel continued, "Secure the DMD to your bracelet, then visualize the structure you're looking at on the screen and give the code. Everyone, connect so Guleed can escort us to the delightful location the Principalities chose for us."

The group landed near the huge structure they'd seen on the tiny screen. It was overwhelming in size and splendor.

"What is this place?" Nate asked. "It's unapologetically unique and beautiful in an almost indescribable way. It strikes me as both building and art."

Uriel offered, "This structure is Heaven's Creativity Atom. It's a source of pleasure and creativity for angels and humans who are recipients of ideas generated here. It's a place of ideas and experimentation, of serious creation and whimsy."

Jo asked, "Are these circles on the ground like the song containment cubes we saw around the Heavenly Host's Choir Chambers?"

"They're similar, but much more varied than just components for unwritten music and finished songs," Michael replied. "You see, this center has nine different spheres arranged like a crystal's atom.

Each sphere is a workshop where angels can come to work on an idea they had, or just relax by creating something, or by doing something they love doing. Different kinds of creation happen in each sphere."

"Like what?" the trainees chimed.

Uriel could hardly contain his enthusiasm. "The central sphere is the Sphere of Inventions and Discoveries. Many great scientists and inventors linger there working on ideas that have been planted in their minds. They work until they've brought their ideas to reality. The perfected ideas are then delivered to living humans or other species to solve pressing problems. The angels who were great inventors and scientists before they transitioned were fueled this way and now continue their passions here and pass sparks to current scientists and inventors. It's an amazing system of advancing humankind as well as species in other locations of the universe."

"So, da Vinci, Edison, and Alexander Graham Bell come here?" Micah asked.

"Yes, all of them and many others. Benjamin Franklin is one of the most frequent visitors from what I hear," Uriel confirmed.

"Why does Benjamin Franklin come so much? I thought he was a Founding Father of the United States, not a scientist," Ariel murmured.

"Franklin was many things during his earthly life, including statesman, inventor, and scientist. His first documented invention was a pair of swimming fins when he was eleven years old. He also invented the Franklin stove, lightning rods, street lamps, bifocal glasses, the odometer, and the flexible urinary catheter. He's a quite the creator." Kirron continued, "He never made lots of money from his inventions, though, because he never patented any of them. He once said, 'We should be glad of an opportunity to serve others by any invention of ours; and this we should do freely and generously.' He still practices that by sending new ideas to Earth regularly."

"Inventions and Discoveries is in the center sphere, what happens in the other spheres?" Dina asked.

"The other eight cover creativity in the areas of Visual Arts, Writing, Motion and Dance, Theater, Fiber Creation, Puzzles, Magic, and, lastly, Humor and Pranks," Uriel informed them.

"There's a sphere for Magic and another one for Humor and Pranks?" Gabe asked.

"Yes, God loves illusions and has quite a sense of humor. He instills those gifts in some. Laughter is one way of spreading love."

"I wish we had time to visit every sphere, but we do not. We can go inside one, if everyone would like to do so, but only one. Then we must get back to business." Uriel smiled. "How are we going to decide which one to visit?" "We could take a vote," Aniela suggested. "I know which one I'd vote for if we only get to visit one of them."

"Is a vote acceptable to everyone? The sphere with the most votes is the one we go into for a short visit?" Gavreel asked.

Head bobs confirmed their agreement.

"Very well. Aniela, what's your nomination? Which sphere do you want to visit?"

"The Motion and Dance Sphere would be a good choice for all of us," she announced. "All of us love enhanced speed and agility, and everybody on this team except me was athletic before transitioning. I wasn't athletic the last few years of my life because of being in the wheelchair, but I was a good dancer when I was younger. I think Motion and Dance would be the one that would interest the whole team, not just a few people."

"Are there any other nominations, or should we accept Aniela's suggestion unanimously?" Gavreel asked.

"Motion and Dance," sounded from the team, followed by a snicker.

"Follow me to the entrance for the Motion and Dance Sphere," Gavreel directed. "When we go inside, please, stay together and be silent. We don't want to distract any of any dancers or athletes who are practicing moves there. I'll motion you when we must depart."

The ensemble flocked after Gavreel, gracefully swarming in the direction she led, trusting her to lead them to the correct place. She put her finger to her lips as a reminder to remain silent as they stepped through the door she opened.

They entered the bottom of the support pillars and saw a spiral staircase winding upward. Like geese in migration formation, they followed Gavreel to the top. She pressed her hand on another door, swinging it open for them. They entered an observation deck, about halfway up the height of the sphere. There was a stellar view of the entire space.

The sphere thumped with activity. It was organized chaos, like being at a fair. Crowds milled around the many activities that were happening in every open space. One group on a raised platform gyrated in smooth moves as they perfected a street dance routine. On another raised platform, ballet dancers capered through spins and leaps. Before them stood several raised stages, each one featuring a different style of dance. Aerialists swung on trapezes and walked on raised wires. Gymnasts balanced and flipped in ways none of them had ever seen. A number of people climbed a rock wall at the far side of the sphere then bungee jumped from a platform at the top of the wall. An obstacle course challenged all who tested themselves. This sphere was a testament to the innate desire to move.

Gavreel motioned the spellbound trainees to follow her as she led them out the door they'd entered and down the staircase they'd just climbed.

Comments bubbled from everyone when they made it back outside. The visit had delighted all.

"Guleed, do you remember the code for the training center? We must get back there and resume training," Kirron asserted.

"WHL6TCB1," Guleed replied as he placed his hand on Kirron's shoulder.

When they returned, the teens still chattered about their favorite dance routine or other activity they'd watched during their short visit to the Atom.

"We knew you'd like that place," Uriel said. "Guleed, how do you feel after your second transport from one sector to another?"

"I feel like I always feel," he crowed. "I like everyone and everything here. I am so happy."

"We're all glad about that and delighted that using the tessellation has no ill effects on you. It's yet another way you're like your teammates. Not one person on this team has had ill effects from space travel. We're now going to move to our next section of training," Uriel told them. "It will be vital on the mission we've been assigned. Are you ready to communicate telepathically?"

TELEPATHY

All eyes locked onto Uriel as he continued speaking.

"All of you have received telepathic messages from us. Remember when you learned metamorphosis? Your trainer stayed with you and sent the mental command to change forms. You were able to hear the messages we sent. That was telepathy."

Michael pointed out, "Telepathy is a gift we all possess. Telepathic communication is much more natural than one might think. God gave humans this ability to connect with the consciousness of others, and it has been passed down from ancient times."

"That's right," Kirron concurred. "Telepathy is really another sense, one that's been allowed to go dormant in many humans. The ability is within everyone, though. When we align our consciousness with the grid of another's consciousness, we're able to communicate telepathically, using no other senses."

Gavreel added, "Another way of thinking about telepathy is to think about what's inside you as vibrating energy. You have many frequencies. Everyone does. When we're able to align our frequency with the vibrations of another, we can communicate telepathically. We no longer need to use other senses because we have direct connection into one another's minds. Twins are particularly good at using telepathy with one another. Because they formed together in their mother's womb, they're born with the same frequencies. As they get older, twins often know when their twin is in trouble or is worried. Some couples also develop telepathic communication with their partner, especially if they're soulmates. They know what the other is thinking and can finish one another's sentences. It's more than just practiced familiarity."

"Young people are better able to embrace their telepathic abilities because they trust their guts. They don't try to explain why they think a certain way, they just trust their instincts when they get strong feelings about something. This lets them connect with the frequencies of others." Uriel took a breath. "Also, telepathy often happens during dreams. It's often how important messages are sent to those who need them. Sometimes the dreamer will remember everything, especially if it's a dream visit from someone they've known and loved, but sometimes they'll just wake up with an idea or a feeling about something."

"So, were we using telepathy when we visited Bilan?" Guleed asked.

"Yes, that's why you had to be physically attached to me and Jo to Michael as we moved through her brain. We were using telepathy with Bilan to map our route to reach her cortex. You hadn't yet mastered telepathic communication, so we extended our abilities to you. Sleep is a time when brain waves are at a frequency that allows data to flow in and be processed so it is an excellent portal for telepathic communication."

"Sometimes you'll hear the thoughts of someone with whom you've connected, but other times you'll just know what they're thinking. Telepathy and empathy are closely intertwined. Empathy is the ability to completely understand the feelings of another and relate to them, whereas telepathy focuses on actual thoughts. Both use frequencies that are aligned." Michael grinned. "All of you look like we're about to ask you to run naked through this training center."

Nervous laughter filled the air. "You aren't going to send us a message like that, are you?" Aniela worried.

"Of course not," he chortled as his fellow trainers tried to contain their laughter.

"We are going to have you try some techniques that have helped many improve telepathic abilities. Some people improve quickly, and others need more time and practice. Remember, though, this is a gift that's already inside everyone," Uriel remarked. "Are you ready to try the first technique?"

"If everyone's comfortable in the place you're seated, we're ready to begin. First, you'll be learning to meditate. I don't mean sitting cross-legged and chanting 'Om.' I mean training your mind to focus. You're going to focus on God and the gifts that have been bestowed upon you. Telepathy is one of those gifts. Close your eyes and focus on God and telepathy. If your mind starts to wander, refocus. Repeat mentally, 'Glorious God, thank you for the gifts you have given me. Help me now retrieve the gift of telepathy from within my essence.' Say it over and over until a thought from me enters your thoughts, then tell me the message." Uriel waited while the trainees meditated.

Jo spoke first, "You said that some people are better telepathic senders, and some are better telepathic receivers."

"That's right!" Uriel praised. "Now send me a message mentally, Jo. Say it over and over in your mind while you visualize me, the person to whom you're sending the message. By visualizing me when you repeat your message, you'll be aligning our frequencies."

"I think you're great!" Micah blurted.

Everyone stared at him.

"Sorry. I just heard Jo sending that message. Isn't that right, Jo?"

"It is, but I wasn't visualizing you, Micah. I was visualizing Uriel. How did he get the message instead of you, Uriel?"

"It wasn't instead of me. I heard it, too. It was in addition to me. You and Micah are already using the same frequency, probably more often than you realize."

"Let's keep going. Everybody, repeat the Glorious God mantra and focus on my new message. Raise your hand when you think you know the message I'm sending telepathically."

Jo, Micah, Aniela, and Dina raised their hands and waited. No other hands went up, so Uriel asked, "All of you who think you got my message, what did I say?"

In unison the four declared, "When it comes to telepathy, practice makes perfect."

"Exactly!" he announced. "Dina, will you send a message now? Visualize whomever you want, or more than one if you want to try multiple recipients. We'll see if your sending skills are as sharp as your receiving ones seem to be."

Dina closed her eyes and began repeating her message.

Jo and Gabe instantly spoke. "Humans can communicate telepathically if they're on the same wavelength and love one another."

The three smiled at one another, realizing again how connected they'd become.

"I heard that, too," Gavreel said. "Were you sending it to me, too, or just Jo and Gabe?"

"I sent it to you, too," Dina said smiling.

"Michael, will you send a group message this time? Again, raise your hand if you hear Michael's message."

This time, eight young hands waved almost immediately.

"Really, all eight of you got Michael's message that fast?" Uriel inquired. "What did he say?"

The group chimed, "Time to take a naked lap around the training center!"

Uproarious laughter shook trainees and trainers, causing nearby groups to stare, trying to figure out what was so funny. Bruno stood on his hind legs and cocked his head repeatedly.

"Daddy, you're so bad! You know we're angels and wouldn't do such a thing!"

"Part of what makes it a funny joke. That and the fact that nobody's near their closet platforms," he chortled, still pleased with his ability to make everyone laugh.

"Everyone's advancing with this skill, but we need to practice more. Let's break off in pairs and try sending and receiving messages. Each individual trainee will be paired with every other individual trainee at some time during this exercise. The four of us will observe your communication skills with each member of your team. It will be vital that you can communicate effectively with everyone. Girls, pull your chairs in a row along here, and boys, line up your chairs facing them. Everyone will move to new partners when told. To start, face the person directly across from you and focus on them. Girls, you send the first messages and guys, you try to hear them. Raise your hands when you think you received the message that was sent to you."

One after the other, hands went up.

"Okay, Micah, what was Jo's message?"

"My dad thinks he's so funny!"

"That's right," Jo affirmed.

"And also correct," Michael added with a grin and a wink.

"Gabe, what was Aniela's message?"

"I wish I could've joined that street dance group at the Atom."

Aniela beamed. "Yes! And I do, too."

"Nate, what message did Dina send to you?"

"I'd like to watch you create something in your studio."

"You got it," Dina confirmed.

"Guleed, what did you hear Ariel say in your mind?"

"She said she would do whatever she could to help my sisters."

"That's right, Guleed. I'll try to help Bilan and Fatima when we go on our mission."

"This is going splendidly," Uriel praised. "Now, we'll have the males send a message to the same partner to test the reciprocal responsiveness. Guys, visualize your partner and repeat your message to them mentally."

Jo blushed as she raised her hand, sooner than the other girls. Shortly, all female hands shot in the air. Their messages were voiced and confirmed. The boys moved one seat and faced a new female teammate. Again, the messages were sent and received accurately.

They changed partners several more times until each teammate had successfully exchanged thoughts with every other teammate. They practiced group messages successfully next, amazing their trainers with the speed at which the entire team could telepathically communicate.

"One more test before we declare full mastery of telepathy," Kirron told them. "Dina, Jo, Nate, and Micah, stand up and connect with me. We're going to tessellate to several locations, starting with your home. I'll send a message to the other trainers when we're ready to receive a message. You'll need to tell me who sent the message and what the message is when you get it. I'll verify if you're correct and tell one of you a message to send before we move to a new location. I'll be in constant telepathic contact with the other trainers to determine accuracy before proceeding. Dina, please, move us to your home."

As soon as the five disappeared, Gavreel said, "Aniela, please, send the group this message: 'If you stumble, make it part of the dance'."

Gavreel beamed. "Message received by all! Listen to the response Nate sent:

'Dance is art in motion.'"

Kirron's group transported to the training grounds and received the message, "I choose to be unstoppable!"

Micah responded, "This is very true. We're an unstoppable team!"

When they moved to an unknown location, they all heard, "You are more than who you were." Their final stop was the steps of an ornate building. Their message was, "God has a purpose. Believe and trust."

The traveling group reunited with the rest of the team at the training center, excitedly chattering about the messages they'd sent and received from far away.

"Before we move to the final level-two training section, I need to stress something to all of you," Uriel broke in. "Please, listen and heed what I'm going to say."

The group quieted and turned their full attention to Uriel.

"Telepathy is a gift from God and must be honored as such. Using mental communication is not a game. It must be used sparingly, only when necessary. It's not meant to replace other communication. It's a tool for missions and training, just as the other divine gifts you've received. There are some who feel telepathy is a tool of the evil one, the one we all serve to defeat. It's not. It's a gift from God to be used for good, but there are evil entities who have honed the skill and use it for dark reasons. Like other powers, telepathy can be misused. Always use it only to serve God. Is that clear?"

Somber nods answered his question.

"Very well. Examine these Thought Transference tokens and they'll be added to your growing collections. He passed out charms that looked like the top view of two whirlwinds overlapping one another. Where the circular spirals intersected looked surprisingly like staring eyes connected, yet separate. The shiny silver whirlwinds were mounted on a bright blue oval. The back was engraved:

"God is able to do exceedingly abundantly above all that we ask or think."

The Bible: Ephesians 3:20

"In spiritual communication, mental telepathy is the beginners' course."

Guru Sri Chinmoy

CHOOSING GIFTS

"The next step of your training journey may be confusing, or it may delightful," Kirron told the group. "Many trainees never receive a Choosing Gift, but if they do, it's not until the conclusion of level-four training. This team is so fast-tracked and the mission so intense and important that we've been directed to take you there now."

"What's a Choosing Gift?" Nate asked.

Gavreel spoke softly. "It's another divine gift, but not every team member will receive the same gift. When we enter the Armory, one of us will be paired with two of you until everyone is inside. We'll wander the aisles together until your first battle weapon chooses you."

"What does that mean? How can a weapon choose a warrior?" Gabe asked.

"It's part of the gift. The weapon has been waiting for the right warrior to come. There'll be an instantaneous connection with your essence that makes its power and effectiveness multiply."

"How will we know when something chooses us?" Aniela asked.

"It will be obvious," Uriel assured her. "Sometimes weapons glow when the right warrior is close, then fade if they move away. Sometimes they flash. Some actually wrap around the warrior's hand or arm. It depends on the weapon."

"As soon as all of you have your gift, we'll begin training you on their proper use, as well as defensive moves you may need in battle," Michael declared.

"Everybody, stand up and connect for transport to the Armory," Kirron directed.

They found themselves standing by the far edge of the Council Edifice's stairs. Another massive structure loomed to the side.

"The Armory is next to the Council Edifice," Uriel announced. "Follow me. We'll break into groups of three and stagger our entrance."

As they gathered at the door, Gavreel spoke. "As you go in, you'll think you've entered something quite strange. There are lengths of silk fabric hanging from the ceiling. As we walk through, the fabric will jostle around each of us. It's similar to how hanging cloth strips in a soft carwash surround the vehicle and glide over it. The silk is extremely sensitive and will transmit information to the displays about who's entering. It will be quite pleasant, but I thought you should be prepared."

"I don't know what this soft carwash is that you're talking about, but I don't want cloth surrounding me and doing whatever it does. You make it sound like snakes slithering all over us. Why do we have to go through that?" Guleed asked.

The others looked away, trying to contain their snickers as Gavreel searched for her response.

"The silk caress is part of the choosing process, Guleed. It's nothing like snakes crawling on you. The cloth is very soft and perceptive. By interacting with you before you see anything displayed, it helps send sensory data to the many items that are stored in the armory. It cuts down the selection time quite a bit."

"Have we misled you about anything so far, Guleed?" Michael asked.

"No, but I do not like slithery things. I do not want anything slithering on me."

"It won't be like slithery things. You've liked every other gift, so you're going to have to trust us that this will be fine. We need to get going." Michael patted him on the back to end the conversation.

Staggered groups of three stepped through the armory doors and were surrounded by a riot of colors. Vivid silks hung from the ceiling. They draped and twisted together loosely to form an alluring entry arbor. The smooth and delicious fabric formed a ubiquitous yet unique sculpture that arched high above their heads. It ushered them forward into a sea of waving silk strands. Like sails without boats, lengths of silk flapped gently, bidding welcome to all. Carefree and joyful, each streamer billowed and recoiled, creating a spectacular and ever-changing mosaic.

Pastels, bright colors, and patterned cloths waved and stretched, caressing each soul who entered.

"This is breathtaking," Dina marveled. "It's like being inside a kaleidoscope, surrounded by the shifting colors. It's textile art magic."

"Yes, it's quite remarkable," Uriel agreed. "Incredibly beautiful and supremely efficient. We're almost through the silky sensors."

The trainees and trainers reunited as the final three stepped from the silk web. Kirron announced, "We're going to wander through the aisles of displays now. Be watchful. The gifts that have chosen you will give an undeniable sign. Don't be frightened by anything that happens. Nothing in here will hurt any of us. We'll explain what each gift is and how it's used when it has joined our team."

They'd only advanced a few steps when a pile of shiny pea-sized pebbles and flat disks flashed. They ignited in blinding flames, engulfing Aniela. She calmly extended her hand. The flames extinguished immediately, but a smoky swirl spun around her arm, a leather pouch, and a sizable mound of the glistening bits.

"We have the first choosing gift! Aniela's gift is a set of mirror disks and balls. They are tiny, but powerful. When thrown individually or in small numbers, they flash, spewing blinding radiance from within. If more than ten are hurled simultaneously, they seem to ignite and generate heat, but the flames are an optical and tactile illusion. They're not really setting anything on fire, but enemies don't know that. Their effect in battle is impressive. They have a magnetic connection to the warrior they choose. They'll return to

Aniela after they're thrown, and their radiant power's been dispensed. They recharge a short time after they return to their angel warrior. This gift will be welcome on many missions, Aniela. Scoop that pile into the pouch and bring it with you as we walk around to find the others' gifts," Gavreel directed.

Near the end of the row, a pair of flying objects zipped around the group, flew away, returned, and clattered on the floor between Micah's and Gabe's feet.

"Pick up your gifts," Kirron told them. "Both of you've been chosen by Valari. It will be interesting using two of them on missions, but I believe we may train using them simultaneously. They're similar to boomerangs. Their aerodynamic structure enables their return to the thrower. Notice that they're made with two limbs at angles, one that's thin and tapered and the other that's rounded. The rounded limb is the handle. The tapered limb is sharp. The thrower can throw it straight or spin it vertically or horizontally. It's lethal if it's spun and hits the neck of the enemy. I suspect your baseball pitching prowess will make this easy for you to use, Micah, and your superb coordination should make it easy for you to master, too, Gabe."

"Dina, did you notice this object's spin when you walked near it?" Michael asked. "I saw it spinning as you strolled past, but I wasn't quite up to it yet. Walk back and let's see if it spins again."

"I thought so," Michael said. "This Maduva, or Madu, has chosen you, Dina. See it still spinning slowly as you stand near it? Your Madu is made of two blackbuck horns pointing in opposite directions. It's a double-bladed dagger and is used in close combat when someone is attacking with a long sword or other handheld weapon. It's primarily a defensive weapon. This one is very ornate with images carved into the blades. It's extremely sharp, too. You hold it by this middle section." Michael handed her the weapon.

As they strolled, a distinctive drumming sound began. It was just a percussive tiptoe when they first noticed it, but the beat and volume intensified as they rounded a corner. Three baseball-size metal weights pounded the table rhythmically, steady and loud like rolling thunder. Jo tapped softly on the table edge, matching the beat of the reverberating sound. A long leather thong wrapped around Jo's arm. When she stopped drumming, the polished balls fell silent, too.

"It appears this bola has chosen you, Jo," Michael announced. "I've never heard one make a musical signal of choosing, but this bola must really understand your essence. Bolas are usually thrown to entangle legs, so their target falls or gets distracted. The weights are light enough to throw easily, but heavy enough to hurt when they hit or wrap their tether lines around their target. This is the part you hold when twirling and throwing."

The group hadn't moved far when three shifting light rays caught their eyes. The light beams settled on Guleed's hands and chest.

Uriel stepped forward. "Guleed, this Kpinga has reflected its light and power on your hands and heart. Kpingas are powerful long-range weapons. They were carried by Azante warriors in central Africa. It's a three-bladed throwing knife. All of the blades are different shapes and sizes, and each one is projected at a different angle to maximize damage. This weapon will require special training. Handle it carefully."

They wandered up and down several walkways with no obvious signals that weapons had chosen Nate or Ariel. Many whips hung on the wall. Most were wound tightly, but a few hung down, showcasing the length or material of the whip. None seemed do anything except hang there, though. A subtle hissing caused them to loiter near the wall of whips. As they stood still, the sound grew louder.

A golden whip freed itself from its hanger and slid down the wall. It slithered to Nate and thrust its handle into his hand.

"That's a Serpent Spine Whip," Kirron informed him. "They're very rare. Notice the elongated, forked spear tip on one end and the serpent head at the opposite end. The chain links that form the whip itself flow from the serpent's mouth, like a very long tongue. As a matter of fact, the length of the whip can be as long or short as it needs to be. The serpent head recoils or extends links in synch with the wielder's vision of the target. It's impressive when handled correctly."

"It's beautiful, in a weird snake-weapon kind of way," Nate remarked. "I've never seen anything like it."

"It's quite artistically designed," Kirron agreed, "both in appearance and function. Snap it out in this open lane and it should retract for easier carrying."

They approached their starting point, having made a full trip around the armory.

"We must have missed a signal," Gavreel declared. "Sorry, Ariel, I guess we need to loop around again."

Gavreel had no sooner spoken than two silk streamers, one red and one gold, fluttered loose and wrapped around Ariel. At the end of each piece of fabric was a flat gold piece that had attached to a matching piece still mounted on the ceiling.

Uriel stammered, "I've heard of this, but I've never witnessed it before. Have any of you?"

Gavreel, Kirron, and Michael marveled, "Absolutely not."

"You guys are freaking me out," Ariel confessed. "Why am I wrapped up like a mummy in red and gold silk? What kind of weapon is silk?"

Uriel finally spoke. "The silk itself isn't the weapon. You've been chosen for a very rare and utterly important task, Ariel. In the many eons I have served, I've never witnessed it before. I did hear about it once several centuries ago, but you'll bring it to life again."

"Still freaking out," Ariel muttered. "Bring what to life?"

"One of God's rarest creations," Uriel told her. "It's been dormant until the right person came. It's chosen you and this team."

"I still have no idea what you're talking about," she blurted.

"I often feel that way," Guleed told her. "They sometimes say funny things."

Gavreel smiled. "Ariel, look at the shape of the gold pieces on the ends of the cloth hanging over each of your shoulders. What do you see?"

She pulled the cloth far enough from her body to be able to look at the metal closely. "It's an intricately carved bird. It looks sort of like an eagle, but it has many longer feathers like a quetzal or bird of paradise. What is it?"

In unison, the four trainers declared, "It's a phoenix! You've been chosen to be the keeper of the next phoenix!"

"You're kidding, right? I thought they were just mythological birds."

"We're not kidding," Gavreel assured her. "Take the two gold birds and press them together with both of your hands over your heart."

"The metal is getting warm in my hands! I feel a vibration, too. What's happening?"

"The phoenix is awakening," Uriel told her. "Keep your hands around the two pieces until it bursts from your hands."

Ariel stood motionless. Sensing the transition was near she declared, "My hands and heart have brought warmth back to your body. Come forth now, my feathered friend. Join your team."

In a fiery burst, wings of red and gold flapped above the onlookers' heads. The silk that had encased Ariel transformed into glowing feathers. The magnificent bird circled the group once and descended, coming close to Ariel before ascending once more. Its blazing body changed course and circled the armory near the ceiling, carefully avoiding the silk sea where it had once rested. Arcing with outstretched wings, the phoenix delighted in its rhythmic flight. Each feather shone as brilliantly as stained glass as the fire within burned with pent up frenzy. After several laps around the ceiling, the flames extinguished and the bird dove toward the group. It landed lightly on Ariel's shoulder. Its brilliant red and gold plumage accented sapphire eyes that stared intently at her.

"What am I supposed to do now?" Ariel asked the elders.

"Well, you're supposed to discover the name of the phoenix. Using telepathy, try asking the bird," Kirron said. "Many creatures cannot speak, but they do understand many words. If you ask, it may be able to send you a mental message."

"I'll try," Ariel declared. She stared into the pools of blue that had not dropped their gaze.

"Sage," Ariel relayed tentatively.

"That's a perfect name," Uriel bubbled. "It makes perfect sense. Sage is both a culinary and medicinal herb. Burning sage is an ancient spiritual ritual, sometimes called smudging. Sage also means wise through experience and reflection. Since a phoenix is reborn from its ashes when it dies, it's had many experiences and time for reflection. Yes, Sage is fine name for the creature."

"Is your name Sage?" Ariel whispered.

The phoenix rubbed its head against Ariel's cheek.

"Your connection to the bird is already strong," Kirron observed. "That will be very helpful during training."

"The bird is a female. She's very lightweight," Ariel told the others. "I'd think she'd be heavy as big as she is, but she isn't."

"She's beautiful," her teammates chimed.

"What do I do with her when we're not training or on missions?"

"She'll want to be close to you. She'll likely bond with your teammates, too, which we encourage, but her connection to you will be strongest. She'll live in your quarters with you, as Bruno lives with Gabe. Like the other creatures here, she won't need to void so you don't have to worry about messes."

"Does she need to eat?"

"Need? No. Want? Probably. Eating is a pleasurable activity for most creatures. She's been dormant for a very long time, so she will likely want to eat when you return to your home. I'm certain she'll want water to quench that parched feeling that comes from her fire within." Uriel gazed at the beautiful bird as he spoke.

"We're finished here," Kirron announced. "We need to move to the training grounds to develop your skills with these gifts. Please, connect, and I'll take the group there. Ariel, you should probably hold Sage as we move through the tessellation. I don't know if she's ever had the experience before, so make sure she doesn't get loose in transport."

CHOOSING TRAINING

The team scanned an area they'd never seen before. The training ground was a vast expanse, grassy and flat as far as they could see. Far to the right, several targets were set up. They could barely make out the bullseye because of the distance. Far to the left, they viewed what looked like a grotesque collection of figures of all different sizes and shapes.

"Where are we?" Jo asked.

Michael replied, "This is a level-five training ground. Remember that Kirron told you that many warriors do not receive Choosing Gifts, but if they do, it's at the end of level-four training? This area is known as WHL5CGPG."

"Let me guess," Jo speculated, "Warrior Heaven Level Five Choosing Gifts Practice Grounds."

Gavreel winked. "I do believe you have this acronym system down, Jo."

Michael commented, "Before we break into small groups to practice with your gifts, we want to demonstrate some basic defensive maneuvers and have you practice those until we feel you're prepared to go into battle. You haven't been issued swords yet. Usually, that doesn't happen until level five, but you can use defensive blocks, jabs, and kicks. These are particularly effective when you're invisible and your opponent has no idea what just hit him."

"Like with the gargoyles and bugbear on our first mission," Dina remarked.

"Yes, but we want to show you how to improve your stances and power of your jabs and kicks. With a bit of practice, your offensive and defensive moves will be strengthened. Bruno, sit, stay!" Gavreel commanded.

He immediately sat, his gaze fixed on her.

The four trainers each took two teens and practiced martial arts style moves. It wasn't long before all teammates were proficient at powerful strikes with their hands and feet.

"We're going to send you to different sections to become proficient with your gifts now," Uriel told them. "Micah, Gabe, and Guleed are going with me to the target area. You'll practice throwing your Kpinga at the target, Guleed, trying to hit the smallest circle in the middle. Gabe and Micah, you'll throw your Valaris at different targets, first using straight throws with no spins. You, too, will try to hit the bullseye and have your gift return to you. If you catch it, it must be by the rounded end, not the sharp tapered end. I'll demonstrate both weapons when we get there." The four of them trotted near the targets.

"Dina, your Madu is a close combat weapon so we'll stay where we are, and I'll work with you on defensive use if someone is attacking. I'll show you how to fend off swords and several other long-range weapons," Gavreel told her.

Kirron announced, "I'll take Aniela and Nate into the wide-open area past the targets and statuary army. Aniela, you'll practice throwing one disk or pebble at a time and calling it back, then move to multiples thrown at the same time. Nate, I'll have you practice cracking your whip in different directions and recoiling it, then have you try to hit objects I throw. If that goes quickly, we'll see if you can hit any of Aniela's disks. That should be interesting."

"Which means, Jo and Ariel are going to the monument army to practice throwing the bola and toppling the statues. Ariel will practice sending Sage away and calling her back on command. When those tasks are accomplished, we may see if Sage can take some of Aniela's disks and pebbles and drop them over the sculptures. That, too, should be interesting to observe." Michael smiled at the girls. "Are you ready?"

The group spread out to their designated areas. A buzz of intense voices underscored the seriousness of their instruction. Before long,

Uriel's voice boomed,

"That's the third consecutive bullseye, Guleed! Your quick mastery of the Kpinga is impressive. We'll move to the statuary army next. Back up a little further and try some more throws until then."

Gavreel had Dina crouching and thrusting her Madu at holographic images. Gavreel controlled the holographs with her hands and sent them at Dina from all different directions. "You're very accurate, Dina. I knew you had excellent eye-hand coordination because of your artistic ability, but I believe you could defend yourself against any and all attackers with the Madu that chose you."

"Thanks, Gavreel. The Madu seems to be in charge of my hand, not the other way around. It seems to be protecting me with its power. Is that possible?"

"All things are possible."

Laughter rang out from the far end, beyond the target area. Gavreel and Dina turned their attention toward the sound and saw Kirron jumping up and down. His excitement was undeniable. "Another first!" he cried. "Everybody, come over here and see this. You have to see it to believe it!"

The group gathered near Kirron. "Aniela and Nate, do it again. Show them what you're able to do together."

Aniela's and Nate's grins prefaced their actions. Aniela tossed one mirror disk in the air. Nate snapped his serpent spine whip and struck the disk. Sheet lightning illuminated the sky as the disk rained down in many perfect pieces. They repeated the maneuver, but this time Aniela sent a mirrored pebble soaring. As Nate's whip struck the bead, forked lightning streaked above them and dozens of perfect pebbles hailed down. Aniela held out her hands. New disks filled one hand and new pebbles filled the other.

"Together, they made new mirror disks and pebbles! Nate's accuracy at striking the flying disk or bead with the golden whip actually produces more. We can go into battle with unlimited flash bangs and fire!"

"I've never even heard of this before!" Uriel exclaimed. "God has bestowed limitless light power, trusting these two to use it wisely."

"That was cool," Gabe cried. "What happens if your whip hits more than one at the same time? Have you tried to strike several of them at once? Or have you thrown them with a spin rather than straight, Aniela? I wonder if something different happens with different motions."

Everyone stared at Gabe.

"What? I just know when I change my moves, different things happen. I thought it might be the same with these new weapons."

"I believe we should look at the possibilities," Kirron responded. "Aniela, try taking one disk and flipping it up, like you would if you were flipping a coin. We'll observe what happens when the whip strikes the somersaulting disk."

Aniela's first attempt at flipping a disk did not go high enough for the whip to reach it. The expected brilliant flash happened, but nothing else.

"Try it again, Aniela. If you can launch a bit higher, the whip may be able to reach the flipping disk."

Her second flipping went significantly higher and further from the group. As the forked end of the whip struck, waves of pure energy rippled from the disk. Like heat shimmers, the energy was visible to everyone. It spiraled around Aniela, wrapping her in iridescent waves of energy.

"What's happening?" Aniela squeaked.

"You've just been infused with energy waves, Aniela. You have great power within you now. This is so rare, I've never worked with one who received energy waves," Kirron marveled.

"What do these energy waves do?"

"The energy can do many things," Michael explained. "Your mind and body will work together to send energy through any kind of matter. With concentration and practice, you'll be able to send forth waves, spirals, rings, pulses, or bursts of energy.

The energy from you will be able to damage, destroy, push, paralyze, bind, or heal. It can be extremely harmful or incredibly helpful."

"Perhaps we should have Aniela test her energy on some of the demon and creature figures," Gavreel suggested. "She can try sending different forms of the energy so we can all see what happens."

"Excellent idea. Let's move nearer the statues and see if Aniela can send different forms of energy to those objects. Are you ready to practice?" Kirron asked.

"I guess so," Aniela told him. "I don't really know what to do, though."

"We'll give you suggestions," he reassured her, "but none of us have ever been with an angel infused with energy waves, let alone trained one. We'll have to work through this together, learning as we go."

The group had just moved near the edge of the stone army when Kirron directed, "Try focusing on that gargoyle right there and make a pushing motion toward it with both of your hands."

As soon as Aniela gestured, the gargoyle statue toppled over in a flash of brilliant light, shattering into hundreds of tiny pieces.

Her teammates and trainers gasped.

Kirron announced, "Now we know that a straight pushing motion sends out waves that can knock over a heavy object and pulverize it. This time, focus on the gargoyle statue that was behind that first one and point the index finger of one hand toward the statue. Make poking gestures over and over as you concentrate on your target."

Blips of energy like sparks pulsed from Aniela's finger as she stared at the second gargoyle. The stream of pulsed energy superheated the statue. It glowed red hot then melted into a puddle.

"So, straight pushing motions topples heavy objects and destroys them, and poking motions results in super-heating and melting.

This time, try making a circular motion with your index finger. You choose the statue to focus on and don't tell us. We'll watch the field and see if we can figure out your target."

Aniela stared straight ahead while making repeated clockwise circles with her finger. A funnel of energy surrounded a gigantic tusked mammoth. It rose higher and higher as Aniela continued making circles in the air.

"Stop gesturing now. We need to observe what happens when you stop sending the spirals of energy."

The mammoth tumbled to the ground, knocking over several other statues when it crashed. The surrounding area looked like a bomb had been dropped on it.

"Aniela's circling gesture causes an object to levitate until she stops sending the energy. A heavy object like that mammoth becomes a bomb." Michael shook his head. "This gift is hard to fathom."

"Let's test bursts of energy next, Aniela," Gavreel suggested. "This time, focus on the debris of the first gargoyle while you repeatedly make flicking motions toward it with both hands like this." Gavreel's hands snapped as if she was flicking water at someone.

As Aniela flicked her hands, energy bursts sprayed from her fingertips. Some streams were straight, while others were zigzags, and still others resembled stretched-out spirals. As they converged on the debris pile, the tiny shards and pebbles arranged and rearranged themselves until the reassembled gargoyle statue stared at them.

"Amazing," Uriel blurted.

"You can bind and heal as well as destroy with your energy, Aniela. Do it again, but this time with the melted gargoyle."

Aniela's energy flicks soon made the assemblage feel like they were watching a movie in reverse. The molten remains of the gargoyle streamed upward until the gargoyle was back intact.

Without being told, Aniela turned her flicking motion on the crumbled mammoth and piles of wreckage that surrounded it.

Chunks of debris rose and dived, floated and tumbled until the mammoth and its statue neighbors once more filled their spaces.

Aniela beamed. "That was the best puzzle I ever put together! I like assembling things with this energy."

The others gawked at her, too stunned to say anything until she asked, "So what now?"

Uriel reasoned, "I think you should try to make rings of energy and see what that does. Any ideas on how Aniela might send rings?"

Dina suggested, "She could try curling her fingers, so they touch her thumb and make an O, like when you pretend that you're looking through a telescope." She demonstrated the position. "Maybe if she pumps one or both of her hands in that position, energy will exit her through the O and make rings."

"I'll try it." Aniela turned her attention back to the gargoyle statue she'd just restored. Perfectly round rings oozed from her hand. Coin-sized as they left her, each ring shimmered and expanded as they approached the target. One loop after another piled around the statue, encasing it with energy hoops. She stopped pumping her hand when the gargoyle was completely shrouded from view.

"I wonder if she can remove the rings by reversing her pumping motion," Michael murmured.

"And what happens to the rings if they do come off," Kirron added.

"There's only one way to find out," Aniela asserted, clearly emboldened by using the gift. She formed the O with her fingers and reversed the pumping action. One by one, the bands lifted from the statue and headed back to Aniela. The rings shrunk en route and disappeared into her gesturing hand.

"So now we know." She grinned.

Gabe asserted, "See what flipping the disk did? It gave Aniela all this infused energy, and now she can do all of these amazing things. I think Nate should see if he can hit more than one of the disks or pebbles at the same time. Who knows what will happen if he does?"

"Gabe's right," Kirron agreed. "We need to assess what happens if there are multiple strikes with one whip crack. Let's move back to the wide-open area and see if Nate can hit more than one with the serpent chain."

Aniela flung ten mirrored disks. Nate's snap of the golden whip hit one disk. It burst into flames in midair. The others fell to the ground and blazed on impact. Flames roared over a wide section of the field. As quickly as it started, the blaze went out. There was no damage.

"That fire is like the one at the training grounds when we were learning how to stop enhanced running," Dina observed. "It's a fire simulation, but it doesn't do damage."

Kirron grinned. "The effect on enemies is powerful, though."

"It was powerful on me, too, as I recall." Dina grinned back.

"Keep trying to hit more than one, Nate," Uriel called. "It may take a few attempts, but I'm sure you'll accomplish it with practice."

The field blazed with several more simulated fires as the whip missed its mark or struck only one.

"Maybe Aniela should throw more than ten or twelve at a time," Dina suggested. "If she launches both fistfuls, Nate would stand a better chance of hitting several because they'd be closer together."

Aniela nodded. She tossed two handfuls as Nate stood ready to strike.

The expected miniature sonic boom of the whip's snap sounded as Nate flicked it outward. The crack was followed by the sound of rolling thunder as the serpentine chain met several mirrored disks and pebbles. Lightning flashed along the whip's length, causing the golden links to glow and pulse. The kinetic energy roared through the handle and surged up Nate's arm, crossed his chest, and flowed down his other arm and hand. The golden glow dissipated after it reached his second hand's fingertips.

"That was weird," Nate maintained. "I don't really know what just happened, but I feel like I've been shocked, and my arms and hands still have that strange fluttery, tingling sensation."

"The whip infused you with some of its kinetic energy," Uriel explained. "The real question is, what will that extra power enable you to do?"

"I have no idea," Nate replied. "What do you want me to do?"

"Let's test it the way we did with Aniela. Try focusing on one of the statues and make a pushing motion toward it. We'll see if anything happens," Kirron suggested.

Nate turned toward the statues and pushed outward with both hands. The stone figure moved away until he stopped the gesture.

"Do it again with a bigger one this time," Michael said.

The giant mammoth traveled backward slowly as Nate made the pushing motion.

"You seem to have electrical telekinesis now, Nate. You can move objects by extending your power toward them with your hands," Uriel told him. "Try moving a different one faster, by pushing faster."

The gargoyle flew backward and slammed into another, knocking it over.

"Now try moving an object in different directions by focusing on it and moving your hands in different ways," Gavreel uttered.

Nate successfully moved all shapes and sizes of statues in all different directions. Slow hand motions moved the objects slowly, but quick snaps sent them sailing at high velocity.

"This is truly unprecedented," Kirron marveled. "Nate has the gift of electrical telekinesis; Aniela, the gift of infused energy waves; Ariel, control of a phoenix; Jo's and Micah's soulmate power of vapor manipulation; and, of course, Gabe's pyrokinesis through his feet. I wonder what we'll discover in Dina and Guleed."

"Maybe we don't have anything like the others," Dina murmured. "Maybe we're just regular warriors."

"That may be true, but I doubt it," Gavreel soothed. "Because of the greatness within this team, your unique divine gifts are yet to be discovered."

"I am happy with all that I have been given," Guleed declared. "If I receive no more than enhanced speed and agility, levitation, invisibility, metamorphosis, languages, and using the tessellation to move, I say it is all good. Oh, and my kpinga, my bed, and the food around here. Those things are all good, too."

The group burst into laughter as they chimed, "Exactly!"

MORE INFORMATION

"**W**e should head back to Team JAMBANGGD's home. We can discuss proper stowing of their gifts and the pending mission. We'll give them some time to refresh before departing. They've been training a very long time." Gavreel blanketed the group with her soothing smile as she took Dina's hand. "Bruno, come! Connect for tessellation transfer, please."

Bruno bolted to the group and sat on Dina's feet. She scooped him up, nuzzling his face. "Good boy. You're ready to go home, I see."

The group landed on the porch.

"Let's sit down here and talk," Uriel suggested. "It is a lovely spot."

The team settled comfortably and looked at their trainers. Sage fluttered to the railing and preened her feathers while Bruno settled on Dina's lap.

Kirron spoke first. "You were astounding during training. Guleed is now caught up with the team. You learned basic offensive and defensive moves without a weapon. You each have your choosing gifts and learned how to use them. You'll be heading into a very dangerous mission with us, but we know you're as prepared as you can be after two levels of training."

"We feel you need to know more about Somalia before we go there," Michael told them. "Guleed's homeland is fraught with problems and danger."

"That's right. The more you know, the better you'll be able to handle things when you get there," Gavreel added. "Somalia is a very poor country. There's been drought and famine for many years, as well as extreme violence. Malnutrition and diseases kill many, as does the violence from the warring factions within the country. You saw glimpses of the country when you saw Guleed's life, but it will be overwhelming to see the magnitude of the situation when we get there. There are over 150 different armed groups in Somalia. You'll likely witness the effects of mortar rounds, improvised explosive devices, and targeted attacks. We must stay focused on our particular mission, though. We'll not be freeing Somalia from all of its woes, but just one small section for now."

"Some question why God allows such situations to exist, why there's such suffering for some and not others," Uriel declared. "I want to tell you again that God is love and that God allows free will. Lessons must be learned to fulfill individual life plans. Sometimes that involves suffering to learn certain lessons and develop certain skills. Your families have all suffered since losing you, but they're learning and growing from that devastating experience. Let me stress this again: God does not create evil, but evil evolves and grows. Evil overtakes some people and places. All things are connected, though we often cannot see the connections when we're directly involved. But, with a different perspective, things get clearer."

"Like with me," Gabe offered. "I always thought I had it so bad, that everything was unfair. I didn't understand why no one ever helped me. Things are clearer for me now that my perspective has changed. I know about my dad's life and how hard it was. Seeing Aniela's and Guleed's lives before transitioning put my own life in perspective. Mine wasn't nearly as hard as theirs. And now I know Gavreel watched over me and gave up Bruno to save me. I see things more clearly now. I understand a lot more."

"You've grown significantly," Uriel assured him. "You're an excellent example of perspective and connectedness. Based on your own experiences, you sensed Guleed's need. You saw his vulnerability and refused to leave him when you found him in the cockatrice den. You knew nothing about him nor why he was there, but your essence connected you to him. You sensed you were there to save him."

"Bruno came to you when the time was right," Gavreel uttered.

"Just as we came to one another when the time was right. All things are connected."

"We'll be going to Bilan when the time is right, too," Michael told the team. "She's suffered unspeakably, but she's now old enough to manage the next phase of her life and fulfill *her* destiny. She'll be saving many more after we depart."

Kirron noted, "There's still much you must understand before we depart. The median age in Somalia is eighteen and a half years. That means half the people are younger than eighteen and half are older. Over seventy percent of the population is under age thirty! It's a very young population and very poorly educated. Only six percent of Somalians go to secondary school. As a matter of fact, two thirds of adults in Somalia do not know how to read and write. Which means, there are few opportunities for Somalians to improve things for themselves. In addition, because of the starvation, diseases, and violence that are rampant, evil has gained a stronghold there."

"Many demons inhabit Somalia. We also have reason to believe that a particular demon, Aka Manah, has gained control of many souls. Aka Manah is the third son of Satan and lives up to his name's meaning, evil mind. He's regarded as the most violent demon ever born. Born to corrupt all he possesses, he leads others to evil thinking and evil purposes." Michael looked grim. "He's capable of toppling civilizations, which appears to be what's been happening in Somalia for several decades."

Kirron proclaimed, "I have faced Aka Manah before, many eons ago. He's a powerful warrior for darkness. I sent him back to the dark realm with my sword, but we believe he's surfaced again. The only thing that can slay him is a seraph's or archangel's sword infused with heavenly fire. There will be four of us with this weapon. We intend to purge Somalia of his presence. Your weapons and the weapons of man will have no effect on him or other demons. Your efforts will be centered on protecting innocents or possibly slaying evil mortals who intend to harm innocents."

"Gabe slew gargoyles and Pukwudgies on the first mission with his internal fire. He's imbued with heavenly fire he can call forth in battle. He may have to assist us if the demons are too numerous," Michael informed them. "Gabe is a natural in battle. With the extra training he's received since his first mission, I'm sure he'll be very effective."

"We'll be departing for Somalia when our DMD flashes our orders. Aka Manah is in control of Afweyne and will be coming to the compound soon. We believe Afweyne is a mortal whose heart is pure evil, but we'll offer him an opportunity for redemption," Uriel told them. "If we can save humans from evil, we will always try to do that, regardless of things they've done while under the control of dark forces." He shot a warning look at Guleed. "He is to be slain only if he cannot be saved. Is that clear to everyone?"

"We'll land on a flat rooftop and observe the compound and the area surrounding it while in invisibility mode. The DMD will make it clear where the demons are. They may be mingling with innocent mortals like Guleed was. We'll attempt to free as many innocents as we can," Kirron explained, "but our primary mission is to free Bilan of Afweyne's control and set up the compound as an orphanage with a school. Using Afweyne's assets for this purpose will serve a great need."

"So, what are we supposed to do, exactly, if only Gabe is going to help you guys slay demons?" Micah asked.

"We'll have a better idea when we observe the entire compound for a while. This team was chosen for this mission, so we know you're crucial in making the mission a success," Michael replied.

"Before we leave you to refresh, you need to know how to stow your weapons for transport to Earth," Gavreel commented. "Just like the DMD shrinks and adheres to the bracelets, your weapons can shrink and be returned to full size when needed. Our swords are shrunken and in our bracelet's storage compartment right now. Only your essence combined with your bracelet will accomplish this with your weapon. Your third bracelet on your left arm is the storage unit. To shrink your weapon, circle the bracelet with the four fingertips of your right while holding the weapon in your left hand. When your fingers have made the full circle, the side will open, and the weapon will have shrunk in your hand. Slip it in the slit you see and trace the entire bracelet again. The slit will close, and your weapon is secured. Never try to carry your weapon if you transport from Warrior Heaven. It must always be securely stowed if you leave your home sector. Leave it in storage when it's not being used. Everybody but Ariel, stow your weapons now."

When all weapons were stored, Gavreel told them, "To retrieve your weapon, circle your storage bracelet the same way. When the slit opens, remove the miniature weapon and put it in your left hand. When you circle the bracelet again to close the opening, your weapon will expand to its full size. Try it."

Full sized weapons filled their hands once more.

"You've got it. Go ahead and stow them till the mission. You'll have some time to refresh, but we really have no idea how much. We'll monitor the DMD and come for you when it flashes the code for our landing spot. Be ready to depart quickly when we come again."

"So now we can eat?" four young male voices chimed.

Over the laughter, Gavreel sputtered, "Yes, now you can eat, you teenage-eating-machines!"

She raised her arms and gestured just before opening the door. Delicious aromas wafted to them on the porch. Young men and a little dog led the charge to the feast that was set for them.

THE MISSION

Intense prolonged knocking didn't bring anyone to Team JAM-BANGGD's door. Kirron, Gavreel, Michael, and Uriel entered the lounge, but found no one.

"They must all still be in their chambers," Kirron observed. I guess we'll have to rouse them."

Faint yips drew their attention. "It sounds like Bruno's outside. Let's check the backyard before we go into any of their private areas," Gavreel suggested.

When the trainers rounded the back corner of the house, they saw Ariel and Dina working with Sage. The pair trained her to watch for hand commands and fly back and forth between them, landing lightly on either of their shoulders or extended arms.They also saw Gabe teaching skateboarding techniques to Guleed, Nate, and Micah. Jo and Aniela stood near the skateboard ramps encouraging the novices. Bruno ran and tried to catch every skateboarder as he went up the sides of the practice bowl. Laughter and intermittent barks proclaimed their shared fun.

"It's good to see you having such a good time, but we have to interrupt. It's time to suit up. Our mission is at hand," Michael declared. "Everybody, hustle to your closets and get in uniform, then meet us in the lounge."

The group paraded around the house and headed to their closets while the trainers settled on the sectional.

"Gabe had the other guys doing pretty well on those skateboards," Uriel remarked. "He seems able to teach skills as well as practice them himself. That will be useful in the future."

"Seeing Ariel work with Dina and Sage was impressive, too.

Ariel understands there may be times when her focus won't be on the phoenix, but the bird may need to be moved or go with someone else. Having Sage get used to a teammate was excellent forethought. Ariel sensed Dina's feelings about not having discovered her internal weapon yet, so letting her become special to Sage was thoughtful."

Enthusiastic teens bounded to the sofa, in uniform and bright eyed. Sage perched behind Ariel. Bruno hopped onto Gavreel's lap.

"Bring your DMDs up to full-size and make sure everyone can see the screen," Kirron instructed. "If you can't see, move to where you have a better view."

Aniela and Gabe brought the team's two screens to full-size, while Kirron enlarged a third one. The scene was the same on each and the code flashed intensely.

"This is Afweyne's compound in Mogadishu. He has acquired favor and wealth for his obedience and service to the darkness. As you can see, the compound consists of several buildings besides the large house. The entire complex is surrounded by a steel reinforced concrete wall. It's well-guarded at all times. We believe the guards are a mixture of men and demons posing as men. We'll try to save the men if we possibly can, but sometimes men have become so evil that saving them is impossible." Kirron stared at the screen.

Michael picked up the conversation. "As you can see, it's night there. We'll arrive under the cover of darkness, landing on the flat roof of this building. It's a huge garage that houses a variety of vehicles, but also many weapons and ammunition. An important man, Afweyne's boss, is scheduled to visit and inspect today. He likely wants more than that. We believe this man is really the demon Aka Manah, masquerading for his own evil purposes."

"We'll wait until we see this man arrive," Kirron announced. "I'll know if it's Aka Manah in whatever form he's taken. He's a primary target. Your weapons might distract him, but remember, he can only be sent back to the dark realm by heavenly fire. He may be surrounded by many demons in his entourage, so the battle will likely be intense."

"Most of the time, you should remain invisible. You may need to be seen if innocents are close, but you will know if or when that's required. Trust your instincts and training. Watch out for one another. Protect one another." Gavreel smiled reassuringly. "We'll free this facility from evil control and convert it for good."

"Hold Bruno and Sage and connect for transport," Uriel commanded. "Remember, maintain silence on the roof. Telepathic communication only." He raised his arm.

The black sky, illuminated with countless stars, gradually faded to gray. Dawn besieged the luminaries, prodding them to hide their brightness. As if sensing someone or something was coming from which they should hide, the stars disappeared. The birds' dawn chorus began as brilliant orange poured across the horizon. Furrowed clouds glimmered in every shade of pink. Delicate yellows infiltrated the pink rows as the sun rose higher, sparking the birds' flight as well as their songs. Golden light dribbled over the land, bringing everything into clear view.

Two pairs of armed men emerged from a building near the entry gate. They marched in opposite directions around the perimeter, inspecting the walls for any sign of intrusion. They met in the middle of the back wall and reversed their routes. No signs of anything amiss. The men who guarded the doors to the main house joined them near the gate. They were alert and clearly waiting for someone to arrive. None sensed they were being monitored from above.

Afweyne joined the group. "They're not due for two more hours, but we'll be ready if they come early. Did you make sure the warehouse is ready for inspection?"

"It is. All inventory is organized and on display."

"Good. Bilan wants to bring the boys outside to play before it's too hot, so they'll be in the side garden. I do not want them out of the house when our visitors are here. When you see the caravan arrive, send her in. Is that understood?"

"I will personally see to it," a young guard declared.

Guleed saw his sister and nephews descend the stairs and head to the side yard. She carried a colorful ball and small riding toy. He nudged Jo and sent the message that they would soon need to contact Bilan and make sure she got the boys to safety. They could let them play outside a little while, though. She would have an easier time getting the boys to cooperate and go back in if they had played some. But *they* would need to send her in, not one of Afweyne's men, so she would know the mission to save her was happening.

Uriel, Kirron, Michael, and Gavreel huddled near the front of the roof, watching the gate and counting how many guards were on duty. They counted thirty. No way of knowing if they were demon or man until the fighting began. It would become obvious once they showed themselves.

Childish laughter wafted to them as they waited. The sound was soothing, a reminder of the true purpose of this mission, to save the lives of many children.

As the sun climbed higher in the sky and the morning warmed, Kirron sent the message for Guleed, Jo, and Bruno to visit Bilan in the side yard. He ordered them to remain invisible and make sure she was alone with her sons before showing themselves. As soon as they left, a motorcade approached the gate.

Guleed and Jo, holding Bruno, found Bilan tossing the ball to her older son as the little one scooted around on a wheeled toy. No one else was with them. They materialized right before her.

"We have come, Bilan," Guleed told her. "You must get the boys to safety and stay inside, no matter what you hear or see."

Jo set Bruno down next to her. The youngest boy pounced on top of him, squealing. Bruno's tail flipped joyfully as he licked the baby's cheeks. It was hard to tell who was more delighted.

"Get that creature away from my baby!" Bilan screamed.

"Bruno won't hurt anyone," Jo soothed. "You can see how happy they both are, but you must get the boys inside. Pick up your son and get the older one's hand. They must leave the yard right now." She lifted Bruno and disappeared.

A tall young man rounded the side of the house.

"What is this?" he bellowed.

"Aadan, this is my brother Guleed. He's visiting. My son is named after him."

"We were not told that there was a visitor in the compound. When did he get here?"

"Last night. All is well. We were just headed inside. The day is warming up early."

"I will escort you inside," Aadan told her. "Afweyne's visitors are arriving and he wants you and his sons out of sight during their visit."

"That won't be necessary, Aadan. You have been a good friend, and I appreciate your offer to help, but Guleed and I can get the boys inside. You must be needed elsewhere if visitors are here."

He nodded, staring at Guleed before turning.

"Aadan has always been kind. He's a hard worker and likes seeing the boys. I like him better than anyone else who works here. He seems different than the others," Bilan said. "Here, Guleed, bring your ball and take my hand. We'll go in and have some fruit and milk."

"I must return to my team," Guleed told her. "Get the boys to safety. Get the metal box. You will soon be in charge. Be strong and brave. Do not let anyone convince you that this isn't your property. Contact the orphanage right away and ask for their help. I'll always love you, my sister." He raised his hand and vanished.

"Where did that man go?" young Guleed asked.

"He had to go back to work," Bilan replied as she pulled him through the front door. "Would you like some mango or banana for your snack?"

Several armored vehicles lined up at the compound's entrance as Afweyne's guards searched them before allowing entry. Finding no explosive devices attached to any of the Land Cruisers, the heavy gate opened. Afweyne and several guards stood near the large building's entrance.

The convoy pulled forward, parking near the garage-warehouse. Heavily armed men poured out of each vehicle and stood near the third in line. The driver scurried to open the back door. As soon as the tall man emerged, guards who'd exited the other vehicles surrounded him. He strode forward confidently.

Afweyne greeted him warmly. "You'll find everything you requested is ready for you, sir."

"We shall see."

"We can survey our fine inventory if you are ready. We have more than enough to fill the order. The pirates haven't bought as much as they used to buy, so we have a healthy stockpile."

Kirron sent a message to the team. "Exit the roof. Engage enhanced speed and agility but stay invisible. Bring your weapons to full size and spread out around this building. We don't want to fight inside if we can avoid it. Let's have Bruno create a distraction. Send him running from you, Jo, to Dina. He'll be visible when he's not held tight, so that should create quite a stir. Move to a new location as soon as you have him in your arms again."

Guleed sent the message, "See that man by the corner of the building? My sister says his name is Aadan and he is kind. He might be a good man who should be spared. Bilan will need someone she can trust to help her guard the compound."

"We'll save Aadan if he doesn't morph into demon form," Uriel assured him. "We'll try to save the men who haven't succumbed to the darkness."

"I'll become visible to battle Aka Manah," Kirron hissed. "He'll sense my presence even if I'm invisible, just as I can tell it's him in his tall human form. He must be sent back."

"We go forth in service of God!" rang from the team's mouths as they leapt to the ground. Confused men looked in every direction to spot who'd yelled the strange words they all heard but none understood.

Their confusion mushroomed into shock when they saw a small wild dog streak across the grass and spring into a young strangely dressed woman's arms. Then they both vanished. Something utterly peculiar was happening.

"We must get out of here!" one of the guards cried. "Back to your vehicle, sir."

"This is a trick of some kind. You cannot overtake me with your tricks, Afweyne!" the tall man growled. "I am in charge, not you. You are who you are because I made you and I can destroy you!" He flicked his hand toward Afweyne, who was lifted several feet off the ground and slammed against the wall. He held him there, powerless, by some invisible force. One compound guard tried to pull Afweyne loose and found himself plastered to the wall with his boss. "Fools!"

One dagger then another flew from Aka Manah's hand and plunged deep in Afweyne's and his loyal guard's chests. Crimson sprayed all who stood too close before the bodies slumped to the ground. "We'll leave when I say so," he declared.

"I say the time for you to go is here!" Kirron barked as he appeared with his blazing sword. "But, you'll be going back where you really belong, not the place you call home these days."

"Kirron! You won't defeat me again. I know your ways. I have a legion with me this time. You're a mighty warrior, but you cannot defeat a legion." Aka Manah's smirk contorted into a snarl.

Kirron parried toward his enemy who'd morphed into his true form. "I'll start with you!"

Aka Manah zigzagged away from the blade and jumped on top of the vehicle parked closest to the building. He shouted, "Loyal legion, make yourselves known! We will defeat this intruder who would destroy our mission!"

His closest guard morphed into another huge demon.

"Ahriman! I should've known you'd be where so much corruption and destruction have been rampant for so long. My blade can take care of you, too."

"How about all of these?" Ahriman asked as he waved his hand. All but five of Afweyne's guards and all of Aka Manah's morphed into gallu demons. More poured over the wall.

Before he could say another word, a pair of blazing swords struck from behind. Ahriman collapsed to the ground as a pile of black ash.

"So much brave talk and yet so easy to slay," Kirron taunted. "Your turn, Aka Manah. Come and get me."

Kirron's footwork demonstrated his expertise as a swordsman. While his technique, timing, and perception made him formidable, his grace provided a balanced center from which he could lunge, advance, pivot and retreat. Whatever move was needed, Kirron's instinctive skill and eons of practice allowed him to make them without thought. He was a master of the game of mathematics and physics that sword fighting required.

Aka Manah leapt from the vehicle, intending to knock over Kirron and seize his sword. Kirron deftly pivoted. His thrusting sword thwarted the advance of a pair of gallu. They dropped as smoking black piles next to Aka Manah. The other gallu backed away.

"Those guards aren't much good now, are they?" Kirron piped. "You have to face me yourself, Aka Manah. Your gallu and your kinetic force won't help you. Nothing will."

Aka Manah evaded Kirron's thrust as he slid sideways, then jumped and slammed against the armored side of his Cruiser. His ricocheting body almost caught Kirron, who quickly evaded the impact by leaping on the vehicle's hood and vaulting over Aka Manah. The pair spun and charged over and over in combative grappling. Kirron maneuvered Aka Manah away from the growing throng of gallu, the building, and caravan of vehicles.

Aka Manah charged, intent on grabbing the fiery blade's handle and wrestling it from Kirron. He would pierce the warrior with his own fire and take him to the darkness! This sword would be his greatest prize, a weapon worthy of his hand. Aka Manah's hand wrapped around Kirron's and squeezed. He leaned back next to Kirron's body so the blade could not reach him, squeezing harder and harder, trying to force Kirron's hand to relinquish its hold. The two scuffled for the blade, neither lessening their grips.

"I will never surrender my sword to you, Aka Manah!" Kirron bellowed.

"You will. And soon," his enemy countered.

From nowhere, scarlet and gold feathers swooped between the adversaries. Colossal feathers beat the sultry air as the majestic bird winged upward, its talons scraping Aka Manah's face as it ascended. The demon roared and swung at the bird, momentarily forgetting his struggle over the sword. A moment was all Kirron needed. The sharpness and heat of his sword slashed through Aka Manah's chest as the master swordsman delivered blow after blow. Aka Manah's final wail cut through the air as piercingly as Kirron's blade had cut through his body. His crumpled body smoldered into ashy debris.

Kirron turned back toward the warehouse. About a dozen gallu slammed against the door trying to knock it from its hinges. Uriel's, Gavreel's, and Michael's blades cut down demon after demon, but more poured over the wall. A pair of well-thrown valari, a kpinga, and a bola knocked them over and slowed them down. The demons turned on one another, snarling as they got up and charged toward the angel warriors with the flaming swords.

Kirron charged into the melee as a pair of flamethrowers launched from the top of the wall. Four blazing swords and a pair of flamethrowers were grossly outnumbered. Aka Manah's bragging about having a legion of demons was true.

Aadan and four other human guards clustered together by the corner of the building. None of them had any idea what was happening or what to do. The roaring demons furiously worked at getting inside. So far, the locks held, but how much longer would that be true? If the demons reached the mortar rounds or explosive devices, the compound would be leveled. The men knew they had to keep that from happening. Maybe they could get inside from the back door and cut off the demons if they broke through the main door. But the keys were still in Afweyne's pocket. Shooting off the locks could result in unplanned and deadly explosions and draw attention to them.

The same girl who'd caught the wild dog appeared next to them, brandishing a Madu in one hand and the dog in the other. She was clearly foreign but spoke perfect Somali. "You must help. The demons' numbers are too great for my team. We can not fight them alone. They must not break into this warehouse and get the explosives inside."

Aadan stammered, "We could enter through the back door and shoot them if they break down the front door, but the back door is locked, too. The keys are in Afweyne's pocket. His body's near where those creatures are. We cannot get the keys with them so close."

"I'll get them," Dina declared. "Make your way to the back door, and I'll meet you there." She disappeared.

They exchanged shocked looks, but stealthily crept to the back of the building.

Dina pilfered through Afweyne's pockets until she felt the keyring. She carefully slid it out so that it did not jangle and draw the attention of the gallu who still slammed warehouse entrance. Just as quietly, she bolted to the back and became visible, arriving just before the guards.

"I hope you know which of these keys fit these locks." She extended the ring toward Aadan.

He nodded, cautiously grasping the ring. He quickly unlocked three locks, and they slipped inside.

It was dim, but Dina could make out the arsenal of weapons

and vehicles stored here. There were even more than she'd feared. It was more than enough to destroy the complex and several surrounding miles.

"Those demons cannot be killed by bullets," she told the five men. "Only heavenly fire can slay a demon. Are there flame throwers in this arsenal?"

Aadan nodded. "There are a few, but it's not the most favored weapon in the market Afweyne served."

"Show me," Dina ordered. "It's our only hope of stopping them if those demons breach the door."

Aadan led the way to a back corner and pointed. "These are the flamethrowers. Those are tanks of propane. They hang on the back of the person shooting the weapon with these straps. This hose attaches the tanks to the firing mechanism just below this valve. The fuel valve has to be open and so does the mechanism valve. The propane's ignited as it exits the barrel through the piezo ignition, right here at the end. Turning this valve starts and stops the gas flow. If it's open, the gas pours out and ignites when it reaches the end of the barrel. If it's closed, the gas is cut off and the flame goes out. It's a dangerous weapon to operate."

"Help me get one on and ready to use," Dina ordered. "I'll need to be close to that door, so I can shoot the demons as they try to enter. All of you, move the explosives as far back as you can."

"Bruno, I can't hold and cloak you with my invisibility while I fire this flamethrower. I'm going to drape you around my neck. You need to stay there, no matter how much I move around. Don't try to jump down. Can you do that, boy?"

She lifted him carefully, tucking a front leg under the tank strap on one shoulder and a hind leg under the strap of her other shoulder. "Those straps should help a little, keeping you balanced in place. Stay still up there, little buddy." Bruno pressed his head reassuringly against hers. They both stared where frantic pounding and shrieks grew more intense."

Aadan reappeared next to Dina with a flamethrower in hand and tanks strapped to his back. "I can't let you do this alone," he told her. "I must help protect Bilan and her sons."

Dina declared, "If they break through, let's aim our flames at the center of the entryway. Our streams of fire will merge and may be more powerful."

Aadan nodded and took a ready-to-fire stance, his barrel pointed at the door.

Outside, countless gallu and heaps of black ash piles littered the grounds. More demons streamed over the wall and spread out, trying to access the big house.

Kirron, Michael, Gavreel, and Uriel dropped their invisibility in an attempt to lure the demons away from the warehouse. The warriors leapt and spun, zigzagging in all directions, their fiery blades slaying gallu with every slash. Gabe's flame-throwing feet cut down many that congregated close together, but more poured over the wall unceasingly.

They heard Jo's and Micah's voices rising before any of the battlers saw them standing at the bottom of the stairs leading to the house's front door. They, too, had become visible. They held hands, which they raised above their heads. They faced the demons rushing toward the house, crooning, "Spark up the flame! Spark up the flame in me!" Their harmony grew louder and more intense as the vapor spewed from their mouths. They repeated the lines over and over, the vapor building as they sang. Spiraling from their mouths, the vapor thickened and blew outward. Dozens of gallu streamed toward them, intent on gaining access to the house. Fire shot from Jo's and Micah's mouths with each word they sang! While their individual streams of flame braided together and shot outward with tremendous force, their fiery notes slew the gallu who came close. Several tried mounting the stairs from the sides rather than the front. Jo and Micah turned, still singing and flaming. The demons who'd approached from each side dropped in mounds of black cinders near the door.

Jo and Micah took several steps forward as their prayerful chorus, steamy vapor, and flames poured from their mouths. They kept the front of the house free of gallu. Many smoldering piles accumulated between the house and warehouse as the pair vigilantly guarded Bilan's home.

Black mounds pocked the grounds, but still more gallu poured over the wall. There seemed to be no end to their numbers.

The gallu who'd determinedly slammed the warehouse for so long finally knocked loose a hinge. The door wobbled with their next body slams. Their frenzied squeals and intensified attack proclaimed their understanding that they were close to entry. A few more slams and they'd swarm the warehouse and gather the coveted weapons!

As the door crashed to the floor, the first demon charged! He was only one step inside when two streams of flames struck. They spiraled together, united with a thin band of blue. The powerful blaze encapsulated their target, incinerating him. As the others tried to gain access, they, too, were met by flames that meant cremation. Gallu after gallu met their fiery fate at the warehouse entrance. None were allowed access.

By the wall, a golden whip struck shiny pebbles that sailed in the air. Lightning flashed and a brilliant red and gold bird dove at the gallu who approached. Ariel stood on the wall about twenty feet from where the demons streamed across, signaling Sage to squawk, soar, and dive over the far side of the wall. The pair distracted the demons who approached, slowing them enough to allow the warriors to slay more of the legion who'd already breached the wall.

Aniela jumped atop the wall, about twenty feet from the demons' crossing zone. She was about fifty or sixty feet from where Ariel stood. She spied a sea of gallu streaming toward them. Frantically, she jabbed toward the encroaching demons. One after another melted as she sent her energy waves in their direction. The molten pools cooled to black ash.

Sage circled and dove as Ariel commanded, distracting demons who were farther and farther from the wall while Aniela continued to drop all who came close. Sage repeatedly circled over one spot, drawing Ariel's attention to it.

"I see it!" Ariel shouted. "The demons are pouring out of hole about a hundred feet from this wall. It's a straight line from where they're crossing. The wall might be big enough to cover it if it is flipped over the top of the hole."

Nate shouted, "I'm going to push the wall! Maybe we can seal their entry portal! Balance if you can but be ready to jump to safety if you can't."

The girls shook their heads, acknowledging his words.

Nate nodded as he pushed. A huge section of the compound barricade broke loose and moved outward. Aniela's energy pokes had slowed the flow of demons, but many were still on the ground between the barrier and their entry portal. As the wall moved, the girls were closer and closer to the source. A hot wind reached them, carrying an overpowering stench. The noxious sulfuric odor, like nothing on Earth or in the heavens, reached their nostrils. Even as they gagged, they held their positions.

The heavy wall acted like a bulldozer blade as it scraped the ground, displacing ashy mounds with its scouring movement, leaving behind only black burn marks on the ground. Each marked where a demon had been slain. The pile of embers grew higher and higher as the wall got closer to the hole. Demons stumbled as they tried to scurry over the remnants of their comrades. It slowed them just enough for more to fall as the wall approached its target. The mountain of cinders reached the hole and poured inside. No new gallu emerged as the remains rained into the portal.

Sage shrieked as she dove toward a huge cairn of rocks, many of them the more like boulders. Ariel shouted, "Sage is showing us those rocks and boulders. Maybe those can seal the entry hole rather than using the compound wall. I think God-made materials would make a stronger seal than manmade. Do you think you can move enough of them to block the hole before more demons flow out?"

Nate jumped up and looked where Ariel pointed.

"Yes! Between Aniela and me, we can move those rocks. We don't know how deep the portal is, but I suspect the boulders will need to be bigger than the hole. Otherwise, they may just fall out of sight and do nothing to seal the opening."

"Maybe Aniela can melt some smaller rocks around that big one to make a seal around the edges," Ariel suggested. "Or maybe even all over to make a layer of molten rock over the first layer."

"I'm starting with that boulder that's just to the side of the others. It looks biggest from here. I think it will cover the hole. Then we can pile more around it and on it." Nate pushed slowly and the gigantic boulder moved slightly. "It needs to come this way, toward the hole, so I'm going to try pulling it rather than pushing it. I hope it works." He slowly dragged it toward the portal. It covered the hole, except a tiny gap visible on one side. "We need more. We can't leave even a tiny gap."

Nate and Aniela concentrated so hard on moving stones that they didn't see the pair of gallu approaching from the compound grounds, intent on retreating to safety. The pair leapt on the teens' backs, knocking them from the wall onto the rocky pile surrounding the boulder. The demons pinned their adversaries' arms to the ground. Hatred spewed from their eyes as drool spewed from their mouths. The gallus' claws scraped the rocks as the two young warriors struggled to free themselves from their grip. There was no doubt about the pure hate and evil radiating from these grotesque creatures.

As Ariel leapt from the wall, Guleed's kpinga struck the neck of one gallu. It knocked the demon off Aniela, just as Ariel and Sage pounced on the other. The bird's wings flapped furiously as she dove at the demon's face. Ariel wrapped her arm around the gallu's throat and pulled it back, freeing Nate from its grip. The enraged incubus flipped Ariel over its head, slamming her on the rocky pile. It sneered as it pounced on top of her, baring fangs that dripped green drool, and clawing at her throat. The phoenix's screech warned of its attack, but the gallu paid no attention. The bird's strike was furious, her talons and beak ripping at the demon's flesh. Aniela poked her finger at her attacker, dropping it on the rocky pile. She wanted to slay the demon that attacked Nate and Ariel, too, but was afraid of hitting Sage instead of the demon. The gallu thrashed, trying to free itself from the bird's wrath. Guleed's kpinga hit it right between its evil eyes. The beast stumbled as several red feathers rained down. Aniela's energy found its mark as soon as Sage took flight. It melted near its fallen comrade. The demons' charge at their enemies, their intent to drag them to the underworld, had not worked out.

"Thank you, guys," Ariel rasped. "That thing was really strong."

Sage circled overhead before landing on Ariel's shoulder. She gently preened Ariel's hair with her beak, conveying her love and concern.

Ariel reached up and stroked the bird's back. "I'm okay, girl. Thanks for helping rescue me from that demon. You really let that awful beast have it!"

Nate and Aniela worked together quickly to stack the rest of the rocks and boulders on the mountainous pile that now covered the portal. Aniela melted many but left the largest chunks intact. The molten stone became a bonding material that held the heap in place.

"Maybe we can have some of your mirror disks and pebbles, Aniela. We could see if Sage could drop some to create a distraction wherever the others are still fighting. There are no more coming since their hole is sealed, but there were so many already in the compound." Guleed held out his hand.

Aniela piled a handful in his outstretched hand. "It's definitely worth trying."

The four young warriors vaulted to the top of the wall and surveyed the battleground. Black speckles stretched from the warehouse to the main house, around the caravan of parked vehicles, back to the guardhouse at the gate, and along the fence line. They spotted Jo and Micah singing, spiraling vapor and flames rushing from their mouths with every note. Their fiery spray cremated several demons who tried to enter the house. They saw Gabe leaping, ricocheting off vehicles and the warehouse, his flamethrowing feet incinerating every gallu he kicked. They saw Kirron, Michael, Gavreel, and Uriel attacking, their lunges and thrusts slaying all who met their blazing blades. They also noticed a mass of gallu swarming the top of the vehicles. Several of them held something and watched intently, clearly waiting.

"There. Let's see if Sage can drop the pebbles by the cars. All those demons on top are up to something. We need to distract them and stop them before they can do whatever they're intent on doing." Guleed pointed to the crowded vehicles.

"You're right, Guleed," Nate agreed. "Ariel, can you get Sage to drop some of the pebbles near the vehicles?"

"Yes! She follows my hand signals well, and we practiced dropping small stones back at home. Hold your hand out, Guleed, and I'll have her grab some of them and send her to the cars."

Ariel signaled Sage to grasp several pebbles in her claws then sent her flying. She circled overhead, intently watching Ariel. As soon as Ariel's hand made a flinging gesture, Sage dropped her load and headed back.

The bright flash when the pebbles landed created the desired distraction. Agitated demons squealed. One group threw what they held in their hands, a large throw net. It landed squarely on top of Uriel, snaring him in its webbing, not allowing him to wield his sword effectively. About a dozen gallu held the weighted perimeter of the net that would not burn. Uriel struggled to free himself and slice through the mesh that held him.

The team of gallu pulled the net, knocking Uriel over. They chanted, **"Waad nana raaci kartaa!"** You can go with us.

More and more gallu joined the tussle as they worked to drag their huge captive and his flaming sword to the underworld.

Another bright flash stopped them. Flames engulfed the group. Their terror mounted as a kpinga and golden whip's lash knocked one after another from the net. A scarlet streak dove at them time and time again, its talons striking accurately with every dive. Only four still held the net over their prize. They found themselves rising upward, the net still in their claws as they rose higher and higher. Ariel extended her hand to Uriel to pull him to his feet.

"Hey! No slacking. There's still a few more of these nasty creatures hanging around. Get that sword back to work!" She grinned at Uriel as he sprung to his feet and jabbed the gallu that had sneaked up behind her.

Uriel turned his attention to the group huddled atop the first vehicle. They held another net ready to throw at whatever enemy came close enough to snare. They studied streams of flames that raced all over the grounds; if only they could capture whatever made such fire and moved so fast. Nate sneaked around the far side of the vehicle and made a whipping gesture.

A golden lash knocked over several gallu as bright flashes blinded them. Uriel's thrusts and slashes left mounds of black cinders dotting the roof of the Cruiser, held in place by the fireproof net.

Dina and Aadan stepped out of the warehouse door, flamethrowers at the ready. One gallu bounded toward them and met its fate as their weapons sprayed flames at the unsuspecting demon.

Michael and Gavreel danced around a pair of snarling gallu, who dodged and bolted in different directions. The seasoned warriors shocked their foes by leaping and landing in front of the fleeing creatures, flaming blades dropping them before they could escape.

The warriors scanned the compound-turned-battlefield and saw only two demons left, each trying to evade the blades of Uriel and Kirron. They rushed toward the final pair, intent on helping end the battle. A pair of flame streams beat them to Uriel's opponent, reducing it to a smoldering pile.

Kirron danced around the final gallu, who somehow dodged every thrust and slash. A golden lash encircled the beast, pulling it to the ground. Kirron's flaming blade sunk deep in the demon's chest. Its charred remains became another smoldering pile.

"Come back to visibility now," Kirron called. The team gathered around him.

"What should I do with those four?" Aniela asked, her finger still pointing upward.

The team followed her finger and spotted the four gallu who floated overhead, still clinging to the net and clearly trying to scramble free but unable to do so.

"Bring them down a bit. Aadan and I can dispose of them before they make it back to the ground." Dina grinned. "I've improvised with this manmade flamethrower, but it did the trick. Are you ready to blast the final four, Aadan?"

"I—I guess so."

Four young men slinked from the warehouse and plastered themselves against the wall, staring at the compound grounds and the group that stood with Aadan.

Aniela lowered the demons, so they were only about ten feet overhead.

"That should be just fine. Everybody, stay clear of the impending ash storm." Dina nodded at Aadan. Together they destroyed the last four attackers. The narrow band of blue entwined with the inferno from each flamethrower was unmistakable.

As soon as Dina lowered her weapon, Bruno licked her cheek, scrambled to her shoulder, jumped down, and ran to Gabe.

Aadan lowered his weapon and stared at the twelve warriors, small dog, and phoenix. "Who are you?" he stammered.

His fellow guards eased closer so they could hear the answer to that important question.

"I am Kirron, Seraph in service of God. This is a team of angel warriors sent here to save lives and protect the innocent. We have freed this compound of the demons who controlled all that happened here. We have freed Bilan and her sons of the evil that surrounded them. We have also freed you and those other four men from the evil that had almost entirely engulfed this place."

Aadan turned and saw four men he considered his friends standing against the building. "There are only the five of us left? Afweyne employed one hundred guards so there was protection around the clock. You killed the rest of the guards?"

"These creatures we destroyed were not men. They were gallu demons who had taken human form. They lived among you. The gallu are wicked. They feed on humans and drag their souls to the underworld. The five of you are lucky you survived this long with so many gallu surrounding you. It speaks to the goodness within each of you. Two other powerful demons were slain here today, Aka Manah and Ahriman. You saw Aka Manah murder Afweyne. He's the most violent demon ever born. We destroyed evil and depravity today, not men. The only men killed died by Aka Manah's hand."

Guleed stepped toward Aadan. "I am Guleed, Bilan's older brother. I am now a warrior angel. I was murdered by Afweyne. That man murdered our mother, too, and stole Bilan when she was only eight years old. I do not know how many other people he murdered and hurt in unspeakable ways, but the man was evil. Bilan told me that you are kind, Aadan. She will need someone to help her, someone she can trust. I hope you and your men will be trustworthy advocates of the continuing mission she will be overseeing here."

"I am very fond of Bilan and the boys. I will help them if I can," Aadan assured him. "I am sure these good men will help, too." He gestured toward the four still listening intently at the edge of the warehouse.

"Good. We should start by trying to put the place back together the best we can." Uriel smiled warmly. "You'll be amazed at what else this team of angels can do, besides slay a multitude of demons. Aniela, can you put that door back on the warehouse, please, and make sure it's secure?"

Aniela stepped closer to the trampled door and flicked her hands repeatedly. The heavy slab, its hinges and the surrounding casing danced in the air and rearranged themselves until the assembly was back in place. It looked a bit battle worn but was strong and secure hanging where it had hung before the melee began.

Aadan and the other compound guards stared at the freshly hung door.

"We need to survey the grounds to see exactly what needs to be done, so please excuse us a few minutes while we look around from the roof of the warehouse. That will give us the needed perspective." Uriel pointed to the flat roof where the mission had begun. Each team member leapt and landed where Uriel pointed. The five guards gaped up at them, eager to hear what they said from the roof.

"There's so much black everywhere," Guleed remarked, "and funny marks."

"Each black pile marks where a demon's life was extinguished from Earth and sent back to the underworld," Michael told him. "Those symbols are Adinkra Symbols. They are powerful messages."

"Dina, you made that one just outside the warehouse entry. It's called Denkyem and means *adaptability, being able to adapt to circumstances.* The crocodile is a strong creature and able to function powerfully on land and in water. You adapted to the needs of the mission and used a manmade flamethrower. It was strengthened by joining with a flame controlled by a strong human who hadn't succumbed to the evil all around him. The flames from both weapons were united with a powerful band of blue. God was with you as you guarded the warehouse." Kirron pointed to the symbol a few feet from the door.

"I didn't have a sword or powers to slay demons, but I knew they couldn't get in the warehouse and get the explosives. I had to do something to keep that from happening," Dina explained.

"You did well. You slew many gallu as they tried to storm the building. You saved the humans in the compound from what would have been massive and deadly explosions. You saved the buildings, too, because all would have been destroyed if this building went up."

Michael pointed toward the house. "Jo and Micah, you two made those two symbols flanking the stairs. You kept the demons from getting to Bilan and the other humans in the house. Because of your actions, the home of a mother and her children was preserved. The one on the left side of the stairs is called Obaatan Awaamu. It means warm embrace of the *Mother*. It's a symbol of compassion.

The one on the left side of the stairs is known as Akoko Nan. It translates as *the leg of a hen, a symbol of nurturing and discipline*. It reminds parents that they should be protective and corrective of children, that they should nurture, but not pamper. This place will rear many children by this directive."

"So, both of the symbols we created are related to motherhood, like Bilan and the other woman will be to all of the orphans who come here," Jo murmured.

"That's right. You and Micah ensured there will be a home for many children to be mothered by Bilan and Afweyne's other widow."

"That one over there, near where the compound barricade used to be, was made by Ariel, Aniela, Nate, Guleed, and Sage. Their energy combined to form Aroma Ntoso. It means *linked hearts, a symbol of understanding and agreement.* It's symbolic of people coming together usually for the purpose of working together, which is exactly what they did." Gavreel smiled. "They certainly worked well together."

"I had no idea we did that," Guleed marveled. "All I thought about was helping my teammates."

"Which you and your kpinga certainly did," Gavreel praised. "Why did you move the compound wall? What were you doing on the far side of it?"

Ariel answered, "There were so many gallu pouring over that you couldn't get ahead. More came than you were able to slay, even with Gabe mowing through the swarm and Micah and Jo stopping them from getting to the house. I didn't know Dina was cremating the vile creatures at the warehouse entrance, but the number made it seem like impossible odds. I thought Sage might make a distraction to slow them down, so I directed her to circle and swoop. Nate used his whip on Aniela's pebbles, too, to make flash distractions. It slowed them a little, but they just kept coming. I could see Sage circling in one place over and over. She had spotted a hole, an entry portal for the demons. So many streamed out that we knew we had to seal the hole or there was no hope."

Aniela spoke next. "When I jumped up on the barrier, I could see what Ariel saw. It was a terrifying number of demons, all coming this way. I used my energy pokes to melt as many as I could when they got close, but more kept coming. We decided Nate would try to push the wall to the hole and we'd knock it over to seal the opening. Ariel and Sage distracted some of the demons as the wall moved while I slayed as many as I could with my energy. Then Sage showed us a huge boulder and a pile of other rocks. When Nate pushed the wall close to the hole, the ashes of the cremated demons merged into a huge mound. It was hard for the gallu to move in the deep ash, so I was able to slay the ones trying to navigate the cinders. Nate jumped up on the wall with us and saw the rocks. He used his electrical telekinesis to drag the gigantic boulder over the hole. We kept moving more and more and piled them all around the hole and on top of one another."

"Aniela and I concentrated so hard on moving the stones that we never saw the two gallu who attacked from behind. They knocked us off the barricade and pinned us to the ground. Guleed's kpinga knocked the demon off Aniela. She quickly slew it when her hand was free. Ariel jumped on the back of the one who had me pinned to the ground. The demon turned its wrath on Ariel, and Sage turned her wrath on it." Nate smiled at Ariel. "Ariel and Sage saved me from the gallu."

"I wanted to melt that gallu, too, but I was afraid I'd hit Sage instead," Aniela reported. "Then Guleed's kpinga hit it right in the neck, and it rolled off Ariel. As soon as Sage fluttered up, I poked that thing to death!"

"We finished the cairn, and Aniela melted some to make a seal between the bigger rocks. No more demons were coming, so we came back to this side of the wall," Nate continued.

"And saved me from the gallus' net," Uriel remarked. "See that symbol near the cars? It's where the net had me struggling on the ground. My sword made that symbol as I struggled to get free. It's Nyame NTI and means *by God's grace*. The stalk is the staff of life. It is a symbol of faith and trust in God." Uriel stared at the symbol.

"Gabe you made that one with your flaming feet," Michael pointed to the grassy area between the warehouse and gatehouse where much of the battle had raged. "You kept circling and rico-cheting off the warehouse wall and those trees which caused your feet to burn that symbol. Its name is Nyame Biribi Wo Soro. It means *God is in the Heavens*. It reminds all that God is in Heaven and listens to all prayers."

"I didn't know I made that, but I kept looping through that area because there were so many demons charging. I kicked a lot of them."

"Yes, you did. We might not be here surveying this battleground if you hadn't been with us." Kirron pointed to the last symbol they could see. "Uriel, Gavreel, Michael, and I made that one with our swords. Our swords created the Onyankopon Adam Nti Biribiara Beye Yie symbol. It means *by God's grace, all will be well*. It's a symbol of hope, providence, and faith. It's one that we often see after an intense battle with evil."

"It looks like a heart with four lines connecting it to the center, an inscribed cross," Dina observed.

"That's a good description," Gavreel said. "We need to finish here. We should move the cinders from the compound, adding it to the mountain of rocks and ash that Aniela and Nate made over there. Then we should get the compound fence back where it belongs."

The team bounded to the ground, landing near the five men who had witnessed and survived the carnage.

"Do you have brooms and shovels?" Kirron asked. "Someone should sweep the ash from the porch and stairs. Others could sweep the piles from the driveway. We'll help you clear it before we go."

Aadan directed the men to get the tools and start the cleanup on the hard surfaces as Nate and Aniela pushed piles together on the grassy area. Before long the ash mound was as tall as the warehouse.

Together, Nate and Aniela pushed the ebony heap toward the perimeter. Aniela spun her finger and levitated the cinders high above the rocky barrier that laid on the other side. A slight push moved the remains over the cairn. She released it so it rained down over the rocks, completely shrouding the stones from view. She melted it in place. A solid black dome encased the rocks, providing one more layer of protection.

Nate and Aniela jumped to the far side of the wall and pushed. The barrier slowly moved back to its original position. Aniela made some adjustments, and the concrete and steel fence was solidly connected and even stronger than before. She and Nate jumped over the obstacle, high-fived one another as they landed, and rejoined their team. Except for black polka dots everywhere and Adinkra symbols burned into the ground, the compound was back in good shape.

The men stood speechless. They'd never seen nor even imagined the things they had witnessed today.

"We will be leaving now," Uriel told them. "Our work here is done, but yours is not. Bilan has a mission to complete, and I know she'll be grateful for your help. She knows what she's been called to do."

Aadan stared at the large warrior, then scanned the grounds and the rest of the team who stood near Uriel. "This is so unbelievable. The things that happened here. These symbols on the ground. Am I under some enchantment or something? I have so many questions."

Michael told him, "I'm afraid we're needed elsewhere, so we must go. Let me assure you that you have not been enchanted, but you have been enlightened. A bit of enlightenment will bring greater enlightenment if you allow it. What you choose to do with your insight is up to you. No one is going to finish this puzzle for you. You must seek wisdom and guidance from God. Talk with Bilan. You may be an important part of her mission that's beginning here."

Uriel smiled at the gaping men. "You are blessed. You witnessed God's power today. God can do all things, but God only acts through willing hearts and willing minds. Our mission here is done. Your mission is not. Help Bilan. See that good continues to triumph over evil."

The warriors placed hands on one another as Uriel raised his hand. They disappeared.

"Enlightened, not enchanted?" Aadan murmured as he and the other guards stared where the warriors had stood.

MISSION ACCOMPLISHED

The team landed at the front of their home, into a crowd of trainees and experienced warriors. Those who gathered stared at the team and nodded, but no one spoke.

"What's going on?" Jo whispered. "Why are all of these angels gathered here? Why are they looking at us like that?"

"The word of this mission must have already spread," Uriel declared. "It was an extraordinary mission. The most extraordinary I've ever been a part of, and I've been on a great many missions."

"We don't even know yet how many demons we destroyed," Kirron added, "but ridding Somalia of Aka Manah and Ahriman, as well as those gallu, was a remarkable feat. Sealing the portal so more demons could not flood out was miraculous. The compound turned orphanage will do so much good in a place where evil has been rampant for so many years."

"I am grateful we freed my sister and nephews," Guleed murmured. "I am grateful I was allowed to be part of this mission."

"We're grateful you were with us and that you have been fully redeemed," Uriel told him. "You proved yourself in battle. Your guilt for things you did in the past led to good. You seized your redemption when you became part of this team and accepted future consequences for past mistakes. You soldered that redemption into your essence when you didn't think about yourself in battle. By putting yourself aside and concentrating on your sister and your teammates, you proved the purity of your heart in spite of the things you did in your lifetime. You freed yourself from the tyranny of lingering guilt. You passed God's test by fully forgiving yourself as you were forgiven by God."

Bruno squirmed to be let down. Gabe said, "Okay, boy. You've been held a long time. Stay close, though." He stroked the terrier's head as he set him by his feet.

Sage fluttered from Ariel's shoulder and circled the crowd. She glided overhead, her aerial laps quite low, narrowly missing some taller angels' heads, clearly searching for something or someone.

"What's that bird doing?" Nate asked.

"I have no idea, but she seems to be looking for something. She's flying so low," Ariel remarked.

The crowd parted, forming an opening to the returning warriors. A subtle murmuring proclaimed the arrival of someone important.

Two Melodeans, like the ones they'd seen at the Heavenly Hosts Choir Chambers, approached. Their tentacles caressed the air, but no music radiated from this pair.

Sage landed on the shoulder of the larger one. Bruno leapt in the arms of the other. "Welcome home, Warriors. Let us congratulate you on your successful mission. It was beyond impressive."

Uriel bowed his head before speaking. "Cadence, Melisma, I'm surprised to see you here. What called you from the Council chambers?"

"This team called us. We've been waiting a long time for the power this team possesses. Our planet needs this team before there is nothing left to save."

The team exchanged glances but remained silent.

Gavreel spoke, "We are here to serve God. If God has already determined our next mission, we will answer the call. Perhaps we should enter the home of Team JAMBANGGD and discuss what brought you here, away from this throng of onlookers."

The Melodeans nodded. "Very well. There is much to discuss."

"I see Bruno still remembers you well," Gavreel remarked.

"This is one of the best creations ever," Melisma cooed as her tentacles gently caressed the dog who snuggled in her arms.

"I agree with that. In fact, I'm sure this whole team agrees with you."

Sage preened the tentacles of the larger Melodean. "I have never forgotten you either, my phoenix friend. You have aligned yourself with the perfect angel for this lifetime."

Michael said, "Gabe, please open the door for these important guests. We'll follow them into the lounge and hear what they have to say."

Melisma and Cadence led the troupe up the stairs. They scanned the porch before stepping into the lounge.

"Please, make yourselves comfortable on our sofa or at the table," Jo offered as she stepped in behind the pair.

"Thank you, Jophiel. You are as gracious as your father." Melisma smiled as she made her way to the sectional and settled on one end, Bruno still comfortably nestled against her.

Cadence sat next to her. Sage hopped to Melisma's shoulder and rubbed her head against Melisma's neck, clearly enjoying the tentacle tickles she received. She returned to Cadence after greeting Melisma and stared at the warriors who stared at her.

"Please, all of you, sit with us. We know you need to refresh after the mission you just completed. We will be as brief as possible."

As soon as everyone settled, Cadence spoke. "We are prophets on the High Council. Melisma and I are Augurs from the planet Melodea. We stay apprised of what is happening all over the universe. Part of our duties is to match the right teams to handle the worst situations. We focus most of our attention on the hot spots in the universe, like the one you just visited in Somalia. You slew a huge demon population that has plagued that area and sealed their entryway. Do you have any idea how massive your victory is?"

Silent head shakes confirmed what the prophets already knew. This team fought for God and good, not for personal glory.

Melisma smiled. "You set an all-time record for a single mission. Twelve warriors, one remarkable dog, and one magnificent phoenix slew Aka Manah, Ahriman, and more than half a legion of gallu. Your exact number was 2,944 demons slain. You enlightened the five human guards and left the compound ready for the next phase of the mission."

"One of you, please, open one of your team's DMDs," Cadence instructed. "When it's open, I'll project the image on your screen so everyone can see it."

Gabe quickly removed the DMD from his bracelet, brought it to full size, opened it, and handed it to Cadence.

They stared at the image projected before them. It was a colossal monochromatic scene. Great leafless tree trunks stood among gray monoliths of stone under a churning mass of dull gray clouds. No life stirred, but rolling dust plumes screamed of desolation.

Cadence explained, "This is one area of our planet Melodea. It was once as vibrant as Earth. It's where many great species were created by God and trained by our people. God made prototypes of so many splendid things and we worked with those creations to make them as useful as possible before they were introduced to ecosystems and civilizations around the universe. Sage here is one of my favorites. She was one of the first creatures I personally trained. She's lived many lifetimes since then and served well." He stroked her feathers as he spoke.

"Many lifeforms have grown sicker and sicker the last two centuries. Some have become extinct. Asag is the demon of sickness. As you can see, much of our home planet is sick. We believe the demon Asag and his followers have invaded Melodea. Not all of it is as barren as this scene, but it is growing worse. We'd like this team to go to Melodea and seek Asag." Melisma paused. "After you've had time to refresh, of course. The young members of the team must finish the third training module. You are so fast-tracked that there's plenty of time for both to happen before you depart for Melodea. Bruno will enjoy his return, I'm sure of that, even if I am not with him." She lovingly caressed his head as she spoke.

"We'll go when and where we're needed," Michael declared, "but everyone is weary. Refreshing and reflecting on the mission we just finished is crucial. Did you say 2,994 demons were slain? Did I hear that correctly?"

"You did, indeed," Cadence replied. "When this team makes up its mind to fulfill a mission, it fulfills the mission. Mission is at the heart of what you do as a team. As you elder warriors know, part of a warrior's mission is to foster the success of others. Greatness is part of the mission, not by any single warrior being better than anyone else, but by every warrior striving to be the best he or she can be and bringing out the best in others. All of you do that naturally."

Melisma added, "I hope you can see the recording of this mission before you leave on your next one. This team's success was guided by synchronistic moments, moments when members acted together instinctively. You filled one another with more inspiration and energy. Your energy level merged two dimensions into one, so the men saw that angels were working tirelessly to free them and raise their level of awareness."

"The power of faith is real. Your spiritual perspective keeps you balanced. This team's combined faith garners great power. You know that every thought is a prayer because spiritual awareness resides within each of you. The strength of your synchronicity accelerates as you fulfill your destiny. Each of you has the power to light the way. Together, you are a beacon." Cadence smiled as he held out his hand. "We're honored that we were asked to present these tokens to your team." He rose and walked around the sectional, dropping an amulet in each waiting palm.

"This token, the Mission Commemoration, is rarely issued. It honors this team for gallantry in action, intrepidity, and acting above and beyond the call of duty. Each of you is part of something greater than yourselves. This team's camaraderie, synchronicity, and shared experiences have fused a bond. Examine your tokens and they will be added to your chains. I'll take Bruno's so it can be added to his collar."

The gold charm sparkled in each of their hands. It was a circle surrounded by a wreath of stars, each star radiating rays of light in every direction. The front of the circle was inscribed: **Only God creates a calling, but missions of destiny are fulfilled by those who answer the call.**

The back was also inscribed:

"A small body of determined spirits fired by an unquenchable faith in their mission can alter the course of human history."

Mahatma Gandhi

As soon as the charms snapped into place, Bruno jumped from Melisma's lap and zoomed around the room. He circled the table then stood on his hind legs, his gaze traveling from the tabletop to Melisma, then back to the table.

"I see some things never change," she snickered. "Your appetite is one of them, Bruno."

"That's my boy!" Gabe crowed. "Food is one of the great bonds among us. We all love it."

"Well, then, let me aid further bonding," Melisma smiled. "I'd like you to try some foods from our homeland. No doubt you'll find everything delectable."

She waved her tentacles and arms toward the table and kitchen island. The table was set for twelve with sparkling china and crystal. Bubbly striped liquid filled each glass. Enticing scents none of them could identify wafted to them.

"We'll leave you to refresh. Enjoy your feast and get some rest. You certainly earned it."

Sage perched on the counter, devouring the platter Cadence had left for her while Bruno attacked the overflowing bowl before him.

"If Melisma's half the cook you are, Gavreel, this should be tasty." Gabe smiled lovingly. "And you don't have to cook!"

Gabe's laughter was like ripples in a still pond after a rock has been thrown into it. It radiated outward through the room. Laughter, light as feathers, bubbled up inside each of them, then exploded as they saw the mountain of food he'd already piled on his plate. The laughter that rocked the room wasn't a chuckle, but a whole-hearted guffaw. The giggling mess of warriors filled their own plates and followed one another to the table, each of them grateful that laughter was a natural part of this group.

Laughter was the balm for the stress of things they had shared and the springboard for whatever would come next. They were genuinely happy together. Shared laughter elevated their spirits, lifted them from the mire of whatever they faced on missions, and gave them the will and the strength to go on.

Made in the USA
Middletown, DE
19 December 2021

56655864R00189